James Lynch

The Fit Country[1]

A Group of Workers' Children

Shortly before the First World War

[1] 'What is our task? To make Britain a fit country for heroes to live in.' David Lloyd George (Earl Lloyd-George of Dwyfor). Extract from a speech at Wolverhampton November 23 1918, quoted in *The Times*, November 25 1918.

In loving memory of my father

Contents

Prologue

Not for one moment did Jimmy Kelly dare to think he would survive that day. He could feel death in his bones. He was resigned, willing to accept his fate without hesitation. Though not a religious man, he clutched at the dog-eared St John Bible in his pocket and made the sign of the cross. Not for the first time in this war, he was convinced that this was going to be his last morning on this earth. Somehow, though, this time was different. Shivering with primeval fear yet determined to do his duty by his Pals, he considered that he had at last found a long-sought-after peace of mind.

It was a little before quarter past seven on what promised to be a fine, warm July morning. The year was 1916. The air was hazed by the early morning warmth and it elicited an almost surreal profile of the features in the ravaged and pocked landscape. An early brightness with just a hint of a thicker early morning mist over the horizon augured well for fair, balmy weather in the day ahead. *It's good to be alive*, he mused.

How sweet the morning seems, Private Jimmy Kelly, Number One Lewis Gunner and erstwhile wool sorter at Rowbottom's mill in Ryaton, thought as he relished what he imagined to be his ultimate samples of the fresh morning air. *Enjoy it while you can*, he ruminated broodingly. He tipped his head back and raised his eyes above the brim of his tin helmet, prudently keeping down well below the top of the trench. Seeming to be cautiously invoking some higher being, he contemplated the few puffy white clouds, edged with silver, scudding across the hazy azure-blue early morning sky.

Likening the clouds to wool dumped for sorting on the mill bench, his brain began to drift back lethargically to random scenes from his prior life: his loved ones and his co-

1

worker Pals from the mill, who were now at his side. They had enlisted together with the promise of fighting alongside their friends and neighbours, one of the many Pals battalions. He revisited his workplace, the large Canaletto-style mill, neither dark nor satanic, aligned with the banks of the river where he'd fished, and parallel to the railway, on which he'd never travelled. He called to mind the squalid rows of back-to-back houses where he'd dwelt and the open-air market with diverse food and textile stalls, where on Saturdays he sat with friends over a half-penny worth of mushy peas with salt and vinegar.

All these images contrasted with the well-polished and impressive Mechanics' Institute building where he had heard lectures which strengthened his socialist faith and aspirations for a better, fairer world. Apart from the churches, it was probably the one place in the town where the social classes intermixed. It was a building that lifted his mentality to the skies, and to which he travelled on the swaying, rattling double-decker trams that also took him on his journey to work.

Distracted for a moment from his reverie, his eye was drawn up to a tiny robin, momentarily resting on the dead branch of a blasted and tortured tree, as it greeted the day with a series of bright chirrups. Its song was accompanied by a tragic Greek chorus of symbolic twittering from other small tits, redcaps and warblers, some stoically and optimistically rebuilding their shattered nests in the skeletal remnants of bushes nearby. Overhead, a skylark too was already in full song.

It is a day when, surrounded by your mates from the same mill, it should be a sheer joy to be alive.

Given the day's plans for him and his friends, all the beauty and promise of the day seemed totally incongruous and his gaze fell nervously to the mire-covered duckboards beneath his feet.

In the very marrow of his bones, Jimmy could sense the high tension in the air around him; he was filled with an all-consuming sense of doom. Trembling, though not from cold, and in common with his mates around him, he had nervously gulped down his allotted final tot of rum already. He and his chums, all from the textile mills at Ryaton, were now glancing furtively at each other, some forcing weak smiles while others stared the hollow-eyed gaze of the already lifeless.

Wild thoughts and fantasies coursed through Jimmy's intellect; recollections of people, times, places and events passed across his mindscape in rapid and muddled succession, frightening and yet endearing. At first, his reflections were dominated by searing dread, anticipated pain, and imminent death. What would it be like to be unalive? *Let it be quick* was his godless plea addressed to no particular deity.

As his restless gaze alighted on the blue ribbons tied to the haversack shoulder straps of his nearest workmates — now warmates — he found his feelings travelling swiftly to the nearest and dearest women in his life: his ever empathetic sister and surrogate mother, Kitty; his gifted and spirited girlfriend, Kate, the woman he should have married; his long-dead mother, Bridget, brutalised at the hands of his long-gone drunken and violent father, Thomas. They all paraded in their turn through his anguished attention.

And what of the young men he and his pals had slain in a frenzy of slaughter? We were great at murder. They were Boches, true! For all that, they were human beings like him. And the executed prisoners? What about them and their families, mothers, wives, sisters and children? What of the young boy who was bayoneted? The boy had his hands in the air for god's sake. He'd thrown his rifle down. He was defenceless. Or those prisoners? Could they forgive? Could any god, if such there were, ever absolve him? *If there is a god up there, please help me*, he muttered inconsolably.

His wandering attentions were interrupted by the order that magazines should be charged to the full, with one round in the breech. He nervously checked his equipment and gave his near friends a last symbolic handshake, uttering to each a mumbled, barely audible, 'Good luck, mate. Good luck, lad. Put it there, pal.

'Fifteen minutes, lads. Fifteen minutes to go.' The invocation went down the line, followed closely by an ear-splitting hurricane bombardment from the Stokes mortars that only served to heighten Jimmy's inner tension. Then, what seemed like only a couple of seconds later, the murderous rumble of man-made thunder increased with the creeping barrage opening and carpeting the way forward.

At seven twenty, wafted by a gentle breeze, a smoke screen appeared to cloud the crystal-clear morning; whistles blew along the line and instantaneously all hell let loose from the German side with Big Bertha engaged to join the symphony of death. Shells, machine gun and rapid rifle fire were already taking their heavy toll on the Pals. Shortly afterwards, at seven twenty-eight, the mines exploded throwing up the sides of a new valley and a new knoll in the landscape. 'My god,' Jimmy said to himself. 'Can anything still be alive? Those poor devils.

'Stick the bastards,' came the call.

'Stick the bastards,' echoed choir-like down the line.

'Stick the bastards,' peace-loving Jimmy heard himself mutter under his breath and then more boldly out loud, his voice amplified by the sheer terror in his belly.

At half past seven, and all too soon for Jimmy, the platoon officers' whistles gave the shrill signal for what was left of the Pals to go over the top of the assembly trench and to move forward in formation slowly and steadily, without bunching, through the smoke screen the short distance to the frontline trench. He cast a fleeting glance behind him and spotted, in the background behind the last of the volunteers, the much reviled and resented trench police hovering threateningly like wild animals stalking their prey.

From now on he knew that other higher powers had cast the die for him. While it had been his decision alone to volunteer, he now recognised — more clearly than he had ever done before — that you cannot stand against fate. There would be no escape from whatever fate that beautiful day would bring him.

No sooner had he ascended the assault ladders to the parapet and commenced the advance, than the persistent shrilling of the officers' whistles seemed to trigger, semaphore-like, at first a fearsome roar, like the noise of uncountable approaching express trains, followed by a hellish cacophony of competing noises as the all-seeing Germans barraged the British assembly lines. The rattle of machine gun and rapid rifle salvoes and the deafening boom of high explosives and exploding shrapnel shells surrounded the advancing soldiers, with the enemy gunners directing their murderous barrage towards the area at the front of the assembly trench.

Grotesquely, bodies began to take wing into the air like clumsy grouse, some headless or limbless with viscera hanging from opened abdomens. The sky responded by raining down foul-smelling earth and sods mixed with body parts, blood and excrement as the incoming whizz-bangs and sausages exploded in the soft earth, taking their deathly toll and menacing to spike-bozzle all earthly human life. The whiff of death was everywhere.

By the time the Pals had advanced to the frontline trench, it was already body-strewn, clogged with corpses and body tissue and the grotesque forms of wounded men from A Company, some of whom were known to Jimmy. By god, some of them were from the same mill. Joining with the remnants of A Company, those that were left of his own unit slowly moved over the top and advanced from the frontline trench. Even as they did so, the ear-splitting noise grew in a truly deafening crescendo.

By now, the harsh shrilling of the officers' whistles was completely vanquished by the staccato rattle of enfilading heavy machine guns, which were raking their lines with a deadly accuracy. This merciless onslaught was augmented by the hiss of passing bullets and splinters from the shrapnel streaking across the landscape, and the screaming whoosh-whoosh noise of the Minnies, the German *Minenwerfer*. Then, there was the addition of rifle grenades, some shot from hides in no-man's-land that had remained relatively untouched by the massive and prolonged British artillery barrage. Incongruously, a handful of skylarks fluttered high above this Armageddon, seeking to override the monstrous tumult of ritual carnage with their song.

The more the Pals advanced up the gently sloping ground towards the German trenches, the more the lethal barrage took a toll on their ranks. As if scythed like corn, the men from his town and his mill at each side of him fell like toppling dominoes. The gory carnage grew with every step that he took. His feet felt like lead and his uniform became encrusted with a mixture of dark brown and red, as both soil and the bloody carcasses of his Pals were splattered on to his attire like some grotesque work of modern art. The perspiration of fear drizzled down his face and neck, and he gritted his teeth. Though trembling and shaking like a leaf in the wind, he carried on moving forward. With rounds flying around him, over his head and between his legs, he stalwartly sustained his advance.

Before they had gone fifty yards, the already thinned ranks of his Pals were dropping to the ground on either side of him, scores of them, wounded, lifeless and dying, silent, groaning and screaming, until his company and others were almost entirely expunged.

There Jimmy stood, solitary amid the human detritus, accompanied only by a chorus of moans and groans, whimpers and wails, and appeals to mothers far away, interrupted every so often by forlorn appeals for stretcher bearers and medics. Amid this bizarre chorale of tormented voices which cruelly tortured his ears, he pressed on up the gentle slope towards the unseen enemy.

The choral concert of death was amplified by a mellow orchestral accompaniment of artillery and small arms fire. Then, like some great god had perceived a need to entirely fill any imaginable noise vacuum, the uneven lethal chatter of the machine guns increased once more. By this time, Jimmy knew that he was not more than a few dozen yards from the enemy machine guns.

In a supreme, single-minded act of naked human courage, he walked on regardless. He had volunteered. He was no coward. And if death was his destiny on this day, so be it — although not at the brutish hands of the trench police. He did not hate. He could not hate his unseen tormentors. He would fulfil his destiny with pluck and without rancour. Kate and Kitty, the loves of his life, would be proud of him.

7

In spite of everything, he kept on tracing along the tape on his left, desperately hoping it would give him some magic protection, still advancing, apparently untouchable — for the moment — up the gentle incline. He floundered, slithering and slipping in the slimy blood-freckled morass and into the red-flecked shell holes and past the enemy redoubt, stumbling clumsily over the corpses of his mill chums, through the remnants of the blasted enemy wire and still onwards towards the German trenches.

His heart raced, his stomach tightened painfully and the flow of sweat aggravated the irritation of his coarse clothing against his scratch-reddened skin. He gripped the rifle tighter; somehow it seemed lighter, less burdensome than it had ever done. The rat-a-tat-tat of the enemy machine guns continued to scourge his brain and the small, high velocity whizz bangs joined in, drumming into the ground. The din attained such a pitch once again that he could scarcely bear it. His eardrums would surely burst. So, this was what the end of the earth was like? His personal Armageddon had arrived.

His turn could not be long, however it would occur. Would he perish cleanly? Would he lie fatally wounded, in agony for days, in no-man's-land? Would he be confined for long painful months in a military hospital? Would he, heaven forbid, be physically maimed for a life of living hell in a soldiers' home, from which only death could ever give relief? An otherwise alert mentality in a useless shell of a body? Any of these fates might be what he deserved for what he had done.

A commotion of strange rattling noises prompted his last reflections, once again of his loved ones: the lissom and intelligent Kate, his sweetheart, and his treasured and bright sister, Kitty.

Finally, an invisible force jerked his body upwards, where it quivered and writhed like a rag doll thrown into the heavens by an almighty yet concealed power.

Chapter One

Shooting bolt upright in bed on the first morning of the official walkout, Jimmy woke with a sudden jolt, screaming from the effects of his nightmare. *Rat-a-tat-tat! Rattle! Rattle! Clatter! Bang! Bang!* Where was he? In the gloom of the tiny foetid bedroom, the windowpane shook perilously as the padded stick slammed against the outside of the cracked and murky net-curtained window. For a while, private citizen, former Lewis Gunner, millennial socialist and Union activist, Jimmy Kelly, sat up rigidly in bed, regaining his bewildered senses while he slowly opened his sleep-deprived and war-weary eyes.

Every night this week he'd had a nightmarish occurrence like this. *How much longer can I go on?* He asked himself. Once again, he had had a rough night, and once again waking up found him in a cavernous slough of depressive melancholy. He felt utterly exhausted. *And me to lead the picket today?* He squeezed his runny eyes again. Once more he closed them, straining to shut out the recent wartime images from his wayward psyche. He grimaced and reopened his eyes to make sure that he was back in real time, and not in some faraway Elysian Fields, another expendable foot soldier fallen in battle for someone else's war.

In what had become a familiar pattern since returning home from France via Italy, his sleep had once again been filled with long haunting nightmares, graphically recalling his horrific life on the Western Front. Time and time again he found himself borne back to grotesque scenes of skeletal and dismembered soldiers past, his dead and maimed friends in the Pals, scenes garnished with vivid images of putrefying human debris amid the already dead and dying. Apparently in some kind of time warp, he frequently re-lived his troglodytic existence: the doses of trench foot and trench mouth, being constantly tormented by the ubiquitous cooties (lice) and the brown rats in the malodorous bog. The cold of a punitive winter had only temporarily relieved the ubiquitous mud, yet at the same time bringing such afflictions as frostbite as an unwelcome substitute. All these torments were accompanied by the deafening cacophony of unceasing artillery bombardments, the intermittent crack of sniping, and the dull thud of a falling comrade.

The demons of his memories just would not release him.

And yet, however horrific the prelude, however numerous the parading ghosts of Pals gone before, however boundless the crippling, painful anxiety, he always seemed to end up in his dreams alone and consumed by a bleak hopelessness in no-man's-land. Last night, in a shallow sleep, he had plummeted once more into a frighteningly realistic imagination. He had relived in graphic detail great assaults and night sorties into no-man's-land. He was there with his heavy Lewis gun, always oddly alone and without canisters. And no number two. What could that mean? How could that be?

Regularly in the middle of the night, he awoke shaking and bathed in perspiration to debilitating panic attacks with the ear-splitting burst of an explosive directly overhead. Only then did he realise that it was the wind forcefully moving some of the broken windowpanes, before falling back once again into a restless sleep of utter exhaustion.

Several months had elapsed since his belated return from the Front via Fiume in northern Italy. His Unit had been posted there at the end of the war on the Western Front to keep the Italians and the nascent Yugoslavs from each other's throats. Yet the depravity of war was still burnt into his night-time dreaming and his daytime reflection.

Against the background of his humdrum, split-shift daily life in the wool bins and spinning shed at the local textile mill, he had to face the implications of his Union activities and his nomination as one of the stewards in the present walk-out.

Jimmy was profoundly conscious that his personal relations with those he loved were unsatisfying, for him and for them. Even his ravenous pre-war appetite was now profoundly curtailed. At times he had the feeling that he was not part of the real world, nor did he feel that he deserved to be. At intervals of intolerable headache, the notion even went through his mind that this was all part of an inexorable slide into utter insanity. How could he ensure the gossamer-thin fragility of his own sanity? The question bedevilled his waking moments; the evidence of his hopelessness and decline was manifest in each of his sleeping ones.

Thus, the knock on his window interrupting his resumed sleep was not at all welcome, nor was it necessary today of all days. Since his return from France and Italy, he never seemed to sleep well and, when he did wake up, he always felt utterly worn out. This morning, on awaking, he had been afflicted in addition with another splitting headache and a parched dry throat. Today of all days he regretted taking on the role of organiser of the strike pickets at the Rowbottom mill. As if he needed anything else to harass his troubled spirit.

Of course, the sore throat could be simply a harbinger of the onset of that dreadful flu, which last week killed forty people in this town alone. Subsequently, in a fit of self-compassion, he reflected that at least such a fate would bring swift relief from the unceasing mental agony he suffered nowadays. His worries about the dispute and his disappointing relations with his sweetheart, Kate and his beloved sister, Kitty — herself the sweetheart of his fallen friend and workmate at the mill, Tommy — were leading in only one direction.

Whereas he could not know it at this moment, it was to be many months before he would sleep more peacefully, and probably years before he could conclusively tame his demons, if ever. At this moment, however, he had other things to worry about. Last night, he had tossed and turned in the damp covers of his bed and found no resolution to his worries about the strike. He had reflected on what would be the fate of his co-workers and their families if the strike were protracted, or even, perish the thought, if it should be unsuccessful. That would imply returning to work on the employers' terms: a ten per cent reduction in wages at a time when prices were soaring like uncontrolled rockets. Plus, the owners would pick and choose which men they took back, and the families of those not taken back would be thrown out of their houses and into homelessness and penury.

After one or two seconds, the padded extremity of the long-handled pole crashed one final time against the loose and cracked window causing it to rattle precariously. *One of these days John Willy is going to break that window*, Jimmy worried as he reluctantly threw back the heavy, moist blankets. In his half-dazed state, he wearily levered himself out of the large shallow trench of the clammy flock mattress which, on top of the iron frame, formed his bed. The stench of damp lime plaster assailed his nostrils. *At least the mattress is better than those flea and bug-infested paillasses that we had in France*, he told himself in a rare turn of optimism.

All at once he was distracted by the muffled chatter of mysterious voices outside. Was it John Willy Earnshaw, the bow-legged and hunchbacked knocker-up? If so, who was he talking to? John Willy was hardly a chatterbox. In any case, he didn't usually have time for a chat at this time in the morning. He needed to get round his group of houses promptly. Otherwise, folk would be at work behind schedule and they would be locked out for the day. As a consequence, he would lose his pay and his customers.

But were those voices real or imaginary? Was Jimmy's own reason playing tricks on him again? Placing his bare feet gingerly on the cold, uneven wooden boards, he shuffled slowly, hugging himself for warmth, across the otherwise empty room to the now silent window. The only murmur was the quiet whine of the wind through one of the cracks in the glass.

Standing at the window, Jimmy pulled back the dirty, threadbare curtains and sneaked a quick glimpse out of the corner. He peered onto the deserted yard below, which appeared even darker and more foreboding as the steady drizzle coated the drab buildings and stone flags with a polished sheen. Only the puddles formed on the uneven cobbles and the heavily worn paving stones of the yard reflected the weak early morning light.

There was no sign of John Willy Earnshaw, the great rattler of loose windows from Tumbling Hill Street. Had it all been a figment of Jimmy's imagination? Clearly John Willy had done his work and moved on already. He had other customers to wake up this morning if he were to earn his weekly coppers.

With neither great care nor protracted attention, and with eyes still wearily glazed, Jimmy glanced across at the other windowpane, on which he imagined he had heard John Willy knocking so vigorously a few seconds ago. Through the ancient ragged curtains, he observed that there was a diagonal crack across one corner of the dirty pane. He knew that the rope in the sash window was worn away. He never needed to open the window anyway.

14

Why does that man always knock on the same windowpane? He wondered irritably, fully aware that John Willy had a choice of only two panes and that both were wobbly. He ruminated for a while on the silver thrupenny dodger a week he paid John Willy to wake him from his pain-ridden sleeps. *At least it beats being in the army*, he reflected. And at a stroke he felt a little happier with himself and with John Willy's unwelcome intrusion.

As he lingered to gaze over the foul middens to the soot-blackened row of seedy houses opposite, a movement directly below distracted his attention to the tiny yard, not more than a few feet from the house. Through the early morning half-light, shadowy, ghost-like figures flitted into the mouth of the passage below the window and out of his sight. Like great reapers dressed in sack-like robes, each bore a dark shape on his shoulder. Was this his latest hallucination? Were his wits fooling him again? Then, to his relief, he realised that the men collecting the night soil were late. For reasons of delicacy, they were usually finished well before daybreak.

Jimmy's eyes focussed on one of the men, a cadaverous straggler, as he emerged from the foul den in the middle of the midden and came into full view. With ghoul-like movement, and without raising his gaze, the man emerged from the cell-like centre of the midden — where he had presumably disappeared some time before — closed the two-part door and crossed the few feet to the mouth of the passage. A large round bin was balanced unsteadily on the dirty sack which covered his left shoulder.

Through the faint morning light, the man's grim body seemed somehow misshapen, like that of a severely hunchbacked spectre. As the man moved across the cobbled yard, an unpleasant discharge dripped from his shouldered

15

bin onto the large stone paving slabs, temporarily discolouring them. The man held the handle of the bin firmly in his right hand as he hobbled into the entrance of the passage with his dripping load of odorous discharge and disappeared from sight.

What a job, Jimmy thought. *All the same, at least it's a job and it's pretty secure. No one shooting at you. No punishments. No short time there. I just hope they don't leave any of it on the road in front of our passage.*

Jimmy conjured up past images of the powerful Shire horse and the deep, two-wheeled cart which would be waiting for the man down at the bottom of the passage, its load dripping the brown, foul-smelling liquid onto the rounded stone cobbles beneath. The rain would wash it clean. Time will tell. His recollection of the Shire horse brought to mind a conversation with Kitty's sweetheart, Tommy, just before Tommy's martyrdom.

'You know, Jimmy,' he had begun. 'Those pipsqueak officers treat their horses better than they treat us men.' One of the other Pals joined in out of earshot of the officers and NCOs and said, 'It's the way we speak, our accents, that are the reason the officers ridicule us. They take it as proof, if any were needed by the superior officers, of the lack of intelligence and education of us common soldiers. They just assume, with their cut glass accents and sophistication, that we rough-spoken soldiers are simpletons, ignorant beasts. Their take on the situation is that we genuinely enjoy the severe and often brutal regime under which they place us. They see us as perfectly willing human cannon fodder. No more and no less.'

And Tommy added tellingly, 'In Britain, social class prejudice does not sleep hidden. If it were not on the surface, it's still ever present. Just below the surface, maybe.

Nonetheless it's there in various forms. Every tide has multiple currents. Take the case of the Anglican padres that we never see. They're all upper class and practically all cower behind the lines in relative safety, except for the Sally Army chaps and Catholic padres. They're different.

Jimmy's recollection of the discussion reminded him that, to be fair, the men did also mimic the officers. On the other hand, whereas the men did it behind the officers' backs, the officers were not beyond mimicking the men to their faces. Tommy was right. Social class was an important way in which people routinely defined each other as superior or inferior. That was also a divide that was carried over into how deaths were recorded. The Brass were recorded by name in the battalion diary and the ORs were not. Only officers were rated worthy of being recorded. In life, even the brothels were similarly graded: for officers, NCOs and private soldiers. In death, it also regulated how they were buried.

What a bloody mess it all was, he considered. *Now the world has changed. Things are not going to be the same ever again. Horses will no longer be worth more than men. And a man's accent will no longer be taken as the measure of his intelligence, his education, his ability or his dignity. We fought for this and we're bloody well going to have it.*

He visualised the horse wagons on the Front in France that came up the line to collect the groaning wounded and transport them to the field ambulances. Even worse were the blood-dripping, two-wheeled carts of death that were used to carry away the corpses and body parts of his dead Pals — at least the bits and pieces that were left after they had been shredded by the Hun's potent weaponry and its lethal shrapnel.

In his nostrils was the stench of excrement and human detritus mixed with mud which had collected at the bottom of the trenches, the detritus having rained from the sky and joined with the leakage from the trench privies after a direct hit. The stench singed the sensors in his nose, at once acrid and sickly sweet with death. Jimmy was consumed by an overpowering nausea and a sudden dizziness seized him. He rocked to one side and steadied himself on the side of the trench ladder, or was it the window frame? In the bubbling mental cauldron of his thoughts, he observed the swamp of obnoxious matter on the base of the trench, some of which was oozing from the latrines excavated from the sides of the trenches. Some also that had pathed its way down the trousers of the men too, rigid with trepidation in anticipation of going over the top of the parapet, whether on night patrol or for an all-out assault. There they waited for the whistle, too rigid with fear even to scratch themselves in pursuit of the lice that tormented them.

Jimmy imagined himself going over the top once again on that fateful July morning, when the Pals were decimated and he lost most of his school and workmates in one, single, bloody, hellish hour. 'Over you go, boys.' Scores of them were just that: boys. He recalled the anger of the Pals — all volunteers — at the message that the battle police had been ordered to shoot anyone who might refuse to go over the top on that fateful morning. It hit those boys hard in their pride.

Coming up from the depths, Jimmy asked himself why these memories were still swirling around inside his head to the exclusion of all else so long after his return home. He was a stranger even to himself. Was this what men were talking about when they spoke of being on the verge of a nervous breakdown? How could he free himself from the shackles of this hell on earth?

Steeply surfacing, like a man rising belatedly from a boundless sea, Jimmy's intellect gasped its way up and back to his contemporary reality again. He leaned forward to steady himself on the windowsill and switched to reflecting on John Willy, the severely handicapped knocker-up who had just stirred him from his troubled sleep. John Willy had shared the blind, misguided fervour for war at the outbreak, and he had not wanted to be left behind.

But he had missed the call-up, because he was not only bow-legged; he was hunchbacked too. At that time the services were still able to be choosy. They were only taking the best specimens and John Willy was far removed from that. Later they were not able to be quite so pernickety. In any case, better to survive inside a body like his, than to fertilise the fields of Flanders like countless others had done.

John Willy had found himself a wife whom he worshipped. Worked at the mill, she did, and they now had a fine young son, Dennis, who was perfectly normal, physically and mentally. Indeed, more than that, he was athletic and mentally gifted. And John Willy and his wife both adored their son; they lived for him. Dennis had just won one of the few paying scholarships to attend the junior section of the local grammar school. Jimmy, however, had no son and no prospect in the near future. Crippled though he was, John Willy truly was one of the fortunate ones.

In fact, John Willy's wake-up knocking was not so urgent that morning. The mill hooter would summon the workers in vain that day. The boilers would still be stoked and, in the bowels of the mill, the huge pistons of the mill engines would scribe their powerful circles. The difference would be that the leather straps would not be engaged to drive the scores of carding, spinning and weaving machines, each hierarchically on their own floor, like the ranks of the army. All those machines would stay idle, whatever floor they were

19

on, even in the depths of the wool bins or high up under the fanlights on the daylight-brightened top floor of the burling and mending room.

The managers would have no one to manage, the foremen would have no one to supervise, the overlookers no lasses to touch up and the gaffers would fret their hearts out for their lost profit. The floors would not resound to the massed castanet-like clatter of the machines, nor the yards to the lads' and lasses' clogs on the cobbles, nor to the metallic grating of the horse's metal shoes and steel cartwheels across the rutted paving stones. Neither would the sickly sweet smell of the horses' steaming droppings rise to assail the nostrils of the workers. His comrades would not crowd their way to the time office in the clock tower at the mill gates, pushing and shoving, hastening to punch the card and beat the clock before the door was slammed shut in the face of any latecomers. No! For today was a strike day.

They would all be on the picket line. Pals again to join the fight against the mill owners. The dispute had been brewing for some time. Just about since the day Jimmy had finally returned from Italy's Fiume. Since the armistice, the mill proprietors had wanted to turn back the tide of hard-won concessions that the workers had obtained during the war. They had never been happy about such improvements and several of them considered that the workers were getting above themselves, above their allotted place in society. They were earning more than they deserved, and certainly more than the industry could afford in the present economic situation of the woollen textile industry.

At the beautifully ornate, neo-gothic wool exchange the owners had met and co-ordinated their policy reaching a unanimous conclusion. They were all proposing a wage cut of ten per cent for the same hours and conditions as before. The men were totally unwilling to accept such a regressive step, and the Union swore to fight the proposals tooth and nail. Other Trade Unions had pledged support and a joint action committee, the Central Council for Action, had been set up to solicit public backing for the men's case.

Jimmy had reluctantly agreed at the recent Mechanics' Institute meeting of the Central Council for Action, which represented all the Trade Unions in the town, to lead his a picket at the front of the Rowbottom mill, which had been chosen because it was the largest. They hoped to attract greater public attention and to concentrate picket numbers, thus strengthening the picket lines and upholding morale. Jimmy had never been so clear about what he must do. It would be make or break for the strike action.

In line with the decision of the Council, he was committed to a non-violent dispute, which would not harm vulnerable members of the public in such places as schools, orphanages and hospitals who were not participating in the dispute. At all costs, he wanted to avoid a clash with the Bobbies too. It was said they had been called in by the frightened president of the Mill Owners' Association, Sir Arthur Rowbottom, and his members. In a knee-jerk reaction to an unaccustomed challenge, he had exhibited all the hubris of a no-nonsense upper class man expressing superiority and entitlement. But, was it really so unaccustomed? Surely he could have anticipated the response of his workers.

So, the strike was now official, and a massive public relations campaign was being undertaken by the Central Council to make sure that essential public services were not adversely affected and that their actions stayed within the law. The explicit aim was to woo public opinion to the side of the strikers and in consequence to offside the employers' case.

But there were also a handful of imponderables. Jimmy knew that Arthur could be unpredictable. Would he act sensibly and responsibly this time? Or would he seek popularity with the other mill owners with some inflammatory action such as bringing in volunteer workers to replace the strikers? Or even by squaring the police to request that the army be brought in? Would some of Arthur's own men drive him to precipitate action by encouraging him to act unreasonably?

Then there were questions about the police. By what wide measure could the local constabulary be relied upon to be impartial in a dispute like this? The history of their action in such disputes seemed to engender neither even-handedness nor leniency.

Last, though by no means least, was Jimmy himself up to it given his record since his return from the Front? It could be that his hopes, his dreams, of a peaceful and successful conclusion to the industrial action were all pie in the sky. It was certainly going to take a great deal of discipline on both sides and an awful lot of luck. Could he keep discipline amongst his own men? He knew that he had a number of hotheads, who might want to even the score with the police for past excesses. And exactly how was he going to outfox the consummate fox, Arthur?

Chapter Two

Still worn out, and yet obsessed with the likely challenges of the day ahead, Jimmy reflected with a certain nostalgia on the comradeship of times past. He cast his mind back to his time in the wool bins, in the dark bowels of the epic mill building, in which he had first worked on leaving school as a thirteen-year-old part-time elementary school pupil. At first, he had nurtured ambitions to move up to the spinning room, possibly as an overlooker. Thence, in the long term, he hoped to become a gaffer in the burling and mending section, where the lasses worked at the top of the building. Up there, in contrast to the practically subterranean existence in the wool bins, radiant daylight streamed in through the limpid glass roofing to light the delicate activity of textile repair.

He smiled weakly as he reflected on the youthful millennial speeches he had made as an activist before the war. He had perched like some Roman god-emperor orating on his soapbox in the centre of town, to a sparse crowd of a few dozen if he was fortunate, one or two if not. He called to mind the subsequent arguments he had had with his audience, amongst whom had been his sister, Kitty, and her friend Kate, who was now his sweetheart. Affectionately, he reminisced that it was on just such an occasion that he and Kate had met for the first time, disagreed on politics and decided to court. He had loved her from the outset for her beauty, her extensive knowledge, and her combative, independent and sharp intellect. This was no ordinary woman!

As it turned out, he had graduated from the wool bins and had stayed contentedly for the most part as a machinist in the spinning shed until, along with most of his mates, he volunteered at the town hall for the Citizens' League Army as soon as war was declared. How naïve and idealistic he had been. How evident and simple things had seemed at that time. How uncomplicated. How straightforward. It would all be over by Christmas. All pals together in the Pals. They would show them Huns.

Although of different social classes, even Jimmy and Sir Arthur Rowbottom, the mill owner, had seemed to be of the same mind on some issues in their pursuit of the welfare of the workers and their families, and the defence of king and country against the wicked old Kaiser and his mob. And when war came, it was evident that everyone had to knuckle down and pull together — workers and owners — to preserve their freedom, their way of life and to fight to stop the vicious Hun.

Thus, for all the animosity and personal bitterness of this industrial dispute, Jimmy was obliged to concede that Arthur was a humane and high-minded man. He had clearly demonstrated in the past that he was committed to the welfare of his workers, second only to his own profit, social prestige and advancement.

Good works formed an essential part of the straight pathway to salvation, which Arthur and his wife had so religiously mapped out for themselves and their two daughters all their lives. Kindness and concern for obedient and passive workers was a duty. Coincidentally, and never explicit, it could likewise lead to a seat in the House of Lords. Jimmy also had to acknowledge that Arthur, in his own way, had always tried honestly to do what he judged to be the best for his workers, just like his father before him.

Like his father, Arthur was a man washed with countless waters. They had both, father and son, patently indicated their paternalism in the lovely model village that they had built, its accommodation and facilities, and in the construction of civic buildings, not least the grandiose Mechanics' Institute. That unity was one of the factors, which made the current strife so complex and difficult. Now they were in profound conflict on behalf of contrasting social camps, where unity of purpose would be hard to obtain, maybe even practically impossible.

Jimmy, Kate and Kitty had encountered Arthur socially from time to time before the war at some of the meetings at the Mechanics' Institute, and they had always found him an amenable and intellectually sharp man. Although totally self-confident, superior and firm in his religious, social and political convictions, they found him lukewarm in his association with what he deemed to be his social inferiors.

It was obvious that Arthur could be a reconciler, potentially a compromiser. Conceivably, his social poise and prestigious education at the local fee-paying grammar school made him seem arrogant towards, even patronising or intolerant of, other points of view about the direction and content of social progress and the structure of society. And, like countless citizens from the large middle class at the time, he was becoming frightened by what he perceived as the rising tide of socialism and post-war Bolshevism — even bloody revolution as in Russia.

Yes, nowadays the ruling classes were scared stiff of a similar revolution in Britain, and they would do whatever was necessary to avoid it. Arthur's biggest weakness might be, however, that he failed to comprehend that the pre-war attitudes of paternalism towards the workers were no longer either valid or effective in the turbulent post-war era. That had all changed for ever.

At a personal level, Jimmy estimated as he mentally drafted out a rough cameo of his opponent, the mill owner had always been a pleasant person to meet, even engaging, although oh so arrogant and superior. He always seemed to have a twinkle in his eye and a quiet sense of humour, which he trusted to get him out of any difficulties he may encounter in his privileged life. However, he was a bit Janus-faced: he had his feet on the ground and proved that he knew how the other half lived, though if need be he could be ruthless.

Arthur certainly felt himself a self-made man, despite his father's legacy of a thriving business. He had done well out of the war too. Khaki uniforms had been in great demand. He had been fortunate, and shrewd, although of course Jimmy certainly did not hold that against him. There were thousands of others like him, some of whom had accumulated their sordid wartime gains in more dubious ways.

Thus, on reflection, Jimmy perceived Arthur as a good man who was flawed by major weakness. The reason for his weakness in the face of his fellow mill owners was plain for all to see. For Jimmy, he was patently an insecure arriviste. He surmised that because Arthur wanted so much to be accepted fully into the top drawer of British society, he had become the plaything of politicians and the tool of his fellow owners. Arthur's dearest, unexpressed wish was to sit in Westminster, preferably in the House of Lords.

On the first morning of the strike, Jimmy needed to be at the mill before the other workers to make sure that there was no provocation that could give the proprietors reason for official complaint, let alone afford those pugilist Bobbies their chance to corner, beat up and arrest any of his fellow workers. He did not fully appreciate the reason why the Bobbies seemed to relish having a go at the workers. They were, after all, from the same social class as himself and his fellow strikers. In any case, to circumvent such eventualities, the discipline of his fellow Trade Unionists would be crucial. There could be no organisational laxity such as had sunk the previous strike.

Jimmy tried to rationalise the behaviour of the police by reflecting that the Establishment was quite clever, deploying representatives of the workers' own social class against the workers themselves. In that respect, nothing had changed since the war. Other things had changed fundamentally, however. After all the suffering, people thought differently, and they would act differently too. The mood in the country had been transformed. The promised 'fit country for heroes' was a country in which heroes should hold sway and should be able to freely demand justice for themselves and their families. One day before long it would come about.

Walking to a recent strike meeting, Jimmy had met two of his pals, Wilf Oldridge and Joe Ogden. Joe had sported a square-ended, sharply pointed skewer, which the workers used to fasten the tops of the large bales of wool. In the wool bins, the sacks were hung from hooks in the ceiling and filled with wool. Two men would feed the wool into the sack and two more would trample down the wool in the sack, like French grape treaders — although without the sunshine or the same pleasant end product.

'This'll come in handy, if those bastard Bobbies try any rough stuff again,' Joe said belligerently, screwing up his face in a contorted expression of sheer hatred for the police, and flourishing the skewer threateningly in front of Jimmy's face.

Jimmy knew that Joe, though rough-cut, unpredictable and quick to anger, was not really a violent man, although he had suffered the violence of France, which had marked Jimmy too. After all, you don't slaughter other men day in and day out and stay the same. Joe felt strongly that, as a family man, he had to fight for his wife and children. He was fed up with the gratuitous state violence which often faced him and his mates when they tried to organise and demonstrate for a fair wage and decent working conditions for all.

Like Jimmy, Joe expected a major revolution in the way demobbed soldiers were treated by the proprietors in the new fit country for heroes. Joe had lived through the catastrophic strike of 1909 in the town as a youngster, although the Union had been adamant that the young apprentices would not be part either of the strike or the associated demonstrations and pickets. The stories, legion though apocryphal, associated with that strike were told nightly in the pubs. As a young part-timer from school, Joe had undergone first-hand the penury, humiliation, tragedy and consequent embittered relations between management and workers which had ensued.

'Joe, we must remember the 1909 strike and learn from it. We can't make the same mistakes again,' Jimmy advised him. 'Bear in mind that the action at that time was driven by some unwise and hot-headed workers. It was emphatically not instigated by the Union. The big mistake it made was that, although the action was unofficial and officials realised that they were on weak ground, it was reluctantly resolved to back the men's action. The action was precipitate, and the men were not well organised, and even less well disciplined. The Union leadership even less so. Neither did they have the public with them. The dispute lasted for weeks and weeks. The company offered a return to work on humiliating and degrading terms. When the men refused, the company proceeded unrestrained with its aggressive and uncompromising attitude and sacked those who did not return promptly. One chance was all those men got!'

Wilf, who was always one for telling the tale in detail, added, 'I fully accept what you are telling us. To make matters even worse, the company brought in blackleg labour from outside the town to replace the striking workers. The story went around that they were all Irish immigrants, the Irish still being the subject of much prejudice and antipathy in the town at the time. After all, the Micks, as they were known, not only poached jobs from the locals. They were Catholics too. The company brought in extra bluebottles and arranged for the volunteer workers to be ostentatiously transported in rather grand green wagonettes to the front entrance of the mill. This manoeuvre was carried out during the day through the crowds of striking workers with the assistance of large contingents of local and neighbouring constabulary officers. They wanted to send an unmistakeable message to the strikers. The workers, with their families starving, interpreted this message as an intolerable provocation, intended to humiliate them and to emphasise their impotence.

Jimmy nodded his assent.

'You will recall it was at that point the strike got out of hand,' Wilf added. 'In a flash, the mood of the crowd became rancorous and inflamed. A mob of unruly strikers broke open the mill gates and burst through shouting, cursing and screaming. They descended on the manager's house, throwing stones, breaking windows and forcing entry. They ransacked the house and damaged other mill property, smashing up anything in their path. As was reported in the local Press that evening, they frightened the manager and his kinfolk half to death. Riot reinforcements were called in, batons were drawn, and the Riot Act was read by the chief constable on the short flight of stone steps at the entrance to the mill. In the process, a bottle, thrown by one of the strikers, struck him in the face. With blood streaming down his face, he persevered rather courageously, and the Riot Act was formally read. Soon after, the striking workers were baton-charged by the Flatfoots. Some were injured and umpteen were detained, particularly the leaders who were paradoxically seeking to calm the situation. Those detained were given a good hiding by the Bobbies in a side street, before being dumped into the waiting Black Marias.

'And by their rash action, they lost the support of the general public. Although possibly they never had it,' Jimmy intervened. 'I do remember that the local paper at the time lauded the resolution of the forces of law and order. Consequently, the strikers lost the publicity game as well as the dispute.

'And not a few lost their jobs as well,' Joe interjected emotionally. 'And more. Those arrested were rapidly hauled up before the Justices. Virtually all were found guilty and severely punished by the magistrates, some of whom were owners of mills in the town. Some strikers got six months in prison with hard labour.'

'The strike collapsed, the workers gained nothing, the families of the jailed strikers starved and were evicted for non-payment of rent, and the owners could pick and choose who they wished to re-employ. Those allowed to return to work went back cap-in-hand and the mill was de-unionised, although innumerable workers kept up their Union attachment surreptitiously. Beware the lessons of 1909!' Wilf concluded. With that admonition, Joe made to depart rather imperiously.

Jimmy did not relish the prospect of having to grapple with such catastrophic outcomes. At the very least it could bankrupt the Union. No, maintaining public backing was essential to a successful outcome and for that, they needed discipline and organisation within the law. Looking at Joe, who was still wielding the skewer, Jimmy added with disapproving brows, 'Look, Joe, we can never win with violence. Violence just does not work. For one thing, the powers that be will always have more power than we do.

Their force will be greater. They have the coppers and the army, all the resources of the state available to them.'

'Well, maybe,' Joe said grudgingly. 'But at least we can show them.'

'Show them what, Joe? That we're more stupid than they are? No, we have to be canny and play to our strengths. We can capture public goodwill, the one thing that they are afraid of. A bad press frightens the hell out of them. And, with the public and the newspapers on our side, we can definitely win. It's as simple as that.'

'And what exactly might our strengths be then?' Joe asked contentiously.

'Our discipline and our organisation, our solidarity and the justice of our cause. And we need to deny the bosses, and the state, what they want.'

'And what might that be?' Joe enquired.

'Profit,' Jimmy replied unequivocally. 'If we can starve them of their profit, which is after all what they are in business for, it will hurt them. The state will lose revenue and they will have to settle, most likely even on our terms. Remember, just in the short time since the war, that tactic has worked for untold hosts of workers in this country of ours: the railwaymen, the cotton lasses, and municipal workers, even the Bobbies, and countless others as well. Discipline and organisation, that's what will win it for us, not violence.'

'I have the same view as Jimmy,' Wilf concurred, rather unconvincingly.

Grudgingly, Joe allowed himself to be swayed. Jimmy managed to coax him to ditch the skewer down a drain. He asked himself how many of the other workers were carrying skewers? Or even more deadly implements? That would be just the excuse the authorities needed for more drastic action, such as using batons on the defenceless workers, reading the Riot Act, and worst of all bringing in the troops. Jimmy needed to keep the dispute peaceful and to have the backing of the public for the workers' aims. So, he had to be tough with his striking workers — as tough as he intended to be with the employers.

There had been a firm pledge by the government of re-employment, or alternatively unemployment pay, to the returning soldiers. Yet, there had been only spasmodic employment available since those who remained of the Pals had gradually returned from the Front some months previously. The city tramways had begun sacking their female clippies to make way for the returning soldiers. All the textile mills were introducing short time working or laying off workers, the women first. The biggest mill in the north was not even taking on any of the returning soldiers, at least for the time being.

Jimmy had heard only that morning that further out from the town centre, Hardener's and Hubert's mills were in financial difficulties. Even non-textile factories, such as Newton's and Slingsby's, which made railway rolling stock, were laying off workers due to lack of business at home and the loss of markets abroad. Furthermore, the local paper had reported that during one of the frequent periods of industrial unrest in the town, there had been mysterious blazes at two of the larger textile mills on the outskirts of the town which had totally destroyed them, likewise cutting the employment pool available by not quite a thousand workplaces.

Of course, the mill owners had seized on this 'wilful act of arson' as a stick to beat the workers with and, castigating the Unions, had spitefully and falsely blamed the conflagrations on Luddite workers, skilfully canvassing their version with the press. This stratagem had further subverted the rather shaky lingering confidence between workers and proprietors.

One of Jimmy's aims was to rebuild that confidence while, in parallel, winning the dispute. With that in mind, he hoped to use his somewhat tenuous connection to Arthur from before the war for this purpose. He determined to speak to him directly by phone and he hoped to do that from the nearby mill timekeeper's office. The timekeeper, Billy Dolan, would surely not refuse to telephone Arthur for him. He was one of the workers after all. At least, he had been until his unfortunate accident.

As a complementary exercise, Jimmy mulled over the workers' misfortunes. In the long rows of dingy, unsanitary houses spreading out from the town centre and encompassing the street where he and Kitty lived, the clog-footed, lice-ridden children were ailing and starving again, and the curtains were continuously closed. Rationing had been introduced in 1917, just before the conclusion of the Great War, as a measure to make food allocation fairer. It was also seen as a panicked political response to the article in the *Daily Herald* entitled 'How they starve at the Ritz'. There was little doubt that the food shortages had adversely and disproportionately affected the poor. At a time of declining household incomes, prices were rising rapidly, especially in the corner shops that served the run-down back-to-back houses. In those damp and unhealthy households, consumption (TB) was rampant and usually deadly, and childhood diseases too were killing thousands of children every year.

With the onset of the winter of 1918/19, the papers reported daily that flu had begun to scythe the weakened and malnourished women and children of the industrial slums first, adding to the numbers of those who expired from pneumonia at that time of year and to the army of children at any time who still routinely died of measles, diphtheria, scarlatina and other common childhood illnesses. Families that had already lost one parent to the war now had the additional tragedy of losing other members as well.

All these factors made Jimmy appreciate how weak the position of the workers was in this industrial dispute. He had voted for the strike and he shared the responsibility for its organisation and for its success. His troubled viewpoint imposed on him the conclusion that the fit land so fulsomely pledged was not fit for the vast army of the poor, who had already borne the brunt of the 'war to end all wars' with their bodies, sanity and deaths.

Jimmy was due on the picket line at the mill in an hour. At that moment his wandering and unfocussed thoughts were diverted by a loud metallic scraping and rattling from the one downstairs room. The fearful sound of metal on metal recurred repeatedly.

His sister, Kitty, was raking the cinders from last night with the cast-iron poker. Having moved back the clothes horse with yesterday's still damp washing on it, she would shortly be preparing a bed of tinder for the day's fire in the soot-blackened, cast-iron range that she had laboriously coaxed to a rich black sheen the previous night. It was she who, after a long and hard day's scrubbing and cleaning at the hospital, invariably undertook the arduous and filthy task of black-leading the range and shining the top of the brass-looking fender a couple of nights a week.

Once alight, the flames would heat the soot-encrusted kettle for their first warm drink of the day: sugary sweet, steaming hot tea with the watered-down milk that was being traded to the poor. How Jimmy looked forward to that first whistle of the day from the kettle. The blue circled, white-enamel pint pot of tea would accompany their breakfast of dripping and bread sprinkled with lots of salt. The drive of his empty stomach began to take over and his mouth watered. He thought about the rum-laced tea that they had received at 'stand down' most mornings in the trenches in France — none of that for him nowadays, alas.

Jimmy dragged himself away from the dismal view out of the window and trod across the bare wooden boards to the door of the gloomy bedroom to collect his musty-smelling clothes from the wooden hook at the back of the door. He pulled on his damp collarless shirt, baggy, patched working trousers and his 'Guernsey', He shivered as their cold damp surfaces touched his warm skin.

Having pulled his braces over his shoulders and fastened his leather waist belt, he put on his threadbare waistcoat with the white chequered lining and he left it unbuttoned. In his waistcoat pocket he fingered his one prized possession: a cheap pocket watch bought from the local shop of the immigrant Sicilians, the Tartorinis, who had come to Ryaton from Italy at the turn of the century and now had a successful jewellery shop in the centre of town. He retrieved his much-darned socks and work clogs from under the bed, loosened the laces and inverted each in turn to expel any fugitive black clocks that had found haven there during the night.

With weary tread, he left the bedroom and entered the pitch black of the stairwell. He held on to the plastered wall shared with the house at the front to steady himself as he descended the cold stone steps. They were narrow and twisting towards the bottom to the extent that those who passed away upstairs could not be carried down in their casket; they had to be lowered in their coffins with ropes from the upstairs window.

A faint shaft of weak yellow light was cast on the last few steps as he opened the door at the bottom and watched the cockroaches and silver fish make a hasty retreat from the light. He stepped down into a twilit small room, dimly illuminated by a single gas light, still turned down to dim it for the night. Its fitting was precariously attached to the peeling white-washed wall now facing him.

He entered the room, still totally immersed in consideration of the picket today and his unsatisfactory interactions with his sweetheart, Kate. The newspaper that was being used with the shovel to draw the blaze, visibly browned on either side of the small shovel. Then it burst into flames, colluding with the weak yellow gaslight to throw momentarily wondrous, ghostlike shadows on the grey walls. His attention drawn at last, he dashed to the hearth, quickly retrieved the small shovel, and crumpling the paper in his hard and calloused hands to smother the flames, he threw the parched tangle onto the now flaring coals.

Picking up his front stud from the mantelshelf, his gaze wandered to the cut-throat razor, beckoning him from behind a cheap vase. He took it and delicately opened its blade, regarding it for a second. He stropped it on the belt hanging at the side of the mantelshelf and stared again intently at the newly honed blade.

He lifted the blade towards his throat. It would all be so easy. So final. All his problems solved in one go. Did he have the mettle, however? He had never lacked guts with the Pals in France. He could do it here and now and finally free himself of his demons.

Chapter Three

Kate scarcely felt in a fit state to go to work. It was not just that she was feeling awful, coughing blood again and had had another sleepless night. She was also seriously troubled about her rapport with her sweetheart, Jimmy. Most of all, however, she was acutely afraid of her workplace and what trials and hazards it might hold for her in the coming day. She thought about that terrible mill manager and what he might attempt to do if he caught her alone in the house where she worked. She was a nervous and physical wreck, but she knew that she had to go; she needed the money badly.

The house where she lived was in a similar street of squalid houses to the one occupied by Jimmy and Kitty. It was not half a mile from where they prepared for their day's activity, sharing the same cold, wet and miserable morning.

Kate was commencing her preparations to depart for her day as a domestic cleaner at the manager's house at the Rowbottom mill. It was the residence of Herbert Radcliffe, and his wife, Mabel. Kate had already set and lit the coals and boiled up the water for her menfolk's breakfast drink of sweet tea. Similarly, she had put the bread and dripping on the table ready for them. Now her task was to get herself out of the house, catch the early tram and get to the site of her work as quickly as possible. She dared not be tardy. She had to have the money, if only for the family.

The house where she was employed had in the past been the home of the mill owner, Sir Arthur Rowbottom. But, with increasing yields from the business, he had moved out several years before the war to a more palatial, bespoke residence in a small village on the outskirts of town where the railway had gone through in 1865 and had carried on up the beautiful and historic steep-sided dale to the site of the old Cistercian monastery at the side of the river.

Following this move, Arthur had assigned the house on the mill site where he and his kin had lived for many years to his manager, the sleazy and untrustworthy roué Herbert Radcliffe. The manager's house was in the grounds of the mill, where Jimmy normally worked alternate shifts in the wool bins and spinning shed, and outside of which the first major strike picket was to take place that day.

A month or so ago, Kate had lost her well-paying steady work as a pay clerk at the mill, where she had worked since just after the opening of hostilities in 1914, to make place for the returning soldiers. It was at that same manager's house that she had managed, with great difficulty, to obtain a menial and poorly paid employment as a drudge cleaning the house.

She recognised that it was through the influence of the man, whose persistent sexual advances and downright promiscuity she most feared, Herbert Radcliffe, that she had obtained the job. Spurred on by her resistance to his advances, it was he who had won round his wife to the belief that Kate would be the safest pair of hands for their treasures. He had always fancied Kate and his real motivation for giving her the work was a source of some apprehension to Kate, and likewise to her sweetheart, Jimmy.

A raking cough seized her whole body, and she gripped a chair to steady herself. She took out her handkerchief and expelled a red mass into it, replacing it in her apron pocket without examining it. She knew what the handkerchief would look like. She was by no means well. During the night, feelings of outright exhaustion had been succeeded by alternate bouts of a terrible ravaging fever. This succession had only been broken when she had fallen into an intense exhausted sleep. This respite helped her to recuperate some of her strength, though she was wet through when she woke up. In any case, however tired, she absolutely had to go to work.

For, no matter what she felt like, as the only daughter in a house with five men, she could not alter her normal circadian rhythm. She had to rise early and help her mother to get the house going, setting and lighting the tinder in the grate, making the tea and cutting the bread, so as to get her brothers and father out promptly to seek work. She had to prepare the men's lunches and their mashings, a mixture of dry tea and sugar which needed only the addition of hot water to make a nourishing drink. Afterwards, the sandwiches and the mashings all had to be fastidiously wrapped in clean newspaper. That day, however, she was preparing the men for a wholly uncommon purpose: to join in the picket of the mill.

Unfortunately, the shared and stinking middens for her house were some distance down the street, past several frighteningly shadowy ginnels and through a foetid little snicket into a desolate cobbled yard oozing with unpleasant effluvia. Because such a visit provoked great emotions of insecurity and vulnerability, especially in a woman or girl, it was a trip that was always put off, and entered into only in reluctant obedience to the natural demands of the body, or the exigencies of emptying the overflowing night slops. Today that obnoxious task of carrying the overflowing white enamel slop bucket fell to Kate. The exertion tried her physical weakness and slowed down her already slow morning progress.

Even the weather conspired against her this morning. The drizzle and cold, against which her shawl extended little protection, made her visit all the more difficult and uncomfortable. Fortunately, at that time in the morning, there

39

were few others around and she gained instant access to one of the group of ten cubicles. Nonetheless, by the time she returned she was convulsed by a fit of shivering and needed to warm herself and dry her shawl at the hearth.

Gradually, she warmed up and began to get herself ready so that she could get to the mill to do her cleaning at the manager's house. She knew that she had to be on time as this was the only employment that she had been able to find after she had lost her wartime position. She found it grossly unfair that the women had been dismissed to make way for the returning soldiers. It was as if they had done nothing for the war effort, as if they were second class and second-rate workers whose services could be dispensed with at the flick of a shawl's tassels. Sadly, that was the way of this grossly unjust and unequal society. For instance, she reflected, all men over the age of twenty-one had been given the vote, whereas only women over the age of thirty had been accorded the franchise. How could any fair and decent person justify such unfairness?

After Kate had eaten her breakfast of well-salted dripping and bread and drunk her strong, sweet tea, she picked up the sandwiches she had prepared for her lunch. Given the rationing in effect, she had sparingly smeared them with a thin coating of jam before wrapping them in clean newspaper. Along with a grubby and much fingered copy of Dickens' *Great Expectations* she put the sandwiches into the pocket of her pinafore and pulled her shawl more tightly round her shoulders.

As she depressed the latch on the door, she called over her shoulder. 'Bye, mum! I'm off to work.' Only faintly hearing her mother's sleepy, 'Bye, love!' she closed the single door of the house behind her and stepped directly onto the steep rain-glazed pavement of Milton Street — pretentiously named after a literary giant. It was a street which, not unlike thousands of other dreary streets at that time in the industrial north, was still deemed fit for returning 'heroes'. She sighed faintly and gave a gentle cough, filling her lungs with the shock treatment of the damp morning air, which was replete with the ubiquitous smell of coal smoke from the early morning chimneys and the early stoked boilers of the multitudinous textile mills.

Glancing to her left, up the sharply ascending street that disappeared like Jacob's ladder into the dim morning mist, Kate heard the metallic clatter from the steel wheel-banding on the uneven cobbles. The milk cart was filled with churns of fresh milk from a farm on the outskirts of the city. She relished the evocative odour of the horse and the familiar sight of the white heat mist rising lazily from its back and from the steamy fresh droppings on the cobbles.

Albert Hardcastle, the stumpy local farmer, was plying his trade in the street, ladling out the milk from his reniform churn with a long handled can into each house's saucer-covered jug as he had done for all his long life. The clacking of the milkman's hobnailed boots on the stone cobbles, and the chafing of his brown polished leather greaves, were followed by the clinking of the milk bucket's lid.

As Albert walked ahead of his cart and shouted out 'Gee-up', the obedient and powerful Shire horse would advance, with a loud clip-clop of its steel-clad hooves, to where he was standing and halt at his command 'Whoa'. The same routine would be repeated unceasingly down the street and onto the next one until Albert had completed his morning round and was ready to return to his farm for breakfast.

As Kate trudged painfully slowly up the street she called out, 'Morning Albert!' to be greeted by a cheery return, 'Morning Missy, is tha well today?'

Despite everything, Kate's family always had fresh milk first thing in the morning ready for breakfast tea. Albert never missed a day; he was immensely reliable. He'd been doing this for years and his father afore him. His customers trusted him, and he trusted them, even in difficult times. No watered-down milk from him!

Kate was perspiring and feeling absolutely worn out. As she approached the tram stop at a snail's pace, she reflected on her experiences of the previous evening, highlighting her abiding feeling of disappointment with Jimmy and their courting life. Had he really changed so much? He seemed so mercurial. He certainly wasn't the man who had gone to war. The funny, good-natured man was gone; he was good company no longer. Now and again he seemed so tired of everything — even, on occasion, of life itself.

Or was it she who had changed? Possibly she had. After all, the position of women in society had changed radically. Women had proved themselves during the war and were still proving themselves after it in straightened financial circumstances. Additionally, there were manifold cases where women were caring for physically maimed and mentally impaired husbands and other sick loved ones as well. It could not have been won without them.

Then again, had they both changed? They were both now living in a world totally unlike pre-war times, one where working women had different hopes and aspirations from those they held before the war. She just couldn't understand him. Should she take his infrequent protestation of love with a very large pinch of salt? He was no longer the man she had fallen in love with before the war.

Kate's tram approached the stop. The nondescript early-turn driver, Brian Farrelly, knew her well, for they had been to the same slum elementary school under the shadow of the

42

largest textile mill in Europe. In Miss Benson's class, they had even been seated close, though decorum mandated not on the same double bench. Both had attended the Socialist Sunday School and had chanted the Ten Socialist Commandments. They had learned them by heart under the able tutorship and inspired leadership of the indomitable socialist activist, Mrs Maggie Braithwaite. She was the maiden sister of Jack Braithwaite, and she worked during the week at the local Co-operative store on the corner of Middleton Street in the bosom of the local community. Street wisdom has it that that she could be a tough arbiter of who was given tick and who was not.

Kate also knew Brian because her best friend Dorothy had been one of the women conductors or 'clippies' recruited during the war to keep the tramways running. Thanks to his cushy, he had been one of the early batches of men to be demobbed. Dorothy teased Kate, asserting that Brian looked out for her eagerly each morning, even risking his job to halt the tram before the official stop to let her mount the platform if she were delayed. That day, his eyes did seem to light up when he caught sight of her, although it could have been her vivid imagination. He was certainly brighter and more amenable than Jimmy was since he had come back from the war.

The single-trolley tram rattled in front of her and slowly ground to a screeching halt, as metal wheels skidded on wet metal rails. Its bright inside electric lights brought a welcome illumination to the dull morning, which to Kate's damp, cold and aching frame spoke of a warmth and cosiness that she badly needed. The tram's white lights contrasted with the dull yellowy glow given out in pools by the single gaslight of the street lighting.

'Morning Kate, love. How are you this morning?' he cheerfully asked her, doffing his peaked cap. Before waiting for a reply, he ventured encouragingly, 'You're looking well. What ye been up to?'

This latter remark was typical of Brian. He was always chatty, now and again to the point of intrusiveness. He even let down the safety cord and pulled back the sliding door behind the driver's platform for her, as he knew that she preferred to ride inside rather than outside on top.

Kate ignored his last comment and addressed his enquiry concerning her health. 'Morning, Brian. I'm champion, thank you much,' she lied. 'And how about his nibs?' Without waiting for a reply, she added, 'Workers' return, please.'

'Very well, my love. That'll be …'

She interrupted him rather bad-temperedly. 'I travel this route every morning except Sunday. I know how much a workers' return costs, Brian Farrelly.' She handed him two coppers.

Brian ignored her rather haughty and ill-mannered response and selected one of the red-striped tickets from the row of various coloured tickets in his ticket holder. He pinged the ticket with his punch and proffered it to her.

'There we are, my love. Thank you very much.'

If Kate had hoped that would be the end of his chatter, she was to be sorely disappointed. 'Still working at the Radcliffe's then, Kate? Managing to get on with Mabel?' Then he added in a voice vaguely tinged with sarcasm, 'Keeping out of Herbert's way, no doubt?'

Kate ignored what she took as his provocative irony. Though tempted to give him a mouthful, she received all his tedious questions with grace, seeking to side-step further

44

conversation. 'Yes, I am.' In truth she did not feel like talking, not least about her work at the Radcliffe's. Oh. I just thought that with this strike … and you being Jimmy's girl …'

She saved him further embarrassment and stated emphatically, 'Well, you thought wrong then, Brian, didn't you?'

With that curt response, Kate put the ticket in the pocket of her pinafore and pulled her shawl defiantly round her shoulders. Passing close to Brian and staring him straight in the eyes defiantly, she entered the downstairs inside compartment without a further word. As she heard him closing the sliding door loudly behind her, she reversed the adjustable bench seat, so that she had her back to him and slumped down onto the hard wooden seat. There was no one else in that section so early in the morning and she was left to her own reflections.

The bell rang twice and she heard the whirring of the electric motor as they moved away. She took out a copy of yesterday's paper from her canvas bag and asked herself, somewhat petulantly and uncharitably, why people don't mind their own business.

The newspaper made for sombre and depressing reading. Forty deaths a week from the flu in Newcastle. Elementary schools closed and indoor gatherings barred in that city and elsewhere. High prices for meat, other food and for commodities. She looked at an article about the *Federationist*, the publication of the General Federation of Trade Unions, which was still being published. She moved on to a piece about the United Textile Workers, who were still pressing their claim for a forty-four hour week at the same wages as for fifty-five hours. How utopian! And with the country bankrupt and on its knees, and she on only five shillings a day.

After that, Kate's eye alighted on a brief report about the increase in moonlight flits: people unable to pay their rent owing to a drop in household income because women were being replaced by returning soldiers. Some of these tenants decamped with their household belongings at night-time to dodge the rent man. She hummed a little of the new song 'My old man said follow the band' to cheer herself up, smiling at its content. *Women always get left behind*, she mused bitterly.

Turning the page, she encountered a report of prosecutions for watering the milk. Only a very few of the culpable had been caught, brought to justice and punished. The newspaper was eloquently indignant about the scandal of the price of milk and the fact that watered-down milk was being sold by some unscrupulous milkmen at the same price. The report stated that, although the local Food Control Committee had taken it extremely seriously, proving anything was difficult and sometimes impossible. Don't we know it! She read further. The coal shortage was getting worse and had not been helped by the miners' strike and the free reparation coal from Germany. Innumerable essentials were still available only on the ration, and in some parts even those were unobtainable. For the well-off, everything was — of course expensively — to hand on the ever-ready black market. Jam and jelly were still rationed, although honey and syrup were not. Anyway they were expensive; again, an example of unequal rationing against the poor.

On a lighter note, the film *Better late than never* was showing at the local picture house, the Little Vic. She would have loved to see that. But, in her straitened financial circumstances, it would be too expensive. Finally, there was a small advert addressed to maimed and disfigured ex-soldiers, offering them assistance. *And not before time*, she thought to herself.

Gradually, the paper dropped onto her knees and Kate's attention wandered, as she resumed a painful visit to her encounter the previous evening with her sweetheart Jimmy. He really was the limit. So wrapped up in his own quandaries — at least those he had brought back with him from the Front.

She had spent the whole evening with him, something which she had been looking forward to immensely since the beginning of the week. He had come to pick her up at home, sporting a clean white collar to his striped shirt, a red tie and his battered trilby. He had clearly freshly pressed his trousers and polished his black working boots. All in all, he looked like his former young and handsome self once again.

Her parents and her grandmother were at home when he turned up with a cheery knock and a prompt and sociable entry. He got on well with Kate's relatives, although her father, resplendent in his newly home-knitted jacket and without his separate shirt collar, was a bit mistrustful of him. Notwithstanding that slight caginess they all engaged in a little humorous banter, while he was waiting for Kate to finish getting ready upstairs. After all, her parents knew him well. He had wooed Kate for at least a year before the war and her father had worked with him at the mill.

Finally, the door to the stairs opened and she appeared smiling and — according to her mother — looking pretty. Jimmy had graciously commented how radiant she was with a lovely rosy bloom in her cheeks, and she had valued it a good omen for the evening. She took her outdoor coat from the hook at the back of the house door and buttoned it up deftly. Taking her hat from the top of the sideboard, she secured it with a long hat pin and put on her best leather gloves. When she was ready, she and Jimmy bade cheerio to her parents and grandmother, who warned him not to keep her out too long as she had work tomorrow, and they left the house.

Jimmy had unhesitatingly and unusually taken her hand. But, sadly, there seemed to be an uncanny distance between them. It was almost as if he felt repelled by the closeness of her body to his. Well, if not repelled, at least embarrassed. Even holding hands was a cold enterprise that evening.

On the other hand, he seemed to want to please her. Almost at once he had asked her, 'Would you like to go to the Tide and have a ride on the Shamrock and Columbia? If not, we could go to the Civic Playhouse this evening if you like, love. Otherwise, would you prefer to go to the picture house? I looked it up in the local paper and *Daddy-long-legs* is on with Mary Pickford at the Little Vic and *Anne of Green Gables* at the Oriental.

'It's up to you, love,' she had answered obligingly. 'Although I'd love to go to the theatre. It's so long since we went. Before you went away, isn't it? And I hear that there is a new play by Shaw the well-known pacifist and socialist. Can we afford it? Going to the theatre always seems like a special occasion, more so than going to the pictures.'

'For you, nothing is too much this evening. The theatre it is,' he said confidently, while appreciating that such a visit would likely clean him out.

As money was scarce and they had plenty of time, they had walked down to the playhouse, hoping to see *Pygmalion* by Shaw. Like Kate, Shaw had affirmed opposition to the war throughout its duration and suffered great opprobrium for it. Kate had joined in the women's demonstration for peace, and she had read Shaw's *Heartbreak House* and firmly shared the ideas expressed in it.

On their way, they passed successive soot-blackened mills. Their nostrils took in the lanolin smell of unwashed wool as they passed the town beck, known locally as the 'mucky beck'. A little further and they entered the shopping area of the town and embarked on a walk up the hill to the Prince's. They halted briefly several times and window-shopped for items for her unofficial bottom drawer. On one occasion they pored over a selection of inexpensive diamond rings in Trattorini's display window and chatted amicably, even if somewhat guardedly, about their mutual plans for the future.

Neither of them had much money, so they had had to buy standing places at the back in the gods. Whilst it was a rare treat these days, they both enjoyed the experience of theatre going. There was always plenty to talk about after such a visit.

Shortly after Jimmy's return, they had savoured going to the music hall in town and had seen the *Maid of the Mountains* seated side by side in the gods the previous December. As things had got financially tighter, and she had lost her wartime work at the mill, such luxuries were usually beyond their slender financial resources.

However, the lectures and discussions were free at the Mechanics' Institute and visits to the library were frequent, for they both liked reading, especially the political tracts, and discussing them. Additionally, there was the Socialist Club, where the Independent Labour Party had been inspired. It helped to keep them mentally alert and intellectually alive and to keep up contact with their circle of radical friends in the town and beyond. Since the war, it had been an important source of news about the rampant industrial unrest in the

49

country. In its new venue at the Textile Hall, Jimmy could have a game of billiards or snooker with his pals, while Kate had a chance to have a modest drink and talk to her friends. Off and on, they would go into the singing room, where all in the room sang sentimental wartime songs — not particularly harmoniously.

The performance of *Pygmalion* by GBS, as the author was known, was hugely popular among their friends from the Socialist Club and they met up with and spoke to several of them during the interval and after the performance. As soon as Kate and Jimmy bade farewell to their friends after the performance, they engaged in quite a vigorous conversation about the performance as they strolled home. They first talked about the actors, the scenery and the production, before moving on to a more critical discussion about the philosophy of the piece and its message. Although Kate had enjoyed that part of the evening walk home, she was also ambivalent about their subsequent discussions, which on the whole had not lived up to her expectations.

At base, she graded the play as being a rather chauvinist, middle class and socially loaded piece of writing, and it was that which she had been eager to discuss with him. The alleged superiority of a middle class male lording it over a working class female offended her notion of what true socialism was about and what the emancipation of women entailed. The lead female was excessively mercurial and too pliant for Kate's liking. Real working class women were not like that at all. She wanted to know if Jimmy held a similar point of view to her. *How did he see it?* She asked herself.

But, somehow, it was not a detached discussion of the philosophy behind the drama which followed. What emerged was an expression of the enduring conflict between Jimmy's dry emotional detachment and Kate's passionate commitment to their romance. What burst to the surface was her profound frustration with his apparently distanced behaviour since he had returned from the war. And this was paralleled and reinforced by her conviction of the contemporary betrayal of her gender by society as a whole.

After all the energy and self-sacrifice that uncounted women had put into espousing the war effort, what had they gained? Their gender was not esteemed worthy enough for all adult women to have the vote in the same way that men already had. Although Jimmy could not be held accountable for this, it was his gender that was perpetrating this treachery of the highest order. The result of this mixture of personal and social grievances was an explosive melange, which gained expression in a way, far removed from her original intention, which had been aimed at an objective discussion of the play. That explosion was to have unforeseen implications for their future relations.

For starters, she asked, why had she not been able to vote in the last election at the end of the war? The legislation stated it was because she was not old enough, although men of the same years were held to be sufficiently aged. Was it because of the old saw that women were appraised as not being intellectually inferior to men? Or else deemed to be socially or financially less trustworthy? Otherwise, was the distinction based on some other characteristic, which she simply could not conceive of?

Jimmy's response was that her government would fix the injustice before long.

'Don't call it *my* government. This government is none of my doing. I didn't vote for them. I couldn't have voted for them even if I'd wanted to anyway.'

'Well, you know what Lloyd George's view of women is, don't you? He thinks that work, which demands a five-year apprenticeship can be done by intelligent women after a couple of weeks' training. So, he obviously esteems women mighty highly, though you have to take whatever he says with a huge pinch of salt.'

'Don't attempt to trivialise the matter with flippant comments like that, Jimmy. I am deadly serious, and the issue is serious too. Don't you agree?'

His attempts at levity dismissed, he answered more seriously, 'Well, of course I do, love. You know that I strongly support your stance on this question. Men and women should be equal, and it does not take a visit to the theatre to see a play by an armchair socialist like George Bernard Shaw to convince me. It is a manifest denial of justice and the quicker it is remedied the better. But don't go on at me about it. I wasn't responsible for the legislation.'

'So, it's nothing to do with you? You can wash your hands of it then?'

'That isn't what I said, Kate, love. I agree with you and I find the restrictions on women having the vote illogical and unjustifiable, especially given the way they kept the home fires burning during the war. Then, my class is not in power so far. When we are, we shall rectify that injustice without further ado. Mind my words, we shall have a socialist government in soon. Then those toffs had better watch out.'

With the head of steam which the play had generated, Kate found Jimmy's response offensively supine; she found his efforts to rationalise such injustice rather patronising. His words irritated her even more, arising, it seemed to her, from an underlying male chauvinism that she believed she perceived in him, despite his politically correct protestations to the contrary. Was he not conscious that, in the same way that innumerable men like him had been radicalised by the war, so too had countless women, although this process of radicalisation of women had originated long before the war under the banner of the women's suffrage movement.

As far as Kate was concerned, the Suffragettes had been predominantly upper crust women and there was little in their demands for the mass of poor, ill-educated, oppressed working class women. If the lives of such high-born women were socially restricted and intellectually inhibiting, how much more so were the lives of their working class sisters? Their modest success only highlighted how little had changed for working class women. Kate's take on women's difficulties were, first and foremost, abysmal poverty, inadequate health care, slavery to the home, unwanted multiple pregnancies, tawdry and dangerous backstreet abortions and inescapable domestic violence.

Would these pressing women's difficulties be for another generation to attack, even after the triumph of votes for all women on the same basis as men? Kate would never accept the ongoing domestic tyranny over women, which existed especially for poor and impecunious working class women. With every fibre of her body, she would rebel. She would fight it. It had to be broken. Otherwise, women would never be truly emancipated, even when they all had the vote. After all, the vote was merely a symbol of equality. The reality was not the same.

At least the Suffragettes, despite their cultural and social limitations, had set in motion a long-term agenda of greater independence and equality for women that could no longer be denied. Given the vast contribution of women to the war effort, men now had to recognise that the nation worked better when women were received as fully fledged and equal citizens.

This background of radical politics and her dissatisfaction at Jimmy's responsiveness combined to bring to the boil all the disappointments that she had suffered about their relationship since his return. In the background was another feeling that she could not quite come to terms with, namely the love that she had found in his absence with his sister, Kitty: love of a different kind, though no less genuinely felt. If truth be told, was she actually blaming him for returning from the war? She felt drawn into an utter confusion of conflicting pressures, and this boiling pot of emotions now welled up and spilled over in a new distressing explosion, which she knew could only have a further destructive impact on their relationship, which she was powerless to eschew.

'Women will never be fully equal,' she retorted more sharply than she had ever intended. 'Men are afraid of equality, and in any case, there is no way that men are fit to take over the child-rearing responsibilities that women have to undertake in addition to their other work in and out of the house. That will take another couple of generations at least … if it ever transpires. In the interim, we should have equal political rights straightaway and get equal pay for equal work. There are more women in the labour force now than there ever have been. Somehow, in spite of their espoused principles, I don't notice a rush by your socialist heroes demanding that equality. Do you, Jimmy?'

'In principle, I endorse the equal pay claims, though it could have the unintended consequence of putting off employers from employing women? Moreover, a man is expected to provide for a household, whereas a woman's wage is usually a second wage in the house, more like spending money, if you like. Given a finite quantum of profit available for wages, won't more for the women automatically imply less for the men, and by extension their families too?'

Kate countered with incredulity, 'So, you're arguing now that such claims for equal pay for women are justified, although you don't espouse them at the level of practicality? In your opinion, they're not in actual fact justified? Isn't that a bit contradictory? Isn't it downright illogical and even glaringly hypocritical?'

'No, that's not what I was trying to say at all, love. You're misinterpreting my words, Kate. What I wanted to say was that justice has to be seen in terms of responsibilities as well as deserts. From each according to his ability and to each according to his needs.'

'All these are mere pretexts for not conceding that currently women are unequally and unjustly treated across a gamut of controversial issues, not solely wages. In marriage, divorce, property ... they're just slaves to the males in the population, sexually and financially.'

'Kate, I see eye to eye with you about your aspirations for women. Of course I shall support you when the time comes. Although ...'

'Thank you very much!' she interjected combatively. 'When the time comes? Any time in the future, only not now. That's what you mean. I am not sure any more, whether you still believe in good conscience in all the socialist principles that we both espoused before you went away to that crazy war. I don't know whether perhaps you're simply pretending in order to placate me.'

Kate did not like hypocrisy and his words smacked of it to her. Wiser counsels succeeded, however, and she decided to let it rest. For his part, Jimmy, feeling distinctly ill at ease at the turn their conversation had taken, made a last desperate attempt to obviate further conflict by endeavouring to draw that aspect of their conversation to a close.

'Kate, I am a man of my word. I believe what I say, and I say what I believe. Not least to you. One thing is certain, however, and that is that neither of us will be around to see the day of full equality between men and women that we both accept should come as soon as possible.' Then he followed up, half-jokingly, 'But, as for men taking over child-bearing from women? Well, it's clearly a biological impossibility, isn't it, Kate?'

Chapter Four

Having restated their respective positions on the injustices perpetrated by British society on women, Jimmy and Kate had experienced a sulky lull in their conversation that night. Seizing the opportunity and seeking to heal the gaping wounds, he'd pulled her towards him. She acquiesced, a little reluctantly at first, though before long she was pulling affectionately on his arm and steering him slowly and strategically towards a more immediate objective.

They had come to a row of shops and, as they both gazed into a jeweller's shop window, an atmosphere of warmth seemed to return between them. Having admired the selection of rings at some length, and drawn her sweetheart's attention to several of them that she valued as affordable including one she told him she particularly liked, Kate made a decision to exploit the opportunity to open up the pressing issue of their future.

'Jimmy, love, when will we be likely to have sufficient money put by to buy the engagement ring? After all, I've waited patiently for four years for you. I've spent the whole of my youth waiting for you and paying the price for your misplaced idealism.'

That last sentence was the wrong approach and she immediately realised it. It could be her feeling of constant exhaustion making her unusually slapdash with her choice of words. Then again, maybe it was that unrequited ache for fulfilment, combined with a realisation that her time was limited. But, no doubt, they were the wrong words, and it was the wrong time.

Of course, he felt guilty that she had had to wait for him during the war. It was a wasted part of her life. Then, it was also a wasted part of his life too. Then, that was not the same, for it was he who had made the choice; it was he who had volunteered after all. In a way, he reflected, Kate had been fortunate. Inestimable numbers of women had waited for loved ones who had never returned. That was the case with his sister Kitty, whose loved one, Tommy, had fallen at the battle of the Somme. In any case, that initial emotional reaction to her words was overshadowed by her last comment. In actual fact, that's what had cut him to the core, all the more so because he knew that what she had implied was true.

She was right when she insinuated that he and his Pals had been duped on a wave of chauvinistic euphoria into supporting — nay, *providing* — the endless supply of expendable soldiery for an unnecessary, unjustified and dehumanising war. And all down to the contretemps and jealousies between countries headed by three royal cousins.

Jimmy's already raw feelings did not hurt less for the accuracy of what Kate had stated. On the other hand, because the first part of her comment had made him feel responsible and sorry for her misfortune, he recognised that he had to submerge his negative emotions at her second comment. He would ignore her critical comment as an unintended slip, and he would bridle his tongue. He mustered all the affection towards her that he could.

'Well, I'm not sure, love. With this strike, finances are not in a healthy state. Immediately this strike is over and won, Kate, I promise you we shall give it priority. If we win the strike, we shall get engaged straightaway. That is, if you'll still have me?'

Decidedly unhappy with what she regarded as his evasive reply, which she considered a delaying tactic, she did not reply directly. Instead, she steered him away from the window and they dawdled on down the street.

His response, however, had brought up the thorny issue of the strike, on which they had somewhat divergent outlooks — not, let it be said, about the aim, rather about the tactics. She knew she would regret pursuing the issue of the industrial dispute, mainly because she knew that it would be likely to put a stop to their brief moments of tenderness. Since his return, she had been single-minded in assisting him to reconstruct his pre-war character. So was that selfish of her? It was her dearest wish that he should be once again the man he had been and that she had loved. She loved him and wanted him desperately. On the other hand, she did not want him to be under any illusions that she would permit their tryst to be conducted entirely on his terms. When she spoke of equality, she meant in marriage too. When she spoke of justice and fairness, she included their life partnership. Could he understand that?

Their conversation had left her feeling unwanted, directionless and resentful. Thus, in spite of herself, the words tumbled out, propelled more by her hurt, dissatisfaction and feeling of neglect than by any rational consideration of what she wished to achieve.

'Talking of work, I fancy you are confident that this strike is worthwhile, that it can be won?'

'In no doubt at all. If I wasn't, I would not have voted for it. I am one hundred per cent for this strike and so are the vast majority of my co-workers.'

'Yes, Jimmy, I know that. My question is, is this strike winnable? It may be justified. It may command wide backing. For all that, given the history of strikes in the mills in 1890 and 1909, where the men ultimately went back on their masters' terms, can it actually be won? Will the men have to go back with their tails between their legs and take what they are given, as they have done after previous strikes? Under worse conditions than before?'

'It can certainly be won. And, no, the men will never accept a return on worse terms. This time we will stay out until hell freezes over.'

'You know that the employers have issued a nasty statement blaming your mates for the conflagrations at those two mills?'

'How underhand! That's a load of twaddle. There is no evidence that any of our members were involved in those blazes. In fact, there is no evidence that those two infernos were anything other than accidental. Nor, before you mention it, were any of our members complicit in that boiler explosion at Briggate Dyeworks, where that chap was killed and a handful of workers were injured. I gather the explosion took place independently in the economiser and subsequently engulfed the six boilers in front of it. At least, that's what the local daily is reporting, and it's usually pretty accurate. I am sure that they would have made more of it, had there been a glimmer of suspicion that our lads had done it. In any case, it would not be in the workers' interests to burn down their own places of employment and make themselves redundant, would it?'

'Well, it's been done before. And I overheard a conversation the other day that implied otherwise.'

'Well, whoever you were listening to was wrong. It's evil-minded say-so. More it's systematic and pernicious spreading of false reports in an effort to undermine our morale, damage our cause, and destroy the justice of our claims. The challenge for us is that people do not, in general, appreciate that some employers could possibly spread such malign tales to bolster their own situation and to harm our case. It just goes to show how desperate some employers are.'

'And I heard that they are going to strengthen the security at the mill today, and they are ready to read the Riot Act at the first signs of any trouble. If necessary, they'll send for the army. The army has already been alerted to the possibility.'

'It's only what I expected. That is why I intend to make sure that there is no trouble and that they have no excuse for such an intervention. And all my colleagues in the Central Council of Action are fully behind me on this.'

'But did you know that the bosses are already preparing to request assistance from the army?'

'I didn't know, although I guessed as much. We did consider that eventuality at the last Central Council meeting. We're prepared. Don't you worry!'

'Jimmy, why don't you accept what is currently on offer? Grab it while you can. Needless to say, it is better than nothing. With all the illness and food shortages, it's not perhaps the best of times to call the men out on strike over a few coppers. You know that it's the women and children that'll suffer. They're already exhausted after the sacrifices they made during the war and with the deficiencies under rationing. All that combined with the illnesses which are raging through the town.'

'That's exactly what the owners want us to do, and as soon as they have that concession, there will be another demand, and another and another. It's not just a few coppers they're after. They want to roll back all the concessions that we won during the war. Before we know where we are, we shall be back to the sixty-hour, six-day week at starvation wages. I can't allow that to happen to my workmates, umpteen of whom fought alongside me and their Pals for their country. It would be an act of infidelity to those who survived against all the odds, and it would disrespect those who did not make it.'

'Well, I don't know how you are going to stop the employers this time. You know, it seems to me that you don't stand a chance. The odds are all against you.'

Jimmy felt provoked and retorted rather gracelessly, 'We'll see about that! It's about time the mill owners were made to shell out. No one is talking about them having to take less of a profit. I hear reports of some having paid a seven to eight per cent dividend to shareholders. No, they live pretty grandly and they can afford to share a little more with the workers. Some of them have done very well out of the war too, thank you very much, and are living in imposing houses on the outskirts of town. I don't hear of them being hit by the rationing. Their kiddies are not dying of measles, not even of the flu or the other illnesses that decimate our children.'

'Now, you know lots of them have been pretty open-handed over the years to their workers and their families.'
In spite of Kate's radical views on women and society, Jimmy occasionally felt that she had a rather old-fashioned, even recklessly rosy, assessment of the mill owners and the reasons for their generosity.

'We don't want their charity, nor their wives' bountifulness. We want justice.'

'Yes, though someone like Arthur Rowbottom ...'

'Arthur Rowbottom moved some time ago with his wife and baby daughters to a rather grand mock French-Empire,

Lutyens-designed palace outside the town. He's not going short. I don't see him reining back his spending. Apart from which, I'll bet he will want to avoid the bad publicity surrounding a long and bitter strike, not least if he tries to break the strike. His friends in London would surely hear about it and that could finish his chances of a seat in the Lords. He wouldn't want that, would he?'

'Don't count on it, Jimmy. If you are going to win this strike, you have to take a crack at considering what the bosses are thinking,' Kate advised fervently. 'What are the reasons that persuade them that they're right and can win? What is their motivation? For, in the same way that you have compelling reasons for what you are doing, they must have compelling reasons for their positions on the issue too. Remember, mostly they're not wicked men, although you may disagree with them.'

'I do not believe that they are wicked either. Certainly not Sir Arthur. That said, I am convinced that he will act in his own self-interest. I also suspect that he is being manipulated against his better judgement by the chicanery of a small cabal of the other less scrupulous owners, like Arthur J Barraclough and Edward P Thackray.'

'Exactly. In other words, like me, you regard him as a decent, rational human being, who sees his interests threatened, like you do. Even the other two you mention, it may be simple fear that motivates them rather than naked malevolence towards their workers.'

'No, Kate. The underlying rationale of the owners is purely unadulterated greed with a little selfishness added for good measure. Maybe they've got used to big and easy profits during the war, employing cheaper labour and all that. Now the squeeze has come, and they want to protect their profits even if that is at the workers' expense. We are not willing to allow that to come to pass.'

'I don't think it is as simple as that, Jimmy.'

'Its simple economics,' he interrupted. 'The size of the cake has shrunk so they want more of the smaller cake to make up for their deficit. The outcome of that policy is that we have to be forced to take even less. That's their rationale, as you call it. What's fair in that? Where's the justice there?'

'Jimmy, love, do you honestly believe that there is a constant size of economic cake? Do you? After the war and all?'

'No, I don't. Trade has always fluctuated and so have profits. It's always been up to the owners to smooth out the ups and downs. Their resources are greater than ours to average out the operating profits — the good times and the bad. They cannot expect to delight in the fruits of the good times, and then expect us to subsidise them in the bad times.'

'I am not so sure about that. I don't think they would see eye-to-eye with you. The point is that the textile industry is in terminal decline. It has been for some time. There aren't the markets anymore,' Kate shot back. 'That's why they're so afraid.'

'I do know that some of the proprietors did pretty well out of the war. When they employed women to replace the men away at the Front, they paid them less. Oh yes, it was all dressed up as patriotism. The outcome was, though, that they could increase their yield from the smaller inputs. Their margins increased enormously and so did their spoils. Now that the government is making them take back their men, they are squealing and wanting to pay them what they paid the women. That's the top and bottom of it.'

64

'They allege that trade is bad. Orders are not coming in. The international economic situation is weak and unpredictable, they say. They are adamant that unless the concessions wrung from them during the war are rolled back, it will mean unemployment for countless men. Their position is that higher wages implicitly and inevitably entails fewer jobs. Surely you can fathom their logic even if you do not adopt their position.'

'That's a threat and they're scare-mongering! I don't believe it for one moment. They want each of us to do more work, so they pay fewer wages. Then they will have a pool of unemployed to threaten us with. To keep us disciplined and in line. Do you agree with us? Or with them?'

What she understood as an accusation of egregious partisanship stung Kate, more so because it came from the man she loved and contradicted her basic political beliefs. She signalled her displeasure with silence. She entertained all kinds of resentments. She had spent four years of her young life in a fog of uncertainty, waiting for him. Would he return? Would he return whole? Would he return sane? And for those years of pain and worry, this was the appreciation that she received? An accusation of disloyalty to her class. She felt heartbrokenly despondent about their love affair. Perhaps she should finish it and have done with it!

But her feelings of dissatisfaction concealed a more entrenched longing: an aching to be held as she had been before he had departed for the war, to be loved as she had been then. She yearned for the passionate pressure of lips on lips that she had always savoured in their more amorous moments. His former passion, which she had always feigned to resist, had been replaced by a hollow tepidity, cloaked in the formalism of words she did not recognise and did not know how to cope with. The only man she had ever loved!

But, why, oh why, was he now so changed? So distant, distracted, wrapped up in his own problems? How could she help him to change back, to be like he was before?

There still appeared to be some affection there, although their goodnight kisses were about as good as a formality; they were earnestly intended on both sides, although definitely lacking in any form of sexual ardour. They had skirted past the park on their way to her house, and he had not tried to steer her into the darkened bandstand as he would have done before the war. Yet she knew in her heart of hearts that she still loved him profoundly, and she was satisfied that he still loved her too.

In the latter part of the evening, the topic of her employment at the mill manager's house had come up. On that topic they did not see eye to eye, and their discussion had become quite strained. She knew that the reason was partly that Jimmy felt protective towards her and felt that the job demeaned her. Partly also, she knew, that it offended his loyalty to his cause.

'How are you getting on at the mill manager's house, by the way?' he had asked.

'Very well, thank you,' she reacted curtly, seeking thereby to deter further questioning.

'How are you getting on with that upstart, Herbert Radcliffe?'

'Not so bad. I don't see much of him anyway.'

'He doesn't try …? Well, you know what I mean. After all, he has a bit of a reputation. Especially among the lasses.'

'No!'

'By gum, I'll deal with him if he does. Just you let me know.'

Jimmy's exclamation and his apparent jealousy pleased her. On the other hand she had also taken umbrage at the fact that he considered she would need his assistance.

'I don't need you to deal with him for me, thank you much, Jimmy Kelly. I can handle him myself.'

This exchange was followed by another brief, embarrassed hiatus. After a silent breather, Jimmy broke the atmosphere between them.

'How does his wife treat you?'

'She's fine.'

'I suppose that they are still enjoying the good life, Herbert not having been to the war and all that?'

'Jimmy, stop interrogating me about my job. You know very well that it was the only job available, and I had to take it. I have to make the best of it, at least for the time being, until things pick up again. I need the money. My family needs it as well. It's as simple as that.'

'I know, love, I know.'

'And, if your question about Herbert denotes that he is up to his old tricks trying to touch me up, the answer is no. I would never permit it anyway. You know that. At least, you *should* know that without asking. On the few occasions that he's there at the same time as I am, his wife watches him like a hawk. She must be heedful of his reputation. He seems terrified of her and would not try to pull a fast one while she is there.'

'Really?'

'Yes. I have never seen a man so cowed before. So, I am safe so long as she is there. On the whole, she is charitable to me and often gives me little titbits to take home. Last week she gave me some homemade jam, which came in useful.'

'So, no mention of us, then?'

'No, they never talk to me about my personal matters and certainly not about you. But, now that you mention it, you do realise that the activities of your Union, and particularly this strike, are bound to jeopardise my job in the long run? The fact that they never speak of you does not mean they do not know about your courting me.'

'I don't see why that should make a difference. After all, the strike has nothing to do with you.'

'If Herbert takes a dislike to me on account of you, my job will be in jeopardy. He will only need to win his wife over to his standpoint. You know how good he is at making up stories and engineering people's dismissal. As you know, he's an expert at angling reasons why girls should be sacked, and that makes it all the more difficult for anyone to get another job afterwards. Especially as there are now so few jobs around.'

'What do you expect me to do about that, Kate?'

'Just make an effort to understand. That's all I ask. I need that job, as much as your mates need theirs. I need it to keep my family alive. It's all I've got at the moment. I can't go on strike, you know. Not like some people. And I don't have your Union solidarity to protect me. I am highly vulnerable.'

'That's intolerable for any worker, Kate. It's clearly another reason why, emphatically, it is time we make a stand and bring these bosses to heel. For that, we all need to join forces and demand decent conditions for all workers. It is unacceptable that workers like you can be victimised and not be able to do anything about it.'

'Well, I accept that of course. The question is one for you to answer. What does your Union intend to do about it?'

'We shall see. The proposal to lower the already low wages by ten per cent is totally unacceptable. This time I know that the public are with us and will stick by us to the end.'

'What makes you think that?'

'From the talk in the working men's club and the letters that have been appearing in the local newspaper, people see the bosses' actions as being arrogant and provocative. So, I feel that we have the public on our side. And this time we have the solidarity, discipline and good organisation necessary to win the day.'

'Well, to quote you, Jimmy, "we shall see". Only time will tell.'

'By the way, love, you do realise that tomorrow you will have to walk through the picket line?'

'Jimmy, I've just told you that the job is essential for my kin. We can't do without it, so the answer to your question is yes, I know, unless I am hindered by your thugs. What do you expect me to do? Will your Union pay our food bills and rent? Will it prevent us from starving? Will it pay my doctor's bills? Can't you understand?'

'Kate, I'm not suggesting that you should give up your job, let alone not go tomorrow. And rest assured there won't be any thugs there. This time the essence of our fight will be disciplined organisation and non-violence. We are not going to make the same mistakes as we did before.'

'Well, that's a surprise.'

'Kate, there are no thugs in our ranks. All those involved in the pickets have been admonished to keep the strike peaceful and not to provoke either the police or the owners, and to stay away from the potential strike breakers.'

'Good!'

'And regarding your job, I just wanted the lowdown on it, so that I know what I have to do. My question does not imply that you shouldn't go through that picket line tomorrow.'

Well, that's a relief anyway.'

'But, Kate, you must realise that, though I love you dearly and I would give my life for you, if you walk through that picket line tomorrow, I cannot prevent my mates calling you a scab or other vile names. It could be unpleasant for you. Feelings are likely to be running high tomorrow. Whatever may come to pass, rest assured that I shall be at your side, my Love.'

Kate realised that Jimmy's loyalties were plainly torn between her and his co-strikers.

'So, will you also be calling me a scab then, Jimmy?'

He regarded Kate with a baleful expression, seeming greatly hurt by the posing of such a question.

'Kate, you do not need even to ask that question. You know that I won't. And I shall do my level best to prevent the men from doing it. I shall be there to protect you, Love, even if I cannot be everywhere all the time. I can shadow you to your job tomorrow morning. I do not know yet, whether I may be able to see you home again. Yes, you're right I have to take into account the interests of the men that I am leading into this strike. There are limits as to what I can do and what I can ask.'

Kate adopted a more conciliatory stance. 'I know that, Jimmy, love. Of course the issue may solve itself. Herbert may feel that he has to act in deference to Arthur Rowbottom by getting rid of me. May see it as a way of currying favour with his boss.'

'I don't think Arthur would see it in that light, even if he ever does think about it. You reckon they both know of your relationship to me then?'

'Yes. He and his wife must be well aware of it, since the whole town seems to know.'
'Has the strike made a difference to their attitudes towards you?'

'Well, now that you mention it. It seems that lately Herbert's wife has changed in a subtle way.'

'In what way?'

'I find it difficult to put my finger on exactly what has changed. Although still kindly towards me, of late she seems to be a little bit mistrustful of me. I find her popping in on me more regularly than earlier on. She used to let me get on

71

with the job. She seems to find multiple reasons now to come and see me regularly. And she does not seem as friendly as she was when they first employed me, although she is still quite kindly.'

'Do you ever hear them talking about us?'

'No. Then again nowadays she and her husband seem to be much more discreet about their conversations than they used to be. It's almost like they are regarding me now as some sort of spy in the camp.'

'Well, we shall just have to see how things turn out and hope that they turn out for the best. Time will tell. In any case, I shall be there first thing in the morning to see you through the line to the manager's house, whatever, come what may.'

Kate's heart leaped; she felt uplifted by his love for her and the action he was willing to take on her behalf. She had not waited all those years in vain. He did reciprocate her feelings for him, and his tightening grip on her hand only served to reinforce his affection for her.

'Tomorrow we shall face this problem together. I shall be there at the mill early to make sure that you have no difficulty getting to work.'

'Thank you, Jimmy. I realise that it is difficult for you. I only wish I could help and be your Rosa Luxemburg.'

'That's not a good example. You know what happened to her earlier this January, don't you?'

'Yes.'

'Well, I don't want you to suffer the fate that she and her comrade, Karl Liebknecht, did.'

But Kate's feeling of happiness was short-lived as she continued to bicker with Jimmy on the way home. She tried to reason with him. Nonetheless, on each occasion she came up against a solid wall of bull-headed obstinacy. On the other hand, excusing him, she wondered if it could have been that same quality that had borne him through the hell of the trenches, giving him the courage and determination to survive and return home to her. She should be grateful for his stubbornness.

On several occasions Kitty and she had spoken about Jimmy at length since his return. They both felt that he was still so preoccupied and distant, despite all their devoted labours. On the other hand, Kitty had pointed out with some satisfaction that at least he was not prone to the violence against his womenfolk that afflicted some of the other wives and female relatives of returning soldiers. The big question was what more they could do to bring the real Jimmy back again?

Then again, should she even be considering helping him? Was their affair now beyond salvation? They had seemed totally estranged by the time they parted ways the previous evening. Should she make the break and be done with it? To hell with the effect on his leadership of the strike. To hell with the strike and the damned workers. To hell with Jimmy!

Chapter Five

With a sense of urgency, Jimmy's sister Kitty was busy preparing for her imminent departure to her job as a cleaner at the infirmary. This job was a rare chance for employment, and she could not allow herself to be delayed. She was already fully dressed in a full-sleeved cotton print blouse with a stylish ankle length skirt gathered over the hips and brown button boots. She wanted to look her best for the ordeal ahead.

She was preparing the breakfast in front of the old newspaper-covered table, with its ugly, bulbous wooden legs — a table which had belonged to their now deceased mother. Hurriedly she spread the thick slice of bread she was preparing for Jimmy's breakfast with an abundant helping of brown-streaked dripping and sprinkled it with a liberal helping of salt. *Why do we women always have to do this for our menfolk?* She was grumbling to herself as Jimmy entered the room.

'Morning, Kitty,' he greeted as he entered the downstairs room.

'Morning, Jimmy. Did you sleep any better last night?'

'A bit better last night,' he replied, expressing a forgivable half-truth that was intended to prevent her worrying about him. He knew she did that all the time. 'Another night. Another day!'

He bent to seek his steel-rimmed working clogs beneath the ancient, battered armchair, which had been bought second-hand by his father and mother soon after they wed. He found his shoes exactly where he had left them the previous night and sank down into the springless chair. He pulled the clogs on over his darned socks and fastened the leather laces in a double bow. Then standing up briskly, he crossed the stone paving to the external door, the irons of his clogs scraping on the large bare sandstone paving slabs that formed the floor.

He lifted the latch with a loud metallic click. Walking through the doorway, he passed into the cold damp of the drizzly morning and slammed the door behind him. He strode the few paces to the toilet block across the yard. There was movement in the adjoining houses as people prepared for the day ahead. Despite this there was a peaceful, though rather oppressive, quiet hanging in the misty air.

On his return to the house, he went to the cellar-head scullery, practically tripping over the dolly stick which had been left out of the tub at the side of the mangle on the stone floor. Tucking in the top of his collarless shirt, he filled his white enamel bowl with stone cold water from the brass-coloured tap — the only tap in the house — and began to shave. Then he took the large block of soap and washed and dried his hands and face. Turning to his sister, he tried to convey a buoyant and light-hearted attitude.

'And how are you feeling this morning then, my love?'

'Well, apart from getting cracking on a new job, it's just another day to me. Just another day. They come and they go. Nothing more than that.' Jimmy wondered if she was feeling the loss of her sweetheart Tommy profoundly this morning.

Then she added, 'I need to be at the hospital before six thirty this morning. I can't afford to be late. That would just give them the excuse they need not to engage me. Not least because they now know that I am your sister.'

'What do you mean? Why wouldn't they want to take on a hardworking woman like you?'

75

'As I've just said, happen because of my brother.' She smiled at him, clarifying that there was nothing that he could do to lose her affection.

'But seriously, love?'

'Well, they could offer my job to someone else who would be willing to do it for less. Isn't that the scam that all these employers are playing these days, now that the men are back and there are few jobs for women?'

'Who would they find to take on your job for less and stay the course? You don't need me to tell you that it's hard graft.'

'All the same, loads of women are losing their jobs in the mills and factories, and on the trams and trolley buses, to make way for the soldiers who are coming back. There are tons of women who are now unemployed, and jobs are in short supply. The powers that be needed us during the war. Now it's over, and they don't need us anymore.'

'I see.'

'And with some of the returning soldiers without jobs, and families having to exist on their twenty-four shillings a week unemployment donation from the state, there's many a woman waiting up there each day outside the hospital's employment office on the off chance of a job. There's always a queue, you know. These are hard times for lots of women.'

Kitty was slim and well figured, if small. She was a beautiful young woman in her twenties, fastidious about her appearance. In spite of her current menial job at the hospital, she always took great pains with her appearance and her clothes. She had mellow brown eyes and wavy black hair framing a lucent and intelligent face. When she wanted to use it, she presented an engaging and radiant smile, although such smiles were a rarity in the days since Tommy's death.

Ferociously modern and independently minded, she was nonetheless a perceptive, loving and caring sister. Strong-willed and down-to-earth with neither guile nor pretension, she had a rapier-like intelligence which had no doubt put off some young men at a time when women were not expected to be overly clever. They don't like their women intelligent and well-read in this town, Jimmy often commented. Kitty was not like other working class women of her day. She was neither servile nor deferential in manner, such that she would not willingly yield to others without a fight. Not for her the sentimental and pretentious nonsense which had bewitched some women into assuming the role of second-class persons.

When the others left school, she had stayed on until the age of fourteen in the higher grade section of the local elementary school, learning science, mathematics and literature, all of which opened her eyes to a world of wonder beyond the grungy street in which she and her brother lived. Always an animated person, she read a great deal and explored widely for mental nourishment.

Kitty was an enthusiastic champion of the local Socialist Club and Labour Party. With Jimmy and Kate, she attended gatherings of the group and went to lectures in the Great Hall at the Mechanics' Institute where she had heard some of the most radical politicians of the day. They had inspired her ambition for a better world, not least for women after the declaration of the armistice. It was those encounters that had convinced her that things could not stay as they were; things had to change for everyone's benefit, not just for the few.

On one occasion, Kitty was even invited to tea in the Mechanics' prestigious upstairs restaurant by Sir Arthur Rowbottom after a lecture. She greatly admired the building with its Venetian glass, polished ornate brass and curling mahogany staircase. It had an ambience of venerable dignity cocooning a radical political faith and ideas. Once in a while, she and Kate went to the local playhouse where they were both enthusiastic and critical about the plays, usually buying a cheap standing place in the gods.

The foursome — Kitty, Kate, Jimmy and Tommy — had all taken advantage of the Aladdin's cave that was the free reference library in the centre of town, with its large mahogany study tables, extensive collection of reference works and cubicles for individual study. It was there that they could gain access to the richness of human culture and literature in all its contemporary and historical splendour and read the local and national papers for free. There they gained free access to the WEA magazine *The Highway* and its rich fund of knowledge and they also attended some of the WEA lectures.

In manifold ways, Kitty had been the springboard behind Tommy's conversion to radical socialist dogma. That was before he and his friends from the mill were carried away on a wave of jingoistic propaganda leading to his precipitate and fateful enlistment as a volunteer in the local Pals in 1914. With the benefit of hindsight, Kitty considered it an absurd and impulsive step, too far and too soon. Driven by her love for him, she had alerted him to the potential corollary of fighting a rich man's war. He had paid the ultimate price for ignoring her words.

During the war, in the absence of both their sweethearts, Kitty and Kate had backed Ramsay Macdonald and the pacifist wing of the Labour Party until it split. They embraced the policy of the Independent Labour Party to oppose conscription. After Tommy's death on the Somme, in common with hundreds of other radical and socialist women, they had walked side by side in the women's anti-war demonstration and March in 1917 in the town centre. They had done it in the face of the opprobrium of the neighbours and exclusion from some social groups. On the march they had been assailed by catcalls from hostile bystanders — women as well as men — some of whom screamed out and out chauvinist and lewd comments.

Nevertheless, their steadfastness never deserted them. It was in such pursuits that Kate and Kitty had become very close friends, providing much needed social and emotional comfort for each other while the men were away at war, a surrogate relationship that both found humanly satisfying and fulfilling.

During the war, Kitty, given her high level of literacy and numeracy, took on a responsible job as an accounting clerk in a local tailoring factory making uniforms for the officers of the military. She liked working with her brain and had ambitions to move up in the world. But, with the end of the war and the contraction of the market, Kitty lost her job to a returning soldier and was too proud to take the twenty shillings paid by the government to unemployed women.

She now considered herself blessed to have obtained her backbreaking, dismal and menial job as a cleaner at the local hospital, scrubbing wards, stone slabbed landings and toilets. She still had dreams, however. And she still visited the library, where she read and later professed radical, social and political change in what little spare time she had. Such visits helped her to form a mental picture of an alternative and better society for all, and an improved life for herself and her much-loved brother.

It was hard, even demeaning, for Jimmy to visualise his sister kneeling down to scrub and clean the squalor of the wards in the old workhouse building now used as a civilian hospital. She had not been the same since she had received the news in July 1916 of the death of her fiancé in the futile and calamitous battle of the Somme. Tommy, struck by a shrapnel bullet in the head, had been one of the first of many of the town's Pals — eighty per cent casualties no less — to fall on that fateful first of July. And that was not the worst of it.

Ignominy followed tragedy and personal bereavement. Swiftly, any initial sympathy that there had been for the women who had lost their men dissipated and 'superfluous' women like Kitty were resented, encouraged to emigrate to Canada or Australia, and even defamed by the press.

On some mornings, Jimmy's view was that Tommy had been lucky in a sense. A hot piece of metal in the head had killed him outright as he emerged over the lid from the assembly trench, before he even had a chance to reach the frontline trench and begin the advance towards the Hun's frontline, let alone discharge his rifle. Although impossible for Kitty to recognise, in a way it was a blessing. His death had been instantaneous and his body was recovered. Ultimately, he would be an honoured casualty with a headstone and an inscription in a military cemetery in France to provide a distant comfort to his kinfolk. But, for Kitty, Tommy's death had been a devastating blow from which she would never recover. She would never fall in love again. It seemed to say that on her face and in her premature ageing.

Jimmy reflected with fond affection on those early days of naïve and youthful, blind patriotism and heady passion, which greeted the declaration of war. It had been a wonderful summer with lots of sunshine — an idyllic time of life, not least for young people in love. And he had been so in love with Kate that summer.

He recalled the shared human warmth and happy-go-lucky idealism when he and Tommy had enlisted for the local Citizens League Army. They had so proudly worn their new blue uniforms made locally of coarse material, and the embroidered cap badge with the town's coat of arms emblazoned on it.

At that time, it had all appeared so translucently clear. They had enthused themselves into volunteering without a great deal of knowledge or foresight. No white feathers for them. Save those for the conchies. It had seemed the natural thing to do, although there had been some anti-war discussion among the Labour and socialist groups nationally and in the town.

There had been fun in it too. In that first brilliant summer of 1914, how swanky and romantic their new blue uniforms had seemed, although Kate had remarked at once that they might be mistaken for postmen not soldiers. In spite of that, the girls had loved going to the local park to see them drilling in those glamorous uniforms with their obsolete Lee-Metford rifles. Even the rather comic exercises and the camping out in the countryside up one of the nearby dales had seemed like a brave adolescent adventure.

The bittersweet of their leave-taking from the packed central station had seemed romantic. The air was filled with the music of local bands playing patriotic tunes and the thronging crowds were singing and cheering. The atmosphere had been electric; they all felt like heroes in the making. Kitty and Kate had both come to see them off, and he and Tommy had faithfully promised on that day to take care and be back home by Christmas. The taste of their

81

kisses had been so sweet, garnished as it was with the expectation of an exciting adventure.

How dissimilar it had been when Jimmy had come home on leave after the battle of Loos, where the British army had for the first time used poison gas to slaughter fellow human beings and the British casualties were roughly twice of those of their enemies. In the poor and shabby streets, curtains were drawn and the doleful church bells had tolled all day. As he and Kate vowed eternal love to each other at the dreary central London and North Eastern railway station, she sensed forlornly that he would not come back a second time. At the very least not the same. There were no bands, no naïvely enthusiastic crowds, and no toadying civic dignitaries. Only the dismal, lazy hiss of the steam engine and the dim illumination of the few gas lamps still working. God knows, Jimmy had not wanted to go back. Alas, he had no choice. He had to return to that indescribable hell on earth, to Fred Karno's army.

In any case, soldiers could be shot for not going back; some had been shot already as an example to the others. And there was the consequential unbearable stigma for their families too. To say the least, he and Kate acknowledged that even if physically intact, he would not come back the same. He would never be whole again, like he had been before. Their painstakingly planned lives together for the post-war times could never again be the same. And the Somme was still in the future.

How changed the atmosphere had been beneath the cast-iron arches of the grand central station on that second occasion. The eagerness of the men, the jumbled love, fear and pride of the women, the elation of the crowds, and the pompous bands: all were long gone. Only the hiss of the engine, like a snake poised to strike, interrupted the sombre silence of the platform. Instead of cheering crowds, silent pairs sought the privacy of the shadows, where they cuddled in respectful embrace amid whispered tenderness and the occasional sob.

Profoundly haunted once more by his memories, Jimmy's reflections jumped back to the Pals first posting to the Middle East. It had seemed like a holiday camp in the warm climate, interspersed with a theatrical accompaniment of apparently purposeless games. He had been able to travel with Tommy and quite a gang of the Pals from his area. It had been like a fun holiday for the boys. All for one!

Before that, however, Jimmy and Tommy had had some rather unpleasant experiences. The Pals had travelled by rail to Liverpool, where they had embarked smartly and efficiently and commenced a rather uncomfortable sea voyage. Together with most of the men, Jimmy had been as sick as a dog during the crossing of the Bay of Biscay. Mysteriously, for he was as much of a landlubber as Jimmy, Tommy had managed to dodge the worst of that affliction and to maintain his hearty appetite. Both had, however, suffered from the stomach upsets and other minor illnesses widespread among the men because of the poor food and hygiene and the cramped living conditions. Things improved somewhat when they entered the calmer waters of the Mediterranean. At that juncture they had been permitted onto the deck and into the lovely warm sunshine. After that it was calm sailing to their first landfall at Valletta, Malta for refuelling.

They left behind some men from their unit who were more seriously ill. The rumour running the decks was that some were infected with one of several contagious diseases. Tongues were greatly exercised about the catalyst for and circumstances of contraction. The ship left behind a horse that had given up the ghost from pneumonia, and this demise was the subject of multiple jokes by the volunteers about the comparative robustness of the health of the men and the horses. They departed for Alexandria before sailing and making landfall at Port Said, under cover of darkness in order to dodge attack by submarines.

In that place and at that time, it seemed like a youthful, carefree adventure for the men. Having set up camp nearby, they were allowed to go into town, and Jimmy and Tommy went hunting for souvenirs to send back to their girls. They even tried to learn a bit of the local lingo and get to know some of the 'natives'. Another necessary activity was to purchase local food to supplement their meagre and boring army rations; this activity was, however, somewhat curtailed when a number of men went down with severe bouts of gippy tummy.

This rather carefree atmosphere endured until one of the men was fished out of the canal with his eyes gouged out. This discovery gave rise to great antagonism among the Pals and threats of generalised revenge on the natives. It was as a repercussion from this event that the men were totally barred from entering the native quarter, although they were still permitted to go into the European sector of the town.

Apart from that one incident, the only major nuisances had been the dysentery, flies and lice, the scarcity of water and the poor rations: bully beef, otherwise known as red horse among the men, and sour biscuits. This latter problem had led to the need for some belt-tightening. The officers were not particularly strict and, although some of them undoubtedly regarded the men as inferior and uneducated creatures who had too much spare time to write home, there were few disciplinary charges, even for not saluting.

With time on their hands, Jimmy and Tommy had had a chance to think beyond their relatively idyllic lifestyle. They'd had time to talk of how the world would need to change after the war. How the workers would be better organised, taking over and exchanging their existing class-based, top-down society for a fairer one — more democratic, just and equal for their children. As the routines became monotonous, idle tongues had time to wag and men began to fret about what lay ahead. Reports were seeping back about the carnage in France and hopes of their 'holiday' being over by Christmas were distinctly wide off the mark. The run-up to Christmas and the arrival of a Lady Bountiful Christmas box for each man from Princess Mary, inevitably brought about recollections of their families and loved ones so far away. Homesickness became widespread and persistent.

One day Tommy and Jimmy were left behind on guard duty, while the others were permitted to go to the European quarter of town for their Christmas festivities and lunch. The realisation that the other Pals were doubtlessly enjoying themselves did little to lift their weary spirits or break the ineffable monotony of their task. Jimmy recalled the somewhat maudlin conversation he'd had with Tommy in one of the round tents on a break from guard duty.

Tommy had asked, 'Jimmy, have you ever had it with Kate?'

'What a question to ask of a mate, Tommy. Why do you ask?'

'Well, I just surmised what a tragedy it would be to pass on without ever having had it, even once.'

'Well, you don't need to worry about that. Destined for a ripe old age, you are. And probably a house full of children too. Me and Kate will live close to you with our brood.' He wrestled with his conscience, fully aware that the odds on their both surviving the war in France were not awfully good.

There followed a brief lull in their conversation during which Tommy took a picture of Kitty out from his breast pocket. He stared at it, concentrating hard and seemingly oblivious of all else.

'No, I don't think so,' Tommy continued. 'I can sniff her perfume now. It's just like she was here with us in this tent. I can see her beautiful black hair and feel the warmth of her hand in mine. The tenderness of her embraces, gentle and firm. The feeling of her breasts against my chest. I've never even felt them with my hands.'

'Tommy, stop it. You're just punishing yourself, thinking like that. There's no point.'

Tommy ignored Jimmy's interjection and pressed on. 'I wonder what she's doing at this moment. I can feel the smooth skin of her face. Her warm, sweet, moist lips. She dominates my every thought: every day, every hour, and every minute. I dream of the way she tips her head to the side, smiling gently and throwing a bold glace at you like she's challenging you. I wish I hadn't been so shy. I should have asked her out ages ago. I missed my chance, I did. And now …'

'Tommy! Stop it. There's no point torturing yourself.'

Tommy deliberated for a while then came out with the question that was plainly eating away at him.

'Jimmy, when do you think we'll be going to France?'

'Oh, not for a long time, if ever,' Jimmy responded. He sought to downplay the virtual certainty that sometime — for all they knew it might be in a couple of days — they would embark for France and the hell that was the trenches.

Without a doubt Tommy was feeling rock bottom, judging by his pale face and doleful expressions. So, Jimmy conjured up the best reassuring smile he could muster, slapped him on the back and said cheerfully, 'We're needed here for the foreseeable future.'

'I don't think that's the case, Jimmy. It seems obvious that we're not going to stay here throughout the war. The word among the men is that there have been huge losses in France. The general belief is that it is only a matter of time before Empire troops replace us here and we are redeployed to France.'

'Oh, I wouldn't worry about that, Tommy. They're a bunch of pessimists are the lads sometimes. This sort of tittle-tattle routinely spreads throughout the camp. Too much time on their hands, Tommy. That's the trouble. Too much time to let things prey on their minds. The officers are not always wrong, you know.'

'Well, I'm not so sure about that. Let's just imagine that the first batch of Empires are already sufficiently competent to take over …'

'I doubt it, Tommy lad. You know it will take a long time to train up a large body of men.'

'No, seriously, I can feel it. I know in my heart of hearts that we shall be moving back to Europe in a little while. And I am not afraid, though …'

'Tommy, lad, there is no point in worrying about the future. And you don't need to tell me that you're no coward. I've known you for just about the whole of your life. Since we were youngsters, in fact. Here, have another fag. That'll make you feel better.'

'But Jimmy, if anything should happen to me …'

'It won't,' Jimmy cut in, wanting to close their distressing conversation.

'But, if it does, I want you to assure me that you will always look after Kitty.'

'Tommy, she's my own sister. I love her as much as I love myself. Of course I'll look after her. Anyway, this is all gloomy surmise. You're going to be all right. You're a better soldier that I am, and I am sure you will be okay. You're shooting's better than mine for one thing. Likelihood is much greater that I shall be needing you to watch out for Kate.'

'Jimmy, I had this terrible dream last night. I just know that my number is going to be up when we get to France.'

'Don't be so superstitious, Tommy. That's a silly idea. Probably nothing more than the bully and those sour biscuits being a bit off. You'll be telling me next that you can see the future. None of us can.'

'I'm serious, Jimmy.'

'If we all stay close to each other and watch each other's backs, you will be fine. So, let's have no more of this nonsense. You're just a bit homesick and ill, and you have time on your hands today. And us here left behind on guard duty while the rest of them live it up in town. Trust us to draw the short straw! Forget it. With the war over by next Christmas, we shall be looking back on this conversation. We'll be with the girls — who knows, possibly even our wives by that time.'

'Yes, okay. But I'll tell you one thing, Jimmy.' Tommy was apparently cheered by their conversation. 'If we do get back, I'm not going back to the mill. I'm not returning to the same old master-servant bond and tipping my cap to the bosses. I'm going to make something of myself. I'm going to be something.'

'Good for you, Tommy. That's the way to be looking at things. And I'll be there by your side. And there'll be others of that same view when this mess is over. None of us is going back to the old times. This war has changed everything and the bosses and the powers that be had better grasp that.'

With that, they fell back into taciturnity and stillness as abruptly as their exchange had begun.

Looking back, Jimmy considered sadly the uncanny nature of Tommy's premonition. It made him reflect once more on what a waste it all was. Tommy never had a chance to make anything of himself, let alone to contribute to the changes in society that he had desired, that they had both desired. Along with tens of thousands of others — great and small, rich and poor, geniuses and average decent folk — who could have worked to change society for the better, Tommy's life had been taken from him before he could even begin.

Jimmy's reflections triggered a series of memories as he slid seamlessly into a feeling of intense resentment. It wasn't just the weather that had shifted once they had landed in France. Even on the boat going over, relations had begun to change. On departure the officers had been tetchy and had blocked the men from singing in concert on the boat. This action became a touchstone for a new-found sourness, which turned to bullying and in the longer run became an open and rancorous hostility by some officers towards their men.

Yes, by the time they had moved to France a couple of months after Jimmy's conversation with Tommy, things had changed fundamentally. What a rude awakening they had had. And not just the sub-zero temperatures and the snowstorm in which they had detrained. There was no more holiday adventure. No more leisurely sightseeing, trading with the natives, souvenir buying or bathing in the warm sea. No more relaxed dealings with the officers.

Instead, what commenced was a phase of constant hatchet-faced surliness and obsessive precision about the minor aspects of military discipline. The physically harrowing experience of travel and the change in climate was accompanied by a parallel blow, which was socially disorienting and mentally stressful. The distance between old school officers and working men seemed to grow in proportion to their nearness to the frontline. The officers, always superior, had become downright sods overnight, acting like they detested the men and their culture. They seemed to welcome each small misdemeanour as an opportunity to bear down with their Orwellian social class fixations on their men.

The discipline had become consistently harsh and unbending, even cruel. The Pals were no longer treated as honourable volunteers who could be trusted, rather as lower class soldiers who had to be coerced to obey orders. The objective of achieving the obedient compliance of the volunteers was conducted through wilful denigration, repression and infamous punishments that verged on, nay that *were*, torture. For quite minor transgressions men were tied to a cartwheel and denied food and water over a protracted period. Oh, how it had all changed!

Yet through it all, it was the stoicism of the ordinary volunteer in the face of such belittling and mocking provocation, and their unswerving belief in duty and fair play, that had so impressed Jimmy. Indeed, such adversity only seemed to make steelier their fierce loyalty to each other. The expressions of comradeship among the Pals now grew more profound and somehow more sincere, as did the acute and irreverent sense of humour which enabled them to cope with their new more formal obedience to their masters. Real bonds of friendship had blossomed on those rare occasions when they had been permitted to relish a brief, well deserved visit to the shell-blasted and sandbagged estaminet.

What a bloody terrible waste, Jimmy mused, as he had done so often since his return. They had been deceived with an assiduously cultivated myth of a solely German arrogance and militarism. As if the Germans were the only people in Europe who were arrogant and militaristic. He could name quite a lot of officers who would fit that same bill. They had encountered for themselves the despotic and inhumane cruelty to their own of the British army.

Now there were thousands of widows and single women like Kitty up and down the land, who would never feel a man's hands on them again and whose lives would be a never-ending monotony of lost love. For years to come, there would be an army of women just existing without prospect for the rest of their lives. Some had the consolation of children; countless others did not and never would. And then, there was the army of half men: men without limbs or sight, faces or genitals. Men condemned to a lifetime in hospital, unable to undertake even the humblest of actions for themselves. And what about the inestimable number who, although bodily intact, would carry mental scars and relentless, horrific memories for the rest of their lives? Had it really been worth it?

Jimmy's gaze was drawn to the already fading and curled picture postcards which Kitty had placed as a tiny shrine on the mantelshelf above the range several months previously. This was her place of remembrance and solace. One card had

the words 'I Miss You' with a little verse on the front
expressing a sentimental message, accompanied by a picture
of a soldier embracing his sweetheart. Kitty had received it
from Tommy just a little while before his mother and father
received the telegram notification of his death on the first
day of the Somme.

Tommy, like Jimmy, had been one of the early, eager and
passionate volunteers for the Citizens Army to crowd the
entrance to the recruiting office in the old Town Hall on that
early autumn day in September 1914 — 'aflame for their
own destruction' as Kitty put it after her sweetheart's death.
Some of them were unemployed, attributable to the slackness
in the textile industry; others had good jobs and prospects.
On the other hand they were more than willing to give them
up in exchange for the thrill of going to war. Oh, how they
had jostled and shoved to be among the next group of four to
be admitted into the recruiting hall. Oh, how bitterly they
complained when, brimming over with enthusiasm, it was
announced that the office would be closed for lunch. Closed
for lunch and Tommy was only halfway to becoming a new
Tommy Atkins.

They were caught up on the tide of stirring patriotic
music, rallies at local sports grounds, tramcars festooned
with streamers, and posters clarion calling on God to save
the King, urging British Bulldogs to volunteer, and inviting
John Willie to accede to Kitchener's requirements. There
was a bigwig military man upstairs, pleading with the young
men to volunteer. Crowds came from near and far just to see
the tram and the 'lucky' ones were enlisted there and then.
Fools that we were, he reflected. Brainwashed and caught up
in that romantic nonsense about fighting for King and
country and being back home by Christmas. If anyone
needed saving, it wasn't the King; it was the poor sods who
were rushing to make themselves into cannon fodder.

Jimmy was on the point of moving on to more healthy contemporary matters, such as the organisation of the strike, when his eyes got the better of him and alighted on another gaudily decorated card from Tommy to Kitty. He cast a baleful glance at the words of the song on the card: 'There's a long, long trail a-winding, into the land of my dreams.' On the card was a picture of a beautiful red rose and an evocative long road disappearing into the sunny distance with a young man waving goodbye to his sweetheart. This card, received after Tommy's death, had been his last goodbye.

All that life would ever be for Kitty now was an engraved and fading memory, a fantasy of what could have been, a lifelong and lonely nightmare. A total emptiness stretched into the distant future with only the advent of death as a release at the end.

At least Tommy had been killed in action and had not been one of the two Pals who were executed for getting drunk and being absent from duty. An ostensibly innocent night out on the town had turned into a death sentence for them. Released temporarily from a mire of intolerable stress and profound depression, they had become so drunk that they could not find their way back to their post in time. No one supposed in their wildest dreams that they would be shot for that error. They were brought before a court martial, found guilty, taken out at sun up and shot by their horrified comrades in arms. So, Tommy was fortunate. Or was he?

As Jimmy often did, he spoke to himself, totally consumed by his own internal dialogue, raking up his horrific war experiences again and again. He was obsessed by the fact that the Pals had been sacrificed on the altar of a senseless war, by stupid, class-ridden officers. Pride of place in his rogues' gallery were the generals and politicians who cared so little for the lives of their men and even less for the welfare of their loved ones at home.

The generals' willingness to accept large casualties was born of the fact that, no matter how large, they themselves would not be part of the tally. Nine out of every ten Pals had been killed or wounded or gone missing in one early engagement alone — ninety per cent casualties and few cushies among them. How many generals had been held to account, let alone court-martialled? Who had even been publicly blamed?

And what had it all been about? A minor contretemps between Austria-Hungary and Serbia and the alleged arrogance of one royal clan against the alleged arrogance of another. This war to end all wars had never been the working classes' war. Working men were just the servile-minded fodder. It had all been a cruel delusion. Marx had been spot-on, and Lenin, the new leader in Russia, had been correct too. The further Jimmy distanced himself from the war, the more compelling and incontrovertible became his conviction of its futility and the sharper his determination to make sure that the post-war world would be radically different.

How did Kitty have the courage to carry on? He asked himself. He had been the jammy one in ten to come through it and survive physically unharmed.

Drowsy through overtiredness and drifting now somewhere between sleep and wakefulness, Jimmy's thoughts flicked like a movie camera through a series of vignettes of the loathsome way the ordinary soldiers had been treated by some of their officers. He recalled the way the officers had scornfully battered the soldiers with their upper-class enunciation, bullying them, denigrating them, intimidating them, treating them with contempt and making fun of their regional dialects and accents.

94

It seemed to him that the officers, with their contemptuous attitudes and cut-glass pronunciation, took their men's language as an indication of a lack of intelligence. The ordinary soldiers had been treated as subhuman — worse than the horses. There had been a shortage of horses, so they got priority feeding time. And no horses had been shot by the battle police.

Into the foreground now poured a vivid recollection of one episode which Jimmy had observed that highlighted the distinction between the officers and the others even in the Pals army. It had transpired after a gas attack. The eyepieces of their discarded masks were still dimmed with perspiration; sunk-eyed, gas-wounded men and officers had been mustered in a communications trench. Some of each status were severely affected by the gas, with unseeing eyes and an incessant frothy vomit emanating from their silent mouths. None could move and some were dying. Regardless of the severity of their condition, the officers were carted off on stretchers for treatment in the morning, whereas the men had to lie out in the open all day. Not until the next morning were they led away, each gripping the jacket tail of the man in front as they groped forward, their path often blocked by the throngs of men falling back and clogging the trenches.

To the generals — commanding absolute obedience, even to arrant stupidity — the men had been expendable animals, available in eager and idealistic profusion. Manifestly, the generals were not worried about the vast numbers of cannon fodder, who were slaughtered in what had come to be called the 'theatre' of war. They left the politicians in Westminster to face the flak.

How many of those monocled top brasses would have had the courage to fight in the trenches? To go out on night reconnaissance to scupper a German listening post? And all in the company of the huge brown rats and interminably irritating lice, not to mention the seemingly ubiquitous patrols by Fritz? As Jimmy recalled the croaking of the frogs and the occasional hoot of an owl in the deathly stillness of the night, he automatically scratched at his armpits.

His vivid evocation glazed over as he wrestled desperately to obliterate the images and find solace in his idealism once more. As a best shot at distraction, he turned his concentration to what he had heard of events in Russia, what the workers there seemed to be achieving and their implications for workers here at home. They certainly seemed to have the right idea: get rid of the ruling classes and let the workers take over. He mulled it over once more, affirming his conviction of the need for radical social change in Britain, if it were ever to be truly fit for heroes or anyone else for that matter. Would that ever really come to pass in Britain? The working class of Britain had no backbone for revolution and the middle classes were extremely harnessed to their grace and favour positions.

Even doing one's best to give the lads backbone for a strike to hang on to their existing wages and conditions was challenging. What would it be like to get them to fight for better wages and conditions? They may have had a belly-full of fighting and violence; perhaps they had no more stomach for a fight; they've gone soft. It could be that all the real fighters perished in the war.

Well, we shall see how they frame up in this strike. This is their first real test since the war. Jimmy knew that, as vice-chairman of the Action Committee, he was one of those who had voted for the strike. In other words, he was someone who shared responsibility for leading them into this dispute. He had no alternative but to make the action a success. The strike had to succeed. Otherwise, he would not survive and he'd be out of a job. But, how could he face up to that

96

responsibility, given the sheer nightmarishness of his life nowadays? Bearing in mind his exhausted and downhearted mental state and his flawed human relations with his nearest and dearest? Had he survived one physical hell, only to perish in a mental one? The outlook was bleak indeed.

Chapter Six

The household finances in the jug were in crisis, their rainy day money was exhausted and Kitty was worried where their next meal was coming from and how they were going to keep warm with the colder weather coming in.

'After this breakfast, we're out of bread, Jimmy. And there's no more milk and nothing in the cupboard for tonight's supper.'

His sister interrupted his intense reflections on the inadequacies of the British working class and the unjustified sense of superiority of their useless rulers. She was on the point of seeing his prolonged, brooding muteness as self-indulgent and counterproductive. So, she sought to draw him out of his shell by confronting him with one of the major practicalities of their daily lives: lack of food.

'I need to go to the butcher's today after work if we want a meal tonight. I might be able to get some spare ribs, although it'll have to be on the slate again. Despite rationing, food has become quite scarce and prices seem to be increasing by the day. They're peddling meat on the black market, of course, though it is far too expensive for us. Some can afford it. Most can't.'

'It is truly disgraceful what I have come home to. The shortages, the black market, the selfishness, the greed. I understood that the local Food Control Committee was intended to act against profiteering in such things as meat and watered milk? In fact, against all infringements of the food regulations?'

'Well, that's the theory. Except those that purchase such meat on the black market aren't going to complain. And those that can't afford to buy the meat, don't see it, so can't complain.'

'I was convinced before that we were all in this together and rationing was a measure intended to get rid of any unfairness.'

'The local Food Control Committee hasn't done anything, except warn milkmen against watering the milk. And there's never any jam or marmalade in the shops, even though it is on the ration. And cigarettes are becoming scarce now too. You seem only to be able to get them at the shop, where you have left your ration coupons.'

'And beer is scarce now as well,' Jimmy added regretfully. 'It only goes to confirm what an incompetent clique of national leaders we have. We need a socialist government to sort out this mess, get rid of the parasitic aristocrats and give the workers their just deserts.'

'By the way, the coal place is almost empty, and the coal supply has got worse since the onset of the colder weather. And don't forget the rent man will be coming tonight. And the bowler-hatted doctor's man. You know payday from the hospital isn't 'til next Friday. I don't suppose you have any money, do you, love?'

Jimmy stared past Kitty and into the distance. She was worried about him. He seemed totally at sea. Even more pressing were her worries about their dwindling resources and how they could pay their way in the event of this strike being lengthy. She kept house for them both, as she had done since the premature death of their mother from breast cancer before the war, and she worked long hours as a cleaner at the local hospital. Their father, a violent wife beater, had deserted his wife and family when the children were still young and at elementary school, and nothing further had ever been heard of him. So, Kitty was used to planning the household resources, although they were not usually in such a crisis.

'Kitty, lass. I gave you all the brass I had last week. And you know we're not working this week at the mill, because of the strike. Why don't you ask Mrs Wray if we can have what you need on tick just for this week? She's usually pretty understanding, and we are regular customers. After all, she has our ration coupons.'

'We already have two pounds and ten shillings on the slate. Mrs Wray was adamant last week that we couldn't have any more until that is paid off. You can't blame her, can you? She has to pay her bills too, you know.'

Mrs Wray was the woman who owned the small off-licence shop up the snicket on the corner of the next street. A kindly and sympathetic woman, she had lost her husband early on in the war and had managed the shop by herself since then.

'My wage from the hospital on Friday is not enough to pay it off, and even if it were, we would still have to live for the next week. How do we square that circle? I can't see how, can you?'

'Well then, you'll have to take some of mother's jewellery to the Anchor Fent Shop down the hill and pawn it for a couple of weeks. See what you can get for it. Some of it is good solid gold and silver after all, and several pieces came from her mother. That ring of hers alone must be worth quite a bit.'

'Fine. If that's what you want, I'll do that.'

'You can take my medals from the war as well. Much use they are to me now! See what you can get for them. In fact, take the medals first and save the jewellery for now. We're not likely to be working next week either, the way things seem.'

'Jimmy, I am not taking your medals. You earned those with four years of hard and courageous fighting for this country. We are going to keep those, whatever crops up. It would be a disservice to those who did not come back to pawn them. And in any case, you'll want to hand them on to your children.'

'Well, as you wish,' he conceded reluctantly. He knew that whatever he said, his strong-willed sister would make her own decisions about what to pawn and what not to pawn. She was the one who took the decisions about the house. Had done for years now. And he was immensely grateful to her for doing it, although he rarely articulated it.

He slumped down on a battered three-legged wooden stool at the table. He picked up the pot jam-jar that served as a mug for his sweet morning tea and eyeing the single slice of salted dripping and bread that served as his breakfast, His weary attention was drawn to a sheet of the local newspaper which, with the help of other old newspapers, served as a tablecloth. First of all, he read that, after industrial action, the eight-hour day had been conceded for railwaymen, while another commented on the lack of profitability of British post-war industry. He had read it all before and his attention flitted away to separate article reporting, in the context of widespread industrial unrest, the continuing 'Bolshevist' danger among the labouring classes, whose 'wits' might be poisoned by the events in 'totalitarian Russia'.

He switched off for a few seconds, before alighting an out-of-date copy of the *Daily Herald*. It reported the arrival of British troops in Omsk in January 1919, following deployments to Murmansk and Archangelsk in March 1918 and August 1918 respectively. It also revealed that the government had written to army commanders to make inquiries if their men would be willing to strike-break and whether they would be willing to be posted to Russia. There was also praise in another out-of-date paper for the great landslide victory, which had been proclaimed by Lloyd George in late December 1918 and it restated his much-quoted statement about his task being to build a fit country for heroes.

At that point his perusal of the 'table cloth' was interrupted by Kitty bringing his enamel mug of hot tea, which accidentally slopped over the article and made it relatively illegible.

'You know, you can't win, don't you, Jimmy?' Jimmy detected an unaccustomed note of irritation and aggression in Kitty's voice. Her comment was so sudden and unexpected that, still not fully alert for the day after his bad night, he was rather taken aback. He knew that such warnings arose not from antagonism. Rather they occurred from her love and concern for him. Nonetheless, in this case, she had obviously been brooding on the issue of the strike since she had got up — perhaps even during the night.

'We'll see, Kitty, love.'

'The whole of Tumbling Hill Street knows that you can't win. The whole of the town knows it,' she persisted. 'Only you and your purblind pals on that so-called Central Council of Action don't know it. It's not like it was in France. You may have been fluky there and made it back alive. Here, you're a marked man. Even our friends at the Socialist Club were of the same opinion last night that the authorities have marked you out as an example to be made. The coppers are looking out for you, my lad. You know that, don't you? One false move.'

After his troubled night's sleep and the mental reiteration of his experiences in the trenches, Jimmy was ill prepared for the oral barrage that had now descended on him like the words of some visiting Cassandra — least of all from his own sister, who was usually sympathetic towards him and appreciative of his predicament. How could he possibly respond?

'Kitty love, of course I know it. Then, it's not our fault, Kitty, love. It's the owners. They feel they're in a strong position and they judge that the time is now for them to decrease wages and increase hours. At the same time, they want to shun the introduction of a piece-rate system and other shop-floor practices formally agreed before and during the war. That's effectively a lockout, you know.'

'Lockout, my foot. And your strike? What does it all denote except poverty for the wives and families? And what about the children? What are they going to eat until you return to work — some of you if you are lucky — on the employers' terms? Why can't sensible men just get round a table and take their difficulties to a reasonable conclusion? Why do they always have to have a war?'

'The employers are in no mood for talking, Kitty, love. Their current assessment is that they have us on the run, backs against the wall. We have no choice bar fighting. With the increases in prices of food and other things, wages are already inadequate. We've got inflation running at something like sixteen per cent, so even today's wages are inadequate, let alone a decrease. We just can't let the employers get away with this daylight robbery and let families starve. Plus, one of our organisers, Joe Murphy, has been dismissed for setting up a branch of the Union at the mill. We cannot just allow that sort of thing to take place. Are we supposed to sit back and let him rot at home? What about his wife and children? And if we did sacrifice him, who do you think would be next?'

'Jimmy, it's not just the owners' fault. The moment you raised that red flag, you were marked. And your so-called comrades won't be able to protect you, even if they wish to. Remember, in nearly every country in Europe, the socialists were opposed to the war and that will not be forgotten either. Why did it have to be you? Tell me, Jimmy, why did it have to be you?'

'It was symbolic, Kitty. Then again, why not hoist the flag? We fought for four long years for a free country where no one was oppressed or faced social injustice, didn't we? Anyway, I did it on the mill gate. In Scotland, they put it up on Glasgow town hall only the other day. And I'll tell you something else, Kitty. All in good time, they'll be raising it all over the country. We're fighting the class war now, Kitty. The difference is that this is a war we're fighting for ourselves now, not one for the ruling elite as we were in France. Things have to change in this country, and they won't change unless we make them change. I'm adamant that, at all costs, we must stand firm against what the employers are attempting to do. We just cannot afford to be lily-livered. The workers united, will never be defeated. That's my belief.'

'Oh, that's just idealistic blather. Why can't you just take what the mill owners are offering? Try to understand. They have their difficulties too, you know. At least talk to them.'

'How can you talk to people who won't come to the table? In any case, what they are proffering is a ten per cent cut in wages for the same hours. Textile workers are already earning about a pound a week less than workers in comparable trades. Even the women who are employed in the accounts office at the local bakery get more than we do and for less hours. And they don't have to work in the noisy, dangerous conditions that we do. Where's the justice in that?'

'At least you get a free Christmas dinner,' jested Kitty, doing her best to lighten the intense tone of their discussion.

'Don't make me laugh! And talking of Christmas, don't forget the outcome of the cotton strike. The workers held out and the cotton operatives won a fifty per cent increase on standard wages just before Christmas. That was a better Christmas gift than a charity Christmas dinner. So, if they can do it, what is to stop us? That's the example we should be following.'

'Cotton textiles are not the same as woollen textiles, and you know it. They're not the same kettle of fish.'

'We are all part of the great workers movement now, Kitty, love. Workers of the world unite. That's the spirit. That is our strength. Our solidarity. Workers talk, and so do neighbours, and they know how they compare to other workers in this town.'

'Jimmy, not everyone can have the same wage. Not everyone is worth the same wage. You must see that. Do you sincerely believe that those whose job is in the wool bins should get the same as those who do the spinning, weaving, burling and mending? Should the labourer earn as much as the overlooker, foreman or the gaffer? Should the lasses that serve the tea take home as much as the lasses who do the burling and mending?'

'Well, no. I accept that it would be preposterous to argue that. Not everyone can have the same. Not everyone deserves

105

the same, although it is the wide divergence that seems so unjust. Anyway, I hear your point of view, Kitty. Honestly, I do.'

Implicitly conceding that he had lost that particular argument, he proceeded to change the subject. 'You have referred to the provocation in the raising of the red flag. Was it not like a red flag to a bull when the bosses pushed the proposal to cut wages by ten per cent ... no consultation with the workers or their official representatives either.'

'When the upper classes see a flag, like the one that you hoisted the other day in front of the mill, they're afraid that Bolshevism and bloody revolution are about to sweep the country, even the world. They're already frightened about what came about in Russia. Ask yourself why the ruling classes here in Britain have sent troops there to fight against the Reds?'

'I haven't a clue. I ask myself that question every time I read about it in the paper, and I mull over the fate of our lads fighting and dying abroad again. We've just finished fighting one war. Why get embroiled in another one? It's not even our fight. They're getting our working lads to fight against the workers over there.'

'Will you shut up about the war? It's over, thank god. So ...'

'But we won. We bloody well won. In spite of all the prophets of doom who cast doubt on our capacity to ...'

'I didn't win, Jimmy, did I? And thousands of women up and down the land didn't win either. Their menfolk have gone for ever. The generals won. The royalty and the aristocracy won. The military won and the industrialists won. The little people like you and me, millions of us, we didn't win. And particularly we women haven't won.' She stopped to take breath and compose herself, then pressed him again about his raising of the red flag. 'But why you, Jimmy? Why did you have to be the one?'

'Because I'm a member of the Central Council for Action and I am vice-chairman of the Textile Union. If I don't lead, no one else will. If no one leads, we're all finished. I'm determined. This time we'll have discipline and, like the railwaymen, the Lancashire lasses and the London policemen, we'll win.'

'It's a pipe dream, Jimmy. You know the woollen textile workers didn't win last time. They had to go back for less.'

'Yes! This time though we have a unity of purpose and strong organisation that we have never had before. We have solidarity. I sense that we have the public with us this time. Did you read the editorial in the local rag? "Provocative and deliberately intransigent" is how they described the mill owners' proposals. If we can keep the public and the press on side, I'm absolutely convinced we can win this time.'

'Yes! I am talking about you though. You as an individual! If you set yourself apart, as you have done, the Establishment of whatever kind will go all out to get you. They'll label you as a troublemaker, a communist, an agitator, a good-for-nothing revolutionary. They'll make an example of you to discourage the others.' Then, almost pleadingly, Kitty added, 'I've lost one man to that futile war. I don't want to lose another in peace, especially if they bring in the soldiers.'

As Kitty spoke, she nervously fingered Tommy's locket that always hung around her neck. Jimmy felt a gentle sense of shame at the tension between them about the strike. He remembered going with Kitty, Tommy and Kate to have photographs taken at Novella's in the city centre in their new blue uniforms directly after they had volunteered. Silly, misguided young things. Oh, so proud they were at that time, and so naïve.

'Oh, Kitty. I know, love. And we've had this conversation times without number since I came back. Let's just drop it, okay?' He tried to take her hand tenderly. Jimmy wanted to finish the conversation — he did not wish to upset Kitty before she went to work — though he accepted that she clearly hadn't finished.

'You have the government against you. Not just the mill owners and the local police. And before long the army will be arriving as well. Are you really sure that you can rely on those "brothers" of yours not to shoot you if and when they are ordered to? Do you honestly believe that the lads will stand by you when the going gets really tough?'

'Yes, I am sure they will, Kitty. Of that I'm in absolutely no doubt. There is a new feeling of solidarity and discipline and this time we are going to win. I am absolutely convinced.'

But Kitty, now resolute as ever, returned to the attack. 'Fair weather friends, that's what they are. Think of the strike of 1890, which our parents suffered. The workers were out for six months and still did not break the employers' resolve. At the end of the day, they had to return cap-in-hand because their families were starving, and on worse terms than they had been offered before. That's where you're heading this time as well.'

'Kitty, things are changing. Things have changed already, I promise you. Everywhere workers are winning more rights and even controlling governments in some places. Why, Lloyd George himself is one of us, one of the working class.

He's not one of the toffs, you know. Before long, the Communist Workers Party of Great Britain will have great influence, linked with similar parties abroad, and Labour will soon be in charge of the government. Believe you me, this war has changed things for the working classes and the workers are at the forefront.'

'The only thing the war has changed is that there are a hell of a lot fewer of you for the upper crust to deal with. They'll tame you, and some of your pals will help them. Hilda Pawson up the street was claiming yesterday that her man is not going out on strike, and there'll be others too. They can't afford for him not to work when they have four youngsters to feed.'

'Kitty, the mill girls won their case in the cotton mills of Lancashire because they stood together. The railwaymen got their eight-hour day because they stood united. And there are more to follow. The Yorkshire miners are on strike for their snap break, the shipyard workers in Glasgow are demanding a forty-hour week … and where they have gone, we shall follow. Even raising the red flag if we want to. We won the right to carry that in four long years of blood and tears. Above all, it will be our organisation and solidarity that will win the day for us.'

'Solidarity can be a disappointingly fickle companion, Jimmy.'

'Why even the police have been on strike in London, and they got most of what they wanted. Marched through the capital city, they did. That put the fear of god into those toffs in Parliament.'

'Don't forget that the powers that be are the ones with overwhelming and inexhaustible force available to them. If the forces of law and order can't subdue you, they've always got the army to back them up. If they feel they need it, they'll use it without compunction.'

'Even the army's not so reliable these days, Kitty. Soldiers learned a lot during the war and they are not as pliant as they were at the outbreak.'

'You don't know that. You can't be sure. Don't fool yourself, Jimmy. You and your mates are living in a dreamland. When you join up in the Textile Hall and the Mechanics' Institute down in town, rubbing shoulders with the local bigwigs and downing a couple of pints, you are united in the dream that you can change the world, that you have influence. All men are equal, I hear you telling yourselves. The politicians want you to believe that, to swallow as true their fairy tales about a fit land for heroes. They can't afford to let you change it the way you want to. They cannot afford to let you win. It's you or them, and they have too much to lose.'

'What do they have to lose if we're all equal?'

'Their privileged position and way of life. The elites need to be in charge of the game to make sure that they win and that their children are the ones who control the rules of the game for the next generation. Why do we have public schools and Oxbridge? They will never willingly give up that power. After all, would you?'

Jimmy was off sided by the power of Kitty's reasoning and he felt at a loss about how to react. To cope with the onslaught, he turned to more pleasant memories. With consummate affection he brought to mind how, before the war, he, Kitty, Kate and Tommy used to go to the Mechanics' Institute. There they could nourish their intellects on the words of the great political and social orators of the day and dispute such matters as he and Kitty were now arguing about. After such events, the four of them would go now and again for a pint in the Malt Shovel pub just a brief walk away. There they met other political activists and put the world to right over a pint or two. On such occasions, the ambitions of their idealism knew no bounds.

In the context of these happy reflections, he had to recognise that there was a sense in which Kitty was logically correct. His concessional thoughts were interrupted, however, as his sister carried on with her prolonged and hurtful diatribe.

'And when you talk of Russia and Germany, the upper class here feel intimidated by what has come to pass there, especially in Russia. Maybe that is the reason why the British army is in both countries at this moment.'

'But here we have a democracy, so they have to heed the voices of the people. Democracy is the pressure that will make them change.'

'Your faith in democracy is touching, Jimmy. It is also misplaced. You believe that you have a democracy. In reality, you don't. They still regulate the rules of the game and the power to change them. What do you think the House of Lords is there for? Their descendants have been there since the Norman Conquest. And the aristocracy? The landed gentry? The monarchy?'

'Yes, we know the Lords is still problematic, although that is changing with the first steps taken by the Lloyd George legislation before the war. With the help of the Labour members, he will go for further change in our constitutional arrangements. I am sure that the current state of the country and all those returning soldiers will reinforce the demands for more democratic arrangements.'

'Yes, he pushed the legislation through in 1911. In spite of that, this Prime Minister, of whom you have such high expectations, couldn't change the fundamental power relations, even though he tried before the war.'

'What precisely are you saying?'

'Well, the fact is that the Lords is still there to supervise what the Commons does, because the Establishment has no confidence in the people's ability to govern ourselves. The elites of this country do not approve of democracy and never will. It is not in their interest to do so. Nor that of their children. And they're scared stiff of battle-scarred idealists like you. But, they pulled it over on you once, when you went to war for them, so no doubt they'll believe they can do it again.'

'Kitty, love, you're wrong.'

'No, you're the one who's wrong. Nothing has changed. The higher orders here still have the last word. They're unnerved by the idea of democracy and even more so of the prospect of revolution in their own back yard. You know what Lloyd George's view was concerning the railwaymen's strike? His contention was that the strike was driven by those who were working for a thorough change in the entire social order. In other words, he was accusing them of being revolutionaries. There is no word in the whole English language that is so scary to the elites of this country. That's what the powers that be, including your Prime Minister, are afraid of, and that is why your strike cannot succeed. They're even more scared of revolution now than they were of the Suffragettes before the war, and they see you and your comrades as revolutionaries.'

'Well, that seems to me a bit of an exaggeration.'

'You know the reason why we still have a House of Lords? It's to make sure the Commons doesn't make the wrong decisions, and to stop them in their tracks if they do. So, even if some of you revolutionaries were to get into Parliament, the House of Lords is there to make sure you don't get your way. In any case, the time for this sort of fundamental change was during the war, when the Establishment needed you. You've delayed too long, Jimmy.'

'What's wrong with being a revolutionary? And in any case, it's better late than never and I'm proud ...'

'Your pride will not help you one little bit. Just weigh up what the Bobbies have been told about you, no matter that it may not be true. They are already there in force at the main mill. And the army will be brought in if needed. They have to crush you and those like you. Mark my words, this is a struggle for who controls this country and the elites are winning hands down.'

'Happen it was for this that I was spared, Kitty, my love, when scores of my pals were slaughtered in France. It could be that the good Lord needed someone to speak up for the men after those high-born officers released them from their military and mental bondage. Happen it was for this that I was born. My destiny. Everyone has a purpose to their life, and it just might be that this is mine. As I have faced death so often before, I swear that I have the courage to face up to this and to win. I would rather die than live in the kind of world we had before the war.'

'Perhaps, perhaps, perhaps ... it's all "perhaps" with you, Jimmy. You are still dominated by your memories of the war. It's all you seem able to think of. The time is overdue for you to forgot it all and break free. Live in the real world.

Build a new future for yourself. You have a lot going for you.'

'I acknowledge that I am still dominated by recollections of my experience during the war. Who wouldn't be? Take the crumbs proffered by the toffs or the mill owners? Never! With every fibre of my body, I intend that this will be a land fit for workers, workers who receive fair reward for their labours and are treated with respect by their employers and the political elite.'

'So, you are some breed of latter-day industrial Messiah, are you now, Jimmy Kelly? You're impatient to sweep away what we have, though you're not certain what you would like to replace it with. Is that what you want, a political void? A civil war like they have now in Russia?'

'You know, the other day when I went down to the Mechanics' Institute, I heard a talk by a Union leader from London. Bill Leather was his name. He described how the workers are now organising to exploit the new post-war economy and win a better standard of living for themselves and their families. The brotherhood is on the move, Kitty, and united in purpose we cannot be defeated. This chap underlined the significance of the advance of the Labour Party and their role in transforming this society of ours into a fit country for our heroes to live in. And I'm one of those heroes, aren't I? And so are the other Pals. Isn't that right?'

'Do you believe that Lloyd George really meant that? Or was he just pitching for votes? Being the politician? It was a little while ago that he made that statement. He's probably forgotten what he promised. Anyway, it's going to take them a long time to do what they have pledged, even if they were sincere. And in the interim, the country's bankrupt. We have rationing, poverty, deficiencies of all kinds, rampant disease, insufficient housing ... how many hundreds of years do you estimate it will take them to shift that little lot?'

'You have to start somewhere, love. We can't go on as we were before the war. One day Labour will have the power. Why they'll even be running the government within a couple of years, and at that point we'll see who owns this country. We'll see who gives the orders then.'

'Dreams, all dreams.' And with great compassion, she added, 'Don't go, Jimmy. Please don't go down to the mill.'

'I must, Kitty, love. I have to. If not for me, for all the lads we left behind. I owe it not just to the workers and their families. I also owe it to those absent lads who can work no more,' he explained, finally putting a stop to their continued discussion.

Chapter Seven

Kitty was straining to appreciate, as she had done so many times since Jimmy's return, just how their relationship had altered since he came back from the war. He still seemed so surly and distant, seemingly inhabiting a parallel world of his own. At times he was so engrossed that he did not even hear questions addressed to him, and on some occasions he sat for lengthy periods in front of the empty hearth apparently oblivious to those around him. Occasionally too she could hear him crying out during the night in the bedroom next to hers. He did not seem to be the same man who had volunteered so enthusiastically for war some four years previously.

Was there no help for these ordinary ex-servicemen who were enduring the pain of agonising mental illness? How dare she wonder about it, let alone mention the words in the presence of her neighbours and workmates, given the stigma surrounding it? Where could she turn for help or sympathy? Before the war Jimmy had always been an affable, single-minded idealist, although never radically so in her book. Now, her assessment of him was that he was a complex of differing and competing characteristics: a millennial dreamer, a radical, hard-line Trade Unionist and a brooding introvert, often consumed by memories of his suffering. Why the dickens didn't he — or couldn't he — pull himself together?

As was the case with Kate, and the two of them had discussed this matter almost ad nauseam, Kitty envisaged her role as being to help Jimmy overcome the distress. She would do all in her power to help him put away the memories of his war experiences, despite the fact that he was so fickle and difficult to figure out, so wrapped up in himself, and so difficult to get through to. Lived in another world, he did. Maybe he had always been a little bit like that.

Yet it was his introverted aloofness which worried her, and every so often infuriated her, most. He was just so immersed in his own imaginary world that occasionally when she spoke to him, he did not seem to hear her at all. Those near and dear to him, like Kate and herself, were finding his behaviour challenging. During the day he was irritable and often broody and downcast, always appearing drawn and tired. He admitted that he felt worn out all the time and that his concentration was often less than he would like. Nevertheless, even allowing for all these circumstances and the hell that he had been through, Kitty and Kate were both of a view that they had given him time to recover. Sometimes their patience just wore thin.

'Anyway, this chap spoke of the economics of the supply and demand for labour in the post-war period,' Jimmy said, picking up on a past conversation. 'He affirmed that with the losses of the war the workforce is now depleted, which implies that there will be a dearth of labour and, therefore, according to the law of supply and demand, wages have got to rise, not fall as the employers are suggesting. That would be especially the case if the total wage bill remained the same though for fewer employees.'

'Don't you believe it, love. Those mill owners are no fools. They'll weigh up first the supply and demand for what they manufacture in the markets they know, and how much profit they can make. This country is bankrupt now and lots of industries are going to go under. France is on its knees and Germany won't be importing much from us for a very long while. The street wisdom is that the demand for textiles has dropped like a brick and that will shrink the demand for workers here. So, they are naturally of the opinion that wages should be and can be lowered. Did your Trade Union friend clarify that aspect of supply and demand for you?'

On some things it seemed the two of them would never see eye to eye. He felt guilty about arguing so vigorously with Kitty and, most of all, he felt ill at ease about what he had said about his mates from the mills being slaughtered in France, considering that her fiancé was amongst them. What was becoming of him to be so insensitive to someone he loved so dearly?

'Did you see Kate at the socialist club on Monday?' he asked, desperately endeavouring to change the subject. Kate and Kitty had been friends since school, and he knew that they had looked after each other during the men's absence. The two women tended to have intimate discussions between themselves, and Kitty would never report back to him. She would never breach a trust that Kate had asked her to keep, and vice versa.

'Yes, I did.'

She and Kate often spent time together at the socialist club — not that either of them was a particularly fervent devotee of socialism. In fact, Kitty had introduced Jimmy to Kate at the socialist Sunday school, and they had both been reprimanded for giggling during the recitation of the ten socialist commandments. It was there that Kitty and Kate had had long and painful conversations recently about the problem of Jimmy. Such occasions represented a welcome opportunity for them to unburden their frustrations, and renew their commitment to helping him. Kate had shared with Kitty some of her concerns.

'He appeared intellectually as though he was doing his best to be affectionate and close, yet he was incapable of being emotionally engaged. He has forgotten how to listen, or at the least how to understand those who seek to interrupt his eerily depressing monologues and his long silent periods of solitude. He is certainly not the same affable man who went so happily to war, either in his behaviour or his ideas.'

Kitty responded in like fashion. 'Even as a Trade Unionist he seems much more radical and unbending than before. His expectations of and for the workers are much higher — in some cases unreasonably high — than they ever were before the war. It seems to me that the wounds are beginning to heal, and we shall both need to give him more time. I just know that neither of us can abandon him to get on with his rehabilitation alone. On the other hand, it is my view that we have to be tougher with him in order to be kind. We have no alternative to keeping on having a go at helping and supporting him.'

Thus, they were both of the opinion that they would persevere with their attempts to get him to talk about his experiences to prevent him from bottling up the things that were troubling him. That might also help to move him gradually on to other topics than what he had gone through in the war.

'She did not appear well at all,' Kitty disclosed in response to Jimmy's inquiry about Kate. 'That barking cough of hers is terrible, and she told me that she had coughed blood the other day. She described these raking fevers that she has and afterwards she feels so exhausted. In fact, she feels weak all the time. No energy.'

'She told me that she was getting better. The other evening, when we went to the theatre, she seemed quite well and bright. She enjoyed the theatre.'

'She would say that, wouldn't she?' countered Kitty sharply. 'But it's true she still has that nice bloom in her cheeks and appears quite the young lady. She's a very attractive woman. You should be careful, you know. She just might run off with another young man. There are lots of young Romeos out there who would give their birthright for a beautiful woman like Kate.'

'She's a free agent,' Jimmy mumbled. 'She's not captive to me.'

'But you should come to the club more often, so you can see her for yourself more frequently. She particularly shines when she's in company. She's so vivacious and sparkling. It's a pleasure to see her talking with the other members.'

'Yes, she's a good talker. I don't need you to tell me that, Kitty. And we've had some pretty good discussions among ourselves, haven't we?'

'Yes, we have. Just be warned. She might just get fed up waiting for you and run off with one of the other handsome young men around.' Kitty was half joking, although she worried that he really did not seem to have treated Kate well since he came home.

Knowing that the reality was just the opposite — an undersupply of whole young men since the carnage of the war and a surplus of women — he nodded in Kitty's direction, hoping to stay away from any further points of contention before his departure for a day of picketing at the mill. He would have preferred to concentrate on his responsibilities for the day, except that politeness dictated he made some kind of response.

'Has she been to the doctor?'

Kitty ignored the question and asked insistently, 'When are you going to marry that girl? She waited all those anxious years while you were away in France. Faithful to you all the time, writing to you and longing for your safe

120

return. And you and she, not even engaged. You urgently need to pull yourself together and get thinking, not about the past, rather about the rest of your life with her. Think about Kate. She has a right to the rest of her life too.'

'Kitty, don't keep going on about it.'

But Kitty was tenacious; she pursued her case on a marginally more subtle tack. 'You know, you could have been an overlooker by now if you had played your cards right when you came back. You were one of the first to volunteer. You had a good war record and a couple of medals. You could have been one of the gaffers. You have what it takes for that. You were always good at school and the men always liked you at work. They would have followed you. In that case, you could have married her. That's what she deserves.'

Kitty's censorious tone of voice was beginning to wear on her brother. He just wanted to be left alone to think things through, to straighten out his life, and to make a success of the present strike action.

'Kitty, you're the one who is dreaming, my love. I could never have been one of the bosses. I haven't got the education, the financial backing, the speaking ability or the contacts. It could never have been. I am a workingman. I'm proud of it and that is where my loyalties will always lie. That is what I was born for and to.'

'Jimmy, you're a capable young man with your whole life ahead of you. There is nothing you could not do if you set your mind to it. You could make something of yourself.'

'You know, if you think that the men always liked me, they will follow me in this strike.'

'Jimmy, you have to make the effort …'

'You know, in the army …'

Kitty did not know whether to be pleased or sad. She was getting him to speak out, although perhaps she was just reinforcing his obsession with the past.

'The officers used to look down their noses at us Pals because of the way we spoke. They considered us uneducated. We were subhuman because we did not speak and reason like them, even though a number of us were better read than they were. I hate their class and everything about them. I loathe the snobbery of their class in this damned society, behaving like they were the only ones who counted for anything.'

'Jimmy it's the past. You can't carry on living your life on hate. If you do attempt to do that, sooner or later it will devour you and all those you love and who love you. Build your life on love not on hate. Forget the war and its injustices, violence and inhuman cruelty. Forget what you did to others and what they did to you. Think instead of what you have. You've come out of the war not only with your life. Whole in body as well! You are one of the privileged. What more do you need for a new life? Open up a new chapter in your life. Turn the page. Marry Kate and start a family. Get a grip on yourself.'

Kitty was surprised at her own boldness. Nevertheless she had come to the conclusion that it would not help him to be indulgent. She would aim to shock him out of his trauma. In contrast, Jimmy stared into space; blank eyed, he ignored her proffered guidelines for his future life, seeking once again a haven in the past. It seemed that he was not actually speaking to Kitty as he carried on with his tortured rant. He just had to get the venom out of his system.

'In one case a soldier, an Irish volunteer from Killarney, died under the rigours of field punishment number one. He told the sergeant he did not feel well enough to undergo the punishment, and it was referred upwards. Then, without examining him or even speaking to the poor bastard, the arrogant and insensitive snob of an officer judged the soldier was all right. Thought he was putting it on. Well, he wasn't play-acting when he dropped dead halfway through the brutal mistreatment.'

'Was there no inquiry into the death?'

'No. The officers accounted for his death with a fairy story far removed from how it took place and how the foot soldiers reported it. The public was led to believe that first aid had been given as soon as he exhibited any signs of not being able to cope with the punishment. That was before the real account got out. There was public outrage, wide publicity in the press, a campaign by the *Sunday Chronicle*, a campaign by a crusading MP and exchanges in the House of Commons. But, in spite of all this, no one was ever censured, let alone reprimanded. All the campaigning and public outcry failed to have the stigma of the man's punishment abolished, yet that punishment cost a man his life and his reputation.'

'I agree that's sad, extremely sad. The stigma for the man's nearest and dearest too. Nonetheless, there is nothing you can do to bring him back. If all that campaigning failed to achieve justice, what can you do? Just face that fact. Fight other fights that you may be able to win.'

'You know, on reflection, we didn't need the Hun to slaughter our men. We killed them ourselves pretty efficiently. Just imagine his parents' agony. How many officers were sentenced to field punishment number one?

123

The men deemed it crucifixion. Do you wonder that some people are demanding revolution in this country of ours?'

'Jimmy, you have to recognise what you can change and what you cannot do anything about.'

'In another case …'

'Jimmy, just calm down. You have to let go. You're not doing yourself any good with this persistent harping back to the war. In war there are always injustices. There always will be. The only way round them is to outlaw war.'

'The officers …'

'Christ! Don't keep going on about the bloody officers.' In spite of herself, Kitty was losing patience. 'The war's over now and most of those who were officers are no longer. Many of them are dead. Their class is in decline now anyway. And no amount of blathering on about the dead is going to resurrect those Pals who perished. That is a fact. Learn to live with it. You cannot change it.'

'Yes, I suppose that's true,' Jimmy lamented weakly and with a resignation he had not felt since his return home. In fact, he was doubting his ability to change anything.

'And coming back to the strike, the men might like you. That's for sure! That does not mean that they will follow you into a strike though.'

As if his sister had said nothing, Jimmy's thoughts flicked back to the war and other episodes of utter inhuman barbarity that he had witnessed. 'If any of the lads refused to fight, they were first told to get a grip on themselves. If this failed, attempts were made to shame them in the eyes of their chums. After that, they were labelled cowards in front of

124

their Pals. If social pressure and public humiliation didn't succeed, they were court-martialled and summarily shot, however young and shell-shocked they might have been, whether volunteers or not. The men in the firing squad were punished with the perennial angst of having shot one of their own. And their families were also punished by being labelled as a coward's kith and kin. Even apart from the financial loss for those families, the social stigma in their close-knit communities was horrific.'

Kitty did not interrupt him this time, feeling that it was probably therapeutic to let him ramble on and get it out of his system.

'But there was no such thing as cowardice among the officers. Oh, no, if they were shell-shocked, they were sent off to be examined by a special doctor, a psychiatrist, no less. Somewhere in Scotland it was reported to be. No court martial and no execution for them. No pernicious electric shock torture for them. They were labelled as being sick and in need of free personal and highly skilled medical attention.'

There was such intense acrimony and betrayal in his voice, it was as if he had known all the Pals personally who had suffered the fate of being shot for cowardice or having electric probes inserted roughly into their mouths.

'I hated the war,' he added, voice now quivering with emotion. Could he ever find the words to tell her what he had been subjected to? Did he even want to? 'I hated everything about it, although I have to admit that it was an education for me. It made me see things about our society as I had never seen them before. It made me determined to change things. I swore that if I ever got back alive, I would fight for a better deal for workingmen and their families, a bigger and fairer share of the cake. And, Kitty, there are lots more like me, who've served in the war and are not prepared to let things stay as they were before, not willing to tip their caps to the gaffers and the toffs. It's the workers who have the majority in this bloody country of ours now. It's about time we took control and made the decisions.'

Kitty suspected with regret that, far from helping him to divest himself of the mentally burdensome legacy of the war, her toughness had succeeded only in provoking him into further painful recall of his experiences, even undermining his recovery. Now she herself was faced with confusing choices. It was her irresistible sense of disappointment at his slow recovery that had driven her to push him. Conceivably she had expected too much too rapidly. She had hoped that with love — hers and Kate's — he would recover a more positive approach. Since Tommy's death, he was all she had left. Not knowing whether to feel guilty, she tried once more to steer the conversation into more positive territory.

'Well, Jimmy, let's just consider Kate for a moment. If you can't think of yourself, think of Kate who loves you so dearly. The Rowbottoms own the mill where she works, and may tell their mill manager to sack her, even if he doesn't want to.'

Kitty's comment succeeded in diverting him from his previous obsession; his comeback was more level-headed and rational than Kitty could have expected, given his previous comments.

'Arthur Rowbottom has lots of faults, though being vindictive or petty are not among them. I'll admit that much about him. Mind you, I dare say he's a bit on the weak side sometimes. On the other hand, he's a decent man. A religious man who believes in justice and fairness. He wouldn't do a thing like that.'

'I hope not. Maybe you could help her situation if you wanted to, you know and perhaps help yourself to solve the dispute at the same time.'

'How do you mean, Kitty, love?'

Well, why not give Arthur a ring this morning. He seems a pretty decent sort of a chap and I am sure Billy could connect you from the time office, if you ask him.'

'That's an idea, Kitty! It might just help to smooth the wheels for a solution to the dispute and help Kate at the same time. So, yes, I think I will, if I can.'

Having made what she felt was a bit of a break-though, his sister didn't want to distress him any further. So she elected not to persist with their interchange. She sat down at the table with him, took his hand in her own, and held it tenderly. She stared him straight in the eyes.

'I know that you have suffered, my love. None of us can know how much. None of us can even hazard a guess at what you have gone through. Yet you just have to learn to move on. I will help you.' She squeezed his hand and smiled lovingly at him. 'Please now, get your breakfast, Jimmy. You'll need it today. You'll need all your strength for what you feel you have to do. I'll pray for you.'

She picked up her shawl and wrapped it round her shoulders.

'How's Eric and Irene Wooten's baby?' he asked, referring to the young couple who had moved into the house in front of their own down the passage during the war.

'The baby passed away yesterday and now Irene is down with this damned flu. She was weakened by the birth, you

127

know. Has those fits of feverishness, and after that she just collapses physically. Eric knocked on our shared wall during the night to ask me to go round for a little while to see to her. You were sound asleep. Tossing and turning, though, and crying out as usual.'

'Oh dear, I am sorry, Kitty. And I'm causing you all this trouble. You'd be better off without me.'

'Don't be silly. We are some of the lucky ones that we are here to help each other. And you are all I have now. And Kate, of course.'

'Thank you, Kitty, lass. Do you think the flu is dying down now?'

'It's the people not the flu that's dying. There are dozens of them at the mill who have been laid low. Most are afraid to go to the doctor until it is long overdue. Afraid to lose their jobs, they are. As you know, they don't have the wherewithal to afford a doctor anyway. In spite of that, the hospital is overcrowded. That's the third death in a week in this street and there were reported to be forty in the town last week.'

'Oh dear.'

'The Pogson's child died of measles last week and the Evans's daughter is no longer with us after a diphtheria-like illness two days later. Both followed hardly any days of illness. Similarly, the whooping cough has spread like wildfire, and no doubt there will be more cases to follow. Having said that, it's this flu that I fear the most. People are dropping like flies. They claim that some are well at lunchtime and dead by the evening. Especially the old folks. In town they describe some people as turning black and blue.

The last thing they need on top of this is an impoverished diet due to a strike.'

'Yes, I spotted them washing and disinfecting the trams yesterday at the depot up Skinner Lane.'

'Fat lot of good that will do! That's not likely to halt this flu. I'm not sure that all the nasal and throat douching they recommend will either, or these concoctions purporting to extend immunity. And as for all this business of going around with face masks, like a load of gangsters …'

'Yes, it's not just this flu that's in the air at the moment, is it? There's a lot of gimmickry. What a marvellous chance for all the old quacks to emerge from the woodwork. By the way, I hear that they have closed the elementary schools.'

'Yes, I know.'

Then, as often occurred nowadays, Jimmy abruptly changed the subject. 'What do you think Kate has? You don't think it is the horrendous consumption, do you?'

'It could be consumption, although I don't personally think so. For one thing, that cough of hers is nothing new. She has had it for some time now. That house of theirs is so damp, you know. Nearly as bad as ours. The ceilings upstairs are bowing, and they have to whitewash the walls regularly. There's always a fusty smell when you enter. And there are seven of them in that house.'

'Only six now with Ronny not having come back.'

'Well, six people in three bedrooms anyway. What she needs is a good walk in the country and lots of fresh air. Then I'm sure she'll be champion again. There's no chance of that with you on your current course though, is there?

Can't you just for once put her before your own interests or those of your mates?'

Jimmy fell into a sulky silence again. He loved his sister very dearly except that he wished she wouldn't nag him so. She was a little older than he, and she had been like a mother to him for most of his life, since their mother passed away early in his childhood. Kitty had made sure that he attended school each day, until he left to work part-time in the mill from the age of eleven. She had always encouraged his schoolwork and wanted him to stay on into the higher grade school and go to night class. He had been especially good at mental arithmetic and his handwriting was beautiful, almost copperplate. Night class had been the intention, and then to progress to be a wool sorter. Then the war came.

It had seemed quite romantic to volunteer and leave your girl to go and serve your king and country. He had had not a single moment of doubt that Kate was the one he wanted to marry. But, after what he had lived through in the army, he just could not bring himself to think about marriage, even to Kate. Besides, he had a responsibility to his workmates. If he did not lead them, who would? His dilemma was how he could avoid hurting Kitty, keep faithful to his pals, and still demonstrate his love for Kate?

In the distance, he heard the clang of the early morning tram passing the top of the street. It had improved things since they got rid of the old steam ones when he was a youngster, although it didn't make much difference to him. Horse, steam or electric, he would have to walk down to the mill on foot this morning. Not for him now the luxury of riding — no money for that!

Brian Farrelly, their near neighbour over the low partition wall, had a secure job as a conductor and on occasions as a driver. He was all right. The tramway workers had had their dispute. They had remained solid behind their leaders and they had won. It had only taken four days of strikes for them to get what they wanted. Not for Brian's children the potbellies of malnutrition, although even they could not stay immune to the diseases which regularly took the lives of children on this street. Brian and his wife, Mary Ann, had lost a lass in childbirth and a boy to the dreaded measles.

'Have you any idea how long all this is going to take today, Jimmy? Just so's I know when to prepare the supper, when I come back from my chores at the hospital.'

They were lucky that their father had left him a cheap pocket watch. Not that he had left it as an act of goodwill. He had forgotten it when he left blind drunk after beating his poor wife senseless and had never come back for it.

The Italian watch seller had done well out of his trade with the local workers. He had a fine house on the outskirts of town and a posh shop in the town centre where the burgeoning middle classes could purchase the most up-to-date jewellery designs from Paris and New York. Not for him the trenches of France.

'No. A lot will depend on whether there are any scabs having a crack at breaking through the lines and whether Arthur Rowbottom has tried to bring in any strike-breaking workers from outside. It is probably too early in the dispute for him to have made arrangements to bring in the army. We shall just have to wait and see. Either way, the men are committed. I have no fears about them. The team spirit is good. Discipline is also good.'

'Bring in the army? Heaven forbid!'

'Kitty, I have faced enemy soldiers so frequently in the last four years. I shall not be afraid to face soldiers who are

131

not my enemies. And this time I shall do it for a far more worthy cause.'

'And, by the way, that is a terrible word to use to describe fellow human beings. Scabs! I am surprised at you. You should be ashamed of yourself. Don't people have the liberty to disagree with you any more without being labelled with such terrible names? What has the world come to?'

'Now look here, Kitty …'

A hard knock on the door interrupted them — so hard that it stimulated the latch to rattle in its fixture. Before either of them could answer the door, there was a loud click as the latch was lifted, and the door opened wide. Through the opened doorway, the face of a handsome, perky young lad peered shyly in. The youth of about eighteen had a shock of dishevelled fair hair, covered by a dirty old flat cap. He took off his flat cap as he limped into the room, dragging his clubfoot along the floor.

'Morning Kitty! Morning Jimmy!'

'Ah, Harry. Come on in, lad. How about a nice cup of tea? You're wet through. Come on up to the hearth, lad.'

'Thanks Kitty, love. That would be fine, thank you much.'

'You'll have to hurry up,' Jimmy interjected. 'We're due at the mill in twenty minutes. And we don't want to be late. We need to crack on.'

'Well, in that case, maybe I won't bother then, Kitty,' Harry said, not wanting to delay their departure. He was very fond of Jimmy and held him as a type of model for himself, for the whole man that he would have liked to have been.

'Yes, you will,' Kitty pronounced tenderly yet firmly. 'Never mind, Jimmy. He can drink his tea quickly.'

Kitty understood that her brother held hero status in Harry Shufflebottom's book. She recognised him as an earnest, although gullible, young man and she considered that he was over-influenced by her brother.

Turning to Jimmy, she scolded him. 'You should be ashamed of yourself, dragging a young lad into this dispute. It is too dangerous for him, especially with his disability. He cannot move very swiftly, and they will likely have the Mounties there today to keep you lot away from the entrance to the mill and the manager's house.'

'I'll be all right, Kitty. Truly I will. Don't worry about me. I can keep up with the best of them. And, in any case, this is my fight as well as theirs. I should do my bit, as I did in my own way during the war.'

'Don't you worry,' Jimmy reassured his sister. 'He'll be fine with me, Kitty. I'll keep an eye on him, as I always do, and see that he comes to no harm. He knows to keep well away from any action. In any case, there's not going to be any action.'

'Well, just see that you do.'

Harry gulped down his hot tea and Jimmy finished his dripping and bread.

'Would you believe it?' Harry asked.

'What?' Jimmy and Kitty asked in unison.

'Well, did you hear that Arthur Rowbottom has been elected President of the Mill Owners' Association? It took place at a meeting yesterday, according to Billy Dolan.'

'What?' Kitty exclaimed.

'I can scarcely believe it,' Jimmy said. 'I never imagined he would take such a poisoned chalice. Never!'

'No, it's absolutely true. I just met Billy Dolan going down to the mill and he told me that it is in this morning's *Observer*.'

'If that is true, it certainly puts a wholly altered complexion on our dispute and on Arthur Rowbottom. It may, of course, be a way of easing this dispute. I've always found Arthur a quiet and reasonable man. He has always had great compassion for his workers. A religious man, just like his father before him. Of course, the power may go to his head and he may feel himself boxed in a corner. What's you view, Kitty? He's not a weak man, is he?'

'Yes, I go along with you. Arthur has always seemed to be a level-headed and judicious man. I don't believe his undertaking of the presidency will go to his head, although he has probably sought it as a carriageway to even higher things. But, yes, he seems too equable to let it go to his head. I don't think the snag is him.'

'Well, if not him, who is the obstacle then, Kitty?'

'Well, I came across some of them — not closely of course — when I was clerking during the war. It seems to me that it's the clever and experienced politicians behind him in the Association, like Sir Edgar Crabtree for example, who rule the roost. He is a man of pragmatic and centrist views. To a lesser degree, the usual belligerent hardliners like the rather tactless Joshua Crowther and his crabby sidekick Percy Clitheroe, both well-heeled blood-suckers. The big question is whether Arthur will be able to contain the different groupings, let alone lead them.'

Kitty searched her memory for further culprits. 'Oh, and another one to watch is Sam Baxendale. He has that shoddy mill at Glen Eyre. Besides, he has a successful side business as a lotter, collecting job lots of wool and hawking them as a single trade at a huge gain. He's a real wheeler and dealer, a real tight one if ever I knew one. He'll not give a penny if he can get away with a halfpenny. I met him briefly during the war when I was doing that clerking job. Anyway, this foursome … well, to the best of my belief they're still the power in the Association and Arthur's just their naïve and upright figurehead. Let's just wait and see how it works out. Arthur may still prove us wrong. Will it improve your chances of a settlement? Well, I hope it will, of course. Though who knows. Time will tell. For the moment it's in the lap of the gods.'

'Well, yes, I see what you're saying. It could just be the rest of those fat-cat members of the Mill Owners' Association aiming to manipulate him to put on a kinder public face to gain the headlines in the *Observer* and to win over the common man.'

'And woman,' Kitty reminded him.

But, revising his initial judgement of Arthur, Jimmy added, 'You know, come to think of it, he always came across as a rather weak man. And you seem to me to be right. He has his sights set on a seat in the House of Lords. He'll go the way that best suits his ambitions in that direction.'

'Oh, come on. That seems a rather unjustifiably harsh and simplistic consideration of a rather complex man,' Kitty

135

scolded him gently. 'And, as you yourself have argued, his election may give you and your fellow members an opportunity to solve the most pressing issue and resist the cut in wages. Failing that, it could at least lower part of it, for I doubt that you can resist all the proposed cut.'

'Yes, I believe that his election may give us a slender chance to break off briefly for face-to-face talks. We could ask for further discussions with them, given his election to the presidency. That would give both sides a breather. I'll offer the hand and we shall see if he is ready to take it.'

'Well, there you are. When all is said and done, his election may be a blessing in disguise.'

'But such a move would have to be sold to the executive and approved by our workmates. In their present state, it will be difficult to get that past them.'

'Jimmy, you're nothing if you're not persuasive. It's worth having a go anyway. You have nothing to lose.'

'Except the confidence of my mates. Anyway, that's beside the point. Okay, we shall have to wait until we have confirmation of his election. So, let's leave it there for the moment. I need to get down to the mill. No doubt someone down there will have a copy of this morning's *Observer* so I can read the report.'

With that, both men made for the door. Jimmy took his muffler from the wooden hook, wrapped it twice round his neck and tucked it in to the top of his shabby jacket. He pressed the latch and they both donned their caps.

'Bye, love. Take care and don't work too hard,' Jimmy said to Kitty. 'See you this evening.'

136

'Bye, Jimmy, love. Don't provoke the Bobbies. And look after Harry!'

'I won't and I will, love,' he assured her with a broad grin on his face. 'And I hope that the Bobbies will return the favour and not goad me and my mates.'

Jimmy opened the wooden door, then slammed it behind them as they departed into the early morning drizzle. Kitty busied herself getting ready for her day at the hospital.

'Why these men can't shut doors quietly is beyond me,' she muttered to herself.

Jimmy and Harry walked into the still grey early morning light of a miserable autumn morning. As they strode down the passage next to Jimmy's house, clogs echoing in the gloomy tunnel, they were in no doubt that this was going to be a momentous and decisive day for all involved.

Chapter Eight

Kate had been wholly unaware of the passage of time on her journey to work that morning, the morning of the strike. During the brief ride, she was totally engrossed in reflecting on her relationship with Jimmy and her fears that the strike could only turn out badly and make things worse for him. She was experiencing a dreadful premonition that he would be seized by the police and thrown into prison, when suddenly the juddering of the tram and the gentle screeching of metal wheels on steel rails interrupted her contemplation.

The tram slowed down to halt at the top of the road that led down several hundred yards through the model village to the beautifully designed 'house of slavery' as some of the workers portrayed it, namely Sir Arthur Rowbottom's woollen textile mill. Sandwiched for ease of transportation just below the railway line and above the canal, this building rested above the level of the tree-lined river and beneath the higher ground of the gaunt, boulder-strewn moor on the other side of the dale.

Kate levered herself wearily from the uncomfortable wooden seat, walked the few paces to the door, slid it back and stepped down onto the platform. Brian was upstairs taking fares, so she was pleased that she did not have to face him again and exchange banalities.

She managed to alight somewhat awkwardly, the cool morning drizzle refreshing her flushed features. The harsh clip-clop of her clogs on the flagstones reverberated loudly in the early morning stillness. At this point, the land fell away to the river and she started out slowly down the descent to the mill, all the while faced by a beautiful panoramic prospect across the river to the monochrome sepia boulder-strewn moorlands on the other side of the glen. At this time of day and for these few ecstatic moments of freedom before entering the mill gates, this scene of the wild moor was where she felt most at home. Plus, the walk down the road was the easy part of the day for her: it was the uphill return after a hard day's work that tended to leave her so drained and out of breath.

As she passed the expansive workers' assembly rooms and the library on one side of the road and the elaborately built cottage hospital on the other — all provided through the religious charity of the mill owner — she thought some more about Jimmy. She reflected with a subtle fondness on his threadbare and tobacco-smelling clothing and pictured his good-looking features. Was this love? Certainly, feeling sorry for someone is not a good reason to love them, let alone spend the rest of your life with them. How crushingly confusing were her prevailing dilemmas. She didn't have the strength to resolve them, so she would just concentrate on making it through the working day.

Trudging without haste down the hill, she could not help feeling a sense of foreboding at what she saw. Black Marias were parked in the cobbled side streets. Nearby were groups of Bobbies, relaxing and smoking, with some of them nervously engaged in conversation, no doubt preparing for the coming confrontation. They were commonplace working class men, like the strikers, probably with wives and families. Some of them lived in the same streets, and as children had played street games with the workers now on strike. They had been to the same schools, came from the same bereft social class, went to the same churches. Regrettably, they now found themselves on the opposite side to their erstwhile playmates and friends.

Past rows of similar impoverished houses, which were rented by the mill workers at a favourable rent, she plodded slowly and doggedly onwards, her momentum propelled as much by the downward gradient of the hill as by any energy generated by her own body. She was motivated only by the desire to get to work and earn the wherewithal so essential to her family. She knew that they were relying on her.

She hurried past the neo-gothic grammar school, its lovely carved doors still closed, and she cast a fleeting glance at the porticoed entrance to the assembly hall, also built by the philanthropy and vision of Arthur's father for the education and enlightenment of his workers.

She loved these beautiful stone-built edifices and was appreciative of the philanthropy. She admired the spirit of humanity and caring, which was the root from which they had sprung. If they could do this, the owners could not be all bad. Just as not all the workers were good.

Then, she noticed the spiralling smoke rising from the mill site. Were the boilers firing again? Was the strike over? But, as she neared the mill, she realised that the smoke was coming from the braziers kindled by the strikers. Nearer still and she could see the bright and enticing colours dancing in the braziers that were burning on the pavement in front of the mill.

Like the wrecker's fires on the beaches of old, they were drawing her to her daily fate. In the dull light they illuminated the sullen faces of the striking workers standing around them engaging in muffled conversation. The smoke was wafted by the gentle breeze across the road and towards the beautiful Congregational church on the opposite side of the road, where it climbed symbolically, like incense, upwards to the heavens.

A shudder went down her spine as she weighed the ordeal ahead of her: walking through the picket lines. It was only her indefatigable courage that propelled her forwards to an unpredictable reception by the strikers. She pulled her shoulders back, grasped her shawl tightly in front of her, held her head high and stared fixedly straight ahead. She tried not to notice the knots of men warming their hands around the braziers, although she felt that every eye was gradually turning towards her in animosity.

As she was passing the last row of terraced workers' houses before the mill, two men appeared from one of the houses whose front door exited directly onto the street. She was startled both by the sudden clicking of the latch and their rapid emergence directly in front of her, like characters magically descended onto a puppet stage. At this time in the morning, she was at once on her guard, although she tried not to reveal her fear. She pulled her shawl more tightly around her and quickened her pace once more.

One of the men was older with a sallow complexion and narrow, yellow, wizened face. The other was young, possibly a teenager, quite handsome with a baby face. Father and son off to the mill, she surmised. Was it for work or conflict? Both put their caps on and called back over their shoulders to say goodbye to an unseen person inside the house. The younger one tightened his muffler against the cold and cast a friendly, slightly sheepish glance at Kate.

They stood aside and neither greeted her as she passed, although they stared straight at her. After passing in front of them, she could feel their eyes piercing her back like heated darts. In no time at all they overtook her on the pavement, still without speaking, and made for a group of men round one of the braziers a short distance from the house. A cheery exchange of 'Good mornings' took place among the men, followed once again by an oppressive hush during which they struck their lucifers to light their cigarettes.

As Kate approached the first of the clusters of men, two of the workers with their backs to her detached themselves from the group and turned towards her. She felt like running and struggled to curb her fears and anxieties. How would she react if they were to start shouting 'scab' at her? What would she do if they simply stood in her way, blocking her entrance to the house through those tantalisingly close mill gates? How could she change their disposition to permit her to enter? She needed to work. She needed to earn. Where, oh where, was Jimmy?

As the two men turned fully to face her, her heart leaped with relief as she instantly recognised them. They were clad roughly like all the other workers, muffler-chokered and flat-capped, so she had not recognised them at first. Now she saw that it was Jimmy and Harry approaching her, both of them smiling a warm and heaven-sent welcome.

'Morning, love. Nice to see you. How are you feeling this morning?' Jimmy asked.

'Morning, Kate. Nice to see you. How are you feeling today?' Harry repeated.

'All the better for seeing you, Jimmy and Harry.'

'Well, I promised, didn't I? You didn't think I'd let you down?'

'No, I never doubted you,' she lied.

He gave her a tender kiss on the cheek, put his arm round her and steered her towards the mill gate.

'Come on, Harry and I will walk you through the pickets to the gate.'

Jimmy took her arm gently and led her towards the tall wrought-iron mill gates. There was one clutch of strikers in the direct line of their path, and they seemed to be glaring at her in an unfriendly manner.

'Why is it that she can go in there and cross the picket line?' a rather hostile voice shouted out in challenge. Kate felt Jimmy's hand tighten on her elbow, although he did not slacken his pace. It was Wilf Oldridge, an ugly-looking, stubborn young man, who was speaking loudly and threateningly. Wilf was the same worker, from whom Jimmy had taken the skewer only a couple of days before. The other men in the cluster turned to him to see which way the wind would blow and how it would turn out in what some of them considered a test case.

'Let me deal with this, Kate,' Jimmy whispered in her ear, placing himself between her and Wilf. With reassurance, she felt his warm breath as he spoke, evoking flashbacks to previous occasions in happier circumstances.

As they halted before the group, Jimmy defiantly looked Wilf directly in the eye.

'Now, Wilf,' he rebuked his fellow worker, fixing him with stern eyes and addressing him in the manner of a schoolmaster addressing a recalcitrant pupil. 'You know full well that the picket line only applies to our mates who are employed at the mill. It applies to all grades, and to both Union and non-Union workers. All of them are out. We have solid backing, and we are unanimous that this strike will pass off peacefully and successfully.'

'It will only be successful if there is no scabbing and blacklegging,' Wilf scoffed.

'I am with you on that, Wilf,' Jimmy accepted, doing his best to adopt a conciliatory tone.

'Well, why is she allowed to go in to work then, when we cannot?' Wilf shot back.

'You know as well as I do, Wilf, that it was the unanimous view of the Central Council of Action, that tradesmen and essential deliveries, such as milk and coal, will be permitted through without hindrance. That includes plumbers, repairmen and cleaners. We are not aiming to inconvenience people more than is necessary. Essential work will be permitted to keep on as usual and proceed unhindered.'

'Why?'

'Because we need public goodwill to succeed, that's why. We have to carry the public with us if we are to win. That's why the Council of Action has strongly supported the view that food and milk should be guaranteed for hospitals, schools, orphanages and the general public. Our dispute is not with the general public. It is with the owners, and we have to display good sense in our dealings with other workers. So, please stand aside so that the lady can get to work.'

'I never agreed to that. Never!' Wilf exploded, while glancing round the small clique of men. 'That's as maybe, Wilf, but I have news for you. We here in this Union are a brotherhood. You, like every other brother here today, are bound by the terms set down for this strike by the Central Council of Action, on your behalf and on behalf of all the workers participating in this dispute. That is the strategy. It is our strategy. It is my strategy, and it is your strategy.'

As Jimmy spoke, some of the other men began to mutter. Wilf mustered his optimum oratorical skills and increased the volume of his voice so that all the assembled workers could hear.

144

'I just don't see why she is not the same. Is it because she's your woman?'

Ignoring the barb, Jimmy came back strongly, 'I'll tell you something else, Wilf Oldridge. It is in our interest — yours and mine — to abide by the sensible decision of all the Unions. We have the public with us this time and that will be important in any practicable solution to this dispute. It will weigh heavily with the owners. No one should take any action which might jeopardise the goodwill of the public.'

'You can't pay off the tick with goodwill, Jimmy Kelly.'

'Wilf, we are unyielding in our determination to win this dispute and to get for our co-workers the rate they fully warrant. We shall not budge an inch. We can only win though, if we all support each other and act sensibly. You've seen the Bobbies at the top of the hill. They are there for a purpose, just waiting for us to step out of line. We all have to stick together.'

'Precisely! So why the exceptions? Is it because it's your girl? Special treatment for sweethearts, eh?'

Kate could feel Jimmy's hand tighten on hers as he strove to stay calm.

'Our strength is in our solidarity, not in victimising, harassing or threatening those who are not involved, especially the weak and vulnerable. Anything like that and there are reporters here who will be pleased to write it up for the local paper, and the bosses will lap it up with relish. Such behaviour will certainly lose us the favour of the public, especially if those being threatened are women. We need to stick by the agreed policy, as expressed by the Central

145

Council of Action, and follow instructions. Now, for the second time, move aside please, Wilf.'

Wilf did not budge, and his pals seemed to be closing ranks.

'Wilf, as a good Union member and faithful brother to your fellow workers, you have no alternative. You must stick by the rules that have been laid down for this strike by your own organisation,' Jimmy continued. Or resign and depart from the scene.

'Yes, except breaching a picket line …'

'Wilf, if you do not accept the official policy decision formally agreed on how to run this strike, in concert with the other workers' organisations on the Central Council of Action, the proper way is to challenge it at the next general meeting. That's your democratic privilege, and I fought for your entitlement to do just that for over four long years in France. I did not fight so that we could victimise young women.'

'I fought too, Jimmy, don't you forget that,' Wilf reminded him, adopting a more threatening posture and moving one foot forward.

Jimmy was conscious that the situation was becoming ugly, and he was not finding the words to defang it. He tried again.

'What you cannot do, Wilf, is to go against our agreed official policy here in front of the mill with the Bobbies and local newspaper reporters present. Look up there. The Bobbies are definitely showing an interest in our confrontation. Do you really want that? What good can that possibly do us?'

'Yes, but…'

'Wilf, you remember the deadlock of the disastrous strike of 1909. We lost at that time for two major reasons. Firstly, we did not have public support and endorsement and secondly, we were badly organised, ill-disciplined and disunited. We lacked solidarity. Because we were not united, men went to prison. They never found employment in this town again after they came out. We had to return to work on the employers' terms. And some families starved. Do you want that to arise again?'

'No, but …'

'Well, this time that is not going to occur. I won't let it. If you do not like the decisions of the Central Council of Action, you can resign. Be aware, however, that if you do that, you won't receive any strike pay, and you will still have to abide by the decisions of the Union. You will not be allowed to sabotage the interests of your fellow workers. It will be our discipline that will win this strike.'

'Discipline?'

'Yes, discipline. Look at the Yorkshire miners earlier this year. They were absolutely united in their strike for twenty minutes snap time. There was no need for violence. They spoke as one, and they won. Why did they win? It was their unity, solidarity, discipline and organisation that carried them through to victory and made the owners cave in. And it's our discipline and good organisation that will win us through this time. Not having a set-to with an innocent young lady, who is totally unconnected with the dispute. Now, stand aside and let the lady through. There's a good fellow.'

To Kate's surprise and relief, Wilf spat on the floor, turned away in disgust, and moved to re-join his mates, muttering under his breath. The men seemed to ignore his return and turned their full attention back to staring mesmerised into the flame in front of them.

'Scabs just turn me off,' Wilf ventured loudly. 'Every dog has his day and that includes bitches too. He won't always be here to meet her.'

Kate heard Wilf's menacing comment and the other workers' sniggers. She shivered at the thought of what might take place when she finished her job in the afternoon and needed to walk through the workers' lines again.

Still shaking from the encounter and not feeling particularly well, Kate approached the gate and knocked hard on its thin metal-plate surface. Jimmy was still holding her arm tightly and Harry was also in close attendance. She was reassured by their presence, although she prayed silently that the gate would open with no delay.

After what seemed like an eternity, the small metal gate clanked open and the flat-capped, ruddy-faced figure of the timekeeper, Billy Dolan, appeared in the doorway. Kate regarded him gratefully and turned to give Jimmy a peck on the cheek.

'See you this evening, love,' he said.

'Bye, love. See you this evening,' she reciprocated, stepping high over the threshold and passing through into the mill yard to a bright welcome from the gatekeeper.

'Good morning, lass. Come on in then. There's not been a lot has come in today so far. It's 'cause o' t'strike, tha knows. How's tha' this morning?'

148

'Fine,' she lied, although not too convincingly. 'It's a real relief to see you this morning.'

She coughed roughly into her handkerchief and put it back into her apron pocket. Now all she had to do was survive the day's work and make sure she stayed away from her nemesis, Herbert Radcliffe. She reflected that she would have to run the gauntlet of the striking workers once more after her day's work. And Jimmy might not be there to rescue her and guide her through as he had been this morning.

She shivered, not wholly from the cold, and advanced with as much confidence as she could muster across the uneven, rutted and puddled surface of the cobbled mill yard.

What would this day hold for her? And what about when she came out from the mill campus this evening after work?

Chapter Nine

Stoneleigh was the name of the beautiful, resplendent residence of mill owner, Sir Arthur Rowbottom. Designed by Lutyens, it was a faithful copy of the French style from the period referred to as *le grand siècle*. It was situated on the outskirts of a leafy village beyond the outer boundaries of Ryaton, some fifteen miles from where Jimmy and Kate lived in the slums of the city centre. The house — in fact, more of a mansion — had been constructed to Arthur's father's personal specifications. It was deliberately located a comfortable distance from his mill and the model village where most of his workers lived.

Built of the local honey-coloured sandstone, chunk cut and coursed by the best craftsmen available in the county, the mansion sat comfortably in several acres of classically landscaped formal gardens. If Arthur had glanced out this morning through the French windows of the breakfast room across the stone paved patio, the manicured lawns and the beautifully tended flower beds, he could have seen the gardeners already busy at work.

Through the ornate filigree gates of the garden, he would have been able to see, further afield, an adjoining kitchen garden, where other gardeners were working in front of the large hot houses to produce the exotic fruit and local vegetables for the kitchen of the house and the cut flowers which his wife, Ethel, so cherished for the main rooms of the house throughout the year. Still further afield, he would have had extensive vistas down the dale to local landmark green hills and beyond to the sparsely populated upper valley.

Although absolutely not a sybarite, Arthur had come, through wealth and education, to relish the good things in life. The furnishing of the house was by and large stylishly luxurious. The breakfast room was not the most sumptuous

150

formal room in the house. Nonetheless, it was large and elegantly furnished. The walls were decorated with imitation William Morris fabric wallpaper, and the woodwork and mouldings of the room were tastefully painted in warm, unpretentious colours. Between the large, plush-draped French windows, romantic paintings of local landscapes and classical scenes by local and national artists adorned the walls, and above the marble-effect hearth was the incongruous copy of a bust of a Roman emperor. Brightly coloured Persian carpets were laid on the secret-nailed Columbian pine floors, and a central electric light crystalline chandelier illuminated the room.

On the reproduction Ancien Régime sideboard were further provisions and replenishments for the already ample breakfast. The veneered walnut cabinet with inlaid floral designs, dating from the 1860s, which stood against the other wall, contained displays of curios: an exquisite selection of Wedgwood china, expensive locally purchased silverware, and some choice pieces of Meissen porcelain. At each side stood an upright ornate mahogany dining chair, upholstered in silk taffeta, and to one side a period whatnot, shelves arranged to cope with a variety of drinks. The whole room, although not of one single style or period, exuded a tasteful and harmonious air of good quality and comfort.

Arthur himself was dressed to impress in an expertly tailored three-piece suit, silk tie and handkerchief. Sporting a clean white linen serviette on his lap, he was ensconced at the top of an elegant, French neo-classical style mahogany breakfast table, enjoying his breakfast on a full silver breakfast service.

Not only owner of one of the largest mills in the area, Arthur was now Chairman of the influential Textile Mill Owners' Association. Although of medium height and slight of build, he was an impressive figure with his thinning grey

151

hair, dark grey bushy eyebrows, piercing blue eyes and a jet-black moustache. His slackening jowls indicated the good life to which he had become accustomed and did not detract in any way from the expression of a strong personality and authoritative demeanour. Indeed, his whole presence spoke of a man used to commanding authority.

Sitting now straight-backed on his impressive mahogany carver chair, Arthur was silently engrossed in the pages of the local *Daily Observer*, totally ignoring the other members of his family at the table.

Breakfast and dinner were usually the only occasions when all of them could guarantee to be together, as Arthur was usually out at the mill and other business or political appointments during the day. Often, however, due to his position in the town, dinner was a formal occasion with waitress service for important civic and business guests and for local and national politicians, whom he was courting for favours. Breakfast was the less formal of the two meals and was usually self-service. Despite this familial opportunity and certainly to the displeasure of his loving wife, he habitually used the breakfast time to read the local newspaper and, if he had not completed it the previous day, a national newspaper too, especially the *Times*.

His reading was not even interrupted by the arrival at regular intervals of the primly dressed maid as she slid silently into the room to replenish the teapot and deliver further provisions to the sideboard. On the table, silver napkin rings were blithely cast aside, their fastidiously ironed linen napkins currently occupying the laps of his wife and daughters. His study of the morning paper was hardly disturbed even by the maid's coming and going, to which he reacted with his customary solitary grunt.

The only interruptions he made to his reading were the infrequent side glances at the cherished gold pocket watch he had inherited from his father. It was inscribed on the back of the lid with the words *Presented by the Employees of Rowbottom's Mill to Joshua Rowbottom*. A golden chain was threaded through one of the button holes on his tweed waistcoat pocket with a fob to retain it.

He was particularly attached to the timepiece because it demonstrated how close the connection was between successive generations of Rowbottom mill owners and their employees. It reassured him of the dutiful fulfilment of his religious obligation to care for others. The watch was inconspicuously withdrawn from its hiding place and consulted at table level, not for his own personal benefit. Rather it was out of anxiety that his two daughters should not miss their train to school. For him, schooling was the entrée to the higher echelons of society which he had striven so hard to attain.

At the opposite end of the long dining table sat his lifelong companion and devoted wife, Ethel, who was soberly, expensively and fashionably dressed for breakfast. As usual she was attentive to her husband's every need, a devoted wife and mother to their daughters. What's more, she was dedicated to the efficient and cost-effective running of the house and, her religious faith requiring it, to works of charity outside the house.

At each side of the table, their two beautiful teenage daughters, Imogen and Lucinda, were rapidly devouring their breakfast prior to their five-minute walk to the local railway station where the steam commuter train would take them the fifteen miles to the nearby industrial town.

In common with most daughters of the town's nouveaux riches, his daughters attended the prestigious and well-endowed fee-paying Girls Public Day School Trust grammar school. They had both obtained non-monetary, laudatory scholarship awards from the local elementary school. Their two daughters were the treasures of Ethel and Arthur's lives and both parents were highly ambitious for them, especially Arthur. He had high hopes that both would go on to an eminent university in the south, where the debarring of women that had excluded his wife from higher education had been lifted at the turn of the century.

The local morning daily, the *Observer,* carried a mixture of local, national and a restricted section of international news, some good and some bad. For example, jingoistic and tendentious stories of apparent German atrocities against British prisoners of war were combined with reports of the alleged devious attempts by the Germans at backsliding on the terms of the Versailles Peace Treaty.

On another page an article reported recurrent and widespread industrial unrest across the whole of the United Kingdom since the armistice. According to the article, industrial action had been undertaken with relative success and financial gain by the employed in almost all cases. A diversity of workers, it recounted, from the police and railwaymen to municipal workers, tram drivers and mill girls, had gained increased wages and better conditions, including shorter working hours. The details also referred to rioting, food and fuel shortages in scores of towns, mayhem and civil disorder. The workers were lambasted as naïvely influenced by wild bolshevist ideas. With rising concern, he noted that violence in Glasgow's George Square had led to the Riot Act being read. Further, in Belfast, consequent on a strike by public utility workers, there had been neither gas nor electricity for several days and troops had been deployed to assist.

By this time, Arthur was quite worked up as he evoked the current violence at his own mill in the village. 'Disgraceful blackmail,' He mumbled. 'Outrageous. Deplorable. Unacceptable.'

'You know, my love, you should not upset yourself by reading the morning newspaper at the breakfast table. It is not a good example to our daughters,' Ethel scolded him gently.

He ignored her comment and carried on with his perusal of the news. Returning soldiers were replacing women workers, especially in the mills and in the transport system, and this was increasing production costs at a time when trade was poor, markets elusive and profits weak. Thus margins were firmly squeezed. Additionally, few suitable places could be found for war-maimed soldiers. Both these factors were having a detrimental effect on overall purchasing power for lots of poor families and their standard of living was being drastically diminished by the overall fall in household incomes.

The fact that women and children were being negatively affected tugged at the heart strings of his Congregationalist faith. He decided in genuine concern that he should speak to his wife about the effects of this on his own workers and their families.

'Darling,' he said, placing his paper on top of his breakfast. 'You should have a read of this article on the effects of current shortages on our workers and ex-employees. It is really terrible, and I am sure that you and the other ladies at the church will wish to consider what you can do as part of your charitable activities to alleviate the hardship of those who are hardest hit and are deserving. Let me know straightaway if you need additional funding.'

'Yes, my dear. I shall. We might for example be able to share some of the food from the kitchen garden for the poorest and most deprived families with children. Certainly, for those women who are now heads of family having lost their menfolk, I would hope we could do something extra. And we could add a little additional money. What is your view, my dear?'

'Of course, my dear.'

'Yes, dear, we can certainly do more. If I get time today, I'll have a further look at this matter and arrange for an early get-together of the women's committee to consider what further assistance we can extend. I just wonder what this country is coming to when I see those emaciated children and their mothers in the streets around the mill. In fact, I certainly should do more for our workers and their families. I shall have a word with the head gardener today and see what we can spare. And I am sure that some of the children's clothes that they have grown out of could be given to poor families. Also, the ladies guild is already proposing a bring-and-buy sale for this Saturday. Nevertheless I am sure that we can all do more.'

'I know, my darling. You already do more than anyone could expect of you — you and the other ladies on the church committee. And, of course, the workers and their families must help themselves besides, you know. We mustn't encourage them to become dependent, must we?'

'Of course not, my love.'

'By the way, my dear, I came upon old Charlie Walker at the mill gates yesterday. You may remember him. He lost a leg in the war and he was on crutches when I saw him. We have no safe job for him in the mill, not even sweeping up. Are we doing anything for men like him in the village?'

'My love, the ladies committee has been discussing their needs and our possible assistance recently. All in good time, we hope to commence some more charitable work. We'll see what we can do further for those men.'

He resumed his reading, and the ladies quietly recommenced their breakfasts.

He noted with genuine sorrow that there had been three hundred and thirteen deaths last week from sickness in that one town alone. *God alone knows the number here in the village,* he reflected anxiously. And as if in accompaniment, his gaze inadvertently fell on one advertisement, advising that ammoniated tincture of quinine should be taken as a precaution. Little hope of the poor being able to follow that advice, he mused. The newspaper for its part, recommended fresh air and ventilation, as also nasal and throat douching, as efficacious antidotes against the epidemic. A related report detailed that the number pf patients requiring treatment had overwhelmed doctors and hospitals in some towns, as the epidemic ran its course.

He smiled wryly as he mulled over the excellent hospital and other medical facilities provided by him free for his workers in the model village cottage hospital. The problem was that the general practitioners still had to charge, and consequently in numerous cases people deferred their visit until the illness was just too advanced for treatment, even incurable. Added to this swathe of bad news was the fact that, with the mass dismissal of women workers to make way for the returning soldiers, purchasing power among workers' families was in rapid free fall and even menial jobs for women were hard to come by.

There was also an article about the economic plight of the textile industry. For him, it was self-evident that they had to decrease costs by reducing the wage bill. He knew well that, if mills were to be retained in profit and large-scale unemployment were to be prevented, he and his fellow proprietors would be faced with the necessity of introducing short time working and imposing lower earnings on their workers. It was a difficult balancing act for them on how to cut down production costs yet still preserve employment and maintain the commitment of their workers, all without making their living conditions and the sufferings of their families worse. He was not happy about the options available to the owners; he knew in his heart of hearts, however, that what they were proposing made good economic sense.

This dispute was reflected both in the 'Letters' and 'Comment' sections of the newspaper. As a result of the difficulties faced by the textile industry, employers felt they had to challenge the inflated wages gained by workers during the war. Most considered prevailing wage levels as too high and work conditions as totally unsustainable in the transformed post-war economic circumstances.

Sitting back to allow his devoted maid to refill his cup from the imitation French Empire silver teapot, Arthur had good reason this morning to be both pleased and disquieted. He was pleased because he had last night been elected president of the local Mill Owners' Association at its annual business meeting. This appointment was a big boost to his long-term ambition to be appointed to the House of Lords. The last incumbent of the presidency of the Association had been elected Lord Mayor of the town, and Arthur perceived this route as a pathway to achieving his aim.

But he was perturbed too, because he was not entirely in accord with the organisation's strategy, which he initially found unreasonably aggressive and confrontational. Given the traditional, humane approach to the resolution of disputes supported by his own religious commitment, he would have preferred much more dialogue before such a step, which he personally regarded as a lockout. The tradition of his kinfolk, established from the early days of his father's time, had always been one of care for his workers, even at the risk that the workers may see him as rather paternalistic and patronising.

Additionally, Arthur was conscious that a strike was certain to include all the mills in the town eventually, as well as the dyeing and finishing plants. He recognised that he would be playing a major role in opposing it, or at least negotiating an outcome that would be satisfactory to his fellow mill owners. That was the difficulty: most of them were adamant that they needed an overall reduction in the total wage bill one way or another if they were to survive.

As a first ploy, they had proposed a ten per cent reduction in wages, balanced by a commitment to take back all workers. Their unspoken backup position envisaged a willingness to settle for a five per cent reduction, taking back most — although not all — the workers. Most saw this dispute as an opportunity for a fight against revolutionary socialism and a chance to lance the boil. For that reason, they were adamant that they would not give way.

This was the very matter on which Arthur's conscience was so greatly troubled. Both he and his father were strong, non-conformist believers in good works and humanity as the path to eternal salvation. They were both towering models of rectitude in a society and in an époque when such virtues were greatly prized, admired … and rewarded by the political Establishment.

In their time, both had been and were still much-admired philanthropists in the local community. Arthur's father, a dour and intensely religious man, had been a local working man made good. He had left school as a part-timer at the age of nine, and by dint of sheer hard work and through a determination to improve himself, he had become one of the town's leading industrialists and, in time, one of Victorian Britain's great and good. His determination to better himself had ensured that he wanted others to improve themselves too. To this end, he had sponsored, in a financially prudent way, the creation of all manner of provision for the educational and social improvement of the workers, with whom he still identified.

The older Rowbottom, for example, had been passionately committed to the formation of an early Mechanics' Institute group in the town for the educational recreation and betterment of the working classes. He had evidenced his wholehearted commitment to the educational emancipation of the labouring classes and to drawing them out of their abject and wretched ignorance as well as impoverishment. In his old age, he had been one of the major financial backers of the construction of the fine local Mechanics' Institute building, a costly, neo-gothic edifice in the town centre. Paradoxically, it was there that the early Trade Unionists held their first gatherings that would lead to the creation of the Independent Labour Party.

What is more, it went without saying that Arthur's father felt ardently that it was his social and religious duty to be an active supporter of the new School Boards, instituted under the 1870 Education Act. He had been a committed member of the local School Board, from its inception, specifically for the purpose of advancing the education of the children of the workers. It seemed only natural that later, on the formation of the Local Authorities at the turn of the century, Arthur had automatically been recruited to the new Local Education Committee, a role in which he had followed his father.

Even before the introduction of universal elementary education in the town in the 1880s, the great and good of the town had combined to help the physical, social and intellectual development of the lower orders in other ways too. In the 1860s, for example, outside the dreary, squalid town centre, Arthur's father, though known as a tight-fisted businessman, was urged on by his religious duty to begin the construction of a more environmentally salubrious modern model village for his workers. His own salvation depended on it and he was not about to sell out his eternal life. Each worker had a back-to-back cottage with its own privy across a small yard, the size and facilities of each house being determined by their place in the hierarchy of workers at the mill.

Elementary and grammar schools for the children of the village were constructed, as well as a cottage hospital, a library, an assembly room for educational lectures and meetings and even a feeding room. At the centre of the village was the most beautiful cylindrical-shaped Congregational church imaginable, furnished with exquisite and expensive woodwork, wonderful Venetian glass windows and doors, crystal chandeliers and a resplendent rotunda. The church building was as much a memorial to his own glory as to that of any god, although the financing came now from the more meagre and hard-won post-war profits of the business.

On the opposite side of the road from the superlative church was the large multipurpose, Italianate mill, with its chimney disguised as a campanile. The whole complex was a thing of beauty, even though some radical workers regarded it as an instrument of their enslavement. The mill was constructed of the finest local materials by the best craftsmen, in a beautiful Canaletto architectural style. Acknowledged to be the biggest in the north of England, perchance in the world, when it was built, it covered all the processes from taking in the raw wool to turning out the finished cloth, with the exception of dyeing and finishing.

The mill abutted the canal and the railway with its own station for rapid receipt of the raw wool and the equivalently swift dispatch of the finished goods. Both mill and church had been superbly sited in the dale at the side of the sparkling and shimmering river. Symbolically facing each other across the road, the duality of the mill and Congregational church epitomised a symbiotic philosophical and industrial ethic of hard work, thrift and religious conviction, which included both salvation and profit.

As had always been Arthur's father's ambition, he had left his son with two expressions of that duality: a thriving textile business and strong religious beliefs. His son had followed in his footsteps, being eventually knighted for his services to the Liberal Establishment. Similarly, he had faithfully adhered to his father's traditions of sobriety, philanthropy and religious commitment, matched with business acumen. Furthermore, like his father, he was an enthusiastic member and major financial sponsor of the now thriving Mechanics' Institute and its library. In this respect, he assisted with the expenses for visits by eminent literary, social and political speakers, plus the provision of funds for the purchase of furniture and books for the expanding library.

A regular churchgoing Congregationalist, Arthur expected workers to attend church if they wanted employment in his mill. Additionally, in line with his own commitment to sobriety, he expected them to refrain from alcohol. For this reason, a covenant was settled on all the houses rented by the workers from the company to the effect that no alcohol could be sold anywhere in his model village, in perpetuity.

Arthur had not served in the war, occupying a reserved occupation. In lieu his mill had taken on production of the worsted blue cloth for the uniforms of the local Citizens' Army League, the town's Kitchener's soldiers. This body of soldiers was raised by local civic dignitaries, under the chairmanship of the Lord Mayor. His mill had also been responsible for the switch afterwards to khaki fabric too. Along with most businessmen in the town, he had made a hefty donation to the League, although in turn he had made a pretty penny from the war effort.

'Arthur, darling, do you think that it was wise of you to take on the presidency last night, especially with this strike looming?' His dutiful wife's voice jolted him from his contemplative mode with an unusually provocative question.

Arthur was not a matinal sort of person, and he did not like to be faced with major issues before he had had time to warm up to the day. As a rule, this denoted after breakfast when he had had a chance to read the newspapers, absorb their important content and to weigh up the extent of his day's work.

Sensing the possible gathering storm of a quarrel between their parents — something that transpired very seldom — Arthur's two daughters feigned more intensive concentration on their breakfast. Conflict between Arthur and Ethel might be rare indeed. When it occurred, however, it could be exceedingly potent, a bit like the eruption of a volcano long quiescent. Both he and his wife were decidedly strong-willed.

Seeing that the maid was not currently in the breakfast room, Arthur was drawn to confront the question head-on. He darted an unusually hostile stare at his wife. 'What are you saying, Ethel, my love? This is something for which we have always planned and hoped. As leading figures in the town, it is the culmination of our strenuous exertions to lead the local textile business community and to serve that community. Both our families have always been willing to undertake responsibilities within the local community. Moreover, I have a religious duty to take on such responsibilities if and when they become available.'

'Yes, dear. Don't you think though that it could turn out to be a poisoned chalice? With this strike and all?

'I don't know what you mean, my dear. It is certainly a responsible position in the local community. Our last president, Jacob Benfeld, was nominated the town's mayor last week, as you know, to replace Francis Kasapian, who had a heart attack the week before and can't keep doing the voluntary work. What's going to happen to his carpet business? I have no idea. Anyway, that implied that there was a pressing need to find a person of standing to fill the position. Eli Behrens — you know how gregarious and well-connected he is — kindly proposed me and spoke eloquently in my favour. There was unanimity among the assembled members. No name other than mine was put forward.' Deeply religious he may have been, though he was not above the sin of pride. 'And although it was pure coincidence that this came about as unexpectedly as it did, I am obviously the best man for the job.'

'Yes, I know the circumstances, darling. I'm only thinking of you. You are not getting any younger, you know. And you already do a lot for the local community: sitting on committees and donating to local good causes, patronising the church and sitting on the local education committee. Occasionally, it seems to me that they do not really appreciate all that you do for them.'

'Ethel, you know that what we do, we do in the service of our Lord and Saviour, Jesus Christ, not for any personal gain, let alone appreciation and recognition from our fellow men. We have a responsibility to serve and to engage in good

164

works. In any case, as I avowed, my friends in the Association were unanimous in wanting me to take the job. Was I supposed to rebuff the offer?'

'No, no, my love. It's just that you will now be the centre of this conflict … I mean, this strike, and so will our daughters. Did you consider them when you made this decision?'

'Nonsense! Absolute codswallop, Ethel,' Arthur exploded with an unusually choleric rejoinder. 'Why should my loved ones be worried at all? Why should my daughters be affected? We don't live on the mill site. We don't live in the town. We don't even live in the model village.'

'Well, my love …'

'I don't see why my daughters and my wife should become entangled in this at all.'

Ethel sensed his frustration and mounting irritation and tried desperately to placate him, while simultaneously seeking to make him aware of how it might affect the whole family, not just him.

'Arthur, don't be angry. It just seemed to me that, unlike some of the other mill owners, you have always had such a good rapport with your workers. You've done everything anyone could have expected to take care of them, to see to their welfare, as your father did before you. And now with your taking on this more prominent role … Well, I just worry that …'

'The tragedy of this situation, Ethel, my dearest, is that the vast majority of the workers are not ne'er-do-wells. They are dupes to the extremist political schemers in their midst. These revolutionaries are not in the least interested in the welfare of the workers. Not on your life! Their leaders are the kind who were responsible for the slapdash farrago of the 1909 textile strike, which left the workers worse off than before. Their leaders are mischief-makers, only interested in some millennial fancy of a workers' revolution and paradise.'

'Yes, dear, though labelling them all as revolutionaries would be unwarranted, even perhaps unjust. We know some of them from the church and we know that they are god-fearing men with wives and families. At this cruel time of year, a strike will be hard on the families. You've met some of them at the Mechanics' Institute lectures and you know that lots of them are intelligent people: responsible men, husbands, fathers, brothers …'

'Daddy, we shall be choosing our subjects for the lower sixth form in a little while.' It was Imogen, his younger daughter who, sensitive and astute as ever, discerned an opportunity of shifting her father's attention. 'Do you think I should specialise in ancient languages or natural sciences? Miss Brogan says that I stand a good chance of doing well in Latin and Greek and of going on to Cambridge to study Classics. She thinks that sciences are not for women. Which will be most useful to me, Daddy? What is your view?'

Sir Arthur Rowbottom found himself exasperated by the old-fashioned nature of the advice proffered to them by their teachers. So it was that he found himself compelled to challenge the advice given, promptly finding himself diverted from his wife's contentions and enticed into a completely changed category of combat. Imogen's diversion tactic seemed to be on the cusp of success.

'Well, as I see it, my love — although it is true that ancient languages are not my speciality — there seems to me to be no future in learning to speak Ancient Greek and Latin.

166

They are languages that no one speaks anymore, except maybe a handful of clerics.'

'But Daddy, Miss Brogan points out that they can be a useful discipline for a woman.'

'Humbug, Imogen, my love. It is an unfortunate fact for the fussy Miss Brogan to face, that only a small handful of people around nowadays speak those languages. Unless of course you want to go and live in the Vatican.' He hazarded disdainfully. 'On the other hand, science is advancing at a rapid pace, and there will always be good career opportunities, including for capable young women like you. Especially now, after the war, there is such a deficit of young men missing from the ranks of science, and attitudes have shifted since Miss Brogan last encountered reality. As far as I am concerned, there is no contest. So, you can tell her what she can do with her ancient languages!'

'You will do no such thing, Imogen. I accept your father's view that the future lies in science and technology. That does not give you permission, however, to be rude to Miss Brogan who has given her whole life to the grammar school and the advancement of women's education.'

'Yes, dear. You are right. Forgive me. There is no reason for anyone to be rude, merely firm and steadfast, crystal clear and direct, so as not to be waylaid by superfluous words and notions. That way Miss Brogan knows exactly what your reasoning on the matter is and that it has the full backing of your parents.'

'Yes, that makes sense,' Ethel affirmed.

'I know, mother,' Imogen added compliantly.

'You can be polite and tell her that, as always, your parents warmly appreciate her interest and advice. Having discussed this with you, however, and taking into account your own career wishes, they would prefer you to choose sciences: Physics, Chemistry and Botany or Zoology with Mathematics would be a good combination.'

'Of course, Mummy.'

'Knowing my daughter and her commitment to respecting others, whatever their station in life, I would have expected nothing less than politeness,' Arthur added proudly.

At this point, the maid entered in a circumspect manner and quietly and politely addressed Arthur. 'Sir Arthur, there is a man from the mill, Billy Dolan, on the telephone who asks if he can speak to you. He told me that there is a Mr Jimmy Kelly who wishes to speak with you on the phone. Do you wish to speak with him, sir?'

Arthur meditated for a while, his initial inclination being to decline to speak to anyone during his breakfast.

'I've come across that man Kelly before. At the Mechanics' events before the war. One of those clever socialists. He's a bit of a radical. An intelligent man. A bit of a troublemaker though. I'll bet he's at the root of this dispute. Darling, what do you think? Should I go to the phone? What can I possibly gain by speaking to this man now?'

He tightened his eyebrows in a frown and made a scowling glance of exasperation to his unresponsive wife as he tried to make his decision. Ultimately, it was in large part due to his concept of Christian charity that he was brought round to a reluctant acceptance of the invitation to speak to Mr Kelly. He would have to speak to him without betraying his new position as president of the Mill Owners' Association. At all costs he had to avoid the impression that he had negotiated with the Union side behind his members' backs.

But it might just be worth the risk and it might also be an occasion to take this brash young man down a peg or two.

Chapter Ten

The interruption of his scrutiny of the breakfast newspaper by the maid had left Sir Arthur Rowbottom somewhat displeased, to say the least. He was not in a good mood. Moreover, he had retired to bed late after the business dinner, and although he was fairly satisfied with how it had gone for him, he had a few misgivings undisclosed to his wife.

Most importantly, however, business was business and home was home. He tried to keep the mill strictly separate from his personal life and normal routine at home. For several moments he toyed again with the notion of refusing the phone call. In the end, his religious conviction overcame his chagrin. *Jesus would expect me to exercise tolerance*, he mused.

'Billy Dolan? He's the man who is in charge of the clock office at the mill. And I assume that Kelly is one of the strikers' leaders. I wonder what he wants. But, yes. I'll come to the phone now,' he assured the waiting maid. 'Tell Billy to hold the line. I shall be there in a minute when I've finished my tea.'

With that, he gulped down the last of his drink from the fine bone china teacup and, turning to his wife and daughters, he politely asked, 'Would you excuse me, my loves. We can pursue our discussion after I have spoken with this man.'

His wife consented in her usual acquiescent and sensitive tone. 'Yes, of course, my dear. Please do go ahead.'

When Arthur picked up the telephone situated in the spacious hallway, Billy Dolan, always deferential, was almost incoherently submissive. He was evidently debilitatingly embarrassed at having to interrupt his boss so early and panic-stricken at the prospect of ruffling Sir Arthur's feathers. After all, jobs were difficult to get. And Mr Rowbottom, for all his Christian principles, wasn't above sacking a worker on the spot if he felt that someone had been disrespectful to him. And Billy was only too aware that Sir Arthur did not like being contacted at home — especially early in the morning.

'I regret ... err, I am sorry ... err, very sorry to trouble you, sir ... at this hour of the morning,' he mumbled. 'I know you don't like being ... err ... disturbed at home, Sir Arthur.'

'Yes, you are right,' Arthur barked.

'Sir, I have ... err ... Jimmy Kelly from the Union next to me and ... err ... he claims that you would be interested in speaking with him, Sir.'

'Oh, he does, does he? Well ask him why he thinks that.'

'Well, sir, he ... err ... claims that he has a proposal, which ... he claims ... err ... could help to solve the dispute at the moment ... the strike, I think. I was thinking ... well, I do hope that you do not mind, sir. Err ... I felt I could not refuse him. I do hope that was alright, sir?'

'He's the leader of this damned strike, isn't he, Billy?'

'Yes sir ... well, one of them, I believe ... that's ... err ... why I felt it was so important. He claims ... well, he has a proposal ... a suggestion ... well ... help avoid ... err ... to end ... the strike. I hope I did the correct thing, sir?' Billy pleaded in conclusion, pathetic in tone and phrase.

Arthur knew Billy, as he knew most of the key workers at his mill. Billy was a decent working class man. Not particularly bright, it's true, and not too articulate either. Arthur, however, was able to perceive another side to him. He regarded him as an earnest and sincere worker who had never given any reason for complaint. Moreover, and this was the tipping point in Arthur's decision, Billy was a regular churchgoer; Arthur knew him as a faithful usher at the village's church. He had been injured in a mill accident in the weaving shed and was now partially disabled. That was the reason why he had been given the job in the time office. So, not in any way a man devoid of human compassion, Arthur's heart was gradually melted by Billy's bumbling.

'Yes, yes, Billy' Arthur replied, somewhat more gently although still impatiently. 'It is all right. It is fine to let him use the time office phone. Just put him on.' And after a brief delay, he added, 'Please.'

Arthur's conversation with Jimmy was relatively brief and totally unsatisfactory for his intention. Subsequently, Jimmy was to reflect that it is often better not to react on the spur of the moment and launch into an important conversation unprepared. Arthur, for his part, suffered consequent pangs of conscience, feeling that he had been seized by an unusual rush of peptic arrogance and had dealt with Jimmy in a bad-tempered way.

'Hello, Sir Arthur Rowbottom here,' he announced rather pompously. 'I do not in general accept business calls at my residence, Mr Kelly. So, say what you have to say briefly and let me get back to my family.'

Although not normally a snob, the expression of difference in their titles was intended by Arthur to indicate their separate statuses in the social hierarchy. There were clearly to be no favours, despite their previous acquaintance at the Mechanics' Institute. It was not customary for Arthur to act in this rather high-handed and priggish way. He was usually much more congenial, not least with his own workers. He was well known for turning up in the factory, even at the feeding hall, and engaging his workers in conversation about local football ... although always steering away from politics.

The interruption of his morning's reading, his stalled breakfast, his conversation with his wife, and Miss Brogan's interference had all contributed to his crotchety mood. So, although partially mollified by his religious faith induced compassion for Billy, he was in no mood for trifling with Jimmy.

'Mr Rowbottom, I hear that you were elected president of the local Mill Owners' Association last night?'

'Yes, that's confirmed. Although it's still not official. A mere formality of course. Anyway, what is this about?'

Jimmy's initial feeling was that Arthur was being unhelpful. This latter's tone of voice alone made Jimmy feel as though he was being addressed like a simpleton. Nonetheless, he elected to do his utmost to make the conversation successful.

'Well, I felt it appropriate on behalf of all members of the Union to congratulate you on your election and hope that the spirit of long-term co-operation, which has characterised your approach and that of your father before you, might help us overcome the fundamental difficulties we face today without further conflict and deterioration of previously harmonious relations. We all depend on each other in this community. We all have an interest in overcoming conflicts if we can. Don't you think so, Sir Arthur? We have responsibilities to each other and both sides of our community.'

Ignoring the compliment and the congratulations, Arthur went straight to the kernel of their dispute as he saw it. 'I do not need to be lectured by you, Mr Kelly, on my community responsibilities and my shared humanity with my fellow man. Are you ringing me to tell me that you are calling the strike off, Mr Kelly?' Was Arthur's somewhat ungenerous response.

'No. Rather I believed that your election might be a good opportunity to arrange to meet to discuss the prospects for a satisfactory resolution of our differences.'

'There'll be no talking unless the strike is called off, Mr Kelly. That was the unanimous decision of all the mill owners last night. That is the mandate that I have received as their president. Indeed, I have been formally delegated by that group to insist on that position at all costs, whatever I might think about my own mill and my own workers. My Association's members will be sticking together. You and your cronies describe it as "solidarity" I believe.' Arthur added scornfully.

Jimmy considered the use of the word 'cronies' provocative and uncalled for. This conversation was not going well at all. At this juncture, he was prompted to reconsider the wisdom of his having called at all. Nevertheless, he decided to ignore what he considered to be taunts and carry on, conscious that he was charged with securing the welfare of his fellow workers and their families. He could not afford to be provoked.

'Mr Rowbottom …'

'I am not Mr Rowbottom, Mr Kelly. That is not my name. I am Sir Arthur Rowbottom. Sir Arthur to you.'

Jimmy tipped his cap to no one. Arthur's rude treatment of him so far in this conversation had hit a raw spot, for it reminded him of the way that some of the officers in the Pals had treated their men in the trenches.

'Look, don't you accept that there would be some mileage at least in the two sides getting together informally to see if there is any possibility of solving this dispute without an all-out mutually damaging fight.'

'Mr Kelly, it is not the owners who are seeking a fight. It was you who summoned the men out on strike. As I advised you before, there will be no talking until you all come back to work. And thank your lucky stars that you still have jobs to return to. I'll tell you now, there were voices among us advocating sacking the lot of you and replacing you all with new recruits. Of course, I did not support that view. And one thing further. Since the armistice, trade has been highly unpredictable. Competition is extremely fierce. The wage increases and lighter conditions of work that were extracted during the war are simply not affordable now in these transformed economic circumstances. Most of the owners think that the workers are receiving wages which are higher than they in effect rate. We're asking for a ten per cent cut in wages so that the industry can survive. Otherwise, we simply cannot afford to carry on business and there will certainly be fewer jobs, if any at all. That is certainly not the outcome that we are hoping for, and we absolutely do not want a fight, as you falsely assert. Those are the stark facts, Mr Kelly.'

'Well, the owners would argue that, wouldn't they? For our part we see wages as already excessively low, not least in the context of the current rate of inflation. They are certainly lower in this town than they are in other parts of the country,

175

and lower in woollen textiles than in other comparable industries. From our standpoint, the way to increase production, profits and employment is to improve wages. This will, in turn, stimulate demand in the local and national economies ...'

'Mr Kelly, these are items that can be discussed at the Allied Joint Industrial Council, which as you know represents both sides and was set up to manage wage bargaining and to iron out any little problems that might arise. We all agreed to the setting up of that body and it has an emergency committee to deal rapidly with any local disputes swiftly and effectively.'

'But that is precisely the point. Don't you see that you, the owners, have circumvented that body by unilaterally demanding a ten per cent wage reduction, although the word on the streets is that you would settle for five per cent? It is you who have broken the procedures, not us. That is precisely why we are driven to this strike, which nobody in their right mind wants.'

'Mr Kelly, such matters of dispute can be made in the calmer atmosphere of the Council, if you so wish. That is the arena where such points of economic contention can be advanced, not here with me on the telephone during my breakfast and in the privacy of my own home, when you have already instigated a strike by my workers and those of my fellow mill owners.'

Jimmy could feel the conversation — and his hopes — briskly slipping away from him, as Arthur carried on in an unyielding manner. Quite possibly the idea of the telephone call had not been a good one after all. That may have been a mistake, asking for trouble.

'And before you go lecturing me on your dubious economic theories, Mr Kelly, let me tell you what your stark options are. Costs have to be reduced. If not, we cannot sell what we make and we cannot pay our workers anything at all. That is a stark fact of economic reality. So, it is not a question of retaining the same wages and conditions of work, when and if you return to work. Rather it is an issue of whether there will be the work there for all the men, even at the new rates. If this dispute lasts, not all men may be taken back, because there just will not be the work for them.'

'That will never be acceptable to the any of the Unions.'

'Moreover, the men's jobs will not be available for ever. You will be aware of what came about during the railway strike. The companies and the government were fully complicit in this. They encouraged the use of volunteer labour and threatened to cease further demobilisation of troops. You know Mr Lloyd George's view about the use of replacement volunteers, don't you, Mr Kelly? He is on record as arguing during the war that jobs for which a five-year apprenticeship was essential could be done by intelligent girls after a week's induction.'

'Is that a threat, Sir Arthur?

'Similarly, he is on record as supposing that work which had previously been done by highly skilled engineers could be done by women after only three weeks training. There is a lesson in that pronouncement for all of us here in the textile industry, where much of the work was done by relatively unskilled and emergency-trained labour during the war.'

'In spite of Lloyd George's bravado, the government ultimately had to capitulate, Sir Arthur. In my view, the same will come about here as well.'

177

'I don't think so, Mr Kelly. The railwaymen were part of the triple Alliance set up in 1914 with the miners and other transport workers. They could have brought the country to a standstill. The miners still could. We shall see. Just a handful of striking mill workers in an industrial town in the north of England are not going to do that. You overestimate your strength, Mr Kelly.'

'I honestly believe that it is you who has misjudged the mood at this time, Sir Arthur.'

'I don't think so, Mr Kelly. It could be that you and your Central Council for Action have over-played your hand at this time, as I conjectured.' Arthur countered disparagingly.

'For the very first time, Sir Arthur, all the textile workers are in this as one. The overlookers, engineers and wool sorters have come out with the unskilled labourers. Union and non-union workers have united at what they see as the injustice of the employers' demands, which effectively they see as a lockout by the bosses.'

'I am not intimidated, Mr Kelly.'

'The strikers have set up a Central Council of Action, representing all those workers on strike, and that is the body with which you shall eventually have to negotiate. And by the way, none of the men will go back to work until every one of them goes back, and any attempt to bring in volunteers to replace regular workers will be resisted.'

'If that is the case, Mr Kelly, it is going to be a long day. And by the way, I hope that you are not threatening violence against the volunteer workers.'

Jimmy ignored the barb and instead chose to make one last valiant effort to rescue the conversation and avoid the impending deadlock.

'Sir Arthur. A major strike such as this will do nothing for the reputation of the mill owners, for the town or for you as their elected leader. Surely there is some way that reasonable men can settle their differences. I am sure that the chairman of the Central Council for Action, Vic Noble, would be willing to meet with you off the record if necessary. Indeed, I would myself, in order to prevent what could become a disaster for both sides and for all members of our joint community. Let the two of us meet and talk this thing over. Let us at least do all we can to find a workable solution.'

'Meaning exactly what, Mr Kelly?'

'Meaning exactly what I have said. We are ready to talk and failure to talk … well, there are repercussions for others, innocent parties, and there are reputations at stake also.'

'I see no point in a get-together such as you propose at this time, Mr Kelly, as I have already indicated. Moreover, I resent the implied threat about reputations. As chairman of the Mill Owners' Association, I have already expounded our unified position. Return at the new rates and under the new conditions and our doors are open and we can talk. My members will not countenance any other arrangement. It is no wish of ours to drag in innocent groups or individuals, nor does any one of us wish to undermine what you yourself describe as our joint community. We have no wish to see hardship of any hue for our workers and their families. On the other hand, neither shall we relinquish our position under any circumstances.'

'I am afraid that will never be acceptable for the workers. The matter has gone too far now. And for our side, we shall never relinquish the fight for a just return in the restoration of our standard of living for an honest day's work.'

'Given the official acceptance of our terms by the Unions, Mr Kelly, we will take back all the strikers. Unless, of course, anyone has been found guilty of any legal misdemeanour or breach of the peace. But, until you go back to work, our conversation seems to be finished. And by the way, your time for returning is not unlimited. The owners have a responsibility to the community to keep the mills going, somehow. And now I must return to my wife and daughters and my breakfast. Good day, Mr Kelly.'

With that parting shot, Arthur slammed the receiver down. Furious, he turned and marched briskly back into the dining room. At that moment he was in no way disposed to compromise with this man, his organisation or indeed anyone else in the world this morning!

Only later would he express contrition to himself for his downright bad behaviour to one of god's creatures.

Jimmy thanked Billy Dolan for arranging the telephone call. He felt dejected at the point blank refusal of Sir Arthur to move at all, which was a significant setback to his plans. He was also alarmed by the implied threat of strike-breaking labour in Arthur's last affirmation. Of course, it could have been just a ruse by the wily old man.

Jimmy was likewise disconcerted at his own total lack of success, indeed his ineptness, in his struggle to plead his case with Sir Arthur. He just had to do better. He could not fail his mates. Tight-lipped and with eyes cast down, he left the time office and headed sluggishly back to his mates on the picket line.

They saw him approaching and, sensing his dejection from his gait and his bowed head, they slowly edged aside from the brazier and gathered him in to one of the clusters. Some embraced him and expressed words of consolation, affording him a momentary sense of kind-hearted community. He gratefully received a proffered enamel mug of sweet tea.

Jimmy stood in silent contemplation, still preoccupied in brooding on Arthur's concluding shot about keeping the mills going … somehow. What was he implying by that? Were the owners already contemplating the use of scab labour to replace the strikers? That would certainly incense the strikers, as it had done in the past. It would inflame the situation, making it all the more difficult to settle later.

When strike breakers had been imported before, it had engendered disastrous outcomes for the workers and their families and had entrenched bitterness for years afterwards. Such a move by the employers could be a body blow to the Union's strategy of an orderly and disciplined strike with strong public endorsement. It could totally sabotage the success of the strike and lose them all their jobs. Was Jimmy really the man who could head off such an outcome? Was he up to it?

Chapter Eleven

Dry-mouthed and with a splitting headache, the last thing Jimmy had wanted to do that morning was to lead on the picket line. After the night he had had, he was plainly not up to it. It was only his inherent sense of solidarity and the memory of his former Pals, who never came home, that gave him the strength to get up and to go to the mill.

As he embarked on his walk down the long hill past the cottage hospital and the elementary school that he had known so well in his youth, he noticed the constables relaxing in groups, smoking and drinking tea from thermos flasks. Some were sprawling idly on the pavements with their backs against the buildings. Their vehicles were at the ready nearby. Reassured, Jimmy had noted that there didn't seem to be any horses. Nevertheless, he had asked himself why there were Bobbies there so early. Who had alerted them to which mill the workers would be picketing first? Could there be a sneak in the Advisory Group? No! Unbelievable! If not though, who could it have been?

As he had exited the large olive-painted wooden-doored mill entrance from the time office to approach the picket line after his unproductive telephone conversation with Arthur, he quickened his pace to re-join his mates only a few steps away. No sooner did they noticed his return that there was a swift surge of comradeship from the workers already assembled. Lots of the men ambled up and welcomed him in a friendly manner. It was their warmth which seemed to restore some life to his weary limbs and his exhausted, angst-ridden mind.

Although strongly committed to the aims of the strike and to their role on the picket line, the men wanted to hear if there had been any progress in negotiations with the owners. Conceivably, they were hoping against hope that the Union side had reached their run-of-the-mill and simple goals: the return of all workers, including the sacked Union representative, and at the previous wage rates. They feared the worst, however, and, sensing Jimmy's gloom, they exercised forbearance. Apart from greeting him cordially, they allowed him his silent contemplation for a while.

What were the pickets expecting of him? The telephone call had been fruitless. Apart from that there had been some unfounded and unverified stories of initial contacts between the Unions and the employers — at least between Jimmy and the employers' chairman, Sir Arthur Rowbottom. These tales had spread across the model village with great alacrity. Some argued that they had been intentionally put about by the owners and their allies in the vicinity, the Press and elsewhere. Regrettably, they were merely unsubstantiated rumours. Soon, though prematurely as far as Jimmy was concerned, the pickets could curb their curiosity no longer and the dam of their restraint fractured. Without interruption the questions streamed at him simultaneously, their words gushing forth like a mountain torrent.

Billy Sutcliffe from the weaving shed, an older worker with three grown-up children expressed the unease shared by numerous other pickets. 'Jimmy, have you seen the Bobbies up the road? What do you think it means?'

John Roberts, a young unmarried apprentice wool sorter, asked, 'What was the outcome of the discussions? What was the employers' position?'

Bert Cousins, a communist activist, was more optimistic. 'Have the old gits backed down?' he asked with a gruff smile on his weathered face. 'Have they given in? What are they offering? Has that two-faced bastard, Rowbottom, conceded our demands?'

Doug Ackroyd, freshly promoted to the burling and mending shed as an overlooker, asked wishfully, 'Shall we be going back to work soon? Has the owners' position moved at all? Are our jobs secure?'

Then Bert Cousins shouted out again, stridently over the top of all other voices. 'Let's get to the point. What about our comrades who were taken in by the flatfoots last night for loitering at the Rowbottom mill entrance? They had seven bells beaten out of them by those bully boys for nothing. And what about Joseph Murphy who was only doing his legitimate recruitment duty when he was reported by one of those treasonous overlookers and sacked on the spot by one of the gaffers?'

But it was Jimmy's artless friend Harry, in a rather reedy and hesitant voice, who somehow prevailed with a more open question. 'How did you go on?'

'There have been no contacts so far. We have not heard from the employers' side. So, no change. Keep on as before. The strike is still on. I'll tell you all one thing though. We have to remain united. That's the only way to win. Stick together, lads. We fight on. All for one and one for all. To victory! As we did in the war.'

Bert Cousins sloganised the clarion call enthusiastically, 'The workers united will never be defeated. Stay united, comrades. All for one and one for all!'

Jimmy could feel the tension rising in his head. He was feeling rather hurt by the speculative chitchat that he might have had secret contact with the employers without telling his mates. He needed to keep the morale of the men high and such baseless prate could only be detrimental to that goal. He knew that he had to keep them converted to the notion that they could win, even if he himself was not sure. He had to retain their confidence in him. Resolutely, he raised his hands to quieten their questions and reassured them. 'There have been no contacts and no backdoor deals have been made. Nor will such deals be made. The commitment to the strike is still one hundred per cent.'

Disappointed, the men settled back into their groups glumly, contemplating in murmured conversation the randomly snaking flames of their brightly burning braziers. The braziers had become their solace and the focal point around which they symbolically expressed their solidarity and unending brotherhood — with only the odd digression about the local town football team which, not many years before the war, had won the cup and then taken in its first females for a parallel team.

Jimmy noticed some of the officers redeploying down the road towards the mill entrance, getting closer to the strikers assembled round the braziers.

Right away, the order came from a burly, red-faced inspector. 'Move back now! Let the officers through. Keep the King's highway free! You are blocking the King's highway. Please move back. Clear the road.'

The striking workers on the line murmured and stood resolutely where they were. The seeds of a stand-off were already being sown. How could Jimmy avoid it? He opted to speak to the officer in charge.

It so turned out that Assistant Chief Inspector Jack Braithwaite in charge of the deployment was not unsympathetic to the aspirations of the workers. Certainly he was more sympathetic than his Chief Constable. Indeed, his social provenance predisposed him to be as even-handed as possible, which was possibly the reason the Chief Constable had chosen him for this duty. Braithwaite was a decent man

185

whose kinfolk had worked in the wool business for several generations. Some of them were still employed in local mills. His father had been a wool sorter: a skilled job, ranked as being a cut above the mill workers. Braithwaite lived quite close to Jimmy in one of the larger middle class terraced houses facing onto the main road. In spite of his more affluent residence, he was of thoroughgoing working class origin — more indeed than he cared to admit. Nonetheless, he had managed to gain successive promotions through the ranks by his integrity and hard work, both of which were much admired by his colleagues and appreciated by the local population.

Jack Braithwaite was presently close to retirement. Given his good conduct, he would have an adequate pension, and he would have time to indulge in his main interest of fishing in the nearby river for trout or for tiddlers in the park pond with his grandchildren. It would likewise give him space in his life for time with his grandchildren, of whom he was extremely proud. Although he found negotiating with strikers irksome, he was thus not untouched by their aspirations and their predicament in this difficult post-war period. At the same time, as the upright and incorruptible officer that he was, he accepted that his first duty was to uphold the law with absolute impartiality.

The ranks of the police surged forward at first gently and then more firmly as the strikers sought to resist the pressure with equal firmness. In the process, some of the braziers were knocked over and hot ashes spread onto the cobbles and melted the tar which bound them together. Pickets jumped back as the situation became riskier and more fraught.

Some of the men acquiesced compliantly to the firm oral persuasion of the police, not fully realising what was happening. Others, however, resented what they regarded as the belligerent tactics of the police in support of the antagonistic strategy of the owners, who they believed had decided to bring in replacement workers 'volunteer' labour, or scabs as they were derogatively referred to.

Volunteer labour was a charged subject for the men and consequently some of the more militant workers pushed back vigorously against the advancing police line. As a result, some of the officers became more assertive in driving the workers back, a few lashing out with their heavy hobnailed boots.

Jimmy realised that he had to do his utmost to defuse the growing confrontation between the two sides if the strike action were to stand any chance of succeeding. So, he stepped forward towards the police line. He could see Jack Braithwaite behind the line of officers. As he approached, however, Jimmy was firmly pushed away, maybe because the officer involved sincerely believed that he was seeking to breach the police line. For his part, Jimmy refused to be deterred. He moved back towards the line and tried to remonstrate with the officer who had thrust him back, asking him to let him through to see the inspector. He simultaneously held his arms outstretched to indicate to his followers not to make further contact with the police.

'What the bloody hell do they think they are doing?' Harry shouted close behind him with a note of alarm in his voice. 'What are the Bobbies doing now?'

'I haven't a clue, lad, but I aim to find out.'

At that moment, a well-built, broad-shouldered sergeant in the front row deliberately brought up his heavy boot and caught Jimmy squarely in the groin. The searing pain drove him to the ground instantly where he was jolted by a further blow to the head. This second blow jerked his head sharply backwards and momentarily stunned him. The scene appeared to swim before his eyes, and the notion crossed his fuzzy mind that he was getting his rightful deserts for all those good working men he had slain in France.

In a blinding flash, an excruciating pain in his head and lower body threw him on to his back writhing in agony on the muddy floor of a shell hole. Dully, as if through a thin soundproof screen, he could hear the distanced agonised cries of the wounded Pals around him in no-man's-land. Unable to move because of the snipers' incessant fusillade towards his position, he could not help them. All he could do was await the inevitable counterattack by Fritz, hoping against hope that it would not come to pass before nightfall. Even with the blessed arrival of darkness, a time of fairly safe passage for those not seriously wounded, the wounded were still left untended.

A sufficiency of medics and stretchers was said to have been envisaged for the unbelievable legions of casualties. One stretcher for each sixteen soldiers should be enough, the officers had optimistically prescribed. Only one in ten of the Pals survived unscathed that day. How could they ever have had enough for all the Pals who were laid low on that day? No one in their wildest dreams could have foreseen such a mountain of casualties. No General in his right mind would have planned it. No Prime Minister would have agreed to it. No one with an ounce of human feeling and compassion would have persisted with it.

Then, out of the blue, he felt an arm helping him rise. Had he been lucky? Was this one of the medics, who had come upon him by chance? Would he survive after all? He shook his head, doing his utmost to unblock his brain. He opened his bleary eyes to regard the saviour above him … a stretcher-bearer? Another Pal?

Harry, a kindly and gentle, somewhat Panglossian soul, had been at his side in the picket line when Jimmy was attacked. In a bid to help his friend up, he had bent down to help him. He was straightaway in receipt of a vicious kick, probably from the same officer who had attacked Jimmy. It was only a glancing blow, and the officer fell off balance and rather comically stumbled backwards.

Nonetheless, because Harry was low to the ground striving to help his friend, the heavy boot caught him in the face. He fell beside Jimmy, clutching his face and groaning, blood pouring from his nose onto the scorched cobbles. A group of the more militant strikers, having witnessed what had occurred, had surged forward to afford protection and the police line momentarily receded, giving the two men the chance to help each other up, first on to their knees and thereafter shakily on to their feet. They were both supported by their co-strikers to limp further from the line of constables, now resuming their slow advance.

It took a couple of minutes for Jimmy to come to his senses and realise where he was. He surveyed what was materialising, and what he glimpsed was extremely troubling. The police were now working to split the workers' line, forcing them to either side of the arched mill entrance. This manoeuvre left the two wounded friends further isolated, as the officers pulled back from them to complete the movement.

By now word of what had happened to the two men had spread through the ranks of the strikers and they began shouting and heckling. 'Bastards! Bastards! Bastards!' they chanted. Not long afterwards, with the atmosphere becoming ever uglier, someone hollered out, 'Get the bastards!'

Jimmy staggered gingerly on his failing legs and swayed from side to side, propping himself on Harry, who had sunk back to the ground in a kneeling position. He yanked Harry up in a futile effort to indicate to his striking followers that they were both all right.

With a weakened and wheezing voice, he tried to shout to his own men. 'Get back. No violence.' In spite of his appeal, the general commotion, the obscenities being shouted, and the ever louder and more vitriolic heckling by the strikers doomed his feeble voice. Realising he had to do all he could to get an agreement with the officer in charge to quieten things down, he lumbered and limped slowly, heavily and painfully again towards the police line, shouting to them that he wanted to speak to the inspector in charge.

'Get back or you'll get the same again. You are breaking the law by blocking the road. If you do not move back swiftly, you will be taken into custody. You have been warned once already. Move back now!'

Fortunately, amidst all the shouting and chaos, inspector in charge Jack Braithwaite, had seen Jimmy staggering towards the line and realised that he was one of the leaders who wanted to parley. So, he came out from behind the line and approached Jimmy. As he did so, some of the strikers pressed forward again, fearing that Jimmy and Harry were either going to be arrested or attacked again. Several constables rushed forward to push the men back once more, and this time more vehemently, and this manoeuvre appeared to leave the two men segregated from the other striking workers.

Inspector Braithwaite moved out from behind his men and approached Jimmy and Harry. Eye-to-eye, they stared each other straight in the face. Jimmy addressed the inspector as fittingly as he knew how, without giving him chance to speak first.

'Inspector, I wish to speak to the officer in charge about the policing of the dispute on this site.' He was still groggy and his voice was weakened.

'That's me. I am the responsible senior officer. What is it you wish to speak to me about, allowing for the fact that I could have you arrested for obstructing the highway and attempting to prevent my officers from carrying out their duty?'

'I don't think that would be helpful to you or to us.' Grappling to master the pain and with his head still spinning, Jimmy continued in a reasoned manner. 'That is unless you want another George Square riot on your hands. It is my earnest wish as the responsible leader at this picket to pursue this picket action peacefully. I want to make sure that there is no violence and that there are no breaches of the peace. I am adamant, however, that my workers must be able to engage in peaceful and lawful picketing and are treated with the dignity they warrant. That is their democratic right, something for which I spent four hard years fighting for and for which umpteen of our co-workers gave their lives. I would suggest that you withdraw your men, so that we can discuss tactics and help each other to maintain law and order and prevent further casualties.'

'I can figure out where you're coming from, although your reference to the Glasgow riot is a bit overblown. You might perhaps remember that you and your comrades are not the only ones who sacrificed for their King and country. Umpteen of my men did likewise.' He gestured behind him at his men. 'At any rate, the instructions from my Chief Constable are to make sure that public access to the mill is preserved at all times and that the King's highway is kept free for passage. To be honest with you, who and what passes along that highway, provided their actions are within the law, is a matter of supreme indifference to me.'

'But the surest way of getting that is through negotiation and not by bellicose conduct and violent, sometimes brutal, action on the part of your men.'

'I don't accept for a single moment that my men have been aggressive, let alone brutal. Firm? Yes. Forceful? Aye, when required. In no way unnecessarily aggressive. Your members did not move back and free the entrance to the mill when given a lawful instruction by the law enforcement officers in the course of their duty. So, they had to be moved back, always of course with the minimum amount of force necessary. That is the instruction my men have received, and that is what they have done, so far as I have seen.'

'I don't recall receiving any request for us to move back. I did not hear either message or instruction. You know who the Central Council of Action leaders are, and you could easily have contacted them. In that case we would have co-operated in your request insofar as it was legal. Nevertheless, in no case is violence against unarmed civilians justified. That much we should have in common.'

'You do not realise, Mr Kelly — that is your name, is it not? — that it is not up to you to adjudicate what is legal. In this country that is what the courts are for.'

Jimmy feared the interchange was running away from him and reacted somewhat more abruptly than he meant to. 'Nor is it up to you. In our country, that decision does rest with the courts, which are independent of the employers ... and the constabulary.'

'Of course. And operational decisions have to be taken by the responsible officer on the spot. If in dispute, any decision can be challenged in the courts in due course. For the moment and on this spot, it is my decision, which defines what is legal. Not yours.'

Still stinging and aching from the kick, Jimmy felt his integrity and his suggestion of co-operation were being spurned. He reacted rather more severely than was his intention. 'You're hand in glove with the mill owners. That's the top and bottom of it, isn't it? You'd rather side with management than with the workers.'

'No, that is not the case. We have instructions from the Chief Constable to uphold strict impartiality. We are not for one side or the other. Our job is solely to maintain the peace and keep the King's highway open. It's as simple as that. And that is what we intend to do.'

Jimmy hit back again in a defiant manner. 'Since we are talking about legality and impartiality, one of your men assaulted me and callously assaulted this young man by kicking him in the head.' He gestured towards Harry, who was standing beside him, blood flowing profusely from his nose and his bruised eye gradually closing. 'The evidence is there for all to see. Is that legal?'

'I did not see any such assault. If you can provide me with the name and number of the officer allegedly involved, I assure you I shall investigate the matter further.'

'I don't have the name and number, because I was facing away from your men, struggling to hold back my striking friends, when I was assaulted. I was on the ground writhing in agony when Harry here was assaulted.'

'Without those details, I am afraid I cannot do anything. Rest assured, though, I shall not tolerate common assault on the part of my men. My job, as I explained, is to uphold the law with strict impartiality in the interests of all citizens, regardless of background.'

Jimmy noted the rather more conciliatory tone of Jack Braithwaite's rejoinder and elected to build a united front. Despite the Inspector's previously uncooperative response, he felt that he had to persevere with what he saw as his responsibility to his own men.

'Look, we both have the same objective here, namely to make sure that this industrial action stays legal and peaceful, and thus ensure that no one else gets hurt. Don't you agree?'

'Alright, then, Mr Kelly. Get your men off the road and back onto the pavements at either side of the mill gates and we have no issue. They must stay behind the police lines. And if they press forward again and breach the lines, I shall instruct my men to draw their batons.'

'That would be a foolish mistake, Inspector,' Jimmy responded, possibly underestimating the meaning of what the Inspector was saying.

'Are you threatening me, Mr Kelly?'

'No. I am merely notifying you that to instruct your men to draw batons will only inflame the situation. It won't help you keep order, which is my objective too.'

'On a more human level, Mr Kelly, would you like to pass through our lines to go to the hospital and have those wounds of yours and your friend's attended to? However they were caused, they seem to need some attention.'

Jimmy was taking on board this conciliatory gesture on the part of the Inspector when a murmuring in the crowd of strikers interrupted their dialogue. The lull that had taken place in the confrontation as both sides regarded the dialogue of their leaders, slowly began to erode. A scarcely audible babble of individual voices gradually rose to a co-ordinated crescendo of raucous shouts as a frisson of widespread anger rippled through the crowd of striking workers and the men cried out in unison, 'Scabs! Scabs! Scabs!'

Jimmy and Harry glanced up to see a charabanc turning into the top of the road with its windows blacked out. At first Jimmy thought that it was merely bringing in police reinforcements. But, as it drove slowly down the road with officers on foot escorting it on either side, swiftly followed by another in a similar fashion, Jimmy's suspicions rose.

'What the hell is this?' Jimmy exclaimed. 'This looks ominous.'

Then Harry understood. 'No, the Bobbies can't be so stupid so soon.'

Chapter Twelve

'Christ, they're bringing in scab workers,' Harry yelled.

'Don't you understand?' Jimmy demanded, turning to address the Inspector and feeling that he had been betrayed. 'This will simply inflame the situation. My members will never take this lying down.'

'The decision to bring in the two charabancs with their occupants is not my decision. It has nothing to do with me, let alone the force in general. This is the owners' decision. Theirs alone and it is a lawful act.'

'Like hell it is!' Jimmy shouted back. 'Look at the effect that the appearance of those strike breakers has had on my mates. It's inflamed the situation and made it much more difficult for us to keep the action peaceful.'

'That's as may be. Nevertheless, any attempt to impede the progress of those two vehicles will be illegal, Mr Kelly. It is the job of the force to see that the highway is not obstructed and that those going about their lawful business are not impeded, interfered with or threatened in any way.'

Jimmy turned away from the inspector in disgust and moved hurriedly towards his men, who were now forming a solid phalanx to block the passage of the two vehicles and their escorts. The weight of their numbers pressed the police into the side of the coaches and potentially under the wheels of the slowly advancing vehicles. More strikers were now gathering to prevent the vehicles from moving forward, and banging on the windows, all the time chanting in strident chorus, 'Scabs! Scabs! Scabs!'

As more officers were called in from the side streets to assist their colleagues, the forward crush of the strikers was temporarily halted. Spasmodic scuffles between the police and strikers persisted, however, with some on both sides injured in side brawls. Others, mainly injured strikers, fell to the ground where they were in constant jeopardy of being trampled underfoot. As the tide of commotion surged back and forth with neither side establishing a firm line, Jimmy heard the instruction, 'Draw batons!'

'What the bloody hell does he think he is doing?' Jimmy yelled out to Harry, while running up the road as fast as he could towards the two vehicles to intervene, lest the situation get even more out of hand.

But things were gradually escalating, and the outbreak of rampant violence was as sudden as it was sensational and unpredicted. For their part the police retaliated to workers' resistance with unbridled aggression, now using their batons freely and indiscriminately in a no-mercy pitched battle with the front ranks of the strikers. On both sides men were shouting and cursing, uttering all manner of obscenities. Those at the back of the strikers' ranks were pushing forward bellowing out to encourage those in the thick of it and barging them into an ever-tighter struggle with the police. Fists and boots were flying, banners were being used as weapons, and a fair number of striking workers were being floored by police batons.

Several officers also fell to the ground gripping their shins, and one was laboured around the head with a banner. Several strikers were struck down and left moaning and groaning on the cobbled street. One man was felled by a truncheon blow with great force directly to the top of his head. He fell writhing to the ground uttering a loud moaning bellow, his flat cap falling off and his head opening up, with blood pouring onto the footpath. Both sides were now driven by growing feelings of unrestrained bile and revenge.

Violence and brutality were taking over from reason and humanity on both sides.

Jimmy could see that some of the felled strikers were already being taken away to the small cottage hospital by their comrades. Others were hobbling away by themselves. Inside the hospital they were quickly laid out like cadavers in the narrow crowded corridors, awaiting treatment by the overstretched medical staff, who had been taken totally unawares by the influx of patients.

Other strikers, less seriously injured, were getting up, however dazed, and striving to stand by their mates and fight again. Gradually, with the aid of reinforcements and some newly arrived mounted constables, the police began to slowly edge forward, driving the seething mob of strikers away from the buses containing the volunteer workers. Little by little they were succeeding in clearing a path for the two charabancs moving at a snail's pace towards the mill gates. With every yard that the two charabancs moved forward, the white-hot fury of the workers seemed to grow, and the fighting surged once more becoming more violent and embittered.

At that moment, like an actor entering an already overcrowded stage, a rather ramshackle old steam lorry came lumbering along slowly, hissing and puffing. In a cloud of billowing grey smoke, its entry drew immediate attention from the strikers, who halted its forward progression. A few minutes previously the lorry had made its first delivery of a consignment of soft drinks at the local Co-operative store and it was still half-loaded with bottles of 'pop'and crates of empty glass bottles. Its potential contribution to the battle was directly recognised. All at once, a cry went up from several of the more rowdy strikers, reminiscent of cries at the Front. 'Ammunition! Ammunition!'

Bert Cousins, the well-known, outspoken local Communist Party activist, made a wild rush for the lorry followed by others who scattered the thin police line at the side of the road. The former scuffle at that point spiralled into a riot and anarchy instantly took over.

Fiendishly political, Bert was small, wiry of stature and flinty of character. As an out-and-out product of his time and social and political circumstances, he was of the second generation, whose kinfolk had immigrated to Britain Imperial Russia to Britain in the latter part of the nineteenth century. As an orator, he had a natural twinkly-eyed chutzpah that was magnetic to his fellow workers. Far from being faint-hearted, he could be exceptionally combative by nature and he expressed his radical views eloquently and convincingly to his working class audiences.

Like lots of working men demobilised of late he was still struggling to adjust to civilian life and its challenges, and to leave the trauma of the war behind him. Although occasionally a little short-tempered at home as much as at work, and prone to being excitable in stressful circumstances, he had his finger firmly on the pulse of the workers. His drawback was that to him his Union activity was a fulcrum to agitate for class war, a ragbag of ideas to which all else was subordinate, for which he was an articulate apologist.

He had, however, several saving graces: his sincerity and commitment to the working classes were undoubted, his whimsical nature often permitted him to express hard positions softly, and he was a decent family man to boot. Indeed, all who knew him well considered that he had a good and generous nature and felt that his blemishes were utterly human and fully forgivable. He felt he had a mission to make a change to what he regarded as being a broken world. And, for Bert, the instrument to achieve that was communism, which he envisaged would bring about an earthly paradise for the workers, such as was being constructed in Russia.

He and Jimmy saw eye-to eye about the working classes having been misled into fighting each other for the sake of a squabble among Europe's aristocratic elites. They were, in effect, the working-class victims of capitalist greed and folly. Where their views differed was on the way forward from this tragedy; in this respect they had often acted as intellectual sparring partners. In Bert's world perspective, only a class war could eradicate the dominant elites and the immense economic and human damage they had done. His pre-war zeal for the development of the European workers' movements in Germany and Russia and for the evolution of the Independent Labour Party gave him a unique perspective on the Russian revolution and its significance for the workers in the other countries of Europe.

Though impatient for peaceful and rapid evolution, he was not entirely starry-eyed and utopian in his beliefs, for he was well read in the literature of the working classes, including Marx and Lenin, and in multifarious ways was a highly practical politician. For him, royalty and the aristocracy were parasitic, exploitative, profligate and dangerous. He was fiercely committed to overthrowing the oppressive British aristocratic rule and the tyranny of its spendthrift and snobbish coterie of flunkies. The workers' revolution would give birth to the glorious socialist millennium, like the bolshevik revolution in Russia, and sooner or later a workers' paradise would be born that would eradicate such medieval fairy tales, used to enslave a gullible working class. It was only a matter of time.

Lenin-like, Bert leaped onto the back of the lorry and urged the strikers to action. Inspired by his brilliant encouragement and lured by the prospect of a steady stream of heavier calibre ammunition, they surged round the lorry and formed a chain of men to unload the bottles and to deliver a murderous barrage of exploding glass missiles into the police ranks.

As a consequence, Jack Braithwaite brought in reinforcements, including a small detachment of mounted constables whose startled horses reared their sharp hooves and fell on some of the police and strikers in some cases resulting in serious injury.

A small, tightly knit detachment of police, spearheaded by some of the mounted officers, sought to fight their way through the bustling crowd of riotous strikers towards those on the lorry. Brandishing their batons, the detachment formed a tight group and eventually beat their way through to the fervid strikers around the steam lorry, leaving a trail of trampled and bleeding strikers in their wake. By the time they reached the lorry, however, its load was substantially depleted and the damage to property and their own ranks had already been done. Some few strikers had formed a protective cordon around the lorry; and they seemed to have taken on a single goal, like knights defending a medieval fortress to the death. It was no longer simply a struggle about an exhausted stock of bottles and a united king-of-the-castle mentality, it was a stubborn determination to cede no territory to the constabulary at any cost.

Another group of strikers stood in front of the lorry, road-blocking it, so that it could not move forward. Others shouted a strongly expressed demand to their two 'brothers', the driver of the lorry and his mate, to alight and join them. Meanwhile, a couple of strikers had already scrambled up onto the back of the lorry and, against the vociferous remonstrations of the driver, accelerated the distribution of the remaining bottles.

In a moment of pure farce, one of the more enthusiastic of the strikers, Simon Green, launched himself onto the lorry to join the others. In his blind enthusiasm to be part of the mayhem, however, his foot slipped on the greasy hub of the vehicle's wheel. He banged his face on the corner of a crate and fell to the ground, moaning and writhing with a stream of blood pouring from his mouth and nose. His co-strikers, similarly anxious to get aboard the lorry, appeared unconcerned about one more casualty and Simon was temporarily left to suffer before two of the strikers detached themselves from the 'fun' and helped him to his feet and away to the cottage hospital.

Those who were already aboard had been taking the bottles out of the crates and passing them to those waiting below. As the supply of bottles diminished, men began to jump down from the lorry, and without explicit organisation, the strikers who had been distributing the bottles redeployed into an amateur Saxon shield formation to try to keep back the approaching phalanx of officers.

In the wider battle, with bottles now in short supply, the strikers stopped using them as missiles, instead employing them as truncheon-like weapons to reciprocate the incoming blows from the constabulary. At close quarters, a slogging match had developed; the fighting had become ever more intense and vicious, with many officers and strikers falling injured. The scene was now one of total pandemonium.

Out of the blue, as often happens, there suddenly ensued a temporary hiatus in the violence as some of the men began to drift away to home or hostelry outside the village, while others assisted the walking wounded to the hospital, leaving only the most zealous, fit and patient of the strikers to keep up the fight.

Finally the few remaining bottles were shaken vigorously to increase the explosive impact and thrown to the ground with the aim of frightening the advancing horses of the mounted police. Once again the turmoil inflated again to exceed its previous intensity. The last of the bottles were used as long-range missiles, finding their marks directly onto individual officers as they were launched with greater accuracy. Some strikers were still using bottles as truncheons to beat the opposing forces anywhere they could, including shins and faces. Fallen workers were being kicked anywhere on their bodies, with the hobnailed boots of the constabulary making a dull thud as they met human forms. With more space to strike each other, participants from both sides were falling to the ground in increasing numbers and the street was taking on the appearance of a medieval battlefield.

Strikers were now being scattered in all directions as the Mounties commenced an irresistible advance, gradually forcing the strikers into flight. Resistance was more fragmented and spasmodic, though no less bitterly violent. It became reactive rather than proactive.

Some Trade Union Officials — wholeheartedly convinced that this could do their cause no good — were doing their utmost to restore calm. They were shouting above the furore, hopelessly exhorting their fellow workers to stay peaceful, as well as doing their best to organise some first aid. There were innumerable wounded on both sides now, some of whom were innocently felled as they tried to assist their wounded and bloody mates out of the melee. By this time, the forces of law and order were no longer in total control of the fragmenting scene. Individual officers sought revenge where they could find it for injuries to their colleagues or themselves. All remaining strikers, many running away, were now considered legitimate targets. Fallen workers, injured or not, were being dragged down narrow snickets for a good thumping and kicking before being launched into the waiting black Marias.

Jimmy watched the chaotic, violent scene with increasing horror. In his bewildered anguish, Jimmy's thoughts drifted. With his wounded mates on the ground around him, it was the close quarters hand-to-hand fighting that he had known in France. Repeated deep booms from the devastating explosions grew rapidly in volume and number. Suddenly, the Boches were no longer in evidence and the Minenwerfer were raining death on him and the other Pals. The noise was magnified a hundred-fold and was accompanied by the shouting and groaning of wounded men. The ground was covered with a red carpet of blood. Another man dropped to the ground like a stone with his head split wide open, blood streaming as from a fountain. Somehow, he had to survive. It was kill or be killed. It was fight and win or die. His heart thumped heavily and his breathing was laboured.

He abruptly came to his senses as a bottle shattered at his feet. The scene surrounding him was one of unmitigated mayhem and human torment, for which he felt a profound personal responsibility. It tugged at his acute sense of guilt and he resolved to do all he could to put a stop to the conflict.

'Stop this insanity!' he screamed at the top of his voice. 'Stop! Pull back! You bloody lunatics!'

Any hope that he might have had to calm the boiling unrest rapidly evaporated. It was impossible to make himself heard above the bedlam. In desperation, he knew that he had to cut off the remaining supply of missiles if he could. Some ground had been cleared of strikers now as some tired of the game and many had had enough of the violence. Quite a number were, however, still in his path. He sprinted towards the lorry, barging his way through the midst of his co-workers and, where necessary, casting them roughly aside. Some regarded his actions indignantly, trying to restrain him. All the same, he felt that he had to get the men down, to cut off the supply of missiles, help to restore some semblance of order and if possible to avoid the apprehension of the few men still remaining on the lorry by the advancing police.

He knew that his mates were committing a criminal act for which they could be taken into custody. The magistrates would come down hard on them and, once again, the families would suffer while the men served their sentences. That news would surely be trailed across the local press, damaging the Unions' public relations campaign — no doubt much to the delight of the mill owners.

As Jimmy neared the lorry, he cried out, 'Get down from there, you idiots. Don't you see that this will only damage our cause? This is exactly what the employers want. You'll be arrested if you stay up there. Think of your families. Get down!'

There were three men still on the lorry. Frank Oldridge, Wilf's brother and a doubler at the mill, was one of them and he shouted back, scowling fiercely at Jimmy. 'This is what happens when you let scabs in. The bosses started it, not us. I could have sworn that you were negotiating with them. I assumed that you were on our side. Well, what have you achieved? Useless git!'

'Frank, come on. Be reasonable. Get down, while you still have the time.'

Frank resumed in an agitated voice. 'It's the bloody Bobbies' fault. They made the situation worse by drawing their batons and charging us. What did you expect us to do? Sit down and just take it? We have a right to defend ourselves, don't we? And they have no right to administer a beating to anyone they like. That's not the law.'

'For god's sake, Frank, get down straightaway and leave this lorry alone. We can settle this peacefully with the employers. For pity's sake, can't you see what you are doing? Think of the consequences if you get caught. Think of your wife and your little ones. For their sake, if not for your own, get down.'

'Piss off, Jimmy.'

Adamant, Jimmy had another go. 'Our dispute is not with the forces of law and order. And what you are doing is only making the situation worse. We need to win this dispute. What you are doing is making that more difficult. Come on down. Let's scarper now before they catch you.'

'Get lost!'

Exasperated, Jimmy opted for a desperate strategy. He was responsible for these men. He stepped on the hubcap of the back wheel and, reaching up, deftly grabbed Frank's leg with the aim of pulling him down from the lorry. As Frank lost his balance and began to fall, Jimmy grabbed at his shabby waistcoat, in the process tearing off some buttons. Frank, taken by surprise and off balance, toppled towards Jimmy as the weight of his own body propelled him downwards from the back of the lorry. Jimmy broke his fall. In a gut reaction, Frank lashed out furiously, though fortunately for Jimmy without great effect. Writhing and rolling over the cobbles in the pools of soft drinks from the broken glass bottles, they were both drenched and slightly cut by their bed of sharp glass splinters.

Having wrestled Frank to gain the upper hand, Jimmy dragged him unceremoniously by the scruff of the neck across several yards of the uneven cobbled street and into a side alley, where, struggling and cursing, they both stumbled clumsily to the ground again. Intertwined, they wrestled on the smoother paving, barrelling over and over down a slight incline.

Meanwhile, the police detachment was rapidly approaching the lorry and the police had the two remaining strikers, who had been emptying the crates on the lorry, in their sight. They continued to try to feed what little was left of the 'ammunition' over the heads of the advancing policemen to the supply chain of workers amid shouts of acclamation and encouragement from their friends.

On the ground, Jimmy took a stranglehold on Frank's neck, doing his best to hold him down. Frank was having none of it. In a flash, Frank was free and on top and was about to retaliate by punching Jimmy in the face. Quite a crowd of strikers had gathered to watch them. One man, who obviously wanted to see more of the action, pushed forward in the process knocking Frank sideways. Frank was still clinging to Jimmy, causing them both to topple and roll over and over again away from the lorry.

At that same moment, only a few yards away, police officers managed at last to penetrate through the crowd to the side of the lorry, shouting to the two strikers to get down immediately. Fortunately for Frank and Jimmy, they were far enough from the main fray to be out of sight of the police, who would surely have arrested them for breach of the peace if they had observed them fighting on the pavement. In any case, the officers had their eyes on a bigger prize.

Having surrounded the lorry, the small police contingent halted momentarily. 'Get down from the lorry, you two. Get down immediately. You are under arrest for criminal damage and theft.' After which several police mounted the lorry.

Jimmy and Frank watched in horror as their striking co-workers were pounced on by the constables. The two men were dragged roughly down, while being unceremoniously thrashed with truncheons. They were then frogmarched up the main road, arms forced high behind their backs. Three policemen surrounded each one, while others kept back any strikers who attempted to interfere.

Having observed what had happened to his two mates, Frank gentled his threatening manner, as he extricated himself from his entanglement with Jimmy. 'Thanks,' he muttered grudgingly to Jimmy. 'I could have gone to jail with my mates of you hadn't stepped in.'

'And face a two-year jail sentence? Don't be stupid, Frank. Those lads are going to serve hard time. The charges are extremely serious, and the police will want to nail them for revenge in exchange for what has taken place today. They will not get off lightly. What would your kith and kin have done whilst you were languishing in jail? Starved?'

'They'd have managed.'

'Managed how?' exclaimed Jimmy. 'Look, I need your help with this dispute. You're a good man, Frank, even if you are a bit of a hothead. Come on. Let's see what we can salvage from this fiasco.'

Frank grunted acknowledgement. He shrugged off Jimmy's helping hand to stand up and gently pushed him away. Fatigued by their fight, they both levered themselves up from the cold stone paving slabs.

With the supply of missiles gone, the police gradually gained control and drove the strikers back from the road to either side of the mill gates. Several further arrests were made and soon afterwards the charabancs — with their inflammatory cargo — were escorted down the street and into the main gates, accompanied by loud boos, jeers and catcalls. The large green mill gates closed with a resounding clang, symbolically excluding the men from the source of their employment.

Head bowed, Jimmy returned to the mill gates. There was still a strong police presence concentrated around the entrance, although some of the force had been stood down, as the ranks of strikers had thinned out appreciably. Sensing a lost cause, strikers had departed for their supper, seeking succour in their nearby homes. Others were deserting the dry model village and its teetotal rule, going to seek their solace in the demon drink and an accompanying game of fives and threes in one of the pubs outside the village. Doubtlessly, there would be lengthy post-mortem natters about the day's events.

A relatively peaceful calm was now apparent on the streets surrounding the mill, still littered with broken bottles and other debris. The steam lorry finally departed almost empty of its cargo.

Jimmy was obsessed with the fact that his meticulous planning for the picket had unravelled. He felt a personal responsibility for the riotous shambles that the peaceful protest had become — so far from the outcome he had arranged so scrupulously conjointly with the Executive. Assessing the detritus of the confrontation, it seemed to him at that point that all was lost. He felt thoroughly disheartened. The first day of the strike had been a failure; *he* had been a total failure. The mill owners had won. It was all his doing. How could he have bungled the picket so badly? Perhaps it was the war that had done for him as a leader. He was no longer a leader of men. He was a wash-out, he judged

209

himself, bitterly disappointed at the outcome of the day's picket. He was finished.

Then he remembered his close friend, Harry. He turned full circle seeking him, conscientiously scrutinising the faces of the few remaining strikers. Harry was nowhere to be seen.

Chapter Thirteen

When Jimmy entered the cottage hospital to look for Harry, he was still devastated and scandalised about what had occurred at the mill. He was even more severely shaken by the scene that greeted him as he entered the building. When he saw the cost of the day's events, it appalled him and a surge of guilt at his share of the responsibility welled up in his conscience.

As in some of the field hospitals he had seen in France, there were injured men everywhere, even lying on the floor in the corridors. There was blood on the floor tiles and, in some places, spittle and vomit where some of the men had lain before being removed for attention in the tiny accident and emergency station of the hospital. The reek of urine and stale sweat pervaded the atmosphere. One or two nurses were scurrying from one patient to another, assessing the gravity of their injuries and deciding on treatment. It was patent, however, that they and the handful of doctors who regularly worked in the small hospital were totally overwhelmed.

As Jimmy was picking his way gingerly down the jam-packed main corridor, exercising great caution not to step on anyone, he nearly tripped over the outstretched and bloody leg of one of the injured workers who had a makeshift, blood-stained bandage round his head. The scene was so powerfully reminiscent of what he had lived through in France that, like a flash, an image of a skeletal leg protruding from the slimy side of a stinking trench in France invaded his bewildered intellect. Muttering an unintelligible curse to himself, he found himself lost in his life in France once more.

He entered a vividly haunting maelstrom of recollections of the occasion when he had encountered an assemblage of gassed soldiers from different units, who had been parked in one of the communication trenches. The scene surged into his consciousness, expelling his current reality. He was returning with the survivors once again from a nocturnal trench-bombing mission — three-quarters of the suicide squad were not returning — when he encountered the men. The contorted and discoloured faces of dead, dying and wounded soldiers in that trench gradually took the place of his fellow workers in the hospital corridor.

With blankly staring eyes and tongues lolling out of their sagging mouths, some of the soldiers retched a frothy green substance onto the ground. Others salivated in agony a creamy tight-bubbled discharge from their mouths as they struggled to breathe. Others still — it could be said that they were the fortunate ones — lay keeled over by the grim reaper's scythe, unfeeling and at rest, their agony over for eternity.

His whole body shuddered uncontrollably in revulsion at his involuntary evocation of the horrific Brueghel-like scene. He knew he had to take control. He knew he had to break the cycle. Grinding his teeth in resistance, he broke into a cold sweat that drizzled down his forehead and onto his cheeks. Slowly, by pressing his thumb nail hard into his hand he seemed able to forestall more painful flashbacks. He took a deep breath to help him regain his composure and steadied himself by leaning on one of the large green-painted radiators in the hall, before moving away.

From the entrance hall he entered the large central corridor, all the time hoping to come across Harry. He peered into the curtained side wards and in due course he ended up at one of the small accident and emergency areas. All the way, he was conscious that the injured were so numerous it would be easy to overlook a single person. Then, through a gap in the curtains, he noticed Harry, sitting on the side of a bed being treated by a svelte young nurse. She was smartly dressed in a light blue dress with a white Peter Pan collar, a starched linen nurse's cap with a frilly fringe and a freshly blood-stained starched white apron. She had a certain self-confidence and authority about her. As Jimmy later discovered, her name was Catherine Carney. He switched his attention to Harry, who looked a mess with his enlarged and bloody nose, closed left eye and blood all down the front of his faded blue overalls.

So, with a mixture of feelings — relief at having found Harry at last, alarm at the extent of his injuries, and caution at the apparent authority of the nurse — he made to enter the cubicle. As he pulled the screening curtain further to one side, the young nurse was completely taken aback at his untoward brazenness.

'You can't come in here, young man. I must ask you to leave this area at once. This is a treatment area and contains sterile dressings. You can wait in the corridor if you wish. You cannot stay here. I have just about finished with this patient. Please leave right now.'

'Hello, Harry. I am so relieved to have found you,' he said, ignoring the nurse's admonition. 'How're you doing? You look terrible.'

'Well, thank you. It actually looks worse than it is,' Harry assured him with affected cheerfulness. 'Just a few minor cuts and bruises. I'm lucky considering the kicking the Bobbies gave me. Nothing serious.'

'Well, when the nurse is finished with you, I'll take you home. You can come back with me to our house, though I dread to imagine what the upshot will be when Kitty sees you.'

'Okay, Jimmy. I'm almost finished here,' Harry assured him. 'I was worried that you might have been injured or arrested by the Bobbies. They were seething with anger and clearly out for revenge.'

'No, not me. I am too swift on my feet.'

'Sir, I am tending a patient. I must insist that you leave this area immediately. I do not wish to have to summon the police.'

'I'm sorry. I'm going now. I apologise,' he responded, smiling and conceding defeat. He had already had one encounter with the police today and he did not need another. 'See you at the reception in the corridor, Harry.'

As Jimmy departed the treatment area and retreated into the corridor, he bumped into a young newshound from the local paper, the *Observer*. Mick Bradley was enthusiastically writing up the day's events and compiling accounts in great detail from the police, the injured strikers and any other willing interviewees he could find.

'Well, what comment do you have about today's shambles?' bantered Mick. He was a newly appointed reporter on industrial matters for the local paper and he was patently anxious to establish his reputation swiftly. The current industrial turbulence was an ideal opportunity for him to cut his journalistic teeth. He had joined the *Observer* as an office boy, straight from school, and had been apprenticed to one of the senior editors. Like most of the Pals, he had been a volunteer, except that he had fallen on his feet, insofar as he had been deployed to the *Blighty*, a paper printed during the war for the troops in France. After returning from war service into his old job, he had gained his literary wings as the paper's industrial correspondent. It was de rigueur for him to cover any industrial dispute within a wide geographical radius.

A product of one of the turn-of-the-century higher grade central schools, he was an ambitious, intellectually alert and capable young man, who felt that he had wasted sufficient time in his four years' army service. He had no time to lose, and his aim was ultimately to be employed by a national newspaper in Manchester or London. He needed good headlines and he was currently quarrying for the best piece he was likely to get in the town.

Jimmy had met Mick a while before the war at the Socialist Sunday School, which they had both attended as youngsters. Both had cherished similar youthful radical ideas. Similarly, as children they had both regularly followed the Sally Army band on Sunday through the town — not for the music, rather that there was some soup at the end, and possibly clothing during the winter, if they were lucky.

During the war too, Jimmy and Mick had both served in France and had the joint distinction of being two of the few who returned physically unscathed. It was in the trenches that they had gained an admiration of the dedicated and unstinting presence and generous provisions of the Salvation Army, so close to the frontline. Mick had written it up with the heading 'Always a nice cuppa tea here'. On his return, Mick had been taken back into his old job without any delay and had speedily received his promotion. Latterly, he had reported on some of the economic, industrial and radical political speakers at the Mechanics' Institute in town and had noted the regularity with which Jimmy boldly asked critical questions at those sessions.

'Precipitate and arrogant action on the part of the coterie of mill owners. Heavy handed and unnecessary policing. That's my comment,' Jimmy volunteered. 'Just look around

215

at my mates here. And we are not speaking of a few either. This was totally unnecessary. This is a legitimate dispute. The strikers are entitled to withdraw their labour and demonstrate peacefully. They deserve to be treated with dignity.'

'And you're a member of this illustrious Action Committee. What's it called?' Mick asked provocatively.

'The Joint Council for Action,' Jimmy replied.

'Yes, that's it. Are you going to be issuing a statement?'

'Eventually, yes.'

'Well, in the interim, how do you deal with the official declaration that it was the strikers who opened up the violence?'

'A likely story. Then, that's what they would say, wouldn't they? Do you expect them to admit responsibility? Agree they were the instigators of the violence?'

'Well, no. But …'

'I consider that there is a case for accusing the police of excessive and unnecessary violence and of being secretly in league with the bosses.'

Mick had already interviewed the police officer in charge, Jack Braithwaite, and an official statement had been swiftly issued in an attempt at forestalling exactly the kind of accusation that Jimmy was making. But, while Mick wanted a balanced report, what he categorically wanted to explore most of all was the workers' side of the dispute, with which he had a sneaking sympathy. For him, that side of things was a human interest story that would appeal to his readers, the vast majority of whom were working class, and help to make his reputation as a man of the people.

'What do you reply to the accusation that, with the mill burnings and the sabotage of the mill donkey engine, you were asking for a clash right from the outset?'

'Well, that's just downright untrue. Those blazes were accidental and had nothing whatsoever to do with my members. The same applies to the mill engine explosion. It's not the first engine to explode and no one has been able to put forward any evidence to substantiate such an accusation. In any case, it's so far-fetched to suggest that the workers would want to destroy their own jobs. It's just a scurrilous defamation of our members, probably put about by the mill owners for their own purposes.'

'Well, the Luddites did that sort of thing, didn't they?'

'Mick! That was over a century ago and history has deemed the man who initiated that vandalism as deranged. My men are neither Luddites nor lunatics. They want to preserve their jobs not destroy them. They just want a decent wage, a fair wage for the job.'

'The official report states that some of your members were itching for a fight all along.'

'You know, as I do, that the Central Council of Action issued strict orders to all members to remain peaceful at all costs and to act within the law. It's in the workers' interests to do so. We all recall how it turned out last time when discipline broke and the strike got out of control. The workers lost and their families starved.'

'But those kinds of appeals are all very well as pronouncements. On the ground, however, they can fall on deaf ears, unless there are people there to enforce discipline.'

Jimmy felt himself under increasing pressure to justify and explain the actions of his men, and he felt rather dispirited by Mick's approach. He grappled with finding a convincing form of words and keeping calm, finding himself irritated by the incessant questioning.

'Precisely, Mick. I know that I and the other leaders took direct, effective, peaceful action to restrain strikers and to guarantee good order on our side. We asked some of our members to act as marshals and prepared them for the task. The inflammatory provocation was caused by the owners and the police: the owners by bringing in outside workers and the police by drawing their batons. I told Braithwaite that those actions would make things worse. It seemed to confirm what my members were alleging, namely that the forces of law and order were not impartial. Rather they were in league with the mill owners. I am not suggesting that the police were venal. Just that their views were totally and falsely preformed and they were wrong in their assessment of the situation.'

Mick decided that he had exploited that topic sufficiently and opted to move on to the contentious issue of the leaders detained by the police.

'I'm not sure whether you have heard the reports, that the other Union leaders who were at the mill have been taken into custody and are imprisoned at the town hall Police station? You seem to have been fortunate not to have joined them.'

'I don't know the first thing about the arrests. Do you know the names?

'Well, off the record, I have Paul Brear and John Kenny. There may be others. I just don't have all the details thus far. Please note that it is unofficial and needs to be confirmed.'

'If that is the case, it can only make the situation worse. Those two are the voices of moderation. I know that they were at the forefront of the action, urging restraint on the part of our workers. That sounds like another stupid move by the police. Where did you get that report from?'

'Well, I am not sure that I can reveal my source, although you can take it from me that it came from a reliable source in the police force. Some of your strikers allege that they saw how those two were seized and taken away in a Black Maria. According to these witnesses, they were given a good beating before they were launched into the van, which would have been totally felonious of course.'

Jimmy decided to take the initiative, rather than just react to Mick's questions. So, he changed tack and set his sights on drawing Mick's attention to the plight of his members in the hospital.

'Just glance around you, Mick. This is the result of blind and mistaken policies on the part of the owners and the police. And it will get worse unless someone appeals for resolution of the conflict. That's the Union sides' position and you can quote me.'

'What makes you think that?'

'Look what happened when they arrested Shinwell and those other strike leaders in Glasgow. It didn't make solving the problem any easier, did it? Quite the reverse. Similarly, here, the employers will have to withdraw their unilateral action in seeking a ten per cent wage reduction and they will have to sit down with us and talk — or go bankrupt. And who in our community does that benefit?'

'Is that all?' Mick asked.

'No. The police have to stop acting like they're the enforcement arm of the Mill Owners' Association. It's as simple and straightforward as that.'

'I'll take into account what you are advocating in writing up my report.'

'Well, when you are writing it up, just consider what the dispute is about for the whole community.'

'What's that?'

'It's about the basic principle of a decent wage for a decent day's work. It's also about whether our families are entitled to a decent standard of living. Just think about that. Think of my men and their families. The pound that was worth twenty shillings to them in 1914 is now worth less than ten shillings. Despite that the bosses are asking the men to suffer a further ten per cent reduction in their wages. That does not make any sense. It's just not possible.'

'Fair point. Though they equally have their problems.'

'What are you now, Counsel for the mill owners?'

'No! It seems only fair to me to take into account that, even given that this is a local dispute, it is also part and parcel of a national context of constant industrial unrest, and of an international marketplace that is still weak from the after-effects of the war.'

'Yes, that is true. The Central Council of Action understands that, and they have committed to act responsibly. For example, workers shelved their demands for better wages and conditions during the war as part of the overall industrial truce. The time for honouring the implications of that accord, namely that negotiated settlement would take place when push comes to shove, has now arrived.'

'And your point is that the settlement date has dawned for the textile industry, is it?'

'Not quite so fast. As I advocated before, our industry has been highly responsible. We have not even proposed post-war bids for improvements in wages and working conditions so far, though we shall be doing so imminently. Adjustments for the loss of value of wages during the war have not even been considered up till now.

'So, where does that leave your dispute with the employers?'

'With the stark fact that it is the employers who have brought this dispute about by going in directly the opposite direction to the rest of the country.'

'What do you mean?'

'Well, where most industries are talking about improving wages and conditions of work, and particularly reducing the length of the working week, the mill owners here are proposing not only to decrease wages. They are also seeking to worsen the conditions. So, in the final analysis, this strike comes down to whether a man can provide for his loved ones, whether he can feed his wife and children. Do you honestly want to see children begging for their bread on the streets of the town?'

'Obviously not. Do you realise they will use all the civil and military power at their disposal to fight any major strike in any sector, not just one where your members work?'

'I personally hope that reason will win through. Remember our dispute in the context of the widespread industrial unrest in the country. Every day so far this year an average of a hundred thousand men have been on strike somewhere in the country. That indicates that something is wrong somewhere.'

'And since the Russian Revolution all major strikes have been considered by government as latent possibilities for revolution. For the powers that be they are the potential harbingers of the overthrow of the state.'

'I can't help the fact that government has hang-ups about its workers who have just finished fighting a major war for it.'

'But you realise that your raising of the red flag helps that perception?'

'Look, this dispute is about the retention of a decent wage for our members, not flags.'

Feeling that he had exhausted the possibilities of the interview, Mick decided to terminate it. He had other people he wanted to talk to.

'Well, that's helpful. Helps to shed light on the issues. Can I quote you?'

'Surely. Just make sure you quote me accurately.'

With that, Mick loped down the corridor and continued with his interviews of the injured, using the opportunity to speak to the medical staff when it presented itself.

After what seemed to Jimmy like a long wait, Harry at last emerged from the cubicle. He appeared a little better; he had been cleaned up and learned that none of his injuries were life-threatening.

The two men left the hospital together, turned right and slowly walked up the hill away from the mill and its tight security. They decided to walk back to Jimmy's house to save the fare and they returned home in the fading light of the afternoon, just as Kitty was preparing to cook the stew for supper.

'My God. What have you been doing, Harry?' Kitty exploded. 'And Jimmy, I asked you to keep an eye on him. Fat lot of good that did! What happened?'

'It's nothing, Kitty. Believe me. Just surface stuff. It'll improve in next to no time. It's not serious,' Harry tried to reassure her.

'But how did it happen?'

'Well, there was this police line,' Jimmy explained. 'Things were getting a bit rowdy, so I approached the line to ask to speak the officer in charge to assist in keeping things calm. As I approached, this big, stout sergeant kicked me in the groin. I fell on the floor in pain, and Harry here came to help me get up. Well, he got kicked into the bargain. In the face.'

'Yes, what Jimmy has stated is true. I've been to the hospital and after examining me they tell me that it is not serious and that I should recover swiftly.'

'Well, sit down and let's all have a nice hot cup of tea. And Harry, you can stay for supper. We'll get some hot nutritious food in you before you go home to that cold, damp house.'

'Thanks very much, Kitty. I'd love to.'

'I saw Mick Bradley at the hospital whilst I was waiting for Harry,' Jimmy recounted, wanting to direct the conversation away from Harry's injuries.

'Who's that?'

'You remember Mick Bradley, the chap from the *Observer*. We've met on a number of occasions at the Mechanics.'

'Oh, yes. Mick Bradley. I remember him now. An articulate and ambitious young man. Didn't he take up a job as a newshound when he returned from the Front? What is he doing now?'

'Well, they've made him the chief industrial reporter for the daily paper. He was writing up the strike.'

'What do you think he will report about it?'

'I fancy it's in the balance. A lot depends on which way the political wind is blowing and what manner of response the police and mill owners make to him. I must admit I am worried.'

'Charlie Belfont came by not many minutes before you and Harry came back. He said that they had detained two of the Union leaders at the mill. Paul Brear and John Kenny, he told me.'

'Are you sure of the names?'

'I asked him specifically, because I was worried about you. He was just on his way down to the police station to get confirmation, and afterwards he intended to go and let the families know.'

'What else did he have to say?'

'He advised that there is an emergency assembly of the Central Council of Action on Thursday evening at seven in the Textile Hall. He will see you there.'

'Did he tell you what it was about?'

'Something about a big demonstration and protest march to oblige the authorities to free the detained leaders, to protest at the action of the police and to condemn the action of the owners in bringing in replacement workers. Of course, the aim is also to bring the owner's unreasonable wage proposals to public attention.'

'When is it to take place?'

'The day is not yet set, though he advised that it may be next Saturday in Town Hall Square. He indicated that he would see you at the meeting tonight.'

Jimmy motioned his thanks for the information. Over supper the three of them talked at great length about the day's events. Kitty was upset about what people would think and what the local newspaper would publish.

Eventually, they came round to the topic of Kate and the incidents at the mill gates in the morning. Kitty listened attentively as Jimmy described exactly what had transpired. Then, he remembered Kate and his commitment to her.

'Damn!' he exploded. 'I wanted to be at the mill gates when she finished work. I as good as promised her that I would be there to meet her, after what happened this morning. It must have been rather upsetting for her.'

'You're saying that you didn't meet her?' demanded Kitty. 'I am amazed at you.'

'With all the problems that we have had today, the need to visit the men in the hospital, and with Harry being injured … I just clean forgot. In any case, I probably would not have been there on time. She finishes quite early, doesn't she? I'll go round now and check that she is alright. Kitty, can you put my supper in the oven to keep warm until I return.'

'I can come with you,' Harry suggested.

'No, Harry. You are in no fit state. It's cold and damp outside. Stay here by this nice warm fire, finish your supper and then take yourself off home and go straight to bed. I'll see you tomorrow morning. Kitty, see that he gets straight off home after his supper. And mind you give him some food to go with.'

'Leave that to me. You get yourself round to Kate's pretty sharply and find out what's gone on. I'll see to all that here.'

Jimmy grabbed his coat, leaped to open the door and launched himself into the brief walk to Kate's house at a rapid pace. Despite all his worries about the day's events, his mind was now dominated by his concerns about what might have happened to Kate. He quickened his stride through the cooling rain.

Chapter Fourteen

Escorted by Jimmy, Kate had passed safely through the mill gates and with a few short steps she had entered the drab, formalistic garden of the mill manager's house, where the darkened privets stood dreary sentinel over the austere, soot-blackened portico and main entrance. The house stood directly in front of the mill and opposite the stables, which had been well constructed to shelter the mill's team of impressive shire horses, which pulled the carts of wool and finished products to dye houses for dyeing and finishing.

The horses also transported finished materials to other mills or to the dedicated local railway station for transportation elsewhere in the country, and in some cases abroad. As was still the case with most mills in the town, these horses were the main method of inward and outward cartage for both the mill's raw materials and finished wares, although a small number of steam lorries were still in use and some modern lorries had been purchased prior to the war.

At one side of the house was a large open field where the horses were given their leisure when the mill was not using them or if they had been injured. On the other side of the house were the stables and cart sheds. Behind the house and towering over it was the monumental mill, built of coursed, chunky hewn sandstone in Canaletto style.

Constructed in the same period as the mill for the mill owner, the house dated from the mid-nineteenth century. In contrast to the mill, the house was a plain fronted building, the blocks of stone having been smoothly hewn and finely mortared. Its design was symmetrical, with windows and bays balanced on either side. It had been sturdily constructed from the local honey-coloured sandstone, except that its walls were now blackened with pollution from the adjacent

227

mill. At the front and behind the low privet hedge were rather sadly neglected lawns and, close to the house, unloved laurel, rhododendron and bay bushes.

The large double fronted bay windows framed an attractive porticoed front door with panels either side of delightfully coloured stained glass, encompassing floral and geometrical motifs. The brass furniture was well polished and gleamed a diligent welcome to any official visitor. Red decorated quarry tiles adorned the floor of the entrance. At either side of the front door, set slightly forward, were two large ornamental stone lions and at the right side of the door an ornate, cast-iron boot scraper. Above the front door was a rather ostentatious, rectangular stained-glass window with industrial scenes from the textile industry and a Latin motto — although no one at the mill either spoke or understood it.

The whole house gave an impression of cleanliness, diligence and good, modest bourgeois taste, certainly not of opulence, let alone indulgence. The mill owner Sir Arthur Rowbottom had long departed to a more sumptuous house on the outskirts of town, and the house was now a tied dwelling for the mill manager and his wife, their children having already flown the nest.

But Kate did not enter the house through the front entrance, for that was reserved for the manager and his wife and important visitors. Instead, she passed the front door and went round the left side of the house to the back door, the tradesmen's entrance. As she climbed the neatly white-stoned steps to the back door, pulling herself up wearily with the help of the cast iron banister, she could see the housemaid through the door window-panes, busily engaged in washing the household linens and clothes in the wash scullery below, toiling in the humid atmosphere with dolly stich, scrubbing board and an old wringing machine. A large corrugated tub stood nearby, and the old copper boiler was bubbling and steaming merrily. Monday and Wednesday were traditionally washdays.

Kate opened the glass-panelled door and entered the hallway, with the broom cupboard on her left, where all her cleaning materials for the house were stored. It was here that she left her shawl and collected her overall before the onset of the day's work. After that she went to the front of the hall where she left her hat on the hat stand with the pin secured through it.

As she passed the kitchen on her left, she observed the welcoming fire, merrily blazing away in the large, black, cast-iron range, providing heating for both oven and boiler at either side, and supplying all the hot water for the house, including the cleaning tasks that Kate would have to undertake that day. One of her weekly jobs was to 'black lead' — that is lacquer the tripartite range, embracing grate, oven and water heater — a dirty job, which she hated. Fortunately, today was not the day for that task. On the top of the range was an assortment of iron pans made at the local ironworks, and on the mantelpiece were gaudy floral design vases. Cleaning those was part of her work today, though not yet.

In front of the range and bounded by a well-polished brass fender, lay a tab rug on the bare, dark stained floorboards. To the side of the hearth, on an old worn grandfather chair, sat the black and white house cat snoozing heedlessly in the heat of the flaming coals. On the other side of the hearth was an old worn Chesterfield, with kitschy purple embroidered cushions at either end.

In the centre of the room was a large square dining table with eight round backed, imitation Jugendstil dining chairs, obtained second-hand from a member of the local German business community long before the war. Something of an antique, the set was a wedding gift to Herbert and his wife, Mabel, years previously from Sir Arthur and his wife.

Sitting at the table in the centre of the room were the mill manager, Herbert Radcliffe, and his wife. They were just finishing their breakfast and apparently having some sort of argument when Kate passed the doorway. She had to speak to them, so as not to appear deliberately discourteous. This morning, feeling as she did, she would have preferred not to speak to them or even to see them. Nonetheless, she made herself express a brief word of salutation, as fleeting as was her passage across the doorway.

Herbert's wife was a formidable and intimidating matron with a domineering personality. A forthright, no-nonsense wife who rationalised that she spoke it as she saw it. With her overbearing instincts, she ruled Herbert with a rod of iron in the house, which some inferred was the reason for his aberrant and licentious activities when outside her ambit. Certainly, the word was spread in the neighbourhood that he would flinch every time she chastised him.

Whatever the accuracy of that reputed tale, she was his fiercest defender in the local community, and was believed — somewhat doubtfully — to be a close friend of Sir Arthur's wife, Ethel, even if to all intents and purposes they had little in common. The truth was probably that Mabel identified in her attachment to Ethel the chance for social ascent and greater social recognition, including advancement for her husband.

Mabel liked to boast of the leading ladies of the town with whom she rubbed shoulders at the Rowbottoms' house. But, in fact, she was shunned by lots of them, not least because of her husband's outrageous behaviour, to which not a few poor mill girls had attested. All in all, she was socially ambitious and a flaunter of her connections. She was not, however, a wicked woman, even if Kate knew well from her own encounters that she could be rather spiteful if provoked.

The Radcliffes had two sons who were now grown up and had left home as rapidly as possible as teenagers — one for the army and one to train in a neighbouring mill town as an apprentice wool sorter. Local gossip was unkind about the exact reasons for their early departures.

'Good morning, Mr and Mrs Radcliffe,' Kate greeted them politely as she passed as quickly as possible. She always did her best to be courteous to them — she needed the job and the income desperately — even if she despised them both, perhaps the wife a little less than Herbert. For Mabel was the victim of Herbert's chauvinism more than Herbert was the product of her authoritarianism, as Kate saw it.

'Good morning, Kate,' they chorused overly politely.

It was at that stage that Kate sensed a change in the social atmosphere between them. She guessed they had been talking about her and had been interrupted. It was something that she could not quite put her finger on. Whatever it was, her antennae told her that something had changed. Her keen instinct for self-preservation and for the preservation of her job, however, made her recognise the need to be even more circumspect than usual.

In the fleeting moment of her passing the doorway, Kate had made the mistake of peering into the room. Unobserved by his wife, Herbert stared straight into Kate's face in that way that only a man who lusts after a woman can do. Kate, perturbed by his stare, promptly averted her eyes and made to move on nippily and thus evade his lecherous gaze.

231

'I'll be with you in a second, Kate,' Mabel stated. 'Just get on cleaning the lounge for the moment. Dusting and cleaning the windows on the inside first.'

'Yes, Mrs Radcliffe. Straightaway.'

Herbert Radcliffe was not a bad man. It was just that he allowed his hormones to govern his behaviour rather more than his grey matter. He was well known for it throughout the local community. So far, no one had had the courage to tackle him head-on. Thus, experience had taught him that he could get away with living his life like that. He felt confident that others would break themselves on him, rather than vice versa. Like Jimmy, his first job had been in the bowels of the mill, in the wool bins. He was a born intriguer and by stealth, obsequiousness, and a large helping of good luck, he had risen up through the ranks in the mill that he had joined as a young boy straight from school. In addition, good fortune and his slimy wheeling and dealing ability had provided him with a pathway to preclude military service.

Somewhat tardily, Herbert had volunteered for the Citizens Army along with his pals from the mill, carried away by the general euphoria at the outbreak of war. He had at first been rejected owing to a minor physical defect — in those early picky days. With most of the men at the mill gone to war and replaced by women, and with the strong underwriting of Arthur Rowbottom, Herbert had managed to become first overlooker, then foreman and finally manager of the mill.

Consequently, despite having to appear in front of the Derby tribunal, he was able to remain in his protected occupation which was starred throughout the rest of the war. This achievement was mainly due to his employer, Sir Arthur Rowbottom, who became ever more immersed in his civic duties as the war progressed. He, therefore, came to rely more and more on Herbert for the day-to-day running of the mill and Herbert gradually became the de facto manager.

But Herbert's climb to the top had been neither uneventful nor uncontroversial. A rather sleazy character, he had been an unpopular overlooker at the mill. The source of this unpopularity was that he liked the women and young girls. He had a weakness for touching up his female workers when they were tending the machines and if they complained — which they rarely did — having them dismissed for alleged skiving.

On one occasion when he was an overlooker, one of the bolder women, a spirited lass called Sally Smith, had dared to retaliate by beating him over the head rather hard with a wooden bobbin because he had been touching her rear as she was bending over her machine to repair a broken thread. He fell to the floor dazed and looked up to see the gleeful faces of the girls all staring at him and taunting him in word and gesture. With Sally and the other girls observing his indignity and giggling at him, he felt profoundly humiliated.

But the occurrence did not reform him. It merely accentuated his desire for gratification in further subjugating women. It did, however, prick his unjustified pride to have the girls ridiculing him. He turned nasty. He hauled Sally up in front of his inferior, the mill gaffer at the time who was an aged and weak man, who chose to ignore Herbert's vices in the interests of a quiet life. Sally was dismissed and Herbert was exonerated.

It was little wonder that the women did not hold him in high regard and the men hated his guts for what he tried to do to their women. They all made lewd comments about his manhood, particularly in the context of his having failed his first army medical. He was labelled a coward for not serving

233

during the war. Even after the armistice some men still threatened him not to go out on a dark night.

On that particular day, Kate finished her work downstairs, then took a break to eat her lunch of salted dripping sandwiches in the scullery and talk to the scullery maid. Mabel came in all dressed up. Pleasant and smiling she mentioned to them that she had to go into town to do some shopping. Unusual as it was, Kate felt much reassured by Mabel's unusually good-natured demeanour.

'Ladies.' That was the first time she had ever used that mode of address to them. 'I have to collect some material from Lingart's and go to the indoor market to fetch the meat for tonight's dinner party. They have not delivered this morning and we are having Sir Arthur and his wife to dine with us this evening. I want everything to be perfect, particularly here in the house. You understand. I should not be long. Maybe a couple of hours. You should still be here when I get back. If I am not in time, just go and I shall see you at the usual time tomorrow morning. Before you go, please make sure that everything is spick and span.'

'Yes, Mrs Radcliffe. I'll do t'upstairs while you're in town.'

'Have you finished with the downstairs rooms and especially the front room?'

'Yes, Mrs Radcliffe. I did them last time and I just have t'upstairs to do.'

'Well, then, do the main bedroom first. You know where the clean linen is.'

'Very well, Mrs Radcliffe.'

234

'Bye now.'

'Bye.'

Having given her instructions, Mabel Radcliffe, the would-be socialite of the town, swept out of the scullery and into the hall. A couple of moments afterwards and with a dark foreboding, Kate heard the slamming of the front door and the accustomed rattle of the two loose panes of glass in the door. She would have to be watchful this morning. Extra careful.

This was the first time that she had left Kate alone in the main part of the house, and she was immediately on her guard. True, the scullery maid would be there, although she would be working in another part of the house. Knowing Herbert's reputation, Kate considered sharing with the scullery maid that she was out of sorts and would be going home. For all that, she needed every penny she could earn, and she was not paid for being off sick. So, although she felt vulnerable, she reassured herself that the maid was in the house and Herbert was at his office in the mill. Nonetheless, she resolved to conclude her tasks as swiftly as possible and leave the house before Herbert returned.

'Well, I had better be getting on if I'm to finish the bedrooms this afternoon,' she pronounced to the maid.

Kate worked industriously for about an hour in the main bedroom, dusting the multifarious ornaments, polishing the furniture, cleaning the mirrors and windows with a wash leather, and changing the bed linen. She was on edge all the time, listening for any footsteps on the stairs; she was wary of the slightest inkling of a noise. She dared to hope at each moment that the front door would proclaim the familiar heavy bang that would herald the Mabel's return.

It was as Kate was in the process of collecting her cleaning materials, having completed her chores in the main room, that she heard a creaking on the stairs. Perhaps she had not heard the front door as Mrs Radcliffe returned. She must have closed it quietly for a change, although she had never done that before. When Kate turned round towards the slightly open door she saw the smirking and intimidating figure of Herbert Radcliffe standing at the top of the stairs.

'Well I never! Hello, Kate. How are you today? I've just come up to see if you need a little helping hand.'

He advanced to the door and threw it fully open so that it banged against the stopper and rebounded a little.

'I don't need any help from you, Herbert Radcliffe. And if I did, I would be in a very bad way.'

'Now, don't be like that, Kate, love, I know what you young lasses like.'

'You know nothing! Go away, please, Mr Radcliffe. If your wife comes back and finds you up here …'

'Don't worry. She won't be back for a long time. Plenty of time for the two of us.'

'Go away. Leave me alone. Leave me alone, Herbert Radcliffe, or I swear …'

'You swear what? What will you do? What can you do? You know only too well that I have all the best cards.'

'If Jimmy finds out …'

'What will he do? I'm not afraid of him. If necessary, I'll pass the word to Sir Arthur and have him sacked.'

'Look, just go away. Go away and let me get on with my work.'

'I know your type, Kate. You do not mean it. If truth be told, you don't want me to go away.'

Kate could see that words alone were not going to convince him to leave. So, she decided that a rapid exit was her best strategy. She picked up the bucket and her other cleaning provisions and made to barge past him. Brusquely, he thrust her back. He closed the door behind him and advanced into the room.

'Leave me alone, Herbert Radcliffe, or you will regret it.'

'What are you going to do, little lady?'

'I'm warning you.'

'Now come on. Don't let's fall out. I know what you want and what that beau of yours is probably not giving you enough of. Eh?'

Herbert reached down, dragging the bucket from her hand, scratching her palm in the process. With his face covered in a salacious sneer, he slowly and deliberately advanced towards her forcing her backwards little by little towards the bottom of the bed. Finally, the weight of his body against hers propelled her backwards onto the bed.

In an instant he was on top of her with his hands all over her, lustfully attempting to kiss her. She resisted ferociously, struggling to scratch his face and bring her knee up into his groin. That drove him to viciously grasp her wrists to ward off the attack. Gradually, he forced her left arm behind her back and with his free arm tugged libidinously at her clothing. In the process he tore the buttons from her blouse, which gave him access to her bodice. He dragged it forward to grope her small, firm breasts. All the time, Kate struggled frantically to throw him off her, though the weight of his body and the ferocity of the attack prevented her from moving him. In exasperation, she tried spitting in his face and biting him.

The feel of her breasts seemed to inflame his lustful passion even more; and he moved his hand to try to pull up her apron and her skirts. Over the top of her boots, Kate felt his hand advancing up her leg to the inside of her thigh. At the same time, he tried again to engage her mouth in an imposed kiss. He reeked of tobacco and she could smell his unsavoury breath as well as his sweaty body. Again, she tried to bite him, although the pressure of his mouth on hers prevented it. He was forcing his mouth hard on her teeth to the extent that she feared he might break them. Eventually, with a swift movement of her head, she managed to turn her face from him.

To her horror and revulsion, she felt his fingers trying to find her. Disgusted, she tried to close her legs tighter, to tighten her muscles and deny him entry, to turn her body to the side while struggling hard to free her wrist from his iron grip. Sadly her efforts were in vain. Her strength was waning and she could not stop him. His strength was irresistible, his carnal desire driven by wild and lustful demons.

Then, the front door banging closed, with the familiar rattle of the two panes, came like the clarion call of a saving angel. Herbert ceased his efforts abruptly. Like a bat out of hell, he pulled back although not before she had scratched his face. Athletically he jumped up, rapidly straightening his clothing. Retreating from the bed and nearly falling over in his haste, he cast a rapid glance in the washstand mirror and smoothed his greasy hair narcissistically. Apparently satisfied with his appearance, Herbert made a swift downward check on his trousers and, opening the door, he cautioned her.

'Don't mention a word about this to my wife. You'll regret it if you do, I promise you.'

He grinned salaciously and flounced out of the room like the wild wind as if nothing had occurred. For Kate it had all been a terrible nightmare. She was in shock as she slowly pulled herself up from the bed and got down to arranging her clothes. She straightened her blouse and tucked it more tightly into her skirt, so that the missing buttons were not so obvious. She stroked her hair, inspected herself for a moment in the washstand mirror, and then picked up her bucket and the other scattered cleaning materials from the floor. Shaking with frayed nerves, she staggered onto the landing. Appreciating what a narrow escape she had had, she slowly descended the stairs. As she did so, she could hear Herbert and Mabel having a vigorous altercation in the lounge.

'What were you doing upstairs, Herbert?'

'Kate asked me if I could help her move some furniture, dear. That's all, my love.'

'I don't believe you. Do you take me for a fool? I know you, Herbert Radcliffe. She has never done that before. She has never asked me for help. And in any case, the scullery maid could have helped her. Why would she do that? And you mentioned to me that you would be in the office all day. You lying bastard!'

'No, well, I don't think that the little vixen needed help this time either. She was after something else. You know what she's like, don't you?'

'Is that why you have that scratch on your cheek? The wound's quite deep. Your mouth is swollen as well. What have you been up to this time? I just can't trust you, can I?'

'She is a vicious little tart. She egged me on. She is not suitable as a cleaner in a decent household. We should get rid of her.'

'Don't look to blame her. She is a decent young lass. It's you, Herbert, that's the problem. It always has been.'

'No, honestly, it was her.'

'You'd better get yourself back to work straightaway. Before I do something I shall regret. Get out of my sight. This minute.'

He hesitated.

'Go on! Get away from me, you animal.'

As Herbert tried to give her a parting kiss, she turned her head away. 'Get out of my sight.'

With that admonition ringing in his ears, Herbert scurried out of the room like a frightened animal, slamming the front door behind him as he speedily left the house.

Still dithering with fear from her ordeal and feeling increasingly weak, Kate slowly descended the last of the stairs and joined Mabel in the hall.

'Come into the lounge, love. You look terrible. Sit down.' Mabel patted the embroidered cushion at her side and beckoned to Kate to sit next to her on the horsehair chaise-longue.

'I'm sorry this has worked out like this. It took me longer than I intended in town. If only I had been able to get back earlier. I'm afraid the transport service was disrupted by the strikes in various places.'

'I know. It's all very well. I do understand.' Kate sought to mollify her employer, even though she was still in a state of uneasy numbness.

'Love, after this you know that you cannot stay on here, don't you?'

Kate wanted to remonstrate. Words just would not come. Her knees were like jelly, she was shivering, and she felt nervously befuddled. It was manifestly unjust that she should lose her job when it had not been her fault. She was guiltless, and yet she was to be punished for the wickedness of Mabel's husband who, once again, had got away with it.

'But Mrs Radcliffe …'

'No ifs and buts. It would be impossible for you to stay after what has occurred today. 'You must understand that. Might even be dangerous for you.'

'But Mrs Radcliffe, I have done nothing wrong.'

'I know, love. We both know that. I'm sorry. There's nothing else for it.

Kate's head sank lower. While she was contemplating the injustice of her lot, Mabel was contemplating how she could keep this newest scandal out of the public domain and certainly out of the papers. She opted for an age-old strategy, a bribe.

'Here's ten shillings, Kate. That should more than cover your wages for the hours you have worked so far this week and a little bit more.'

'But, Mrs Radcliffe, I need the job. My father and brothers need the cash. I am the only breadwinner.'

'I am sure that you will find something else. And if you are discreet with your tongue, I would be happy to provide you with a good reference. I shall keep my eyes and ears open as well to see if any of our friends or the ladies that I meet at coffee mornings need domestic help. I'm so sorry, Kate. Truly I am.'

Kate pondered challenging the parting gift that was being tendered. On reflection, however, she thought better of it. She could never win. It was as simple as that. For she realised that to protest too loudly would have no influence whatsoever on the decision to let her go, to dismiss her in effect. That had already been made and was irrevocable. Moreover, to challenge the decision might even jeopardise her chances of getting another job, especially if it were put around that she had egged him on. She might even lose the ten shillings if she pushed it now.

So, although it went against the grain of Kate's character, she sought to make a bid for a little more, hoping to tug at Mabel's heart strings. Keeping her composure, she spoke quietly, politely, and ever so firmly. 'Mrs Radcliffe. Ten shillings will not pay our food bill for the week, let alone the rent and other bills. And what about my damaged blouse? You know that what happened was not my fault. Perhaps you could spare a little more? Maybe a couple of shillings.'

Mabel Radcliffe was taken aback at this unprecedented show of spirit on the part of her usually docile charwoman, although she had always suspected that behind that quiet exterior was a strong-willed woman of gritty character. She did feel a little guilty at having to ask Kate to leave, although covering for Herbert was not new to her. She weighed up the need for discretion in the local community where she had her own position to protect. She ruminated with horror on the tittle-tattle of the local church ladies if the scandal got out. And after all, she was the mill manager's wife — a cut above the rest. She had appearances to keep up, a reputation to treasure. So, she calculated that it would be worth a little more to keep Kate quiet.

She ostentatiously picked up her voluminous handbag and fossicked around inside it. In due course, from the furthest depths, she took out her purse, snapped it open and with her bony fingers selected a half crown piece and placed it with the ten-shilling note on the table between them.

'Kate, here is twelve shillings and sixpence. That's as much as I can afford.' Both she and Kate knew that was not true. 'That should help you out until you get another job, and it's my final offer. That and a good recommendation among my wide circle of good friends in this town.'

Kate understood the threat in Mabel's last words and her assessment was that she had probably bargained as far as she could. She mumbled, 'Thank you, Mrs Radcliffe.'

Only a touch less dejected, she reluctantly consented to take the proffered ten-shilling note and the half-crown. She placed the money in the pocket of her overall. She went back to the cupboard at the back of the hall, collected her shawl and personal effects. Then with head held high she defiantly stepped out the length of the hall to the hat stand. She put her hat on, glanced briefly in the hall mirror, and secured it with a long hatpin. As she was now nearer the front door than the back, she boldly exited the house by the front door — the first and last time that she ever did that.

As she stepped over the front door threshold, she glanced back for the last time at the stained-glass window with its pompous motto 'Labor Omnia Vincit'. She reached back for the brass doorknob and slammed the door behind her, hearing the familiar rattle of the loose panes of glass. As she did so, she sensed Mabel observing her with empathy and relief from behind the lace curtain in the bay window. Kate hurried over the cobbled yard to the mill gate, passing two charabancs discreetly parked down one of the side access roads. They were now standing empty, with windows uncovered, having earlier disgorged their load of replacement workers — or 'scabs' as Jimmy and the other regular workers called them.

'My, you're leaving early today, love. Is there something special on, that I don't know about? Apart from the strike?' It was Billy Dolan the timekeeper-cum-gateman. 'Is something wrong, love? Are you all right?'

'I'm fine, Billy. Thank you very much. I won't be coming back.' She stated baldly.

'Oh, I'm so sorry, Miss. You probably don't want to speak about it. Had it anything to do with that Herbert Radcliffe though? He's a real millstone that one is. You know you're not the first.'

Billy was correct. Kate did not wish to speak about what had occurred. It had all transpired so suddenly and she was still in a state of confusion. In any case, she still had to calculate what she was going to do, and she did not wish to compromise her position.

'Thanks, Billy. I shall miss you.'

244

'I shall miss you too, Kate. Take good care of yourself.'
That was the first time he had used her first name.

'Thanks. Bye,' she called as she stepped through the small pedestrian gate in the larger mill gates and out into the roadway.

If Kate had hoped that her ordeal for the day was over, she was mistaken. There were police on either side of the gate keeping back a sullen group of strikers. Overturned braziers were spread across the road and pavements and police lines stretched on either side to the top of the road. Jimmy was nowhere to be seen.

As she emerged from the mill gate, one of the strikers shouted, 'Here comes one of the scabs now.' Instantly, all eyes turned on her. She felt a shiver go down her spine as she envisaged running the gauntlet of the rancorous mob. To her horror, the shouting escalated, with more and more voices joining in until a chorus of voices were chanting, 'Scab! Scab! Scab!'

She felt like covering her ears against the chanting. She even considered going back into the mill yard. Then, with fiery determination, she decided against yielding to the taunts and insults of the strikers. In any case, she did not want to take the chance of re-entering the mill yard and seeing Mabel — or worse still, her husband — again. So, with no other alternative than to climb the length of the hill to catch her tram back home, she crossed the pavement and, amid the shouting of the strikers, trudged onto the cobbled road. With ever more weary tread she began to plod up the steep incline. Every step seemed to demand such enormous energy from her that her weakened body had difficulty in sustaining it.

She had completed only a couple of weary paces up the hill to the accompaniment of the raucous chanting of the strikers, when one of them, judging the attention of the police to be distracted, thrust his way through the police line and rushed towards her in a hostile manner.

Kate noticed him out of the corner of her eye and guessed his intention. She stepped to the side as nimbly as she could to evade him. In the process, however, she slipped on the edge of the worn and slippery kerbstone and fell onto the wet cobbles. Her hat rolled into the middle of the road, propelled by a mischievous breeze. Without her noticing, her shiny, silver-coloured half-crown fell from her overall pocket and rolled into the gutter, where it came to rest among the broken glass and other debris of the day's fracas.

Laughter at her undignified fall resounded across the road, as the man who had striven to get to her was truncheoned and hustled back, struggling behind the police lines by two muscular constables. She felt thoroughly humiliated. 'What else can happen to me today? What else can go wrong?' she asked herself pityingly.

But there were now some voices of compassion from among the strikers. 'Leave her alone, poor woman. Bully boys! Is this what our strike is about? Persecuting defenceless women? Shame on you!'

A sympathetic policeman moved forward from the police line to help her, as she slowly picked herself up and straightened her clothes. She retrieved her hat from the middle of the road and placed it firmly and deliberately on her head. Then, holding her head high and with her back straight, she made once more to climb up the hill.

'Just a minute, Miss.' the voice of Assistant Chief Inspector Jack Braithwaite called her back. 'Just wait a minute, Miss.'

Her initial reaction to this request was one of horror. *What have I done now?* If she had been able to, she would have run away. On the other hand, she just did not have the strength any more.

So, she turned to face the voice, unclear of what possible further misfortune could befall her today. As she regarded Jack Braithwaite, she felt intimidated by his ample braid and impressive uniform. He had a kindly smiling face, though, as he stooped where she had fallen and rescued something from the gutter.

'I think you lost this, Miss.' He held out the shiny half-crown piece.

Kate rummaged in her overall pocket and promptly realised that she must have lost the half-crown from her overall pocket when she had fallen.

'Thank you very much, officer,' she uttered timidly. 'I don't know how to express my thanks to you. It means so much to me. You'll never know how much.'

'Yes, I can imagine in these difficult times. Are you sure you'll be all right to go up to the main road by yourself? Would you like one of my men to accompany you? If you don't mind my saying so, you seem a bit out of sorts and some of those strikers out there are a bit rough and ready. And they're currently a bit worked up into the bargain.'

'No, thanks very much. It is very kind of you. It won't be necessary. I'm feeling better and I don't believe any of the

247

men would in fact want to harm me. Thanks anyway. And, above all, thanks again for finding my money.'

'You're welcome, Miss. And I shall keep an eye on you as you walk up the hill to see that no one bothers you.'

'Thanks very much. Tara.'

Having turned her back on the officer, she resumed her plod to the top of the road feeling relieved that not absolutely everything had gone wrong today. And she had met kindness as well as wickedness. Nevertheless, she still felt below par and exhausted with every step. As she was passing the showy doorway of the free library, her attention was drawn away from her own travails to an old soldier sitting begging next to the door. With no legs he sat on a small-wheeled wooden platform, with which he could propel himself along the ground with his arms.

'Spare a copper or two, Missy?' he implored.

Moved with sympathy for him, even though she had little enough for herself, she withdrew a couple of coppers from her purse. As she threw them into his begging can, he responded with a heartfelt, 'God bless thee and keep thee, Missy.'

Gradually, to her relief, the chanting abated into the distance and was erased from her memory. It became inaudible by the time she arrived at the top of the steep road.

She sat down in the shelter to rest and wait for the tram to arrive. She reflected on the events of the day. How could she and her family possibly survive now?

There was no one else in the shelter, and a tiny tear flowed onto her flushed cheek. She brushed it away impatiently with her shawl. She sought to come to terms with how she was going to manage with her severance payment of twelve shillings and sixpence and how she was going to tell the menfolk at home of her misfortune.

Her retrospection was ended by a ferocious spasm of coughing into an already reddened handkerchief.

Chapter Fifteen

Jimmy knocked frantically on the door of Kate's house and, like a man possessed by frenzied anxiety, he went straight in without being bidden. The scene that met him was distressing. All the brothers and Kate's father and mother were sitting in a darkly sombre ambience round the hearth. There was an atmosphere akin to doom in the air. Jimmy could feel it. Kate's mother was nervously crocheting a white bed jacket and her father was taking frequent successive puffs of a minuscule tab. The house had a feeling of cold, like a funeral wake.

'Evening all,' Jimmy greeted them, intending to combat the chilly atmosphere with a note of cheerfulness.

'Evening Jimmy,' they all returned rather glumly.

Although Kate's relatives always welcomed him cordially when he visited her house, at this time he had a feeling that they were less than friendly. Indeed, they seemed to be quite cool towards him. Why were they upset with him? What had he done? Why were they all so crestfallen? He ignored his own feelings and went straight to the issue.

'Where's Kate then? Isn't she home yet? Has she gone down to the club or the Textile?'

'I am afraid we have some bad news for you.' Kate's mother intoned glumly.

'What? Is something wrong? Has something happened to Kate?'

'You know that she has not been well this last little while. Since you came home in fact. That terrible cough and those fevers leave her so weak,' she explained.

Her father extended the narrative, perhaps sensing that his wife was too distressed to finish what she had begun. 'Well, she was rather shaken up by what had happened to her at the mill manager's house and then again outside the mill today. You witnessed what it was like at the mill today, and what the state of the men was like.'

'Yes. I escorted her safely through the mill gates earlier this morning.'

'Well, she left early from work because they had asked her to go. In fact, the manager's wife had asked her to go early. So, of course, you weren't there to meet her. No fault of yours.'

'I didn't know she was leaving work early, so how could I be there? I don't understand what you are talking about? Why did they ask her to go?'

'Jimmy,' Kate's father continued. 'We do not know the full story. She was not in a fit state to tell us when she was helped back here by two passengers from the tram. We think that she had a run-in with Herbert. Apparently, his missus was not in the house and he tried to get on with Kate. She resisted, of course, then Mabel came home and concluded that was quite ample temptation for Herbert for one day and asked Kate to leave.'

'But that's not fair. They can't do that.'
'Yes, they can, and they have.'

'Anyway, Mabel's not totally without feeling. She gave our Kate some cash to tide her over. No doubt also so that Kate would go quietly. It's that Herbert that is the problem. He always has been and always will be. He's a womaniser and a rogue. Anyway, Kate had to leave early and when she

251

left the mill, some of your pickets shouted insults at her. She was catcalled all the way up the road.'

'They should be ashamed of themselves. Have they no decency?' Kate's mother added.

'Yes, and one striker tried to assault her, causing her to fall in the wet roadway,' Kate's brother Peter continued. 'But apparently two officers restrained the striker and a senior policeman helped her up and watched her safely up to the top of the road and to the shelter where she could sit down and rest.'

'Who was it?'

'We don't have a clue.'

'She got to the top of the road and sat down to wait for the tram. Then she collapsed on the tram on the way home. A couple of passengers brought her back here and we had to call out Doctor Burkett who examined her and said she needed to go to hospital. He was worried about her. Told your mother to prepare herself for the worst. Kate was coughing blood on the way home before she collapsed, they reported. When Dr Burkett left, dad went straight up to the post office to call for an ambulance to take her to the infirmary.'

'When did the ambulance come?'

'Not five minutes before you arrived. They've taken her to the infirmary in town.'

'That flea-bitten, rat-infested hole never did anyone any good.' Her father interjected bitterly.

Jimmy was thunderstruck, bereft of words to express his emotions. He felt at a loss, partly responsible for what had happened to Kate on two counts: he had not been there to meet her, and it must have been his mates who had initiated the catcalling.

'Kate gave us her twelve shillings and sixpence before she were carried away in the ambulance,' said Kate's father. 'And she asked us to let you know what had happened.'

'Yes, she was intent that you should know as soon as possible,' her mother mumbled tearfully. 'You know, Jimmy, she loves you. She always has. All those years ...'

'Yes, I know,' he confessed, feeling increasingly guilty and responsible. 'Did anything else occur?'

'We just don't know. Kate was too unwell to speak much when she came home, and we were more bothered about getting the doctor and making her comfortable.'

'I must get to the infirmary straightaway,' Jimmy declared.

'I don't think they will let you in. It's not the official visiting time for a while yet. And you're not next of kin.'

'I don't care. I've got to see her. I can't wait.'

'Have a cup of tea, lad, before you go,' Kate's mother offered.

He totally ignored the invitation. 'I'll let you know how she is when I come back.'

Though exhausted from the long day's exertions, Jimmy felt a rush of adrenalin which gave him new energy and provided physical impetus to the urgency of his task. He hastened back to the door and lifted the latch.

'Her mother and I will be coming to see her in a little while,' Kate's father shouted after Jimmy. 'We shall be there at the onset of visiting time and I'm sure that you'll stand a better chance of getting in then. Can't you wait and we can all go together?'

Emotionally driven and irrational, Jimmy had no wish to delay. He wanted to get to the hospital as soon as possible. He grappled with what Kate's father and mother had told him about Kate's condition and what had happened to her that day. *I'll kill that bastard, Herbert Radcliffe. He won't get away with it this time. The dirty bastard.*

But more urgent than his thirst for revenge was his need to see Kate as soon as possible. He had things to share with her that could not wait. Indeed, so urgent was his need to see her that, despite his cash shortage, he chose to travel into town on the tram rather than walk for half an hour. He ran swiftly to the stop, hailed the tram just in time and mounted.

Sitting in the tram, catching a fleeting glimpse of the dirty mills and warehouses as he passed by, he noticed the fluffy wool settled snow-like on the uniform windowsills of the buildings. He smelled the scent of wool all around him. As they picked up speed, the buildings on either side of him flashed by, forming a blurred monotonous background. He slipped automatically into a reflective mental state, mulling over his recent relationship with Kate. Had he been excessively preoccupied with his own problems and experiences since his return? Had he been insufficiently sensitive to her needs? Had he allowed his own cruel self-pity to crowd out his avowed commitment to Kate? Why had he not understood her better? He loved her. Oh, how he loved her. For him the question was, had he told her with his deeds as well as his words? Had he been excessively dismissive when she had mentioned getting engaged? What if she should die? He might be in the process of losing her now. What if she were already deceased when he made it to the hospital? His life would be hollow without her.

Wildly out of control, his restless bout of despair was now dominated by morbid recollections of death, as he mentally glided back to vivid anecdotes of his time in the trenches. He considered the accidental explosion of the Mills grenades which killed some of the men, even before they were marched to the trenches. Others were blown to pieces in the assembly trenches, waiting for zero hour, as the German artillery opened up.

He recalled the fate of one young lad from the Pals. He had been an underage soldier who, carried away by the flush of war hysteria at the commencement of the conflict, had volunteered to enlist at the age of fourteen. Such was his eagerness that he had lied about his age to serve king and country. Cynical recruitment officers had asked no further, although they should have seen that he was exceedingly young looking. Almost miraculously, he had lived through the butchery of the Somme, though after another two years of the senseless carnage, he had had enough. By anyone's standards he had done his bit. He just got up one day and began walking away from the trenches. Where to? What for? He was barely seventeen at the time and possibly he had hoped to have his whole life in front of him. They caught the boy before he had gone a couple of miles. He did not flee. Neither did he offer any resistance. He came back quietly and calmly though his willing return counted for nothing. Still they court-martialled him. After that teenager had given three years of incalculable bravery, the toffee-nosed public school officer who was chairing the court martial had the effrontery to call him a damned coward. The presiding officer sentenced that precious young life to an ignominious death at the hands of his friends, intending to set an example to the others.

Everyone had expected the young lad to be reprieved, but it did not turn out that way. The bloody brigadier general accused him of lacking moral fibre. A 'man of god', an army chaplain, had been complicit in recruiting the divine to champion the murder. The magic words did nothing to comfort the boy, let alone save him. The young lad was dragged to the chair, crying and wetting his pants. His twitching hands and staring, frightened eyes were visible to his mates until the black hood was placed over his sobbing head. Jimmy had been on the firing squad. They, and the other young volunteers, were told that, unless they discharged their weapons into the prisoner, they would themselves be shot for disobeying orders in the face of the enemy. Enemy!

In those few seconds before the order came to shoot, the intense agony of Jimmy's mental state could never in the future be clarified in conventional words. Should he, could he shoot an innocent teenager? To disobey was certain death. But, if he obeyed this order, how could he ever live with himself again?

With a supreme act of will, he made his decision. The shots rang out and the boy was executed by his own pals, themselves all under the same threat of death if they didn't carry out their despicable task. Several of the squad must have shot wide — perhaps deliberately — and the young soldier had fallen, still attached to the chair, and was writhing in agony on the ground.

'Finish him off, Kelly!' The order to administer the coup de grace was addressed directly to him. Aghast, his whole body froze. How could he obey such an order? He would rather die. 'Finish him off, I said. Put him out of his misery.

That's an order. Finish him off, Kelly, or suffer the consequences. You know what they will be.'

The threat was unambiguous. Nonetheless, he dropped his rifle loosely to his side. Like the young and tender boy who lay in front of him on the ground with his life slowly draining away, Jimmy had been driven too far. He had had enough. He was at the limit of his will to live. He was now prepared to die for what he believed in. He could not, he would not, murder for them anymore. The seconds ticked by so slowly that it gave an impression that time had stood still.

A shot rang out from the soldier next to Jimmy and the boy-soldier was no more. His body lay there in silent accusation.

What kind of justice was that? Jimmy deliberated on the lad's fate. He should not even have been at the Front if fair dealing had been done. The government had made a commitment after a public outcry to withdraw all underage soldiers. Such pious pledges meant nothing to the generals, greedy for ever more expendable cannon fodder. The punishment would still have been downright cruel and inhumane, even if it had been wholly deserved by a full-age soldier. For a lad it merely indicated the moral depravity and barbarity to which they had sunk. And this had been visited onto a youngster who had volunteered. So what were the Pals fighting for? Freedom, decency, humanity and reasonableness? Whose? Not the 'lower ranks'! Now Jimmy imagined it was his turn. Hopefully, it would be swift.

Chapter Sixteen

The rattling and high-pitched screeching of a tram passing in the opposite direction interrupted Jimmy's painful daydream and returned him with a jolt to his half-life of today. He was sweating profusely. In disarray, he peered out of the tram window and realised that they were rapidly approaching the halt for the infirmary. In fact, the tram was virtually at the stop, and unless he acted proximately, he would be past it and he would have to waste time walking back.

Dazed, he jumped up swiftly and pulled the leather strap to strike the bell and alert the driver at the front. He had left it rather last minute and, with the tram coming to a sudden juddering and screeching halt, he staggered like a drunk down the centre aisle of the car, pursued by the accusing eyes of the driver who had turned round to see who had rung him at the last minute. Jimmy crashed into the sliding door with some force, swore to himself for being so clumsy, slid back the door, felt the cold brass handle in his warm and sweaty hand, and stepped down onto the rear platform.

As he jumped down onto the cobbled street, he heard the conductor rushing down the back stairs. Jimmy felt that he needed to get to the infirmary expeditiously. So he had alighted like the wind, nearly knocking down a young couple waiting for the tram on the kerbside. He distanced himself at a rapid pace from the tram with the irate conductor glaring at him as it moved away. It was only afterwards that he realised why the conductor had glared at him. He had been so engrossed in his reflections that he had not paid his fare, and he had dared to pull the leather to halt the tram — usually strictly for the conductor to execute. Two unforgiveable infractions from the conductor's point of view. By the time Jimmy had realised it, the vehicle had departed and he was oblivious to any possible consequences of his lapse. He just concentrated on streaking up the road like a man possessed.

At last, out of breath and perspiring profusely, Jimmy arrived in front of the ornate, spired entrance to the grey and sullen double storey neo-gothic building. The infirmary had been constructed in the nineteenth century as a workhouse, through the charity of the local great and good. It was old, soot-blackened, sadly out of date and inadequate for the rapid population growth which the town had known since the epoch of its construction. It was a daunting and unwelcoming place, infested with rodents, cockroaches and other bugs. It was all that the local poor had. With the expectation of visiting time commencing, crowds were forming on the flight of broad well-worn stone steps leading up to the front of the hospital.

Ignoring the press of bodies, and ever apprehensive as to how he would find Kate, Jimmy launched himself forward, bypassing the other visitors and sprinting two at a time up the curved sandstone steps, his sheer momentum driving him resolutely through the crowd. The drab and forbidding, high ceilinged, brown-tiled entrance hall of the infirmary was crowded when he entered, and it was now obvious to him why such a large crowd of people was waiting outside in the chillingly wet evening air.

Inside, the vestibule was extremely crowded. Some people were milling round frenetically, their shrill voices overfilling the already full space, while others were standing forlornly and aimlessly, totally overawed by the surging mass of humanity. The walking wounded were well represented. There were drunks, some assault cases, and some of the strikers and police from the demonstration, plus a mass of accompanying relatives, friends and well-wishers.

The smell of sweat and unwashed clothes was overpowering as Jimmy filtered his way in a rather ill-tempered mood through the jostling crowd and elbowed his way towards the front of the queue. There he joined the line of people waiting for attention, all the time scanning ahead and impatiently counting the number of people in front of him. He felt conscience-struck and absorbed in a brooding agony about whether he would see Kate alive again, blaming himself.

Eventually, he progressed to the front of the queue and was able to speak to the senior sister, an imposing woman in a calf-length blue cotton dress, over which was tightly wrapped a creased white pinafore with crossover straps at the back. Her uniform was crowned by a voluminous white headsquare, tied at the back to form a pharaonic headdress. She was apparently in charge of medical enquiries, including out-of-hours visiting. He gave her Kate's particulars and her approximate time of admission.

'It is not our regular practice, as set down by the infirmary's Board of Trustees, to give out information to strangers, not least to non-family members.'

'But I'm nearly one of her kinfolks. You see, we are going to be engaged soon … as soon as she gets out of hospital,' he ventured weakly, striving to pull at her heartstrings. 'You see, I'm a soldier who has just returned from the Front. We have waited four long years to get married. Can't you help us, Sister?'

But the sister was unimpressed by his attempts at moral blackmail. 'Our visiting hours do not commence for another thirty minutes. Only in exceptional circumstances are visitors permitted outside of those hours, for example imminent death or actual bereavement.'

So, they relax the rules for visits to the dead? That's generous of them! He judged mockingly. In some ways he found the comment rather jocose, although he opted against flippancy and instead donned his most subservient smile.

'Yes, she has just been admitted. Seriously ill with TB, I gather. I just wanted to know how she is.'

The sister remained straight-faced, obviously well used to wielding authority. There had been quite a number like him today: pleading special cases as to why the rules did not apply to them. She was losing patience with all of them. 'If we allowed everyone who wanted access to come and go as they liked, just think of the chaos.'

'Yes, I do recognise that, although …'

'Moreover, there is the cleanliness of the hospital, the risk of infection, not least with TB patients, and the privacy of patients to consider, particularly women patients. Not everyone is very clean, you know,' she added authoritatively, eyeing him up and down. 'There is of course the sheer modesty aspect also to take into consideration. This lady will be on a women's ward in the infirmary. As a decent man yourself, you will be aware of our concern about that, Mr …?'

'Kelly. Yes, of course, I do appreciate that.'

Jimmy found himself overpowered by the mass of reasons given why he should not have access to Kate. He struggled to conjure up any counterarguments, for it had been a hard day and he was feeling exhausted. He realised that his one plus was that she had called him a decent man, so he decided to throw himself on her mercy.

'Yes, but, if I could please just see her for a couple of moments. Or at least find out how she is. Please.'

'Are you family?

'Well, no … almost. As I made clear to you, we've had to wait. It was down to the war. We are engaged,' he lied. 'And we're hoping to get married before long.' Telling a venial lie seemed the lesser of two evils; he desperately needed to see Kate or at least to ascertain how she was. Jimmy regarded the sister's pitiless face and, screwing his cap in both hands, he smiled as sweetly as he knew how.

Looking back over his shoulders at the long queue, she began to waiver. He was obviously one determined young man.

'Well, I am not sure. I shall have to ask matron. What is your name?'

'James Kelly.' He screwed his cap in his hands once again and aspired to make his name sound as impressive as possible and his demeanour as humble as he could. The last thing he could afford was for her to feel threatened.

'If you wait over there, I shall see what I can do for you,' she advised, pointing to a dark wooden bench set against the brown and white tiled wall under a dust covered windowsill. 'But I have these other people to deal with besides, so it will take a while.'

'Thank you very much for whatever you can do, Sister. Much obliged.'

Resigned and exhausted, and recognising from his army service that he was under duress from a system that only served to alienate him, he slumped down on the bench next to an old man. The old-timer's ragged clothes smelt of dried urine and cigarette smoke, and he kept coughing up a bloody sputum. Despite that, Jimmy was so tired that he folded his arms, closed his eyes to the revolting scene and fell into a troubled sleep. Exhausted after the day's events, he seemed to sleep for quite some time. It was so sound that even the trundling and rattling of the trolleys passing him by did not disturb him.

'Are you Mr Kelly?' A voice entered his dream and roused him from his healing sleep.

One by one his senses picked up sensations. His nose detected a strong smell of carbolic soap — far preferable to the stench of the old man when he had fallen asleep some time ago. He felt someone gently shaking his shoulder and fully opened his eyes to glimpse a pair of highly polished black buttoned boots.

As he raised his head, he set eyes on a smartly dressed older lady in a dark blue uniform with a small white Peter Pan collar turned down at the top. Above her left breast, she had a small, sparkling silver watch. She wore a dainty lace-trimmed bonnet on her head, secured by a neatly tied bow under her chin. In her hand she held a large foolscap pad folded over and a mottled green fountain pen, apparently poised to give verdict on his request. She stepped back a little and eyed him disapprovingly. She had that no-nonsense look about her and he knew he had problems.

Anxiously, he gulped. He lacked the knowhow to deal with women of this class who spoke in such an impressive register. He stood up somewhat gauchely, out of politeness and additionally so that he could square up to her on more even terms.

'Yes, that's me,' he confirmed, still bleary-eyed and feeling quite apprehensive about what she was going to share with him.

'Well, Mr Kelly, as you can see, this hospital is desperately overcrowded, what with the flu epidemic, long stay cases such as disabled soldiers, and TB cases. And on top of all that we have the illnesses brought home by the soldiers such as malaria and VD. We're run off our feet. So, as you can realise, we need to restrict visiting as much as possible. In fact, visiting is the least of our priorities.'

'Yes, I sincerely sympathise with the difficulties you face,' he assured her softly, mentally preparing himself for a rejection. 'But I shall be no trouble and I shall not stay long.'

'Well, I am not so sure, Mr Kelly. We run this hospital for the benefit of our patients not for errant visitors. The Board of Trustees has set down rules for a reason, Mr Kelly. They are not arbitrary. They are there for the benefit of our patients.'

She allowed the remark to hang in the air for a moment, and was about to reinforce her point, when, providentially for him, Kate's parents arrived furnishing an opportunity for his rescue.

'We came as quickly as we could. Have you seen her? How is she? Does she need anything? Which ward is she on?' Kate's mother addressed him with a veritable torrent of questions, hardly noticing the matron standing in front of him.

'Are you the patient's relatives?'

'We're her mother and father. Can we see her, please?'

'Subject to the permission of the ward sister, visiting hour has just opened. Do you know this man? Can you vouch for him? He tells us that he is your daughter's fiancé. Is that correct?'

'Yes, we've known Jimmy most of his life. He and Kate have been going out for five years and more. And they are hoping to get married soon,' Kate's mother confirmed, glancing sideways at Jimmy.

'It just so happens that routine visiting hours have just commenced. Medically, in my considered opinion, a visit from *relatives* would be a real tonic for her. But, as she is so seriously ill, you can only see her for a brief period. And only two of you at a time, if you please.'

'That's alright. Dad and I can go in first and afterwards Jimmy here can switch over with one of us.'

'Well, finally it's up to the ward sister. You, Mr Kelly, are not strictly speaking family … yet. Additionally, this is a female ward and there might be other reasons why you cannot have access to the ward. We shall just have to see.'

'Yes, of course,' the three of them spoke in chorus.

'But I believe that the sister may permit you one or two minutes for a compassionate visit. Depending on the condition of the patient of course. The young woman is very weak, and you will be unable to stay long.'

'We just want to see our daughter,' beseeched her mother, as the matron disappeared down the corridor.

When she returned, she said, 'The patient has asked to see her fiancé. So, we — that is the ward sister and I — consider that it might just perk her up a little to see you. Sister will tell

265

you how long you have. She is in Ward B3 on the second floor on the left-hand side. The main staircase is over there to your left. And there is a bench outside the ward where you can wait.'

With a flourish, the matron turned haughtily and disappeared with her nose in the air. The three of them walked slowly across the entrance hall to the imposing sweep of the main staircase and climbed up the two flights of wide stone stairs. When they came to the closed double doors of Ward B3, there were quite a few visitors waiting patiently outside speaking in hushed tones. Shortly, a rather prissy, well-built nurse in a pale blue uniform arrived.

'Visiting time is one hour only. Only two visitors at any one time at the bedside. No smoking and please keep your voices down. Remember that we have some patients who are rather ill.'

With that admonition to the assembled visitors, she opened the double doors and disappeared back into a room marked 'Ward Sister.'

'You two go in for the first half,' Jimmy suggested to Kate's parents. 'I'll wait out here until you have finished.' He was hoping that they would not stay unduly long and that his suggestion would give him a chance to be alone with Kate.

'Right. That's very nice of you. We'll not be too long,' Kate's mother responded.

The twenty minutes before they returned seemed like an age to Jimmy.

'Kate's in the second bed on the left,' Kate's mother said, giving him a motherly glance. 'She just can't wait to see you.'

'How is she?' he asked anxiously. 'How did you find her?'

'Well, you'll see for yourself, lad. Mother and I shall probably see you later.'

'Yes, thanks. I'll no doubt see you presently, possibly tomorrow.'

'Goodnight.'

'Goodnight, and thanks.'

Jimmy hastened to enter the ward on tiptoe lest his hobnailed boots made an unacceptable din. When he found Kate, she was propped up on several pillows, pale-faced and appearing extremely weak. She had on a white crocheted bed jacket, which her mother had made for her, wrapped around her shoulders over the top of her off-white nightdress. She smiled feebly as he approached, beckoning him with a weak wave of her hand to sit down on the upright wooden chair next to her bed. He bent forward over the bed and gave her a gentle kiss.

'I'm glad you came, Jimmy. I feel all the better already for seeing you.'

'How are you really feeling, love?'

'Oh, a bit better. The doctor has been to see me, and they have given me some medicine.'

'I figure you had a rough time at the mill today, what with losing your job and on top of that being heckled by those idiot picketers of mine.'

'Well all things considered, I would not have been able to go on with my job in this state anyway. So, looked at one way, I received more than I would have if I had not been sacked. Don't tell Mabel Radcliffe that though.'

'That old witch! And as for her husband … well, I did tip you off about him when you got that job. He's a slimy character, a snake if ever I saw one.'

'Jimmy, I don't want to have this conversation. We do not have a great deal of time. I do not know how much time I have, and we have some decisions to make.'

'All right, love. What was the doctor's opinion?'

'That is what I wanted to talk with you about. You see, he recommended that I should go to the open-air sanatorium at Essington. They specialise in treating patients like me there. He told me that he is aiming to get a place for me as soon as possible. It could even be tomorrow if they have a bed, although there is great demand for TB beds at the moment with lots of soldiers returning from the war and so much illness in the crowded streets of the town.'

With the word 'Essington' Jimmy's whole being sagged. He was conscious that Essington sanatorium was a place of last resort: 'a waiting room for death' they called it in the town. Only the worst cases were sent there. He hoped that Kate did not know that, and he concluded that it would be best not to tell her. Without altering his countenance, he sought to carry on as usual.

268

'Will you have to go for long? Will I be able to visit you? Do the doctors feel that they can cure you there?'

'Jimmy, the answer to all your questions is yes,' Kate assured him. However, she knew what being sent to Essington could signify. So, she did not know how much time she would have. In any event, she did not want Jimmy to know how serious her case was.

'They describe the hospital as being in a beautiful natural position,' Kate continued. 'With breath-taking views of the river and the rock-strewn fells on the other side of the valley. There are mountains in the far distance, and woodlands on either side. It sounds lovely.'

'But how can I visit you? It's so far out of town.'

Ignoring his specific question in her attempts not to alarm him, she continued.

'Sister assures me it is a lovely place and very comfortable. Lots of the patients who go there come back home in good health. She advised that there is a regular train service that runs up the dale to Lynaton, then there is a special bus that runs directly from the station to the front door of the isolation hospital. After that it waits to take the visitors on the return journey to the station. Visiting is every Sunday, and she told me that lots of people go. No children though I don't suppose that will worry you.'

'Well, that seems okay to me. It must cost a bit though.'

'Jimmy, I just don't know. All the same, I hope that you will feel it is worthwhile and come and visit me now and again, whatever it costs.'

269

Jimmy realised that he had to reassure her and try to help her. He had to give her something to live for, to assist her recovery, to sustain her — for his sake as much as for hers. He had never realised before how much he needed her.

'Of course I will, love. I will visit you regularly until we can bring you home again. In fact, I will bring you home myself. Now, your job is to concentrate on getting better so that we can get married. We've waited too long already, don't you think?'

'Jimmy,' exclaimed Kate overjoyed, her weary eyes brightening in their darkened sockets.
'Does that imply that you will wait for me?'

'Well, you spent all those years waiting for me. And I must have been a bit of a pain since I came home. So why not?'

After the initial shared euphoria, however, harsh reality returned gradually to their conversation.

'But, Jimmy, these are surely just dreams. Where will we live? We have nowhere to live, no furniture, and no means to do it.'

'These are minor practicalities. I am sure that Kitty would not object to our living with her until we got on our feet. After all, the furniture and other stuff in the house was my mother's. She left it to both of us. In any case, Kitty would welcome the company and it would help to draw her back up from that well of despair that she has been in ever since she had the news of Tommy's death. It would be just like old times.'

'Oh, Jimmy. Do you sincerely believe that Kitty would accept such an arrangement?'

270

'Yes, I do. I'll go and get that ring that you liked tomorrow, the one that we both liked in that shop window when we were walking home from the theatre the other evening. And we can get engaged tomorrow, before you go up to Essington.'

'Oh, Jimmy, love, that would be wonderful. Do you truly mean it? I do love you.'

'And I love you too. Goodness only knows where we could get married. I'll find somewhere. Just leave all the arrangements to me.'

'Perhaps, just perhaps, we can get married at Essington. There is a lovely little riverside chapel there. Wouldn't it be lovely?'

'Yes, so something good can come out of this after all. We now have to prepare for the future.'

The conversation had certainly cheered Kate up; she appeared ten times brighter than when he had first seen her less than half an hour ago. He deceived himself into believing that the potent medicine of his words was having an effect. He could now see something of the 'old' Kate emerging, as he knew her before the war. A great ray of hope was shining ever brighter in his thoughts.

'Well, now that is settled, what else is there to talk about?' she smiled.

'We can talk about the future, about our married life, how many children we are going to have and … who's going to wear the trousers!'

She smiled broadly and rather weakly. 'I'd be happy for you to do that. No competition!'

'It doesn't matter, so long as we are together.'

She smiled wearily at him, even though her spirit was slipping. She knew that most of the people who were sent to Essington never returned, at least not under their own steam. They came back in a box. Kate guessed that Jimmy must know that too. He was simply seeking to comfort and reassure her. Did he sincerely believe all that he had pledged? Or was he just hoping to appear tender-hearted because he knew that she was doomed?

'You know, Jimmy, some people go through the whole of their lives without knowing a love like ours. It's the love that we bring, not the length of time,' she said, hoping bravely to cheer him up. In fact, her words had precisely the opposite effect, and she could see that in his face. She resolved to change the subject.

'How did the strike go, Jimmy?'

'Not too well, I am afraid, Kate. It was a bit of a disaster. There was a lot of violence and the whole thing got out of hand. Partly it was my mates and partly it was the police who were at fault. A couple of our Union leaders were taken into custody and several strikers were detained on what seem to me like fairly serious charges.'

'Oh, I'm sorry to hear that. What went wrong?'

'The mill owners bear a heavy responsibility for sending in strike breakers. That's what angered the men and inflamed passions. I just hate to think what the *Daily Observer* will make of it tomorrow. A lot will depend on that. I am not hopeful, however. There's going to be a Central Council of

272

Action meeting tomorrow or Friday to discuss what to do next.'

'It may be that it will all turn out better than you supposed. Often things do turn out that way, you know. Anyway, you will take care, won't you, love'

'Yes, of course.'

'And how is Harry?'

'Well, he is fine, although he has a handsome black eye and a split lip.'

'How ...'

The bell sounded the termination of visiting hour. Punctually, the nurses approached the beds, pulling back curtains and making sure that visitors were not dawdling. Jimmy just had time to kiss Kate gently on the cheek and squeeze her clammy hand firmly.

'I love you. See you tomorrow, love. I have a meeting tomorrow evening. I give you my word that I will come, with the ring. You will wait for me, won't you?'

'I've waited for you four long years already, Jimmy. What difference is another day going to make? Look after yourself. There is so much illness about at the moment. Never forget, I love you.'

'I love you too, Kate.'

He left the ward and exited the infirmary submerged in the depths of a profound sadness, yet elated at her expressions of love for him. The sun was setting, casting long depressing shadows and a surreal rose-coloured light onto the darkened steps of the infirmary entrance. He had never seen the hospital like this before, and the symbolism of the dying day did not escape his imagination.

Wearily, he began the slow walk back home through the growing darkness, the greying drizzle and the oppressive stillness of the approaching night. His reflections were dominated by the words which Kate had uttered about love and the length of time that you are privileged to enjoy it. What was it exactly that she was telling him? Why was he so crippled by a profound sense of loneliness and insecurity? How firm could his commitment be?

After all, it was hate —not love — that had dominated his most recent life: hate of France, hate of the Flanders morass, hate of the Alleymans, hate of the tin hats, hate of the conditions, and the trenches and cooties and the canned corned beef. The list of love was, on the other hand, brief. He loved Kitty. And he loved Kate. Though racked by self-doubt, he felt a new passion awakening in his breast and knew instinctively in his heart of hearts that she was correct. Many people never knew a love like that. Her instincts were well attuned. And for him, it was her love that counted more than anything else, even his love for her.

Jimmy's slow, repetitive, rhythmic footfall on the stone pavement was hypnotic and made the walk seem more bearable. All the time he was thinking about Kate and her illness and about what they had shared with each other. He was occupied by a feeling of immense loneliness. This mental blackness was interrupted only by the bright lights and the noisy clanking of an occasional passing electric tram.

He bent his head. The pavement became a pathway back out towards no-man's-land and towards the German trenches. An assonant rumble of thunder became the bellow of distant guns, the strobing tram lights the enemy flares to illuminate the British squad.

The lights dazzled him as, perspiring profusely and with pulse beating rapidly, he feared that even the pulsating of his rapidly pounding heartbeat would be sufficient to break the stillness of the night and give away his presence to the enemy. Contrasting the mental commotion within him was the absolute and oppressive quiet outside him. It was eerily toe-curling. Not even the frogs croaked tonight and the occasional hoot of the owl usually heard during such reconnaissance exercises was absent.

Soon, all too soon, he was in no-man's-land, his ears and eyes strained to the utmost for any sign of the enemy. Was the absence of the croaking of the frogs maybe a sign of the presence of a hidden enemy unit, lying in ambush? He was quite exposed now. Where was the rest of his patrol? Dimly in the distance, dark figures could be seen hazily through the mist. Was it two or was it just one moving through the darkness? The images of his foe dwindled into the semi-darkness. Was he hallucinating? If not was there actually someone out there in front of him?

Fearing capture, he grasped his fully charged rifle. Cursing himself for his negligence he searched for it in vain. The bloody rifle was not there. Had he dropped it in his fright? He braced himself for the end. He was defenceless. In desperate resignation, he invited them to do what they wanted to him. He had had enough. He could not take any more of it. A living corpse? With luck, a prisoner perhaps … of his own quixotic imagination? There was a bang and he clasped his hands on his head.

'Well, Jimmy lad. Come on in. How did you find our Kate? She seemed a bit brighter when we left.' It was Kate's father whose words interrupted the frightening images of

275

Jimmy's daydream. He had walked to Kate's house. *How did I get here?* He wondered.

'Oh, yes … yes,' he stuttered. 'She did seem a bit better, I believe.'

'What's the matter, lad? You look whacked.'

'Come on, lad,' Kate's mother interjected. 'You look exhausted. Come and sit down for a nice cup of tea.'

Chapter Seventeen

A few days after the strike at his mill Sir Arthur
Rowbottom was once again in his element. Ever a man of
easy charm, he was enjoying an evening entertaining the
members of the Executive Committee of the Ryaton and
District Mill Owners' Association in the impressive dining
room of his magnificent house. This was an opportunity that
he particularly relished: showing off his magnificent house,
furniture, paintings and other cultural artefacts, and vaunting
his wife's cuisine. To top it all off, they were celebrating his
election to the presidency of the Ryaton Mill Owners'
Association.

Although he would never have admitted it openly, he
envisioned this evening as just one more paving stone on the
pathway to his London ambition, when he would be
nominated by the new government as a Liberal peer: Lord
Rowbottom of Ryaton in Cumberdale was how he envisaged
his new title. After all, just like his father before him, he was
a local politician and magistrate, celebrated in the town as a
bountiful philanthropist and a lavish donor to a number of
good causes.

Worshipping each Sunday at the picturesque riverside
Congregational church in the model village that his own
father had commissioned and financed, he and his wife were
esteemed by the whole congregation for the charitable
activity they undertook in their own community. His wife,
Ethel, was centrally enmeshed in charitable good works; she
was a frequent visitor to the homes and families of workmen
who were ill or had been injured at work. With the assistance
of one of her servants, she distributed baskets of food,
medicine and items of clothing — as well, of course, as
plentiful advice on how to live the good life better. Arthur
had already been knighted for services to the war effort, and

while he was not a mason, some of his close friends and supporters were.

There were no wives attending this evening as the meal was intended to be a business meeting about how to deal with the strike that was upon them. Even Ethel had made only a fleeting courtesy appearance in her evening raiment, modestly accepting compliments for the excellence of the reception, while graciously mentioning en passant the contribution of her assistants.

In attendance were the members of the Executive. Sir Edgar Crabtree was a mason, magistrate and key figure in the town. He was the owner of several mills and part owner of the new dyehouse on the outskirts of Ryaton at High Moor, to which textile material was brought for dyeing and finishing from near and far, including across the Pennines from the cotton textile industry 'on the other side'. Sir Edgar was a previous president and had proved himself a worthy and prudent leader through the good times of the war when he had made several fortunes, from khaki cloth amongst other things. The workers tended to typecast him as a rather narcissistic person, mainly on account of his rather pompous and self-regarding assertions. His was contrariwise a more complex and diverse personality than encompassed by that gross generalisation. He was a clever man of great guile and political acumen, as well as some economic and financial shrewdness.

Joshua Crowther, Sam Baxendale and Percy Clitheroe were all local mill owners: not so well connected, untroubled by politics, and with further economic ambitions to expand their relatively small enterprises. They had less of a fortune and less of a footprint in the town. They had also done well out of the war and they were keen to secure their profits and to improve their status. Moses Schuster, like Sir Edgar, was a great philanthropist in the town; he was also a leader of the town's small, cohesive and influential Jewish community. At times he had been regarded with some distrust by his fellow members, particularly because of his alleged pacifism and unwillingness to seek major profit from the war — and also owing to his German-sounding name.

The last member of the team was Michael Majendian, an oddball insofar as his business was effectively in carpet importing and retailing, although he did have a carpet manufacturing factory in a nearby town. Originally from Smyrna, he was a longstanding member of the Armenian diaspora and some of his relatives had joined him from Smyrna after the great Armenian genocide perpetrated by the dying Ottoman Empire in 1915. With the support of his newly arrived relatives, he was committed to seeking new outlets after the disruption of his business during the war.

Arthur had restrained the topics of conversation during the meal and eschewed all reference to the strike. Now that his guests had retired to the study, the ambience was more relaxed. They were consuming the vintage port from the loaded whatnot and some were smoking cigars. It was at this juncture that Arthur judged that the time was ripe to begin the real business of the evening: demonstrating his leadership.

'Well, gentlemen. Welcome. Let me thank you all most warmly for joining me this evening'. His guests smiled benignly at their host, although the competitive ethos implied that they were often at loggerheads. 'The main item that we are assembled to discuss this evening is the Union's reaction to our notification of a proposed ten per cent cut in all wages. We need to firm up what our strategy will be concerning the strike, jointly identify where our best interests lie, and ground that strategy in firm economic interests. Of course, none of us want to see our community impoverished and we need to understand the rationale behind why we are proposing this particular path of action.' He rested for a while, reflecting on his aim this evening. 'Our strategy needs to be one that can carry the local press and the general public with us. It would not benefit us to win this dispute and to lose the confidence of our local community, including our friends in the Ryaton Chamber of Commerce.'

'Have you seen the muckraking comments of that chap Bradley, the so-called industrial reporter in the local *Observer*? Have you seen what he wrote about our proposal for our modest reduction in wage rates? The sauce of the man!' It was the young Percy Clitheroe, ever precipitate and invariably intemperate in his utterances, who interrupted Arthur.

Affording a revealing glimpse into his own political background, Percy resumed. 'He's an out-and-out bolshie is that man. He's obviously been got at by those anarchists and socialists in the Trade Unions, who have friends in Russia and dream of a workers' communistic Xanadu. We should bring to light the role this man Bradley is playing. The newspaper is presumed to be a public service not a propaganda medium for revolution. We should sue him and the local *Observer* for what he's been writing about us and the danger that he represents to our way of life.'

'Now steady on,' retorted Michael Majendian, always the advocate of fair play. Based on the persecuted history of his nation, he always displayed a keen sense of justice and even-handedness. 'Firstly, it seems fatuous to infer that what Bradley has written is actionable. We may not like it, we may deprecate it. We have to accept that it is fair comment. After all, that's his job. Our job is not to alienate the press. Our task is rather to engage them to the justice, good common sense, economic balance and community solicitude of our proposals. Secondly, as I see it we can't tar everyone with the same brush just as all of us cannot be tarred with the

same brush. Bradley is not a communist in my estimate —
not even a socialist. He's an educated and intelligent man
who sees the social and industrial problems in our society
nowadays and tries to relay them in a fair and accurate way.
He may be socialistic in his comments. A socialist he is not.
And he did his bit for the country in France, which is not the
case with everyone in this town,' he added pointedly.

'I'll grant you, the workers' leaders are a motley bunch,'
he pressed on. 'Cut from every cloth. They are not all
anarchists, socialists and revolutionary communists though.
Some are, it is true, though not very many. Others, like Vic
Noble, a staunch member of the Union and a peerless
negotiator for the workers, are plain working men. Were we
in their shoes, would we not do the same? Some, like Jimmy
Kelly, who did their duty in the trenches and afterwards were
called upon to serve again in Fiume, are still traumatised
after their war service on our behalf. Only returned of late,
they are still emerging from a dark tunnel and seeking a
brighter future along the lines of what they were promised: a
fit country for heroes. Who can blame them after what
they've gone through? So, they are not all the same and
therein lies our opportunity. Divide and rule as the adage
goes, with an eye to our public image and an appreciation of
the countless heroes that are involved to whom we all owe so
much.'

'Bugger that for a lark! Public image be damned,' Percy
intervened again scowling fiercely.

He was interrupted by Arthur, who skilfully cut him off
with a liberal plaudit. 'It's interesting that you mention
Jimmy Kelly, Michael. I believe he is one of the main
leaders of the Union and the chief organiser of this strike. He
works at my mill. He's a returned hero if ever I've come
across one, although I hear on the grapevine that he is still
severely troubled by some sort of mental malaise. I've met

both him and his sister, Kitty, at the Mechanics' — by the way, she lost her sweetheart at the Somme — and they both seem pretty decent people. A bit left wing. Then again so are most working men today after the frightful war lots of them have endured. So, let's remember what they've done for their country, for their town and for us. Let's face it, on the whole we did not do so badly out of the war.'

'You seem to be enamoured of our enemies, Arthur. By god, I just don't fathom your attitude,' Joshua said, supporting Percy in his damning assessment of the Union men leading the strike. 'They're just a set of Luddites. Take the destruction of those two mills. Burnt to the ground. If that isn't Luddism, I don't know what is. The workers insist that it was accidental. Accidental my arse! And after what took place outside your mill, Arthur. A large number of policemen injured, property damaged and stolen. A veritable riot by all accounts, and you want to praise one of the main culprits. Well, why not just give the workers exactly what they want and be done with it? Lest they provoke another riot. Just give in to their blackmail.'

'Yes, seems to me that Joshua is correct. We need to think more of our own interests and a lot less about how nice our opponents are and what they have done for us. After all, we have done a lot for them on top. Given them a good livelihood and decent sanitary housing at a reasonable rent. Jobs for their womenfolk while they were away at the war. And just think of all the charitable work our wives do — yours especially, Arthur.'

'There is no evidence that it was the workers who tried to burn down those mills,' intervened the wise and wily old Sir Edgar. 'No arrests have been made and the authorities are apparently keeping an open mind. In any case, I don't see any point in fratching among ourselves. Both Percy and Michael are right in a sense. And if you add up all our comments, what do they signify? They signify that there are three things we must settle today. Firstly, we must be much cleverer in our public relations activities to get *our* message across. We can't have the general public imagining that we are a tight-fisted bunch of Shylocks. That is not what this is about, and we need to tell the public that. As a first step, one of us — and I suggest you, Arthur, as our president — should contact young Bradley. Give him a warm welcome, flatter him a little, put our case to him and ask him to put the businessmen's side of the dispute in his newspaper, emphasising our recognition of our responsibility to our community. Neither he nor his editor can refuse, given their often expressed high and mighty commitment to justice, balance and fairness.'

'Hear, hear!' interpolated Michael Majendian. 'We have to weigh up these things practically, communally and politically.'

'Secondly, we should say yes — and without making any bones about it — to meeting the leaders of the Unions who are organising the strike, under the chairmanship of someone like my old friend, Jacob Berenson. He is a veritable local luminary and someone who we can trust to be impartial. The Union people would also respect him as a neutral pillar of the community. We can tell the press that we made this suggestion first out of compassion for the workers, their families and their plight, and also get around a repetition of the shocking violence between the strikers and the police that we have seen recently. Thus, we get the credit both from the press and from the community.'

'That seems to me like an astute proposal,' said Arthur. 'We have nothing to lose and everything to gain by courting the press and, through them, the general public. After all, we do have the interests of the workers at heart and we are hoping to protect jobs by reducing wages. That's our sincere wish and intention. It's just that they do not see that. I also feel strongly that we have a Christian duty to do our utmost to avoid a recurrence of yesterday's events.'

'Now just wait a minute,' interrupted Joshua Crowther, who had inherited his large mill from his father. The mill was smaller than Arthur's. But, like Arthur's, it did the processing of the cloth from spinning and weaving to burling and mending, though not the dyeing and finishing. 'I'm with Percy. This Johnny-come-lately Bradley has been deliberately attempting to arouse public resentment against us, whipping up public indignation. I would have no truck with him. I don't trust him. He's on their side.'

Edgar resumed steadfastly. 'Thank you for that illuminating comment, Joshua. Thirdly, we need to firm up our strategy. For example, exactly what do we propose to the Union side when we meet them? And, equally importantly, what will our fall-back position be?'

Joshua interrupted again. 'Edgar, you are an exceedingly clever man and there is no doubt that you have a good business head on your shoulders, but …'

'Now look here, Joshua,' Edgar cut him off a little impatiently this time. 'We've known each other for a long time, Joshua, and I knew your hardworking father as a thrifty and diligent businessman, who built up his business from nothing, as lots of us did. I don't want all that to be jeopardised by hasty actions now. For make no mistake: an idle mill produces no profit while continuing to amass financial debts. Our creditors would still want their cash: the banks, the water companies, the fuel companies and so on. And the six pounds a ton increase in the price of coal in July doesn't help either. There are massive standing charges on our mills, all of them. Even if we damp down the boilers, we still have the costs of reigniting them at some time in the future. And all for the want of a little bit of a chinwag with a newspaperman and a few of our own workers? It doesn't make any sense now, Joshua, does it?'

'But by the same token, what do we do about the strike picket which is currently affecting my mill?' Arthur asked plaintively. 'Should we seek to ignore it? Should we seek an injunction? Should we make a formal request for the army to be brought in? Should we consider bringing in more volunteer replacement workers? Do we stick fast on our demand for a ten per cent wage reduction? If not, how far should we be willing to compromise? In other words, what is our negotiating position?'

'You're not the only one affected by the strike action, Arthur,' Percy asserted resentfully. 'My mill is idle and it's costing me a lot of brass.'

'Percy, that's the reason why we have to draw this thing to a close as soon as possible,' Edgar continued. 'We ourselves need a settlement. If not, we shall all be in bankruptcy side by side, as sure as a bobbin is a bobbin. We have a common interest with the men to look for a settlement that leaves us with some face and enables us to last through the slack times. So, let's support Arthur in contacting Bradley and let's help him to get Bradley and public sentiment on our side. We need an endorsing and reinforcing article in the paper this week, as soon as possible. Do we all agree on that?' There was a round of ayes. 'Anyone against?'

'Well, it could backfire …' Joshua retorted weakly, before reluctantly nodding his agreement.

'And do we all go along with the view that we should seek a meeting with the Union side under the chairmanship of Jacob Berenson?' Again, a round of ayes. 'Right. Then now we need to define our strategy. Agreed?'

Arthur intervened to support his predecessor. 'It seems to me that Edgar is spot-on. We do not want to see all that we have striven for over the years go down the drain for want of a little flexibility. So, let's talk to the Union and see if there is a trade-off we can negotiate.'

Sam Baxendale, who had not spoken so far, piped up, 'Are you suggesting, Arthur, that we simply give in to the men's unrealistic demands? Invite them to return to work on the existing terms? Not on my life! I will not be a party to such defeatism. Quite apart from the economic reasons, namely I cannot afford to pay the old rates in the face of increasing standing charges for things like coal and wool that are still fluctuating and unpredictable. It would be economic suicide. We need margins there to allow for the slack times and further government interventions on coal prices, consequent on the impact of the reparations supplies from Germany. We also need to consider other unforeseeable contingencies and increases too. To compromise now is to hide our heads in the sand and face rapid bankruptcy. We would not only lose face. We might even lose our businesses too. And the workers would be back in a heartbeat asking for more. I vote no to Arthur's suggestion. Unlike Arthur, I do not consider my business a charity. My position is: no compromise.'

'Sam, of course you're right in a sense,' Edgar said. 'We cannot disregard the standing costs of the raw materials that we face and their unpredictability in the financial climate nowadays. All that is a given. Neither can we afford a long, drawn-out strike, bearing those standing charges and not making any brass. We are kidding ourselves if we think we can. Just bear in mind the new-found political and industrial power of the working classes. See the large number of groups, from policemen to mill girls, across the Pennines who have gained higher wages through militant though legal action. Through a new militancy, our workers have acquired much better conditions of work than before the years of war. And they know their legal entitlements and how to stay within the law.'

Recollecting his now lost markets in Germany, Arthur added, 'There have been more striking workdays in Britain than in Germany during this year already. It must be obvious that all these workers of ours are asking for is the same wage rate, not an increase. We should grab it with both hands and lock it in for a couple of years dependent on increased productivity. Insist on a two-year standstill for wages. Let's be popular and label it a financial armistice until productivity and profitability improve. That way, unless they work harder, there will be no more income. The value of what is produced will increase. Moreover, our total wage bill will shrink through the fact that some workers who went to war did not return. That's a sad fact, I'll give you that. All the same, we should not look a gift horse in the mouth. Let's go for a five per cent reduction initially and if we can't get it, we'll settle for the same wages with all the former workers taken back unless convicted of a criminal offence. That's what I propose formally to this meeting.'

Edgar added, 'I second that formal proposal.'

'Gentlemen, we have a firm proposal which has been seconded. Return of all men at the same wage rate or five per cent less if we can get it. A two-year wage curb if we can get it, one year if not. And, as an agreement between us, there will be no filling of the vacancies left by those who have fallen, so that the total wage bill is lowered.'

'The package seems to make good financial sense to me. It appears to me to be a shrewd proposal with a good chance of success, and I endorse it,' Sam said.

'Does anyone else wish to speak to the proposal?'

Michael Majendian straightaway affirmed his enthusiastic approval.

'Then we should vote on it and be aware that whatever is approved binds us all.'

'My view is remains that we should go for the full ten per cent as our initial negotiating position,' Joshua said. 'If we cannot get it, go for five. And if we cannot get that, go for a two-year freeze. And I take the point about the bonus for us of a reduction in the total wage bill, although we do not need to mention that in our negotiations.'

'Precisely,' exclaimed Arthur. 'We can afford to be seen as magnanimous while protecting our own interests. As Joshua has proposed, we go in batting for ten, and willing to go with five. If we cannot get five, we go for a two-year moratorium on wage increases. With the most up-to-date rate of inflation standing at about fourteen per cent per month and rising — some project to seventeen per cent by year's end — we have nothing to lose. The worth of our finished goods will be increasing and the cost to us of the men's wages will be a progressively smaller proportion of our total outgoings. So, we can't lose. Can we vote now?'

'Well, I suppose we could adopt that as our position. Strictly hush hush of course,' Percy admitted. 'What do you think, Joshua?'

'Well, I suppose so. There is always a risk that they will see through it though.'

'All those in favour?'

All hands went up except Joshua's.

288

'I take it, Joshua that you are abstaining? Is that so?'

Joshua nodded his assent wearily.

'Carried nem con then,' reported Arthur. 'And that now becomes our negotiating position. Let's hope that we can gain some credit for the sensible way we will be tackling this issue. Thank you all for coming and for being such excellent company. I shall, of course report back on my meeting with Bradley. Anyone for another glass of port?'

Chapter Eighteen

The meeting of the striking workers' Central Council of Action at the Mechanics' Institute building some days later was well attended and tremendously noisy. The major issue facing the rather large and unwieldy gathering of workers was whether they could overcome their own internal differences and produce a united front to present at the upcoming meeting.

When he entered the room, Jimmy was taken aback by the atmosphere of reckless militancy and buoyant optimism in the room. Even the size and diversity of the meeting seemed awe-inspiring, and it would consequently be unwieldy to manage the business efficiently. Although the Council had arranged to meet daily at the Textile Hall throughout the strike, not least to make sure that those not participating were not adversely affected by the action, this emergency meeting took place somewhat ironically in one of the committee rooms which Arthur Rowbottom's father's philanthropy had provided. The previous occupation of the building had been by the local literary and philosophical society founded earlier in the nineteenth century. It was not until later that the accrued literary assets of the society were given a permanent home there. The members of the Central Council sat on captains' chairs, polished by successive generations of corduroy trousers, around a large gleaming oak table with brown inlaid leather in the centre.

The gathering included members of Trade Unions and organisations representing overlookers, wool sorters, engineers, dyers and finishers, burlers and menders, and the other operatives. It was chaired by the imposing figure of Vic Noble, the local branch chairman of the Woollen Textile Workers Union, puffing away like a steam locomotive on his venerable curved pipe. Thick set, red faced and beaky nosed, balding and corpulent although a spry and mentally alert fifty something, Vic was a well-experienced Union activist who had played a subordinate role in organising the ill-fated 1909 textile strike. He bore the scars of old battles, though he also carried the accumulated wisdom those campaigns brought. He was an energetic, self-made man of immense charisma and great stoicism, patient and uncomplaining in meetings and magnanimous towards his opponents.

Although like some of his generation he was slightly bow-legged, he nonetheless had a commanding presence and an authoritative bearing. He had been exasperated with the incompetence of the workers' leaders in the 1909 strike and the crisis-destined folly of their approach. That event made him all the more convinced to implement the lessons learned and to make absolutely certain that this dispute did not culminate in the same way.

Following that strike, Vic had honed his skills, developing into an undogmatic yet profoundly committed Trade Union activist, an unabashed pragmatist in pursuit of the interests of his workers and an outstanding orator. He was popular and well respected among the workers, unionised and free. Resolute and imperturbable under pressure, he was magnanimous in victory and flexible in negotiation. He had learned bitter lessons in 1909 and the errors would not be replicated during this strike. On that he was unwavering. Success was to be the only outcome.

He was the leading force behind the wide-ranging media campaign that the Central Council had so successfully waged since its inception. Indeed, the Central Council had been his brainchild for mustering the community backing that had been so tragically lacking in the 1909 strike. Similarly, he was behind the arrangements for daily meetings of the Council to ensure that the public, particularly hospitals and schools, were not disrupted by any sympathy action on the part of other workers. Yet he harboured no illusions about the difficulties the workers faced.

Vic came from extremely impoverished circumstances and early malnutrition had taken its toll on his health. When he was still a toddler, his tyrannical, alcoholic bully of a father had been killed in a mill explosion. So, he remained an only child. His mother, who worked on a fish stall in the open-air market, brought him up as a strictly teetotal, regular churchgoing Methodist, and there were neither luxuries nor frivolities in life. He attended the local elementary school and the local Methodist Sunday school. At the age of eleven he had begun work as a part-timer in the spinning shed at the local woollen mill and had worked in the textile industry ever since.

By sheer strength of character and personality, and by exploiting his innate ability and integrity, he had risen to the top of the local Union hierarchy. He had developed into an acknowledged orator in local commercial circles, with a penchant for lacerating humour, effectively employed against his opponents and adversaries in situations of dispute. He was much respected by workers and management and had been entrusted by the men with the task of verifying and rectifying the operatives' time-rate sheets.

Also attending were those responsible for managing the strike pickets at the mill. Joe Murphy, the sacked union organiser and baler from the Rawley mill was there too, as were several Union organisers and a further twenty plus senior representatives of local and regional Union bodies: the County Spinners Federation, weavers, doublers, teasers, balers, dyers' operatives, strippers, and so on. At the meeting were also political activists, such as Bert Cousins, the radical leader of the local communist party.

After the previous day's events at the Rowbottom mill, feelings among the committee members were running high, and members' nerves were patently on edge. Opinions about what actions should be taken were vigorously expressed, diverse and divisive.

On the one hand, there were those who criticised the police and mill owners for the violence, injuries and damage to property. They wanted direct, expeditious and energetic counteraction. On the other hand, there were those who argued that the pickets had been badly organised and ill-disciplined and that the strike was ill-prepared. They contended that the workers, and particularly their leaders, should be receiving part of the blame.

Distracted by his own worries and preoccupied with what had happened to Kate, Jimmy casually scanned the cased books along the walls, with the silvered plaque indicating that they had been purchased through the munificence of the Rowbottom family.

Fretting, Jimmy suddenly realised that he had not been aware of the animated conversations around him. Only gradually had his antennae begun to pick up the discussion. It seemed that on some topics there was unanimity: all the imprisoned striking workers must be freed. Again, in the face of widespread indignation at the unjustified dismissal of Union representative Joe Murphy and the unwarranted arrest of the other Union marshals, Paul Brear and John Kenny, there was unanimity. On the action there was, however, divided counsel. Some suggested that they should send a delegation to the central police station to demand the instant release of the Trade Unionists; others were of the view that it was unlikely that such action would result in their release, because the authorities would not wish to be seen to be backing down.

There were those who expressed fear that a lot of public good would have been lost by the actions of the strikers, and that blame should be attributed to the Union leaders who were presumed to be in charge of the pickets.

'Could I ask members of the Central Council to come to order, please?' Vic Noble shouted sternly above the noisy babble. Vic's voice brought Jimmy back to the meeting with a jump. He needed to be alert. If not, his political rivals would be satisfied with nothing less than prompt direct action. He knew that some were after social and political revolution, and they would seek to outplay him.

'I suggest that we speak briefly about the action to be taken in the case of our brothers, Paul Brear and John Kenny, who have been unjustifiably imprisoned,' Vic continued. 'After that, we can get down to brass tacks and move to the main business, the demonstration and protest march to be organised next Saturday. If there are any other matters, they can certainly be taken before the conclusion of the meeting. Is that okay?' There were murmurs of assent. 'In that case, can we move to the first item, the unjust and unwarranted imprisonment of our Union members?'

'We should picket the police station until they are all released,' Bert burst out straight away, playing to the gallery. 'Show them that we, the workers, mean business. That's what we should do. Demonstrate the solidarity of the working-class brotherhood and show them that they can't get away with this type of intimidation and abuse of power.'

Jimmy knew Bert quite well. They had attended the same Skinner Lane Elementary School, although Bert was a little older. He was conversant with Bert's captivation with the Russian revolution and its pledge of an ideal workers' state, even a workers' paradise. For him, such a state would derive its legitimacy from the workers, and be organised by the workers for the workers. He was similarly well acquainted with Bert's post-war estrangement from British society and its rigid class structure. Bert was an intrepid communist and an expert in the ruthless political cut-and-thrust of the Trade Union scene.

But Bert was in no way an empty vessel. Although his major point of reference was the class war, he was not one to robotically parrot the shibboleths of the Russian Revolution. His most fervent wish was for the overthrow of the current elite of British society. He also had another side: an erudite, rational and reflective human being. He was well read, and was a voracious consumer of works in the socialist pantheon of writers, such as Karl Marx and Friedrich Engels from the Free Library. In addition, he was an enthusiast for the ideas of Karl Liebknecht and the Socialist Workers Party. He had read some of William Morris's writings and concurred with the perception of socialism as being an international phenomenon. William Morris the person, however, he considered middle class and anarchic. Like numerous others in Britain, he was totally opposed to the deployment of British troops against the Bolsheviks in Russia and the government proposal to use troops to strike-break in Britain.

'Bert, I understand the strength of your feelings on this matter. Indeed, we all feel strongly about it. The question is how we go about achieving our goal,' Vic advised, aiming to get an early grip on the meeting and also to placate Bert.

At this early stage in the meeting Jimmy wanted to avoid giving Bert any reason to feel that people were ganging up on him. So, for the time being, he allowed Vic to deal with him.

'I should hope so,' Bert jibed in an unusually dyspeptic manner.

'But could I remind you that this Central Council of Action Committee has always adopted a responsible approach to whatever has been proposed. Reacting to autocracy with autocracy is a recipe for disaster, in my view. We are an organisation that is committed to working peacefully and within the law as long as I am the leader.'

'But we stand for *action* not inaction, don't we?' retorted Bert. 'It doesn't seem to me that it could be described as irresponsible to bear witness to the unjust plight of one's fellow workers. In case you don't recognise it. That is what we mean when we use the term workers' solidarity.'

Vic persevered, quietly undeterred. 'This Union is united in making absolutely sure that vulnerable people, such as children, the sick and others, will not be harmfully affected by the strike. Indeed, we have not sought any sympathy action from our brothers at all, knowing that it would be likely to erode public endorsement of our action. What you are proposing would damage that.'

'I am convinced that we should have asked for such co-operation. That's what workers' organisations are for. It was a mistake not to, and I'll tell you that straight. No excuses!'

But Vic was, as usual, unwilling to be cajoled into a course of action he knew could be calamitous for the dispute. He persevered unruffled. He eyeballed Jimmy, making him feel a little uncomfortable that he had not intervened so far. Jimmy had been waiting for the most suitable moment and his verdict had been that for the moment Vic was doing well.

'This is a dispute between the employers and us and, so far as is possible, we all accept that we shall do everything in our power to make sure that no one else is harmed by our actions,' Vic continued.

'Hear, hear!' Jimmy called out enthusiastically.

Vic silently acknowledged the support and, with a lift of his impressively bushy eyebrows, persevered with the elaboration of his line of reasoning. 'Whatever we do has to be within the law. All other actions are beyond the pale and that includes attacking the police, who are only doing their duty. We still have the public with us at the moment and we do not want that to change.'

'What do we do then?' Bert demanded. 'Just sit back and muck around while our brothers languish in jail?'

'No, Bert. We take responsible, legal actions to make sure that this injustice is rectified forthwith.'

'And how do we do that then?'

As the interchange took place, Jimmy's mind wandered. It reminded him of some of the exchanges that had taken place among the seven thousand troops who had protested in Blackpool against the slow pace of demobilisation and the ten thousand who refused to embark at Folkestone. The discussions had been chaotic with each vying with the other to be most radical in their demands. He had taken a leading role in such discussions and had managed to convince the soldiers to rationalise and simplify their demands for early demobilisation, forgetting about other complaints and grievances for the moment. Eventually, his perspective had carried the day and he had been one of the two hundred who were listed to go to Whitehall to pursue the protest by political means. Their protest had hit the headlines and had led to a commitment to a speeded-up demobilisation by the government.

'Well, I am pleased that you asked that question, Bert,' Vic continued calmly. 'Together with the secretary of this

297

committee, Ben Feather of the wool sorters, and of course Jimmy Kelly, the Union chairman at the mill, I have taken chairman's action, which I hope brothers will feel able to uphold.'

Casting a quick glance round the table, Vic detected no sign of dissent. They were all waiting for him to give a report and no one wanted to interrupt — not even Bert.

'We have consulted Harold Green, solicitor to the Textile Union. The feedback we have received is that he feels there is no case to answer in the case of the brothers who were acting legitimately as stewards on behalf of the Union. The officer supervising action at the mill, Assistant Chief Inspector Jack Braithwaite, a decent churchgoing man if ever there was one, has still not charged them and I hear on the grapevine that he does not intend to. With regards to the others, the bottle company has apparently issued a statement to the effect that, in solidarity with the workers' cause, they have withdrawn their complaint. So, my advice is to let the river flow, but to be vigilant.'

'Good thing too,' Bert interjected. 'Why all this shilly-shally. The situation of these comrades is a real hot potato and we should bring the meeting to a close just as soon as possible and go to the town hall and ...'

'I shall need your co-operation in that, Bert,' Vic interrupted, smiling. There was a subdued chuckle around the room.

'But to pursue what I was saying before, I don't expect that any of them will be charged. Harold reports that there is a certain embarrassment among the powers that be at the Town Hall about the arrests of Paul Brear and John Kenny, who are well known moderates of our movement. In any case, what would they charge them with? Endeavouring to

298

calm the situation? Mr Green told me that at the Town Hall they are searching for a face-saving way of quietly — how can I put it? — ridding themselves of the embarrassment.'

'Climbing down, you mean. Saving face,' Bert called out.

'Well, I suppose that's one way of putting it. Use whatever words you wish. But, the fact is that Jack Braithwaite has freely confirmed that the men were playing a conciliatory role in the strike action.'

'So they admit that they made a mistake? What are they going to do to rectify it? That's what I want to know. False arrest needs to be compensated. And what are our leaders going to do?' Bert continued.

'From what we've heard from Mr Green, the likelihood is that our Union brothers will be released tomorrow morning without charge,' Jimmy volunteered, wanting to take some of the stress off the chairman.

'Well, I don't think that is satisfactory. For god's sake, these are our comrades, our mates.'

'Bert, it's going to have to be. I suggest that the early release of our brothers is our first objective, and it is almost achieved. That action alone will help defuse the rather febrile situation that we find ourselves in and enable us all to move on. The situation of the other two is more difficult. Still a pathway to resolution has been endorsed by all parties. It will just take a little time.'

'So, we just abandon our brothers then?' Bert asked contentiously.

'No, we are not saying that,' Jimmy shot back like lightening. 'We must do all we can within the law. All the same we cannot be seen to be condoning the actions of people who have broken the law.'

'Yes, I support Jimmy's interpretation,' Vic counselled. 'My strong advice to this Council is that we should not interfere.'

'I'm flummoxed why we want to hang our brothers out to dry, for that's what is being proposed,' Bert asserted.

'The men who raided the bottles from the lorry at the mill where I was Union organiser did so against my advice and broke the law. I told them at the time, although sadly they would not listen. They have not been put behind bars and charged for going on strike, for pushing and shoving, or calling and shouting. They have been charged with run of the mill theft and criminal damage. The charge could now be withdrawn with the charitable action of the bottle firm, Ramsdens. We just have to wait and see. We have neither role nor power in that matter, although we might achieve some measure of influence.'

'That's right,' Vic agreed. 'Let me tell you that they are lucky that they have not had the charge of riotous behaviour added. It seems the authorities are anxious for a public display of leniency where they can manage it. As they had a formal complaint of theft from Ramsdens, the soft drink people, they had to act. Fortunately for the men, that formal complaint has now been withdrawn.'

'Yes,' Jimmy added. 'The best thing we can do for these men is to make sure that their families are supported and that they have good legal representation if it comes to it.'

Bert found himself outflanked and outnumbered. Wise enough to see the wisdom in what was being proposed, he fell into a sombre silence.

At that moment, a young lad dashed into the meeting brandishing a copy of that evening's *Ryaton Observer*. He thrust the newspaper in front of Vic's eyes and pointed to the headlines.

'I thought you would want to see this straightaway.'

Vic scanned the headlines and, without delay, cited them out loud. 'Owners Aggravate Strike. Police Mishandle Industrial Dispute.' Vic could barely believe his eyes as he shared choice pieces from the article with the Council members. The more he read of the article, the more he liked it, and they did too. There were comments about the 'precipitate and arrogant action of the mill owners' in bringing in volunteer workers at such an early stage in the dispute. In addition, there was a sentence about the 'less than sensible action of the police in arresting the strike leaders who were striving to maintain calm.'

Jimmy listened to this last comment with great relish, reflecting briefly on the much-vaunted power of the press. 'That should turn things around for us,' he roared. 'This is certainly better than we can ever have expected. Who is the reporter?'

'It's by Mick Bradley,' Vic confirmed.

'I knew Mick would come up trumps,' Jimmy exulted. 'Now we truly do have public opinion with us. I never doubted it. I knew that we could win this dispute.'

'Well, this report comes at just the right moment for us. Now, can we move on to the next item, the big demonstration and march next Saturday, which hopefully will reinforce the public's support for us in this dispute?' Vic proposed, aiming to move the meeting along. 'Could you give us a report, Ben?'

'Yes, of course, Mr Chairman, I'd be happy to. Although I should make it plain that the proposed arrangements are subject to the approval of this Workers' Council.'

'Yes, of course,' Vic reinforced the point.

'I have approached all the Unions, including those not directly involved in the dispute. All are willing in principle to participate in a brotherly march with banners and brass bands. Several bands will be coming, including some well-known ones, and they will spread themselves out to march at sundry points along the procession, probably with the workers from their own mills. The march will assemble in Victoria Park and move from there down the main road via Pitt Square to Town Hall Square. We have obtained the necessary permission to march and assemble, on the one condition that it is peaceful, of course. We have spoken to senior police officers emphasising that this will be a family affair, which will be well stewarded.'

'Of course,' interjected Vic. 'We are committed to a peaceful march with families accompanying the workers. Our aim is a demonstration against the unjust proposals of the mill owners and the brutality of the police.'

'That's right,' Jimmy concurred. 'There will be various speakers, and clearly Vic should act as first speaker and master of ceremonies if that's acceptable?' Vic nodded back positively. 'There will be Doug Hodges from the Union Council in Manchester, followed of course by local Union leaders …'

'Including yourself of course,' Vic interrupted.

This was the first time that Jimmy had considered giving a speech, although he had to admit that he was flattered. He remembered the sole previous occasion he had been so challenged, when he addressed the soldiers' demonstration in Whitehall just before he was demobbed. He was, of course, used to addressing union meetings, he reassured himself. It was too good to miss.

'What time are we going to assemble and where?' Jimmy asked eagerly.

'We have booked the Victoria Park, outside the Memorial Hall,' Ben said. 'The Unions have all accepted being in place and ready by two in the afternoon. The transport and car workers will be bringing their bands and I am hopeful that several of the other Unions, who could not give a commitment right away, will be confirming the participation of their bands over the next day or two. The march will proceed down Collingham Lane through the town centre to Town Hall Square, which is where the demonstration will take place with addresses by local and visiting officials. For that, a podium will be erected in front of the Town Hall. That's everything, I believe.'

'Have the City Tramways been put in the picture? Because this is likely to disrupt their schedules down Collingham Lane and in the Square,' queried Joe Murphy. 'And to the best of my recollection there are at least three sets of lines converging on junctions in Town Hall Square.'

'Yes. The circulation of trams will have to be suspended in Town Hall Square for the duration of the demonstration,' Jimmy advised. 'Otherwise, it could be dangerous.'

'Good point, Joe,' Ben asserted. 'Although I have liaised with the Tramways people, it would do no harm to reinforce that. Can you take responsibility for approaching them, Joe? You can stress that we have all necessary permissions.'

'Okay,' Joe reluctantly acceded, wishing he had kept his mouth shut.

'And what are the arrangements for stewards?' Jimmy requested.

'Yes, this is going to be fundamentally important in view of the newspaper report. It seems we have the press and the public on our side for now and we have to keep it that way. We cannot afford irresponsible action, such as we had yesterday. Marshalling the march and the demonstration will play an important role in keeping the public with us. The eyes of the whole community will be on us and there will be reporters from local and national newspapers.'

'With regards to stewards,' Ben carried on, 'Each Union will have its own people as stewards, so that they know each other. All stewards will wear the same armband, so that they can be readily recognised by everyone: the police, the public and our members. They will all receive the same pep talk before we get going, mainly to keep things orderly and prevent any wild elements doing any damage to our cause.'

'Ben, can you confirm that all relevant authorities have been brought up-to-date with regards to the arrangements for stewarding?' Jimmy enquired.

'Yes, and they have advised — off the record — that they will do their best to keep a low profile, provided that the march and demonstration are peaceful.'

'I hear informally that one of the assistant chief constables will personally supervise the policing of the demonstration in Town Hall Square, although Jack

Braithwaite will be in direct operational charge. Jack is an honourable man, and I am sure that he will do his best.'

'Well, he didn't at the mill,' Bert interjected.

Vic hastened to reassure the group. 'That was a regrettable circumstance. Our job is to make sure it is not repeated.' Without giving Bert a chance to come back, Vic continued. 'Well, it all seems pretty well tied up then. We shall have our usual daily meeting tomorrow, at which we can complete the arrangements, deal with any loose ends and allocate any outstanding responsibilities.'

Vic broke off briefly.

'Well, moving on quickly. The local authority has tipped us off that milk is not getting through to the local hospital. Although I know that this is none of our doing, it may be that local authority transport men are working to rule in sympathy, although they have been told not to do so. We don't need their support.'

'We undertook to make absolutely sure that such places as hospitals, orphanages and schools were not affected by this strike or by action taken in sympathy with it,' Jimmy added. 'We have to honour that pledge.'

'Can you contact the transport union and iron this one out,' Vic asked Ben. 'I'm sure it's only a misunderstanding. The Transport Union officials know the policy and indeed were parties to the deal.'

'Can do,' Ben confirmed. 'I am with you that it is important to be seen to be keeping our word.'

'Vic,' Bert interrupted. 'Did we not agree at the opening of the meeting that we would review the incidents at the

Rowbottom mill today? We should do that before we proceed to any other business, shouldn't we?'

Jimmy was immediately on his guard.

'Yes, that's true. Thank you for reminding me. I must be getting old. Would you like to open the debate, as you were at the Rowbottom mill?'

'Well, don't you think it would be fairer to request Jimmy to give a report? He was the Union leader in charge at the mill.'

'Is that alright with you, Jimmy?' Vic asked.

Jimmy agreed to speak. He recounted the events of the day, emphasising his own action to keep order and criticising the actions of the police. He told of how he had visited the injured in hospital and stressed again his own role in doing all he could to get the release of the stewards under arrest. He kept his delivery factual, objective and calm.

When he had finished, Vic spoke sternly, furrowing his bushy brows. 'Jimmy is one of our trusted Brothers who has given a lot of time and personal commitment to the Union and the cause of the workers since he returned from the war. I am not willing to allow this meeting to deteriorate into a witch hunt. We all underestimated the speed with which the employers would bring in *volunteer* workers. We didn't expect the lack of discipline displayed by some of the police and some of our colleagues. We all, and that includes me, have a lot to learn from the hoo-ha at the mill. Let's apply what we've learned to our big march and demonstration next Saturday.'

The speech was impressive. It was Vic at his best and it carried the meeting. There was a chorus of agreement from all sides.

'We've spent a lengthy time here today, and we owe it to our families to give them some time besides. I suggest that we close the meeting now, and request Ben and his committee to report back to us at tomorrow's meeting, which will take place again at the Textile. Is that agreed?'

It was twilight and it had been a very long day for all, so the meeting broke up and the members swiftly departed down the stairs to the entrance foyer, some walking home, others waiting patiently in the pale yellow gas light at the tram stop. Several lit up cigarettes to pass the time, hoping that they had not missed the last tram.

As Bert passed Jimmy, he put his arm round his shoulder and insisted, 'You got off this time, lad. Always remember there will be another time of reckoning. You mark my words. The workers will show these toffs. Just as they've done in Russia. Maybe it will take place next Saturday, maybe some time after … but happen it will!'

With that threat he dodged past and hopped cheerily onto the platform of one of the waiting trams.

Jimmy was determined to return to the infirmary even though he had been delayed by the meeting, which had seemed to take an age. To his chagrin, it had snowballed and dragged on much longer than he had envisaged.

Now, at long last, he was on his way. Having previously pawned his medals with Mr Bernstein at the Anchor Fent Store, he had purchased the ring that Kate had admired so much as they had returned from the theatre the other evening.

He was clutching the promised ring tightly in his left hand, with his hand in his pocket for extra security. Out of breath from speeding up the hill, he passed the Lower Globe Pub, where the discord of gloriously inebriated singing encouraged him towards the belief that miracles could come about. 'Pack up your troubles' they were singing coarsely and jovially, and that was just what he was intending to do.

Finally, he came to the now familiar front entrance of the infirmary. He raced past the ornate nymph-born lamps at the entrance, in high expectation, launched himself through the elaborate neo-gothic doorway and bounded up the front stairs two at a time. His heart pounded from the physical exercise — although in hope too, even expectation. For at long last, he had made a firm decision to suppress the demons in his head. Tonight is the night, he told himself, to tell her exactly what has been going on with him since his return.

He narrowly bypassed an advancing nurse as he crossed the corridor towards the ward. Casting a furtive glance at the now empty space behind the ward reception desk, he arrived at Kate's bed, out of breath and gripping the ring firmly in his pocket.

She was not there! What he encountered was not his sweetheart. Rather he encountered an old woman with a gaunt face installed in Kate's former bed. Kate was no longer there. Had she already been transferred to the sanatorium?

Chapter Nineteen

Jimmy was excited and impatient. He was standing on the station platform sporting a thin-striped, blue working shirt with a clean, detachable white collar and a rather worn blue spotted tie. His threadbare waistcoat was fully buttoned under his rather shabby working jacket. His highly polished best working boots glistened optimistically. Trusty working cap firmly set on his head and a dark muffler around his neck, he was feeling rather out of place in the warmth of the morning sun. That feeling of gentle discomfort was compounded by his embarrassment at carrying a bunch of assorted flowers tied with a length of raffia. He was nursing them as unobtrusively as he could at his side in a 'they-don't-belong-to-me' sort of way.

His eyes wandered aimlessly around the station, watching a discarded cigarette carton dancing down the platform in the gentle breeze. He nonchalantly kicked it on to the tracks. As he impatiently patrolled the platform, he looked up and observed the white smoke rising listlessly from the stone-built station's chimney. The smoke formed an only slightly disturbed near vertical column into a bright blue sky.

After years of neglect during the war, the station's building had been newly painted in the company's blue and cream livery. Newly cleaned metal advertising plates attached to the station's picket fence — Fry's Chocolate, Coleman's Mustard and Bass Beer — sparkled in the morning sunshine. One plate was advertising Gold Flake cigarettes, a reminder to him that he had denied himself cigarettes to pay for this journey, although he carried a packet of five Woodbines in his pocket for Kate, just in case. Lazily, his eyes moved past the adverts to the hanging scarlet-red buckets prominently displayed along the platform's white painted picket fence.

A porter appeared, dressed in a dark blue uniform: striped shirt, white collar, neatly knotted tie, and a matching cap with an embroidered company badge. He trundled a four-wheel cart, loaded with parcels, through the double gates and onto the station platform. Pulling it slowly and steadily towards the goods weighing machine at the far extremity of the platform, he parked it up, putting the handle upright and began a leisurely break waiting for the scheduled arrival of the train. Regarding the passengers sitting on the wooden seats singly or in pairs, he regularly cast expectant glances up the track.

Jimmy's senses were working overtime as he breathed in the beauty of the rusticity with which he was surrounded. It was one of those stunning autumn mornings that surpass even a summer's day in their display. The birds and insects were out and about foraging on the steep banks on either side of the station. A chaffinch was singing its repetitive descending chant and, unusually, the black birds were still marking out their territory with their varied, lengthy and beautiful calls, squabbling from time to time like naughty children over the profusion of hawthorn berries.

The station staff had excelled themselves in growing bedding plants such as antirrhinums, alyssum and lobelia, still late-blooming in ordered brilliance in the stone troughs. They stood out against a rich and verdant background on the embankment of undisciplined cow parsley, ragwort, dock, dandelion and massed rosebay willow herb, all interspersed with anarchic white convolvulus, across which a colourful kaleidoscope of butterflies was on the wing.

The background to the scene was brightly coloured by the browns, yellows and oranges of the first leaf falls of the year from the sycamores and silver birch trees above the embankment and the ripened red, pink and yellow berries from the elders, spindles and crab apples. A trace of the soothing smell of wild garlic wafted towards the platform on a gentle zephyr. Beyond the station in the foreground, the soft-shaped hills furnished a backcloth of indistinct, lush verdure.

The new-born day seemed to throb with life and Jimmy felt good that morning, better indeed and more animate than he had done since his return. This was a good day to be alive. When his mind turned to Kate, his heart soared like the birds that he had just been observing. He gently whistled the song 'If you were the only girl in the world', then abruptly desisted, shy of his emotions.

At that moment, a smart middle-aged man in a gold-braided uniform with brass buttons and an embroidered cap badge emerged from the stone-built station house, sporting a green flag and a sparkling silver-coloured whistle. Simultaneously, the faint, rapid puffing of a distant locomotive and the shrieking of its whistle penetrated the still ambience of the station. The station master took out pocket watch and smartly flicked it open. Apparently satisfied, he closed it, replaced it in his waistcoat pocket, and cast an eye up the track, a model of confident expectation in his demeanour.

Round the wooded bend in the distance came a small, grimy, six-wheeled tank engine, puffing out great clouds of smoke and steam. It was pulling three short-bogey, red-painted coaches and a similarly emblazoned guard's van. As it slowly approached the platform to the hissing of the air pump for the brakes, Jimmy reflected that a fortnight ago he might have seen its approach as a way of rapid delivery from his pestilential trauma. Today, all that had changed. He had something to live for. 'Nothing else would matter in the world today' he sang to himself quietly as the grubby monster pulled noisily alongside the platform, straining as if the challenge were too much for it.

311

He disregarded the compartments in the first and second-class carriage, awaiting the arrival of the third-class compartments as the train came to a screeching standstill. As soon as it halted, the leather-strapped windows were opened with a dull thud and bodiless arms stretched out to grasp the door handles on the outside.

The guard alighted officiously and the porter rapidly commenced his task of throwing the multi-sized parcels into the guard's van. Another railway official, fitted out with rather more gold braid, who had now stationed himself at the picket gate, examined and in some cases retained the tickets from the few departing passengers, systematically examining each one in the apparent hope of finding some irregularity.

The joining passengers began climbing into the carriages under the consistent and attentive supervision of the stationmaster, who was anxiously checking his watch and conscientiously watching the passengers' choice of compartment and carriage. None of the carriages had a corridor, so it was important to ensure that the proper ticketholders mounted the appropriate carriages. In this case, there were apparently no ticket irregularities nor any laggards on that day.

Jimmy sought out an empty third-class compartment, entered and immediately slammed the door behind him. He did not wish to have to engage in unnecessary conversation. So he swiftly seized the leather strap to pull up the window and secure it firmly on the topmost hole. Given that the carriage was non-corridor, he hoped that the closed door and window would give him space and deter any other prospective passenger from entering before departure.

The ashtrays in the compartment gave off a strong stale miasma of tobacco which exacerbated his longing for a

312

cigarette. Should he have one of the Woodbines he had brought for Kate? He elected against it. He placed the bunch of flowers on the metal-rod stanchioned netting that served as a luggage rack and sat next to the door, nearest to the platform, quietly singing to himself as he waited impatiently for departure humming. 'I would say such wonderful things to you. We would have such wonderful things to do'.

At last, the irregular tympani of the slamming doors ceased, and the clarity of the stationmaster's whistle penetrated the cool morning air. With a shuddering, a hissing and a juddering, the little locomotive slowly huffed a gradually increasing pace. It pulled out of the picturesque station, jerkily at first, bidding farewell to the idyllic and peaceful scene with a chirpy toot of the locomotive's whistle. A cloud of white steam and grey smoke traced its way down the side of the carriages and momentarily obscured the beautiful landscape. Rapidly gathering speed, the rhythmic click of the wheels on the rails, the pulsing chug of the engine and the kaleidoscopic passage of the viridescent woods at either side acted to gently hypnotise Jimmy into a timeless half-slumber of reflection.

He was not unhappy in himself — indeed, he felt more positive than he had in a long while — yet his thoughts still strayed to France. He recalled a time when the remnants of the Pals battalion had been pulled out of the line for rest and recuperation. The men were in desperate need of relaxation, all of them physically and mentally stressed and exhausted. Some of them were already profoundly shell-shocked and many suffered from medical problems such as the foul-smelling trench mouth and foot. Strict discipline was still required by senior officers, and a sudden kit inspection was called.

On inspection, one or two of the men on parade were found to be lacking one or more items of equipment. All

313

explanation being cast aside peremptorily, they were sentenced by the battalion commander to one day of the sadistic field punishment number one. This medieval chastisement entailed being tied spread-eagled to a wagon wheel without food or water over a protracted period. This shackling was alternated with temporary release for the execution of futile and pointless physical tasks, including digging a hole to then fill it in again, all under threat of further punishment if the work were not completed in a timely and satisfactory manner. The punishment was cruel, inhumane, brutal, degrading and pointless. Call it what you will. It was officially sanctioned torture.

Jimmy found himself gasping for breath with a desperate tightness across his chest. He could go no further. He could not keep going. He was losing consciousness. He fell to the ground with his arms extended. His arm slipped to the seat and he awoke to the cry of 'Airton, Airton'. As the locomotive screeched to a halt at its first station, he was back in the railway carriage once more.

Jimmy breathed deeply, relieved that no one joined him in the compartment as doors slammed and the stationmaster's whistle blew once more. He turned his attention to Kate, and the last time they had gone out to the theatre. Wrestling with his ceaselessly aching heart, he relived the way he had tenderly and with great self-control helped her to remove her long, fitted overcoat, afraid that he might touch her beautiful body in the wrong place. Despite the coarse jokes and sordid fancies about women that he had shared in those tense and boring hours in the trenches, he nonetheless regarded her person with a certain sanctity. He had noticed her beauty once more, not in any prurient sense. Rather like he had not done since his return from the war. Her shiny black hair, smartly combed back, framed her rounded and petite facial features, blooming cheeks and appealing, dark eyes.

314

He recalled the honeyed tone of her gentle voice as she spoke quietly, the way she looked up at him with her hands clenched below her chin, and her fragrant aroma. He remembered the small droplet of perspiration that moved ever so slowly down her slender neck, sparkling like a costly pearl in the yellow theatre light. That quintessentially feminine touch of tenderness that he had longed for and dreamed of for so long in France. He asked himself, was he any longer capable of meeting his own and especially Kate's expectations?

He recognised now that he had been a fool since his return from France to treat her love so ignominiously. His own blindness and inertia depressed him. More, remembering it made him cringe. Ever since his return, he had left her emotionally stranded — when her illness meant that she needed him most. He had been so self-centred and preoccupied with his own punishing memories. He had to take a grip of himself. He had to commence a new life, turn a new page, forget about France, and live in the present. He missed her so desperately that he could not envisage any life without her.

The rhythm of the train slowed again and the clicking of the wheels became less frequent, taking him back once more to enjoyment of his journey to Lynaton and to thoughts of the sanatorium at Essington and his beloved, Kate. Almost there! He rejoiced. He shifted position on the hard uncomfortable seat, stood up and looking in the rusted mirror, he straightened his tie. Recovering the bouquet from the overhead netting with a swift movement of one hand, with the other he nervously clutched the boxed ring in his pocket yet again.

The slowing had, however, been a false alarm and as the train picked up speed again, he sat down and placed the bouquet on the seat beside him. He glanced up at the sunlight on the craggy rocks and admired the majestic sweep of the bracken-covered fells. At this time of year, heather was already flowering in luxurious purple, more rarely in red or white, standing out amid the motley hues of dark brown and vivid green. On the hillside the timid sheep, startled by the noise of the train, scuttled across the ancient, time-darkened rocks and heather-covered surface. In one of the upper fields in the shadow of the rocky tor a herd of large-horned highland cattle grazed contentedly.

As the train raced onto an embankment, Jimmy cast his gaze down the wooded hurst and marvelled at the sparkling, constantly moving crystal of the river and admired the tenacity and stability of the sandstone-slabbed medieval clapper bridge. The beck provided a haven for an abundant splash of colour, as the kingfishers and dippers sought their prey to the accompanying chorus of a charm of playful finches.

With the increased momentum of the train, Jimmy slipped without difficulty into a light and troubled slumber, daydreams returning once more to France. Charge your magazines fully. Put one in the breech. Set your equipment. Make sure your bayonet is blackened and will slide out of the scabbard easily and quietly. Make sure your boots don't squeak? No noise! Follow me! The soft squelchy splash of shuffling boots on the slimy duckboards. Quiet as you can. Over the top. Tumble into what's left of the long grass. Keep low to avoid silhouetting against any still lingering light. Freeze! In front a sudden rustling in the long grass to the left. Motionless, he tenses. Cold sweat. Don't wipe your face. Don't scratch the bugs. Is your heartbeat too loud? Relief! It's only a rabbit. But! Movement and a cry over there.

'Lynaton! Lynaton! Change here for Carlisle and all stations north. Alight here for Essington Sanatorium.'

Chapter Twenty

Jimmy stirred, finding himself clutching the bunch of flowers rifle-like in both hands, almost crushing them in his nervous grip. Awakening from an uncanny episode, he felt muddled, and then realised that he had to move speedily to get a place on the charabanc to the sanatorium. He gathered his cap and disengaged the leather strap from the metal door peg to open the window.

As soon as the train halted there came a cacophony. The banging of doors resounded as passengers swiftly disembarked and gave the open doors a one-handed slam to close. Jimmy pulled down the window, twisted the outside handle and opened the door. Instantaneously, the results of the rainstorm the previous night greeted his nostrils with the varied perfume of a resurgent countryside.

A large, chipped blackboard on an old easel carried the notice 'Bus for Essington Sanatorium'. Over the bridge and in the lane outside the station exit. Departure 1.30 pm prompt.' Joining the rush and taking the steps two at a time, Jimmy hastened up the flight of metal stairs to cross the bridge, in the company of what seemed like such a swell of people that they could not possibly be carried in the small vehicle that he expected would be waiting for them. Fearing he might be left behind due to a shortage of seats, and eager not to be tardy in visiting Kate, he quickened his pace perilously leaping down the flight of stairs on the other side and, as he passed his ticket to the porter at the picket gate, he was at the front of the crowd.

On exiting the station, he observed a rather ancient Durham-Churchill open-topped charabanc standing in the lane. It was mud-splattered, and its solid wheels did not suggest a comfortable journey on the country road to the sanatorium. In fact, its dull brass head and sidelights and its dust and mud-covered paintwork gave it a rather shabby and neglected appearance. The serried ranks of wooden bench seats, one behind the other like a multi-slice toast rack rose towards the rear of the bus. The worn and cracked soft-top, folded away at the back of the vehicle, did not appear capable of further service. Jimmy was, therefore, hopeful not to have inclement autumn weather to cope with on the final stage of his journey. Regardless of the quality of the transport, his long odyssey to see Kate was almost over and his spirits were high, his expectations soaring.

The driver and conductor were standing at the side of the bus smoking and chatting. Jimmy hastened straight up to them.

'This the bus for Essington Sanatorium?' he asked, secreting the flowers like a bashful schoolboy.

'That's right, mate. Thruppence return. Do you have the small change?'

'How much is a single?'

'Tuppence to you, mate. It's a long walk back from the sanatorium and, if you just go one way, you will probably miss the last train back to town.'

'I'll take a single, please, and take my chance for the return,' said Jimmy, reasoning that if he could save a little here, he could have something towards his next visit, and maybe even a small something for Kate.

Apparently disappointed, the conductor pulled out an orange ticket from a wedge of assorted tickets in the metal clip frame hanging on a leather strap across his portly stomach.

'On your head be it. If you change your mind, though, it'll be tuppence for the return journey as well.'

'Thanks,' Jimmy said, handing him a penny piece and two halfpennies and wondering who would have the task of auditing all the tiny, circular, coloured pieces of paper to check the conductor's takings at the end of the shift. What a job!

'Jump aboard, mate. We'll be leaving shortly.'

Anxious to be off as soon as possible to see Kate, he asked, 'When will that be?'

'We depart as soon as everyone has left the station platform and buildings. Probably in about five minutes. People are usually good at leaving the station promptly as they know there is only one bus. The journey takes about fifteen minutes and we drop you in front of the main door. Take any seat you like. No reserved seats on this old lady. That's service for you. Just like in the old days.'

Not wishing to waste any time at the other end, Jimmy opened a door at the rear of the charabanc for the more elevated outlook it would afford. He climbed onto the bus and sat down on one of the hard, wooden, high-raised bench seats. He slammed the door behind him in the vain hope that he could inhabit that section alone. The other passengers were gradually cramming in to fill the seats on the other benches. The room for knees before the next row of seats was not very great and Jimmy found it rather uncomfortable. He was spreading his legs diagonally across the available space as a rather charming young lady opened the door and got in. He politely shuffled over towards the other extremity of the seat and she sat between him and the door, keeping a respectable, unengaged distance.

To his dismay, however, and notwithstanding his original defensive strategy, a middle-aged couple opened the door to his section and began to climb in. The man was enormous and forced his way straight in using his wife as a battering ram, causing Jimmy to cede territory and squeeze hard against the side of the bench seat on the one side and the young lady on the other. At least, Jimmy hoped, with the man's ample bulk obstructing the door, it would deter anyone else from entering his row. The man's wife suggested that the fat man might be more comfortable towards the middle of the seat, so she stood up and moved, with the result that the first young woman was immodestly crammed between Jimmy and the ample thighs of the large gentleman. The odour of stale sweat was overpowering. Jimmy tried to avert his head and to shuffle his rear harder against the side of the bus. In compensation, he could also sense he young woman's perfume and he could feel her thighs against his own, which to his shame he found rather sensuous. *Thank god this bus is open-air*, he consoled himself.

Eventually, the driver mounted the bus and settled himself into his seat. The conductor took the cranking handle from below the passenger seat and inserted it in the front of the engine. He rotated the cranking handle several times without success. At long last, spurred on by an extra-vigorous turn of the handle, the engine burst into noisy life. The conductor jumped aboard at the front beside the driver and, with a full load of passengers, the vehicle moved slowly away.

As expected, the journey turned out to be rather uncomfortable. The draft of air rushing by, had the effect of dispersing the smell although it also dishevelled the ladies' hair, and both men and women were soon fighting to steady their hats. The solid tyres bumping awkwardly along the unmetalled road were a recipe for traveller pain, with the bus on occasion sinking into the cavernous potholes and

320

bouncing the passengers up and down and sideways on the hard wooden seats. At such times, the guard slats at the side of the bus grated noisily on the limestone surface of the road, especially when the bus left the village and went round some of the sharp bends along the riverside.

At one stage, as they drove slowly up quite a steep hill, the driver fluffed his gear change. There was a harsh grinding and the bus almost came to a standstill and then painstakingly slowly recovered. As they increased momentum, descending the other side of the hill, the driver selected first gear, no doubt to compensate for the probably inadequate brakes.

It was certainly not the most comfortable journey that Jimmy had ever had, and it reminded him of travelling in army lorries in France when the men were transported to holding areas and to working parties behind the lines.

Despite the lack of comfort, however, the drive was otherwise a very attractive one through beautiful landscapes. It was still a splendid autumn day with a suggestion of an Indian summer in the air. Thus, in spite of everything, for the first time since his return Jimmy felt alive, happy and optimistic. The sensation of the young lady's thigh at his side, combined with the warmth of the sunny autumnal day, reawakened his attention to his happy plans for Kate and him in the future life of his dreams.

The sun was now quite high — as high as it gets in autumn — and it had burned off the morning haze in the valley to expose a limpid and still slightly out-of-focus blue sky with only a handful of scattered clouds. Jimmy warmed to the slow pace of their progress, as the bus took them through empty and narrow country lanes, bounded by well-tended dry stonewalls. Some recently shorn fields were ribbed by lines of newly mown hay, while in others the straw was being hand-stooked into irregular and random patterns.

With grinding gears the bus struggled up a hill on the far side of the river to enter the ancient village of Lynaton. They passed through the main cobbled square with its authentic Saxon church and quaint Victorian shops. Jimmy's nostrils were briefly tortured with the wafted aroma of freshly baked bread, which served to remind Jimmy that he had had nothing to eat so far and was now feeling peckish.

Leaving the village, the lumbering old curate's egg of a coach moved tortuously along a potholed and puddled road until it reached a narrow, imposing set of carved sandstone gate posts. Attached was a well-polished brass sign, which heralded their arrival at the 'open-air' Essington Sanatorium.

Immediately, a new vista of broad lawns was exposed, sweeping upwards and interspersed with majestic and mature specimen trees of diverse kinds. At the top of the impressive driveway, the newly built, rather incongruous redbrick, glass-fronted buildings of the tuberculosis sanatorium were coming into sight. The charabanc was driven past the modern utility buildings and halted a couple of yards further in front of the entrance to the main building, which was the only part of the sanatorium that dated from an earlier time of wealthy landed gentry. It contrasted wildly with the other buildings, being constructed of timeworn and weather-darkened sandstone from lower down the valley. The entrance seemed as impressive as any aristocratic country house and Jimmy optimistically surmised that, in such surroundings, Kate would surely recover her strength and her health.

Impatient as he was to alight, he was frustratingly hemmed in and had to await the painfully slow descent of the fat man — with the compensation of a fleeting sight of pretty petticoat worn by the nice-looking young lady.

A smartly dressed and cheery-faced young nurse appeared from the heavy front doors to direct the arrivals to their destinations. When they had dismounted and assembled at the foot of the main front stairs, she addressed them brightly, welcoming them and advising them that they could find the location of their loved ones on a list pinned up on a board and easel in the entrance hall with a map of the sanatorium. They were welcome, she confirmed, to go straight to the rooms indicated. They should of course respect the privacy of other patients and not enter other rooms.

Being one of the last to alight from the chara, Jimmy had to wait tetchily at the back of the group before the other visitors moved out of his way and he could locate Kate's room on the list.

Scanning the alphabetical list, to his great delight Jimmy read the name Kate Melvin and detailed against the name, Room 21..The adjoining map showed it to be situated to his right in the new building and facing out across the valley.

He strode at a rapid pace along a spotlessly clean, half-tiled corridor that smelt of disinfectant. On arrival at the room, he opened the door quietly in case she was asleep.

Chapter Twenty-One

The room was empty of its bed. The broad glass door that formed the front wall of the room had been thrown wide open and the bed had been wheeled out onto a veranda, opening up a beautiful panoramic picture of the landscape sparkling in bright sunshine. The view was stunning, revealing over the treetops the opposing fells of the hillside across the broad dale, surmounted by darkened crags shaped like some assembly of strange mystical creatures.

'Come in, Jimmy. I know that you are there. I heard the door go. I knew that you would come today.'

A white painted chair had already been placed at the side of the bed, and he advanced quickly, giving her an affectionate peck on her blushed cheek before taking his seat, as Kate hastened to secrete a red soaked handkerchief under her pillows.

'Hello, love. How are you feeling?' he asked brightly.

'Oh, a lot better. They're wonderful here and the fresh air is doing me good,' she lied.

Jimmy kissed Kate tenderly on the cheek, almost as though he ran the risk of breaking her frail figure.

'It's good to see you, Jimmy. How are you? How was your journey? Thank you for coming. I hope it wasn't excessively expensive.'

'No, I'm champion and of course the price was next to nought for a chance to come and see you.'

Kate was propped up in bed on three pillows against the bed's gated metal back-rest. Despite her faux-pink cheeks, she seemed pale and fatigued with sunken and world-weary eyes. She had tried hard with lipstick and a little rouge to brighten herself up. She wore the bed jacket that her mother had crocheted for her over her pretty nightie. The jacket was in a pure white wool interspersed with attractive pink and the delicate pearl buttons glistened in the sunlight. Not for the first time, he marvelled at her delicate beauty, oblivious of the reason for that misleading impression. At the other side of the bed was a locker, on which had been placed a jug of fruit cordial and, to his dismay, two lovely bunches of fresh flowers.

'The journey was pleasant and efficient. Everything went to plan. And the valley was a real treasure to behold.'

'How did you get here?'

'I hiked it from home to the station and I took the early train to Lynaton. The chara for Essington was already waiting for us when we arrived and the journey up here only takes about fifteen minutes. They drop you at the front door. It's not a comfortable ride, though it had the advantage of being uninterrupted and pretty brief.'

Jimmy sat down on the straight-backed wooden chair and turned to smile at Kate. She met his gaze, smiling wanly. He was astonished by what he witnessed in her. Instead of the old radiant, vivacious and defiant eyes and marvellously shiny black hair, there was the dimming light of an awesome listlessness in her eyes that really distressed him. Her pale pink cheeks, coloured extra with the help of a little rouge, were surrounded by hastily combed and yet still matted hair.

'I brought you these flowers. I hoped that they would help to cheer you up. Harry made up the bunch for me from his allotment. When he knew I was coming to see you, he

325

wouldn't take anything for them. However I see that someone was here before me.'

'Very many thanks Jimmy. They're lovely. Don't forget to thank Harry. He's a nice lad, isn't he?' Kate said, taking the bunch of flowers from him and laying them delicately on the bed beside her. 'I don't get bouquets too frequently, you know. It was so considerate of you both. These flowers were brought in by one of the nurses this morning from a room where the lady… she … err … left this morning. Mother and father brought the others when they came a couple of days ago. You know father has an allotment near the Congregational Chapel on Chapel Lane.'

'I knew he grew vegetables. I didn't know that he grew flowers as well. They're beautiful chrysanths. So large and with such beautiful colours.'

'Yes, he concentrated on vegetables during the war. With the peace, he has shared the allotment with his real love: pompon chrysanthemums. Anyway, there's always room for more,' she reassured him. 'Especially those cactus dahlias. I do like dahlias and they're pretty hard to get now. There is a great spirit here in the hospital, and we all share. So, if you promise not to tell my parents, I'll let Brenda next door have the others and I'll keep yours here with me. She needs perking up a bit. Had some bad news the other day. Anyway, that's another story. Brenda does not get visitors. She's very young, you know. Only a teenager. Her father fell on the first day of the Somme offensive, and her mother cannot afford the cost of the journey. Now she is seriously ill. Drowning in her own fluids, they say.'

'I fancy these are hard days for lots of people. Many people are going through the wringer. Anyway, how are you?' he asked. 'Are you concentrating on getting better? Do you need anything? Can I bring you anything next time?'

'Oh, they tend to us pretty well here. The doctor comes to see me every day and the nurses bring in anything we need,' she explained, evading his question about how she was. 'We have three wholesome meals a day, so we are well fed. More than I need. I'll be getting fat if I do not look out.'

'I don't think that will happen too soon, Kate, love,' he reassured her.

She did her utmost to carry on leading the conversation, hoping against hope that he would not raise the issue that she had wanted him to broach for so long.

'And on fine days like this, the porters come and open the French windows and wheel the beds onto the verandas. The outlook alone is a wonderful tonic. You can see the vestiges of the old Anglian farming strips from the eighth century on the far side. And that village over there is called Thwaite, an Anglo-Saxon word for a small settlement.'

'Do you know if there are still any old Anglo-Saxons there?' he enquired, grinning broadly all the time.
'No. Although we see some magnificent sunsets from our beds. It's a real pick-me-up. And regarding the Anglo-Saxons, I think that some of the porters here whose families have lived locally for generations have names derived from the Anglo-Saxon language. Certainly, one or two of the local place names are from that time.'

There followed a protracted and embarrassed muteness during which neither of them spoke. Both were wrapped up in what each of them knew they wanted to voice.

'Kate, love. I brought you something else as well.'

Straightaway Kate guessed what he had brought and recognised that he was going to mention the very issue that she did not wish him to at this moment in time. She loved him, true! In spite of her love, she did not wish to possess him. After the war, there were certainly a few young women out there who would be happy to have a fine young man like him. He would have no difficulty in finding someone else to love.

To gain time to think, she asked, 'What did you bring? I hope that it was not cigarettes. I'm not allowed those, you know.'

'No. It's something much more important than that. Before I give it to you, I wanted to tell you something.' He waited. She didn't utter a word. He slowly and reverently took the ring from his pocket.

'I have been thinking things over and I have now recognised that I have been a bit of a chump since I came back from France.'

'Jimmy, don't be too hard on yourself. You know, you've been through a lot.'

'As far as you're concerned, I have been selfish and lacking in sympathy. I have not appreciated your problems and difficulties. I have not sufficiently cherished the wonderful gift that is your love. I am so sorry.'

She was embarrassed. 'That's nice of you, though it doesn't matter. We all make mistakes.'

'Yes, I've realised that I cannot live without you,' he blurted out. 'And I want … I want you to marry me. And you know that ring we inspected in the shop window the other week that you indicated you liked? Well, I pawned my

328

medals and borrowed a little … and, well, I've bought that ring and got it with me today.'

'Good gracious me, Jimmy. I would never have wanted you to pawn your medals.'

'It doesn't matter. I'd like you to take this ring and wear it. That is, if you're still willing. If you'll still have me.'

He waited, watching her etiolating face. She was winding a small, embroidered handkerchief around her fingers. *Have I upset her? Is this the appropriate time? Am I being selfish again raising this at a time when she has not regained her strength?*

The timing of his advance was far from propitious as far as Kate was concerned, and she was in no way convinced that this was a good idea. Sensing his embarrassment, she nonetheless smiled affectionately at him, gently kissed him on the cheek, then fell back wearied into the hollow in her pillow. She summoned all her breath, all her energy and all her courage.

'Jimmy, I've been thinking.' She was straining as she breathed painfully. 'It has been good for me to come here away from the hurly-burly of my life with work, my mother and father, my brothers and the housework, and to have a chance to think about my life … what is left of it. I have thought a lot about you, Jimmy, my love, since I came here. I love you as I have never loved anyone else in my life, and I never will again. Indeed, I'd give my life for you.'

Jimmy was so emotionally stirred and relieved by her words of passionate commitment that he could do no more than utter a rather tearful, clichéd response. 'And I would for you too, my love.'

'But …'

The single word deflated his elation.

'You see Jimmy, to be honest with you, I don't know how much longer I've got. A long life is not a feature of the people who come here, and I know that. Even in the time since I came, I feel I am getting weaker. So, I am not so sure that I should be making a long-term commitment at this time.'

Jimmy felt his heart sink. He had had such high hopes of this visit and it was not turning out at all as he had mentally pre-planned it. He was beginning to find her words emotionally draining. He felt thwarted though still determined.

'Kate, love, listen to me. You've only been here at the sanatorium for a very brief time. You can't expect miracles, you know. These things take time. You must cheer up. You mustn't give in, Kate. And however long we have, it doesn't matter. That's a lifetime for me to be with you.'

'You know me, Jimmy. I'm a fighter and I shall not simply give in without a struggle. For all that, we both have to come to terms with the fact that I may never recover. I may never again travel down that beautiful dale to the industrial squalor that is our hometown.'

Jimmy began to feel resentful — not of her, of course. Rather of the fates which were tugging at his future life with her or rather without her. He could not, he would not, admit the idea that she might not regain her health. She had to get better. What sort of a life would he have without her? His thoughts became jumbled and the words tumbled out.

'Please. Please, Kate, do not be so pessimistic. Buck up and, for heaven's sake, look on the bright side. You will travel down this dale again, on my arm. We will be together again.'

'There is nothing I would like better.'

'Well then?' he challenged.
'Jimmy, I love you dearly — so much that I am not willing to bind you to me, knowing that I may never be able to fulfil your wishes and your aspirations. And even if I could, it would be for only a really short time.'

'You will be able to, love. We shall do it sharing the load. However long it takes, however fleeting our lives, we shall share our futures.'

Little by little Kate was realising that it had always been a forlorn hope that he would appreciate that she loved him deeply and that precisely her love required her to let him go. She could not conceal her love for him, even though she acknowledged that such would have been the only way to make him accept what she was telling him. She was slowly losing that struggle too.

'Jimmy, to take your ring and to know that you are mine and mine alone would be a wonderful fulfilment of my long-held desire. It would be a self-regarding act, however, that would betray my deep and lasting love for you, Jimmy. Try to understand. I am just not willing to do that to you. I love you too much to do it. Please, my love, try to understand and appreciate that.'

'Kate, you have to be positive. I know your fears. I share them. But I can't grasp what your problem is. We would be stronger, the two of us together. We've always been a good team.'

331

'Jimmy ...'

'Kate, I don't know what to ...'

For some moments he stared into nothingness. He turned his face to look full at Kate.

'Don't speak, Jimmy, love. Just take my love with you for all time, wherever you go and whatever you do. I shall always be with you, no matter what. And one day you will meet another woman, who will be much more worthy of you than I ever was.'

'Don't, Kate. Don't. You're hurting me too much.'

'It is the last thing in the world I wish to do, Jimmy, to hurt you. You are so precious to me. The most precious thing in the world. We have to be realistic, however. Unless I am, you will not be. My time is rather limited. In contrast, you have your whole life in front of you.'

'Kate, I can't take this. I can't deal with it. What can I do?' He hung his head in dejection.

Kate looked sympathetically and tenderly at him with tear-filled eyes. She was becoming more and more exhausted. She wondered if Jimmy would ever understand. Could a man possibly recognise that refusal of a ring need not denote absence of love? Rather that it could, in some circumstances, be an expression of a more powerful love.

'Jimmy, I'm unsure whether you can recognise this. So I'll do my best to explain it to you.'

'Kate, there is no need to explain. All I know is that I love you and that I cannot imagine a full life without you.'

332

His comment seemed to confirm her feeling that he would probably never appreciate what she was trying to express. Nonetheless her love for him imposed an obligation on her to help him. So she felt that she had to carry on trying. She told herself again that she owed it to her profound love for him to get him to understand.

'Jimmy, my love, you have to realise that love is not simple, the same at all times and places for everybody. It has varying significances for individual people and it shows itself in contrasting ways at separate times. People don't have uniform ways of expressing their love and they receive it uniquely. There is no direct relationship between the two.' She rested for a while to recover, to seek strength and to regulate her breathing.

'For some people, love denotes seeking to possess their loved one wholly and in every way, physically and mentally. They are expecting a perfect, harmonious overlap between themselves and their loved one. Their love is one hundred per cent all-embracing to the exclusion of the other person's definition of love, self and happiness.'

A protracted cough racked her body and she held a torn piece of fabric in front of her mouth as she made another effort to breathe more regularly and deeply. 'Such love can be stifling to the loved one. It may even suffocate them, for it is no more and no less than a selfish, childlike desire on the part of the lover to fully possess the loved one, as an object.' She feebly wiped away the beads of perspiration appearing on her brow.

'Kate, love, you're so weary. I didn't want to burden you with all this. I'm sorry. You shouldn't ...'

Had he been listening? More importantly, had he understood what she was attempting to tell him? She paused for a second and regarded him with forceful love and compassion in her eyes. The love, which she had tried to share with him, was different from the love she had experienced with Kitty in the four long years of his absence. It was still love though.

'Jimmy, my love …'

'Kate, do you think you should …?'

'Jimmy, what I am doing my best to share with you is difficult for me to put into words.'

'Why try, my love?'

'Jimmy! Can you envisage a love that would always treat a partner as an equal in every way? Would you know how to deal with not just the happy days of full agreement? Rather it would have to deal with days of strong disagreement, without either party being subjugated or the discord destroying their love for each other?'

That was the kind of balanced human relationship that she believed the Suffragettes had fought and suffered for, and that was her belief too. Though she loved him dearly, she could never act as his subordinate.

'Some people love selflessly, Jimmy. They cherish the interests of the other above their own, respecting that person and their separate integrity and seeking to make the other happy. Such a love is not just an expression of the needs of the lover. It is rather an acceptance of the needs of the person loved on equal terms. And equal terms signify that neither dominates. It implies that each absorbs the points of view of the other as they grow in their knowledge of each other.'

With a shake of his baffled head, Jimmy appealed, 'Kate, I am not sure that I can fathom what you are saying. I just cannot think …' he trailed off.

Jimmy looked at Kate. She was so beautiful. Her once defiant nature, however, though still evident, seemed becalmed. Her great energy was now spent, although her intellect was clearly sharp as ever, and her spirit was undaunted. He could see that her determination to make him understand far outweighed the ability of her body to fulfil her intentions.

True, they often had contrasting ideas about things. It had sometimes left him infuriated, though never bored. He had often felt thwarted by her alternative take on his reality. He realised that did not matter now. Indeed, that might well be one of the things that made him love her. How boring it would be if she were just malleable, accommodating to his wishes, like lots of wives were still expected to be these days.

She tried to speak again. 'Jimmy, I can't …' she whispered faintly, sinking back into her pillows, coughing and breathing rapidly.

Jimmy worried that he had overtired her. She would recover. He knew that. She had to. The question was whether his visit had made her recovery more difficult, less likely?

Seized with guilt at his own self-centredness, he contemplated whether to persist. He felt badly about taxing her already weak constitution.

'Kate, I'll always love you,' he insisted defiantly, taking her hand again and gently squeezing it. 'I'll never accept life without you. And my love is selfless. As so often in the past, I'll accept what you want, though I may not always agree with you. I may reason with you. I'll never seek to impose my opinions on you. On that I give you my word.'

Kate turned her head towards him and gazed at his crestfallen face.

'Ours will be a partnership,' he continued. 'A union that expresses the equality between us that you expect. I realise now that I have been blind. I love you because of your independence and your indomitable spirit. That is what I have always loved about you.'

'Jimmy, my love. Every day we dupe ourselves into forgetting that one day we shall all expire. That's human nature. Never forget that I love you, Jimmy. I always will. Not a day goes by when I do not long for you, as you were before … as I was before the war.' Her voice now weak and husky with emotion, she urged him, 'Now go, my love, and leave me. I am very tired and I have a lot to think about if I am going to get better.'

With a feeling of all-pervading wretchedness, Jimmy stood up slowly and bent over her. He noticed the tears like tiny pearls resting on her cheeks. 'I shall always love you, Kate. I shall come back and visit you again soon.' He kissed her tenderly on the lips.

'Come whenever you have the time and the wish. You will always be welcome, Jimmy, my love. For the time being, I shall keep you in my heart.' She smiled directly at him now, not fully confident that she had succeeded in helping him to realise the nature of the love she held for him and the kind of love she wanted from him.

He kissed her again softly on her dry, cracked lips as she extended a trembling hand to touch his arm.

'I'll see you next week, love,' he assured her, containing his emotions as best he could.

Kate knew in her heart that, for her, next week might never come. She had shunned being explicit in her words, so as not to hurt him. How cowardly! She had failed her one big test of the day.

'Yes, love. I'll look forward to that.' She turned her face away to hide the tears she did not wish him to see.

'Goodbye then, love. I'll be back for you in a little while. Take good care of yourself.'

Head bowed disconsolately, he turned and tramped from the veranda outside her bedroom onto the broad, lush lawn and down towards the pebble drive. Deep in thought, he did not look back. He did not look up. He did not wish to run the risk that Kate would see the tears in his eyes and his face so distraught with emotion. He still loved her. The way, in which he loved her, however, had been irrevocably transformed by their conversation today.

It was now the time between the day and the dark. The sky was blackening, although in the West it was still showing those hues of pink, aquamarine and purple, which on fine days betoken a rare and beautiful celebration of the farewell to the day. The sun was now low on the horizon and the shadows of the specimen trees in the grounds of the sanatorium were rapidly lengthening as he walked briskly down the sweeping sanatorium drive.

He dawdled aimlessly just before leaving the driveway, kicking up the gravel on the drive for an instant. Turning he cast a last glance back at the gaunt, barrack-like profiled modern building, bathed in a magical pink hue by the dying rays of the sun.

337

Lonely, he sought refuge in his own thoughts. Though far distant now, he could visualise Kate being wheeled back into the bedroom and the floor-to-ceiling glass doors closed — a portentous symbol of his conclusive exclusion from his loved one. Still at the entrance gate, he hesitated pensively and kicked at the gravel. He turned round once more, taking one final glance back over the rapidly darkening grey-green expanse of the sanatorium lawns and building. Before him he could see the last sparkle of the dying sun in the amaranth heavens, reflected now in the large bedroom windows, facing across the valley, their reflected light shining like a large bank of searchlights. Not normally a man given to showing emotion, his eyes were now full and his heart heavy. As he grappled with contradictory interpretations of what Kate had shared with him, he tried to fathom out how what she had spoken fitted into a future for him and for them … if any.

Then, frantically, he dismissed his own importance, like throwing a piece of dog-eared paper into a waste bin. Most likely, as had been the case as a soldier in France, he was just not significant enough to merit a future. He tried to see beyond his own feelings of hurt and rejection. He faced a host of questions and had no solutions.

As the still incomplete darkness of the evening intensified and the shadows became blacker, paradoxically his perplexing upsurge of doubt, disaffection and self-deprecation finally ebbed. In the way that the tide at its highest must surely ebb next, his attitude of self-flagellation increasingly receded and he gradually felt himself floating free from his pitiful and onerous past. At that moment the moon appeared from behind a cloud illuminating the road ahead of him, lighting the path that he had to take. The clouds moved momentarily and before him he glimpsed the crystals in the moonlit road surface sparkle like assorted jewels. He set out briskly and purposefully on his way to the station and the journey home.

For the first time today, he thought of the strike, his mates and the upcoming demonstration. There had been little action since the clashes at the beginning of the week, and many questions remained unanswered. What did the men he was leading expect of him? Could he meet their expectations? What wage would be absolutely equitable? Would it be a victory if they got what they wanted, a restoration of the proposed cut in wages, if that resulted in fewer men having jobs? He knew that he was expected to give the leadership. On the other hand, he was not quite sure what goals that leadership should proceed towards.

The questions no longer overwhelmed him. He felt passionately that his mission was to speak out against injustice, to fight for greater social justice, to make a positive difference. He gritted his teeth in determination. With the emerging rebirth of his old self, he knew now that all these things were within his grasp if he wished. He was unfaltering in his conviction that his life journey should not go unnoticed.

The charabanc with its load of returning passengers drove by noisily on its way back to the station. He shrugged his shoulders as it passed and turned his attention to the strenuous physical task ahead of him. At a trot, he set out up the narrow, winding, dry-stone walled lane towards the village in the near distance. He could see how one-by-one the shimmering weak yellow lights of the old stone houses were gradually appearing as the dusk deepened over the top of the old Saxon church steeple, which seemed to be a symbolic beacon pointing the way ahead to him to the station and to his new life with Kate.

Then, all of a sudden and with reckless impetuosity, he threw his head back and sprinted full speed ahead, waving his arms and zigzagging down the road towards the first houses in the village like someone deranged. Somehow, he felt giddy, close to delirious. Why he did not know. It could be lack of food. Otherwise, just high on love and the possibilities for the future! He sprinted past an old farmer whose powerful shire horse was clip clopping home to the stable at the conclusion of the working day. The farmer probably feared that there was a madman running through the community. Jimmy just didn't care.

Through the houses he raced, glancing into one or two shops in the centre. The butcher's shop, hung with a few remaining unplucked game, drew his attention and he called a cheery 'Hello' to the keeper as he passed by.

With even quicker step, impelled by the steep downward slope on the near side of the village, Jimmy descended the embankment that led down to the darkly shadowed river. Across the ancient stone bridge he raced towards Lynaton railway station.

Notwithstanding his emotional meeting with Kate, Jimmy felt happier with himself than he had for a long time. Not only did he feel clearer about his relations with Kate and the nature of their love for each other. He also felt more comfortable about his future life, the place of his compelling memories of the war in his life and with regard to the strike. Leadership is not always having your own way and compromise can be a victory. Today had been a momentous day in the growth of Jimmy Kelly. And he had his beloved Kate to thank. As far as he knew, that was what love was about. It changed you. From the pain of childbirth comes life. Now for the future! For Kate and me! And for my mates!

He entered the station building just in time to see the last train pulling in. He hopped right away into an unoccupied compartment and slammed the door as the train began to pull away jerkily.

Chapter Twenty-Two

On the Sunday after his visit to Kate, Jimmy was up
early. It was the day appointed for the Union march and
demonstration. He spruced himself up, put on his best white
starched collar, a stained and wrinkled red tie and his frayed
best jacket. Slipping on his polished best brown boots and
newly unpawned trilby, he left the house quietly, dropping
the latch as gently as he could as he stepped out briskly onto
the deserted street.

There was no public transport at that time in the morning,
and in any case he could not afford the fare. So, he stepped
out at a rapid pace through the dreary early morning city
streets and was one of the first to turn up at the assembly
point. Victoria Park was dominated by the giant statue of a
cloaked Queen Victoria after whom the park had been named
to celebrate her jubilee.

Already a small number of early-bird marchers were
congregating in the park; some were playing football with
their families on the grass. Jimmy's mood was one of
expectant optimism, which was only reinforced by the early
outlook for a splendid day's weather for the march and
succeeding demonstration. He surveyed the scene. It was a
brilliant autumn opening to the day, warm with a gentle
cooling breeze. As on that evocative earlier day in France,
the light early morning mist was being gradually burned off
to reveal a pale hazy blue and promising sky.

The leaves had already begun to take on wondrous
autumn colours of red, brown, orange and crimson. As they
drifted down onto the tree-lined main avenue of the park,
where the marchers were going to assemble according to the
previous arranged marching order, it was almost as if they
were forming a welcoming multi-coloured woven carpet for
the marchers' feet. Through the trees the warmth of ever-

strengthening and brightening rays of the autumn sun were highlighting the changing colours of the trees and casting a mottled shadow on the leafy ground. For him the day had a sense of magic in the air, such as he had not encountered for a long, long time.

On arrival, his highest priority was to assemble the stewards and ensure that they were all appraised of the march's important goal and the appropriate demeanour for its accomplishment. He wanted to underline the crucial need to create an appropriate atmosphere, so that the March and subsequent speeches in the town centre passed off peacefully and with maximum public effect. He called the stewards to him around the waterless ornamental stone fountain, which afforded him the chance to stand on its steps so that all could see him. In his freshly polished footwear and laundered clothes he felt extremely dapper. He cut a fine figure of a man, a figure of authority fully worthy of attention.

There were stewards there from various Trade Unions and other organisations, including those for skilled mechanics such as the strippers and grinders, and from the different mills across the town and beyond. Jimmy commenced by thanking them and their organisations for attending and for offering to take on this hugely important job. He acquainted them with the background to and aims of the strike, emphasising that their cause was just and reasonable and giving examples of other workers, who had already accomplished similar aims — by peaceful methods, he stressed. He was astonished at his own eloquence and his oratory played a major role in confirming their enthusiasm for the day's events.

'Our cause is a right and proper one. Lots of us here fought four long years for our country and we are entitled to a decent wage and decent living conditions. My fellow workers think that the mill owners have made a big mistake, a miscalculation, in proposing to impose an across the board cut of ten per cent in wages. The purpose of this march is to ask them politely to recognise their mistake and to rescind it. We want to draw the attention of the general public to our case too. These mill owners are not wicked men. They are not our enemies. They are members of our shared community. But, in this instance, they are misguided and we want to demonstrate why we, and the general public, think they are downright wrong. For this dispute affects not just us workers. It affects our womenfolk, our children and the wider community of our fellow citizens whose shops we use and whose services we pay for. So, above all, we have no quarrel with the general population and it is our aim not to inconvenience them. We want them to join us.'

He underlined once again the importance of discipline. 'We need the general public on our side. Do not antagonise them. If anyone tries to provoke you, stay calm and polite and just go on your way. There is no scope for anyone on this march who cannot discipline themselves and it is your job to make sure that all walkers behave themselves. No swearing or other foul language. Polite and well behaved all the way. That way, I feel certain we shall win.'

He concluded firmly and explicitly. 'If any of the public complain about being inconvenienced, show sympathy towards them and their plight and express a sincere apology on behalf of the workers organisations. Try to help them to find a correction. There will be women and children on the march and their welfare is absolutely paramount. There is to be no drinking or disorderly behaviour, let alone baiting of the forces of law and order. Anyone engaging in such conduct should be politely asked to leave the march and demonstration forthwith. Any recalcitrance is to be referred to a senior steward or, in extremis, to myself or one of the other top Union officials. Good luck and thank you.'

Jimmy stood down from the steps and set to chatting with the small groups of stewards. The armbands were distributed, and the groups were instructed by a small number of senior stewards on how to deal with any attempt at troublemaking. They were also advised to obey the instructions of the police politely and to the letter.

After he had finished informally chatting to the stewards, Jimmy strolled across to Vic, who was puffing his pipe and smiling broadly. Sporting a pair of horn-rimmed glasses that had been handed down to him by his grandfather, he extended his hand in a gesture of warm congratulation.

'Jimmy, that was first rate, though I say so myself. I was watching you and listening to how you put our case forward and gave the stewards precise instructions about their role. I noticed the positive impact it had on them. You know, you have the makings of a great Union leader in you one day. Your words are smooth as silk, balanced and uncompromising, yet moderate and engaging. Above all, you don't harangue. You coax and convince. You do have a gift.'

Thoroughly embarrassed, Jimmy had no idea how he could reciprocate Vic's comments. It's true that since his visit to Kate at the sanatorium, he had begun to feel his life restored, and he allowed himself a moment of well-deserved self-affirmation.

'Thanks, Vic. That's quite a compliment coming from you. Still, let's stem the euphoria for the moment and see how it works out in practice during the march.'

Vic, although feeling a little under the weather, had been busy greeting and meeting the various Union delegations and representatives from other organisations and associations, thanking them for their backing and participation and explaining what the march was about. As a family man himself, although his children were grown up now, he met some of the families, and spoke with the children.

Ben had had the difficult and delicate task of deciding the order in which the marches, and particularly the bands, would be placed. There were difficult susceptibilities and sensitivities to be considered, and he had managed it with great aplomb. He even managed to sell to Bert and his comrades from the Communist Party the idea that the best place for them was towards the latter part of the march to achieve greater impact and ensure that the march did not just fizzle out.

The national newspapers would have reporters there today. A little overblown, Vic was to be quoted afterwards as having said, 'The eyes of the nation are upon this crucial event of national significance as the struggle of the British working classes for justice continues here today.'

By this time, more Union members were arriving — many with their families — and there was a jovial carnival atmosphere that belied the seriousness of the occasion. Balloons, windmills and streamers were carried by some of the children, and some families had brought a picnic and pop with them.

Although discouraged by the organisers, some vendors were already selling food, drinks and trinkets to the marchers. A large two-wheeled cart was peddling mushy peas at one halfpenny a dish, one penny with black pudding. Another cart was hawking sarsaparilla and dandelion and burdock drinks from large casks. Some of their horses had been tethered to stakes and were grazing contentedly on the nearby lawns, to the disaffection of the football players. Despite that, all was amicable and good-natured. The fairground atmosphere further boosted Jimmy's feeling that the day was going to be a great success.

The bandsmen all turned out in their smart multi-coloured costumes with yards of braid, their instruments gleaming from a final polish. Several of the local brass bands, some quite famous, were present. After unpacking and leaving their cases to be held by the band secretary on a nearby cart, some were now giving their highly polished instruments a preparatory tune. The park was beginning to come alive with a crescendo of discordant strains as more and more musicians joined in. Some were even having a last practice of brief extracts from their repertoires before the commencement of the march. The scene was amplified as it became ablaze with undulating colour as more Trade Unions unfurled their ornately embroidered, multi-coloured banners.

Nervously, Vic approached Jimmy once more.

'Are all the stewards absolutely sure of what their job is today, Jimmy?'

'Yes, they're fine. Although of course there can be no guarantees. You and I and Ben and the other members of the Council will have to play a tight supervisory role, as we arranged at our last meeting. We'll need to be in a hundred places at once.'

'Have they all been given their armbands?'

'Vic, don't worry. They're all ready. They know what is expected of them. We've gone over this a million times. Relax a little. You'll be giving yourself a heart attack.'

At that moment, Ben came running up to the two of them, out of breath and appearing quite agitated.

347

'They've brought in the troops,' he gasped incredulously. 'They're across the path of our march. At least at the side of our route.'

Jimmy and Vic could not believe their ears. This was the last thing they had expected after all their hard negotiations obtaining permissions for the march in what seemed like endless meetings with the police and civic authorities. They were incredulous and outraged.

'What?' they exclaimed in chorus.

'That's impossible,' Vic cried out angrily. 'It's all been arranged. We've agreed everything with the police and told them we shall have stewards to ensure a peaceful march, that women and children will be taking part and that it will be a fun day. What the hell do they think they're playing at? Are they looking for another Peterloo? I don't believe it.'

'I've seen them with my own eyes,' Ben clarified. 'The story is that, with the scarcity of a variety of foods, there have recently been a number of attacks on food convoys and some looting of food from trucks and stores. The Home Secretary has decided that to avoid a riotous situation and to guard the convoys, the police alone cannot cope. They're over-stretched and therefore troops have been brought in routinely in support of the civil power.'

'So, it may not have anything at all to do with our march and demonstration today, then?' Vic suggested, determined to find an alternative more positive explanation for the presence of the soldiers.

'Well, it is not clear. Though that's neither here nor there. The fact is that the troops are in Pitt Square, deployed at the side of the intended path of the march. Many of the participants will feel that their presence is unfriendly, some may consider it menacing. They will ask, if they are not for us, who the hell are they for?'

'This must surely be a mistake. Lack of communication or co-ordination between the police and the army. We have permission for the march and demonstration and the route of the march has been agreed in detail and publicised. All applicable authorities have been put in the picture, haven't they, Ben?' Vic asked.

'Well, yes, except of course for the army. We never in our wildest dreams considered that the army would be brought in.'

'They might be here to guard a number of public buildings,' suggested Vic. 'I hear informally that the Home Secretary has ordered a general deployment of troops for that purpose in places like Goole and Belfast because of the violent rioting that has taken place there. We need to find out before a simple misunderstanding upsets the applecart … our applecart!'

'There is apparently another problem,' Ben interjected.

'And what's that?' asked Vic.

'This is only word of mouth. I have been told that Comrade Bert is intent on providing a little side entertainment during the demonstration in pursuit of his goal of a class war. He and a number of members of the local Communist Party intend to make an issue of the men who have been put behind bars. I have not been privy to any information which is not public, though that's the word doing the rounds. I don't have the foggiest exactly what they are proposing. On the other hand, I am sure it is certain to be disruptive and it may threaten the success of our public relations campaign. Whatever it is, the police will probably

349

assume that, because Bert is a participant in the Central Council for Action, it is our doing. I wouldn't give much for our chances of winning this dispute if he does get up to anything. The press will make a heyday of it.'

'So, he's not satisfied that we got the unconditional release of Paul Brear and John Kenny?' Vic asked.

'No. And he never did approve of our approach to the march with what he called all them bands and other razzmatazz. He wanted a straight demonstration, pure and simple, against capitalist society and its evils.'

'Well, they tried that in Germany with their workers' soviets, and look at what's going on there,' Jimmy snapped. 'Bert may be a complex man. He may be a bit of a political windbag. He is not an unreasonable or vindictive man and he's certainly not stupid. He must know that we have lots of women and children on the march, and that with such a big crowd anything could crop up if he and his comrades begin stirring it. After all, he's not an anarchist, is he? And he has kin of his own on the march.'

'Sometimes good men of ideals are blinded by the power of their own ideas,' Ben commented philosophically.

'We have to find some way of neutralising any possible intention to disturb the demonstration and turn it into a revolutionary proclamation,' Vic recommended. 'We have all worked hard to build up public support in this dispute. We have them on our side now and I want to keep it that way.'

'What do you propose?' Ben queried.

'I may be proved to be wrong. I do not think that Bert and his comrades **will** cause a hoo-ha in Town Hall Square before or during the speeches. I propose that we announce the speakers for the demonstration right at the outset of proceedings. We feature his own talk strongly, and we keep it to the final contribution in the hope that anything that is going to occur will do so after he has spoken and not before.'

'Even though it goes against the grain, we should keep a special eye on Bert and his mates. Perhaps they should be pointed out to the authorities,' Ben suggested. 'Although I know that he would regard that as an infamous fifth column of traitors to the workers' cause.'

'Well, it's an idea worth considering. But, I have to admit, I'm not so keen on it personally,' Jimmy added. 'If Bert and his comrades ever found out …'

'Why not?' Ben rejoindered. 'We're not talking about the sensitivity of one overblown revolutionary manqué. We are talking about the success of a dispute involving thousands of workers, including dependents of tens of thousands. It's their welfare and livelihood that should take precedence. That's what I think.'

'Bert would quote the mantra for workers' solidarity. And while I take to heart what Ben has advocated, I do not think that we should be reporting on our fellow workers. If Bert discovered, it would only confirm his conviction that Trade Unions have been taken over by agents of the state, and that something more radical is needed if workers are to obtain economic advance and get justice. In any case, we have our own stewards and we have to show the police — and the army if necessary — that we have commitment and discipline besides. We can marshal our members and supervisee our own demonstration. That's the way we can put our members first.'

'I think that the interests of the striking workers are paramount and this proposal seems to me like good old-fashioned common sense,' Vic expressed his support.

'Okay,' Ben added a little reluctantly.

'Then will you, Jimmy, as the person in charge of the stewards, make sure that Bert and his group are well covered by stewards. As unobtrusively as possible, mind you,' Vic requested.

'Done,' Jimmy concurred. 'Leave it to me.'

'Well, let's get to our designated jobs then,' Vic ordered. 'I shall be at the head of the march, directly behind the lead banner, as you both know. Jimmy, I know that originally you were to accompany Ben and myself directly behind the lead banner.'

'Yes, that's correct.'

'Well, I'd like you to take on more of a dispatch rider role than we had at first intended, if you twig what I mean. Make sure that any issues along the march are dealt with rapidly and peacefully and that we at the head of the march are aware of what is going on all the way along. You can choose some of the stewards to help you. But, in any case, kick off with that and then seek out the commanding officer of the troops and square things with him.'

'Fine by me. How many people do you think we have here in the park for the march already?'

'Well including the bands, stewards and banner carriers, I would guess at a few thousand. Of course there will be more in Town Hall Square when we get there. Some people, those with families especially, will have skipped the march and gone straight there. Goodness knows the number that will join us there.'

'So do you think that the press campaign, the billboard adverts and handbills were worthwhile?' Ben asked.

Vic was sanguine. 'I believe so. We shall have to wait and see though. That reminds me: have you told the stewards to give out the bills, setting out our case to passers-by as we march along the road and into the square, Jimmy?'

'Yes, it's all seen to.'

With that they parted for a few moments to speak to other prospective marchers. After passing the time of day with some of his Union colleagues, their wives and children, Jimmy had a couple of moments to spare before the commencement of the march and time to reflect. He sat on the back of one of the large ornamental stone lions in the park.

At long last and for the first time since he returned from France he felt in full command of his own destiny, aware of the weaknesses of his education and nonetheless confident of his ability to compensate for those gaps. It was as if he had journeyed through a tortuous passage where his memories were in control of him, to a broad upland of freedom where he was in control of his memories. He felt a mental self-confidence and political zeal that had eluded him for months. No more sybaritic excursions into the painful and soul-destroying memories of France. His dreams were coming back again, and they were not about the war.

His freewheeling reflections led him back to his schooldays at Skinner Road Elementary School. He recalled the teachers who had given him his thirst for knowledge and learning — mostly females with only a handful of men

353

teaching the older children. He smiled as he remembered Billy Wiggins, the head teacher, with his threadbare jacket stained and creased and smelling of cigarettes. He was a dedicated teacher and a visionary human being. He was the first in the town to lead one of the higher-grade schools, which extended elementary schooling by a couple of years and offered a broader and more vocational curriculum.

Billy Wiggins had certainly left his mark on Jimmy. He had cared profoundly about the dirty, ragged-clothed children who attended his school, some of them with huge boils on their necks, septic fingers bloated with puss, weeping sores on their faces or the pot bellies of malnutrition. Billy had adopted them all and willed them to pull themselves out of the mire of poverty and ignorance they shared. Jimmy recalled how Billy used to play the piano to accompany a singsong before school in the mornings. That was one of his initiatives to provide for the children who had come to school early, often with no breakfast, because both parents had to be at the nearby mill for six in the morning.

It was at Billy's school that Jimmy had been encouraged to recognise his own worth and to set his sights high in life. Billy insisted that you should recognise where you could make a difference. You should identify what you could change and change it, and above all not be put off by what you could not change.

Jimmy took out a crumpled cigarette packet from his jacket pocket, struck a lucifer and focussed on lighting and smoking the crumpled remnants of what had once been a pristine Woodbine cigarette. As he blew the first puff of smoke upwards, he raised his eyes to stargaze through the mottled fret of the trees above him. For the first time since his return home, he felt a strong life force in his veins. He would do something with this life of his, which had been spared in the carnage of war. He would make a difference.

His passage through this world would not go unnoticed. He was still determined to marry Kate, to look after her and to love her — in any way she wanted — for as long as she lived.

His reflections were interrupted by one of the bands striking up. It was the lead band from Black Dyke playing the pompous march by Philip Souza 'Semper fidelis', which heralded the start of the march. Jimmy rose, patting the stone lion on the head affectionately.

With a jaunt in his step he went to follow Vic and Ben just in front of the lead band and behind the textile workers Trade Union banner, held by the two released Trade Union officials, Paul Brear and John Kenny.

Chapter Twenty-Three

Uncertainly at first and then eventually with greater confidence, the march had begun to move along the broad avenue to the huge cast iron ornamental gates set into carved stone posts at the entrance to the park. By arrangement with the park ranger, the main gates had been opened for the marchers and out they went — some marching smartly, others ambling in a more relaxed manner with no question of people being in step. They proceeded into the main road to town with the lead band playing 'Take me back to dear old Blighty'. Some of the children were skipping to the catchy tune and the atmosphere was jovial. As they left the park, however, there was mismatched competition as the second band opened with 'It's a long way to Tipperary'.

The last tram brought the few remaining participants from the town centre. It disgorged a full load of waist-coated and flat-capped workers with their mufflers tucked into the top of their collarless shirts, all accompanied by their lively families. The tram then pulled up behind a queue of several others waiting at the side of the park, where they would stay until the march had passed.

Arrangements seemed to be working well so far, Jimmy reckoned as he hastened past the waiting line of trams. The stewards had begun giving out the handbills, which told casual passers-by what the march was about; some of these even clapped the passage of the march fervidly in a gesture of support for the workers. A small number of other spectators heckled the marchers with the result that these few were onlookers were steadfastly ignored.

Before long there was an air of happy celebration along the length of the march, with children tracing their streamers in the air and a mass of Union banners flapping proudly in the gentle breeze. The town had seen nothing like this in years — since before the war in fact. It was hugely impressive. The few police constables along the route were superfluous, often exchanging tongue-in-cheek comments with the marchers and the stewards. It was a real family affair.

Never a model of great military discipline, the march began to stretch out as some bands stepped out smartly and others merely sauntered past the walled gardens of houses that had been the former homes of the great nineteenth century entrepreneurs who had made the town so rich and successful. As the front of the march was entering the town centre, it was already over a mile in length. Moving slowly past the banks, chapels and Brown's departmental store, it wound its way past the Empire Theatre, which was advertising 'The Importance of Being Earnest' by Oscar Wilde and a musical comedy 'Land of Smiles' by the Austro-Hungarian composer, Franz Lehar.

At that stage, on account of the time that the march was taking to pass, the police requested that it be confined to one side of the road to allow the trams to begin running again. This request was efficiently carried out by the stewards without any direct participation of the forces of law and order, a feat that satisfied the police both of the goodwill of the marchers and of their ability to discipline their own participants. The march then continued more slowly down the incline past the pompous entrance to the main London, Midland and Scottish railway station and into Pitt Square.

A surprise awaited them in the square, which caused some consternation and even fear among the marchers, especially the families. Lined up in front of the main post office were several army lorries and a company of soldiers, standing easy and appearing unthreatening. Nonetheless they were certainly seen as rather threatening to the participants on the march. In no time at all, word was

357

broadcast down the line for marchers to adopt a friendly disposition towards the soldiers and the front band broke out into a rousing spontaneous rendition of 'Soldiers of the Queen' as a sign of friendship. Several of the marchers waved as they passed and this was reciprocated by some of the soldiers.

Jimmy, who had been instructing stewards further back to keep the march in single file, dashed up to Vic at the front.

'What the hell is going on?' he exclaimed.

'Jimmy, my friend, you heard Ben say what I heard him say,' Vic reacted defensively. They both turned their attention to Ben.

'What I advised is what was negotiated with the town hall and the police.'

'This is a big mistake on the part of the authorities. It could inflame passions and lead to unrest among the marchers. Maybe even worse,' Vic said. 'I know that Jack Braithwaite will be in operational charge in Town Hall Square. He'll be the senior officer there. I shall bring this issue up with him without delay on arrival.'

'Good idea,' Jimmy said.

'In the interim, you had better make sure that Bert and his group do not in any way provoke the soldiers,' Vic proposed. 'We cannot afford any taunting or jeering. After all, some of them are probably Pals of ours from the war.'

'Yes, Bert's an old hand at the demonstration business. He's not malicious, though he and his comrades can get a bit overzealous on occasions,' Ben commented.

'Jimmy, could you go back down the line now and see that Bert knows about this before he encounters it. Forewarned, he and his group may take the presence of the troops a little more calmly,' Vic proposed.

'Make sure that you treat him with kid gloves,' Ben counselled. 'You know how awkward he can be.'

'Above all, make sure that there is no chance of a disturbance,' Vic added.

'That's the last thing we want. The local newspaper would have a field day.'

Jimmy nodded. 'Yes. It would be just like him and his friends to stir it up, especially when they see the troops. It's part of their revolutionary scenario. Leave it to me and I'll deal with it.'

'You know, I'll wager that when you tell them, they'll see it as a betrayal by us and by the police,' Ben said anxiously. 'They'll never accept that we knew nothing about it. They're always bidding fair to conjure up some spiteful conspiracy theory against us. The presence of the troops will fit their model.'

'Vic, don't you think that you should seek out the commanding officer of the troops in Pitt Square? You could explain to him that this is a peaceful march and that we have families with young children here,' Jimmy suggested.

Vic was coughing and sneezing. He took time out before he grunted a hoarse acceptance.

'Yes, I should. It's true, though we cannot all leave the front of the march. Someone has to stay here and lead. Apart from that, I just do not think I am up to much running around today. I'm getting old.'

'But someone should speak to the military,' Ben interjected.

'What do you think, Jimmy? Could you do that after you have settled it with Bert and his mates?' Vic requested.

'I'll do my best, Vic. Though I'm not sure there will be time as I am programmed to speak on the platform as you know.' At that point Jimmy noticed Vic's face; he did not seem at all well.

'Vic, are you going to be alright? Are you feeling unwell? Do you want to find somewhere to sit down and let Ben and me iron this thing out?' Jimmy proposed kindly, even though he knew that he and Ben did not have the time to do everything.

'Thanks. No thanks!' Vic refused. 'All three of us are needed at this moment in time. We have no time for backsliders. Still, thanks for your concern. I shall be fine. I just have a bit of a cold coming on. Get a pint of beer inside me at the Globe after the demonstration and I'll be fine. Now, let's each get on with what we have to do.'

Jimmy hared back down the column as fast as his legs would carry him. During his conversation with Vic, the police had fortuitously halted the march in order to allow a number of trams to cross in front, so Jimmy had a fleeting chance to exchange banter with members of the column at different points, hoping to reinforce its solidarity.

But, because of the hold-up and not knowing what it was about, some of the marchers were becoming restive and searching for something mischievous to do. Bert and his group were likewise disgruntled about the halt, anxious to get to their destination at the double.

Out of breath, Jimmy greeted Bert who was standing restlessly by the local Communist Party banner. Some of his group had taken the opportunity to light up cigarettes; others had begun shouting slogans about the workers who were still detained, calling for them to be freed from custody.

Jimmy opted for a slow-burn approach to him, seeking to minimise controversy. To his chagrin, however, that was not entirely how things turned out. The holiday-time elation of marchers towards the outset of the march was gradually easing towards a somewhat antagonistic and excitable atmosphere at this point in the column. There was no band at this end. So no singing along, which made the march much more fractured and made the shouting of slogans more effective. Bert's group were standing in line in front of Martin's Bank, which they seemed to recognise as a capitalistic object fully worthy of their vilification.

'Bert,' Jimmy burst in, out of breath. 'I'm glad that I caught up with you. We ...'

'Why? What is all this about? To what do we owe this honour? A visit by one of the Union bigwigs from the front of the column! Have you made a decision to join the workers at last, Jimmy?'

'Listen, Bert. This is serious. There are troops from the Yorkshire Regiment in Pitt Square, and we need to ...'

Bert cut in sharply pouncing on the word 'troops' like a cat on an unsuspecting mouse. 'Troops? Soldiers? Who the hell asked for them to be brought in? I knew we couldn't trust those bourgeois bastards! What the bloody hell are they doing here? Here to break the strike by whatever means, no doubt.'

'Listen, Bert, before we jump to any conclusions …'

'For Christ's sake! This sounds fishy to me and there is only one conclusion. This is a bloody typical provocation of the British working classes by the powers that be. All we're doing is exercising the democratic privileges that we fought for: to march and to demonstrate. They've sent them in to strike break, haven't they? We know from the *Daily Herald* now about that secret letter they sent to army commanders to discover if soldiers would be willing to strike break or even be deployed to Russia. The bastards! Typical of this government. Typical of the British ruling classes.'

'Listen, Bert …'

'This is typical of the bloody deceitful ruling classes in this country. You fight for them and they offer you the earth. Then when it comes to it, all you get is deception and dust thrown in your eyes. They pledge a fit land for heroes and they flaunt democracy and freedom of speech. As soon as they are challenged, they at once resort to state-initiated violence. And you so-called moderates — Mensheviks we call you — are no better. How on earth can you trust them after this? You have a lesson to learn from this today. Hobnobbing with the bosses did you no good, did it, Jimmy Kelly?'

Jimmy was thrown off balance by the strength of Bert's peeved retort and knew that he had to keep a cool head to find a way to calm the situation.

'Look Bert, as representatives of the workers, we have often stood shoulder to shoulder. This development rankles me as much as it does you. I am sure it is all a mistake or misunderstanding. Vic is going to have a word with Jack Braithwaite as soon as the march enters Town Hall Square to discover what is happening.'

'That sounds like a load of claptrap to me! And let me tell you something else, Jimmy Kelly. If the bloody army so much as sets a foot in Town Hall Square, the balloon will go up. There'll be bloody mayhem, I'm warning you. And you can tell that to your Union bosses.'

'Bert, I feel certain that the troops are there by coincidence.'

In fact, Jimmy was not sure at all. He needed to find a way of calming Bert down. 'They are probably en route to their barracks up north at Catterick. They sometimes detrain here. Perhaps this was the most convenient place to detrain them at this time.'

'Mistake? Coincidence? Bah! I don't believe a word of it. And I would not be so sure if I were you, Jimmy Kelly. It would be typical of this town for the mill owners and the police to have met up in the local lodge, had a nice cosy chat in one of their smoke-filled rooms and come to the conclusion to screw the workers.'

Gritting his teeth, Jimmy decided to try yet again. 'Bert, we have women and children on this march. Do you want them to be put in danger, injured or even worse? Is that honestly what you want?'

'Now you're being rather fanciful. Remember, my wife and children are on this march too. It is not me and my comrades who are threatening anyone, let alone putting anyone in danger. It's the bloody troops and those who called them in. Their presence is a real threat to law and order and to the entitlement to peaceful demonstration by

363

workers fighting for their livelihood and decent working conditions.'

'Bert, we're all fighting for the same thing.'

'If things go wrong because the employers have called in the troops, we could be in for another Peterloo. The powder really will go up! Mark my words, Jimmy Kelly.'

'Bert, no one is threatening anyone. In god's name, let's keep things cool and calm. After all, we Union leaders have a responsibility.'

'I'm not sure if your god is going to help you if those troops enter Town Hall Square.'

Jimmy hastened to interrupt before Bert made a threat that could be quoted against him in a court of law.

'Bert, they are not going to enter Town Hall Square, full stop. I give you my word that they will not enter Town Hall Square. Will that do? I am personally going to speak to the officer commanding to settle this matter. Just keep your lads in order as they go through Pitt Square.'

'Delusions of grandeur! Who the bloody hell do you think you are? General Haigh?'

'General factotum, more likely,' Jimmy replied, hoping to defuse the situation with a little humour. 'But as soon as I have finished here, Vic has asked me on behalf of the Council to approach the commanding officer of the unit in Pitt Square and appraise him of the situation and the need at all costs for restraint on both sides. And I'll tell you. I shall not mince my words. Is that good enough for you?'

'Well, maybe, for a fellow worker,' Bert agreed reluctantly. 'But it goes against the grain to let our comrade-workers be intimidated by the powers that be. Me and my group are not so good at forelock-tugging. We're no lapdogs. We leave that to types like you and Vic.'

Although Jimmy was stung by the remark, he forced himself not to react.

'At all events, keep those bloody soldiers away from us. Otherwise, there will be trouble likely as not,' Bert stated coolly and menacingly.

'Fine, Bert. You just make sure that your party members do nothing to provoke the soldiers. Remember, the soldiers are our mates too. We — you and I — fought alongside them in the war. No insults, no slogans, no singing revolutionary songs, no taunts, and no hand signals, okay?'

'We shall have to see.'

Jimmy realised that was as much as he was going to get from Bert and his group. At least they were now prepared for when they would see the soldiers in Pitt Square.

Jimmy turned and sprinted down the hill towards Pitt Square and his next major task. He needed to find out why the soldiers were assembled there, and appraise their commanding officer of the nature of the march, emphasising that there was no need for any intervention on the part of the army. *Hope he's not like those bloody arrogant and socially superior officers we had in France.* Jimmy mused hopefully.

Chapter Twenty-Four

After his brief meeting with the commanding officer, which he judged to have been unsuccessful, Jimmy was sprinting through Briggate, the narrow shopping ginnel that connects Pitt Square to Town Hall Square. He needed to reach Vic without delay and brief him about his meeting. Puffing like an old steam engine, he came upon a large body of police reinforcements assembled with their black Marias in the side street behind the town hall. Some of them were loafing around, chatting and smoking in small groups, while others were sitting on the ground apparently preparing themselves quietly for what they expected to be the coming fray. They largely ignored him.

At first sight, Jimmy was quite alarmed by the numbers of police. Then he accepted that the authorities had to be ready for any eventuality. In any case, the police were presently keeping out of sight of the marchers. So, he accepted that there was nothing unusual let alone ominous in such a contingency tactic. There seemed to be no need for reinforcements at that moment, which was a promising sign as it indicated the police were satisfied with the stewarding arrangements of the Worker's Council. Jimmy's attention was drawn to the commencement of the formal demonstration and speeches in the square heralded by the striking of the town hall clock signalling midday.

On arriving at Town Hall Square and seeing the crowd, he realised that the throng was much greater than the numbers that had first taken part in the march. Town Hall Square was filled to capacity and there was barely room for the few policemen who were on duty around the sides of the square and at the front of the town hall. The crowd seemed good-natured, although under pressure of space. To add to the crush, all marchers had still not arrived and the new arrivals, including one of the bands, were barging forward trying to get nearer the platform to hear the speakers. The throng seemed to be heaving to and fro in waves and Jimmy worried there was a danger of some crushing taking place, particularly of the smaller children. In addition, Bert and his comrades at the back of the procession still had to arrive.

The speakers were all assembled on the podium and the addresses had just begun when Jimmy arrived. Vic was on the platform delivering — or rather, drawling — his prepared text. Jimmy felt anxious because he was a little belated and the chance to brief Vic on the encounter with the army would now have to wait until after Vic had finished speaking. Vic was usually an eloquent and convincing speaker, who was able to get an audience on his side and make them warm to his message. On this occasion, though, something serious was wrong with Vic. He was not his old self. The chairman of the Central Council for Action persisted in labouring on manfully, although it was obvious from the quite painful delivery that he was not a well man. Moreover, he was not relating to the crowd. Quite the reverse, he was on his way to losing their attention; some members were becoming a little restless and even boisterous. Some had begun minor heckling and Vic's address was being sporadically punctuated by jeers and other interventions.

Thus, it was with a rising feeling of disquiet that Jimmy set to pushing his way through the heaving and tightly packed crowd. He needed to move at once to join Vic on the platform and save the meeting.

Jimmy was still preoccupied with his apparent lack of success in his meeting with the commanding officer of the troops in Pitt Square. He had found the man to be an extremely arrogant and unsympathetic person, totally at odds with the civilian world of 1919. Perhaps it did not help that Jimmy himself had stereotyped the officer as one of the old school who considered anyone who did not speak with his plummy brogue as below him, and who just could not recognise the role of legitimate protest in a democratic society.

For the officer, the concept of equal justice for the workers was simply unimaginable, and Jimmy's greatest fear was that the officer might be spoiling for a fight. The officer had stood smugly on the entrance steps of the General Post Office, tapping his officer's baton impatiently on his trouser leg, giving the impression that it was somewhat taxing for him to deign to pay any regard whatsoever to this Union representative, let alone speak to him.

Within Jimmy's earshot, the officer disdainfully asked his adjutant in stentorian tones who this person was wanting to have an 'audience' with him. Wishing to emphasise the social distance he assumed between them, the officer asked Jimmy if he had been in the army during the war and, if so, which unit and what rank. Jimmy understood this as a determination to put him in his place, so he did not reply.

His adjutant, a man obviously promoted through the ranks, stood next to him in posed obedient dumbness, arms sternly by his side. His face was set in marble, although Jimmy very much doubted that he admired the behaviour of his vain and pretentious commanding officer.

In spite of his efforts, the only information Jimmy could elicit from the arrogant officer was that his orders were to place himself at the service of the civil authorities if invited by the chief constable. He hinted obliquely that a request for possible army backup had been received from the authorities at the town hall. Jimmy wondered if that information could at least help to guide the strategy of the Action Committee.

Finally, Jimmy penetrated the last of the crowd and greeted the ring of stewards surrounding the platform. He was about to mount the rungs at the side of the platform when he encountered Mick Bradley, the newspaperman. He stopped with the intention of thanking Mick for his slant on the workers' case in his article.

'Hello, Jimmy,' Mick greeted him. 'How do you think the demonstration's going? Big crowd. Turnout's good. Are you surprised at the numbers?'

'Hello, Mick. No, not really surprised. I thought I would see you here. By the way, thank you for that article in the local *Observer* the other day. It did our cause a great deal of good.'

'Don't mention it. We only report the facts as we observe them in a balanced and fair way.'

'Well, to the best of my belief, the march from the park down Collingham Lane to the town centre has gone well. Quite a holiday atmosphere with the bands playing and all the families who joined us. It's up to the speakers now to make the case and persuade the crowd of the justice of our cause.'

'Yes, I accompanied the march along the way and spoke to some of the participants and passers-by. We're interested in all sides of the dispute, as you know. Courageous and factual reporting, that's what the *Observer* is known for. Plain speaking, and accurate reporting.'

'Well, that's as may be, Mick, and I've just come across something you should write about.'

'What's that?'

'We had reports early on of a large concentration of troops in Pitt Square. Vic sent me ahead to investigate, to

369

find out the reason for them being there. I have just come from a rather discouraging discussion with the commanding officer of the troops there. It would seem that some idiot in the town hall has called them in. You could hardly think of a more unnecessary and inflammatory action if you tried.'

'I don't believe it,' Mick reacted.

'It's true. I have seen the soldiers and their lorries outside the station in Pitt Square and I've spoken to their commanding officer — a rather small, smug, arrogant, moustachioed little man, full of his own self-importance.'

'But the police have their own reinforcements, quite a large contingent. I've seen them with my own eyes behind the town hall. Why would they need the army?'

'That is my question. The arrangements for this march and demonstration have been approved in detail by the authorities. They know that we have a host of stewards who I briefed thoroughly this morning, and who are here specifically to keep order and to whittle out any troublemakers.'

'I know that Vic and the committee have prepared meticulously for this event. Troops? Where do they think they are? In Ireland?'

'More likely in occupied Germany,' Jimmy ventured. Then realising that the restiveness of the crowd was increasing, he insisted, 'Mick, I have to get onto the platform now. Maybe we could speak about this blunder presently. My job at the moment is to make sure that this demonstration is peaceful and effective. It has to be successful. Vic is not so well, and I must get up there and help out.'

'Yes, Vic didn't seem to me to be his usual self. See you later, and good luck!'

There was a bit of a lull as Jimmy climbed onto the platform, and the crowd was already murmuring with impatience. It seemed that the whole momentum of the meeting was in danger of being lost. Vic had finished speaking and he was supposed to be introducing Doug Hodges, and at that moment he was sitting coughing into his handkerchief and wiping the perspiration from his brow. It was obvious that he was not at all well.

'Jimmy, how did you go on?' Vic enquired, between bouts of coughing.

'I'll tell you in a minute. For now we need to get this meeting moving again … and quickly.'

'Oh, yes, I'm sorry. Have you met Doug? Doug, this is Jimmy. You recall that I spoke to you about him.'

Doug and Jimmy exchanged greetings.

'Jimmy, do you think that you can introduce Doug? I don't feel great. I would like to sit down for a while if you don't mind.'

'Yes, of course, Vic. That's not a problem.'

Straightaway Jimmy stood up and introduced Doug — it had to be brief because he hadn't had time to gather any knowledge about him and could thus only repeat what he had heard and read in the newspapers. Jimmy desperately struggled to gain the full attention of the crowd once again. Having been told that Doug was a charismatic speaker, Jimmy made a strenuous attempt to draw the attention of the crowd to the importance of Doug's words and he gradually

371

managed to bring the crowd back on side. As soon as Doug stood up and uttered his first words, Jimmy briefed Vic about his meeting with the army.

'I don't think that you should feel too badly about the encounter, Jimmy. You did your best. I had a word with the Chief Constable and Jack Braithwaite just before we began here, and they stated quite emphatically that there was considerable pressure from the owners to pull in the army after the incidents at Arthur Rowbottom's mill. The Chief Constable, however, assures me that only in the most extreme circumstances will he request assistance from the army. He emphasises the army's presence is mainly because the unit is en route to Catterick.'

'Well, at least that's good news.'

'Off the record, he emphasised that it was very much against his advice and wishes for the army to be called on. He said that all in all he and his officers are confident that they can deal with any eventuality.'

'If he was against bringing them in, who was for it?'

'Well, I can guess. On the other hand, it would not be helpful for me to surmise at this moment, In any case, we now know that the demands for military intervention came from the owners, and which individuals is irrelevant.' Vic mumbled somewhat mysteriously

Doug was speaking at some length about the history of the landmark pact between government and workers at the onset of the war. He cited the amendments to the pact that had been negotiated during the war and the progress of the various industrial disputes since the armistice. As a former Lancashire textile worker, he highlighted the success of the cotton strike in December 1918 and spoke with pride about the successful outcome of their industrial action: a fifty per cent increase on standard wages. *If only we could dream of such an outcome*, Jimmy thought.

Doug spoke of the outcome of the great industrial conference of the previous February and of the aims and organisation of the Textile Industrial Council, a body representative both of workers and employers over the previous few months. He lauded the settlement establishing a 48-hour week for the textile industry from March 3 of that year, as a good example of what can be done given solidarity and discipline on the part of the workers.

On the other hand, when Doug referred to the results of the inquiry into high food prices, Jimmy felt that he was listening to a party-political presentation on behalf of the government, rather than a communique in support of the striking workers. Jimmy knew — and probably so did everyone in the crowd — that it was sheer incompetence on the part of the government to have horded vast stores of food that they were unwilling to release at prices less than they had paid during the war. It was this action of the government that had led to inflated food prices, profiteering and harmful scarcities, especially for the poor.

In any case, lots of this material was ancient history to most of the strikers. The type of thing that they wanted to know was what the national leadership intended to do to sustain the present strike. Thus, a growing restlessness surged through the crowd again. There was erratic and desultory slow clapping. In addition, some people shouted ironic comments and others heckled; each shout emboldened others to join in and to shout louder.

Jimmy breathed a sigh of relief when Doug had finally finished. A ripple of polite applause greeted the conclusion of his statement. Jimmy took over the meeting without delay, thanking Doug for his attendance. He was thinking over his dilemma. Should he tell the meeting that troops were waiting in Pitt Square and risk spreading panic in Town Hall Square among the participants? Or should he ignore the troops' presence and take the criticism in the fullness of time that he should have shared it with the crowd? He tried to put the matter to the back of his mind.

Going straight to the heart of the dispute, Jimmy spoke with a power and fluency that seemed inspirational to those who heard them. With no hint of compromise in his voice or in his heart, he asserted categorically that the workers would never accept the mill owners' strategy to make them take a ten per cent reduction in wages for the same hours. It was simply unjust and unacceptable. In any case, with strong inflation, lots of families were already on the bread line. This elicited a generally approving responsive applause from most of the crowd.

Next, he addressed the workers in the crowd directly, asking for their backing of the Union's position. If they were convinced by that stance, he encouraged them to indicate it by raising their hands when requested. He seemed to have inspired the crowd as nearly everyone in the square voted for his proposal, some also shouting their support.

Then, he turned to the issue of the demonstration. Having drawn the crowd onto his side, he emphasised the peaceful nature of the protest. He underlined the fact that all participants in the strike were taking part freely and voluntarily. There was neither compulsion nor intimidation. 'Was that not what we all fought for? Was it not for such freedom that our comrades from the mills and workshops of the town gave their blood and their lives?'

This approach galvanised the crowd and there were enthusiastic cheers and applause.

He continued. 'In memory of our fallen loved ones, I ask each of you to comport yourselves with decorum this day. That will be our monument to that hard fought war: that we used the freedom gained by the blood of our fallen Pals peacefully and effectively and to its full extent. We used it to defend the basic entitlement of the workers to a decent wage and working conditions, and for justice. The public is on our side. Has not the Labour group of MPs already warned the government about the deteriorating industrial situation and the need to concede reasonable demands by responsible organisations, such as the Trade Unions? United fellow workers we can win this dispute.'

At that point, the last of the march, including Bert and his group, were entering the square, followed incongruously by a swiftly moving tram. Bert and his group seemed to be in jovial humour and, in the absence of an accompanying band, they were singing repetitive, rousing choruses of 'Pack up your Troubles'. In spite of the fervours of their singing, they spotted the tram when they were on the fringes of the crowd and were thus able to quickly scatter out of its path — some others did not.

Tramlines converged in the square from three sides, including some complicated junctions. It had been assumed that there would be no tramcars moving through the square during the demonstration, as they had all been halted as part of the arrangements with the tram company, so some of the crowd were standing on the tracks. When they grasped the danger of the rapidly approaching vehicle, the crowd scattered like fallen leaves. Because they were so densely packed, however, they could not move as rapidly as Bert and his group could.

The word went out that it was a runaway tram, which further added to the panic among the crowd. Afterwards, people reported that the driver seemed as if he were unaware of the large crowd standing in the vehicle's path. Some recalled that the driver seemed to be travelling at a reckless speed, considering the mass of writhing humanity in front of him.

Part of the crowd was struggling to get clear and others were being shunted out of the way. Desperate efforts were made to move the women and children. In the process, some people were inadvertently jostled into the path of the tram, while further away on the fringes of the crowd others hooted and jeered, not recognising the reason for the movement of the crowd.

Harry had been nominated as one of the stewards. Jimmy had nominated him more out of friendship than in the expectation that he would make a major contribution. Ben had opposed the nomination by dint of Harry's disability. Jimmy had insisted and he had succeeded.

Fully absorbed in his role of the good Union steward and unmindful of his own safety, Harry was now ushering a small group of women and children out of the way of the rapidly approaching tram, calling on the men to let them through. His eye was still half closed after the incident at the mill, and his clubfoot was making it difficult for him to move swiftly. To the consternation of those nearest him in the crowd, Harry slipped on the oily wooden sets between the metal rails.

Afterwards, there was speculation as to what exactly had set off the accident. Some people speculated that it was aggravation, even perhaps downright malice, on the part of the driver who was unsympathetic to the march and its aims. Some deemed it the result of a simple miscalculation of the driver's speed. Some people said that Harry's slipping was down to the earlier morning mist that had settled damp on the tracks, combined with his impaired mobility. An alternative theory was that the accident was the result of someone spilling liquid on the track. A few asked if it was simply the result of a miscalculation on Harry's part because of the impaired vision of his damaged eye. Perhaps his handicap simply prevented him from seeing the proximity of the tram until the last minute. Maybe his handicap just made it more difficult for him to move speedily out of the way. A few uncharitably asserted, 'Well, he always was a bit gormless, wasn't he?'

Conceivably, it was a combination of some or all these factors. In the event, it ultimately proved difficult to unravel the reasons behind the accident. It was never possible to identify the precise concatenation of circumstances, and the precise reason for the accident was never exactly defined. The coroner's verdict was simply that it was a tragic accident.

But whatever the reason — accompanied by a high-pitched screeching of brakes and loud shrieks of alarm from the crowd — the tram hit Harry a mighty blow as he knelt between the tracks, struggling to pick himself up. He was spread-eagled across the tracks, dazed and immobile though still alive. Under normal circumstances he would have been driven before the slowing tram by the front guard slats, which had been a legally required fixture for years. In that case, he would have been injured, although probably not fatally. However, the guard slats at the front of the tram were loose. That glitch combined with unevenness in the wooden sets between the lines, which snagged some of Harry's clothes, dragged him beneath the wheels. There were screams of horror and revulsion from those in the crowd nearest to the accident and women shielded their children's eyes from the gruesome sight.

His bruised and bloody body was dragged for several yards, leaving a trail of crimson and some body pieces before the tram finally skidded to a juddering and screeching halt. The sight was ghastly. Some members of the crowd retched, others screamed, and others still, invoking higher authority, made a silent prayer.

After the initial shock, the crowd stood dumbfounded like a mass of still-life effigies in a picture gallery ... just for an instant. In the blink of an eye the mood was transformed and the passions of the crowd nearest the incident immediately became inflamed. Some sought a scapegoat for the tragedy. Several of the more militant strikers mounted the tram's front platform and, with curses and loud swearing, began to assault the driver. The driver fell under a rain of blows by the side of his controls, and two of the strikers tried to drag him out onto the road.

From his vantage point on the platform, Jimmy watched the events unfold with a sense of horror though he was impotent to get to the driver through the tight ranks of the crowd. In any case, much to Jimmy's amazement, Bert and his mates, who were at this time nearest to the tram, moved in to rescue the driver. It was typical of the simple decency of the man, political radical though he was, that he would not have supported such an attack on one of his fellow workers.

Bert and his comrades pulled the other workers away and dragged the dazed driver back to the tram and onto the front platform where two of them stood guard to make sure that no further members of the crowd could attack him. Bert helped the driver to reverse the tram so that Harry's body could be recovered, while some other members of his political group extricated Harry from the tracks. Bert then hopped down and called to people to move back and give them some room. Improvised wound dressings were assembled and a message was sent for an ambulance right away.

After the tram had been reversed to free Harry, his mutilated and blooded body was pulled out. It was apparent that he was in a terrible state, perhaps already dead. His head lolled unmoving on his chest and there were no signs of life. Blood was pouring from open wounds on his limbs and body onto the greasy black stone cobbles. Children were swiftly ushered away from the gory scene, and a group of policemen pushed their way imperiously through the crowd from the periphery of the square to take charge, notebooks at the ready.

With a sense of visceral horror, Jimmy stood rooted to the spot, aghast at the speed with which the tragedy had unfolded. He just could not believe his eyes. He was in shock. What should he do now? Go to the assistance of Harry and desert the platform? Or put the finishing touches to the meeting and draw it to a well ordered close? Should he, could he, jeopardise the demonstration that so far had proceeded so peacefully and successfully? All the people towards to front of the crowd were looking at him expectantly, unaware of what had happened.

Once again, he had to pose the question of where his duty lay. He knew now that the best that he could do for Harry was to bring the meeting to a decorous conclusion. That was what Harry would want him to do, he persuaded himself. He hoped that poor Harry would understand, although he knew in his heart that poor Harry was now far beyond understanding.

Chapter Twenty-Five

Harry's funeral took place at the bleak communal cemetery atop the hill on the outskirts of Ryaton. It was a miserable autumn afternoon, and when Kitty and Jimmy returned home they were both thoroughly drenched. They had stood in the rain at the burial, and afterwards waiting for more than an hour for the arrival of transport after the closure of the proceedings. They were both feeling in pretty low spirits.

As Kitty opened the door, the air from the house that greeted them was cold and unwelcoming. To save what little fuel they had in the cellar, they had allowed the residue ashes to extinguish in their absence. The damp-smelling atmosphere in the house made their depression all the worse.

Kitty noticed a small letter on the doormat in front of her. Though the address was correct, it was not addressed to anyone and was stamped 'Essington'.

'There's a letter here from Essington, Jimmy. I think it's for you.'

Fearing the worst, Jimmy immediately froze. For a moment he was overwhelmed by great apprehension about what it might contain, until he received reassurance from Kitty.

'It's hand-written. It's most probably from Kate. If I'm not mistaken, it's her handwriting. Always so perfect.'

It didn't seem like an official letter. In renewed excitement, mixed with relief, he fumbled to open the letter. 'I'm all thumbs, Kitty. I can scarcely open this letter.' From the envelope he took out one sheet of paper folded in four, on which was a brief note from Kate.

'My love. I thought of you last night and felt that I was rather hard on you the other day when you kindly took the trouble to come and visit me at the sanatorium. So I wrote you a little poem. I know it's not very good and I hope you don't think it's silly. You see from time to time we can express things through poetry, or music for that matter, that we find difficult to voice in prose. Anyway, if you do find it trite, you can always throw it away. It was lovely to see you. Come again before long to see me. Love you always, Kate.'

Jimmy turned the letter over and found two stanzas, written in her beautiful board school slanting handwriting.

For my Love
And when you reach a grand old age
And life has come to its final stage
Remember then what I said to you
True love is found by only a few

Do not lament when I'm not there
Just let my love banish your care
You were fortunate for in your heart
You found true love that will never part.

Jimmy was profoundly affected by the sentiment of the letter and the poem. He sat down by the side of the hearth where Kitty was preparing tinder and read its brief content again and again, glancing aside from time to time at the growing sparks and flames. He felt like pouring his feelings out to Kitty. In spite of their closeness, however, he realised that their bond was not of that nature.

At last, with a strange sensation of pain and joy, he took the letter, replaced it in the envelope and folded it several times so that it fit into his waistcoat match pocket nearest to his heart.

'What did Kate have to say then? How is she?'

'The fresh air seems to be doing her good and I'm more reassured and optimistic now.'

'She's a wonderful woman. You're really blessed, you know.'

'Yes, she's a remarkable … an enigmatic woman. And I miss her greatly. In fact, I can't wait for my next visit to see her at the sanatorium.'

'Yes, I know. She's a woman of great imagination and one who can bear misfortune with great dignity. You know, Jimmy, occasionally love can thrive on separation. Absence makes the heart grow fonder, as they say.'

He paused in silence; neither of them wished to pursue the conversation further. Some minutes later it was Kitty who, feeling the absence of communication becoming oppressive, broke the silence. 'Would you like a cup of tea, love?'

'No thanks, Kitty.' He slumped back into the depths of his gutted old armchair at the side of the range. 'Not for the moment.'

Feeling his pain, Kitty tried to comfort him. 'Would you like me to pop up the snicket to Mrs Wray's off-licence and get you a jug of beer, love?'

'No thanks, Kitty. Anyway, they don't have any. There's still quite a dearth of beer, even in the pubs. And the off-licence shops come last in the queue.'

They continued to render each other mute company while Kitty busied herself lighting the fire with scraps from the tinderbox and what little coal they had left at the side of the range. It took quite a while for the fire to draw sufficiently, during which time each left the other to their silent contemplation.

Finally, Jimmy said, 'You know, Kitty, it was worse than losing a mate in the trenches. Then, you expected people to cop it. Everyone's life was constantly on the line and death was all around you. With Harry it was just a bloody stupid accident. It was just so bloody stupid for it to occur at all.'

'Harry was a good friend to you, Jimmy. And you know, he was tickled to death ... I mean, he was tickled pink by your decision to include him in your Union work. He thought the world of you, you know.'

'Yes, and of you too, Kitty.'

'Yes, I shall miss him. That chummy knock on the door and the tousled head appearing.'

'In spite of his handicap — and he was often taunted about it at work — he was always cheerful and optimistic. He was a lesson to all of us. You know there's none can be as cruel as your own mates, and they used to rib him something awful.'

'Yes, though sometimes it's not intended. In their case, it was always playful and never meant to hurt.'

'No, though it did nonetheless.'

After their rather languid exchange, there followed a further uncomfortable break in the conversation, neither knowing what further words needed to be spoken.

'That was a lovely ceremony,' Kitty said.

'Yes, the minister hit just the right note, didn't he?'

'And there were some lovely flowers too.'

'And the hymns were well chosen.'

'You know "Abide with me" always makes me cry.'

'Well, the large congregation sang with great gusto,' Jimmy added. 'I was amazed at the number of people who were there. I presume the publicity in the local paper about the accident helped. I like singing along with the hymns, though I don't believe in their words. Some of them are downright crass. And the singing … well.'

'The Methodists were always good singers.'

'Yes, and the minister gave a nice sermon. The Methodists were always good preachers, as well as singers. Reverend Matthews had obviously spent some time researching it. I felt that I didn't know Harry as well as I had always considered. A pity Kate could not have been there.'

'Well, she's just too ill to travel,' Kitty asserted. 'And I don't think the doctors would have allowed her. Something about the risk of infection to others, I dare say. Though I surmised that she was past the infectious stage.'

By now the fire was blazing and generating a modest heat; the steam was rising from their damp clothing, pervading the atmosphere with a rather heavy, sweaty stench.

Kitty's comment about Kate reminded Jimmy of something important he needed to ask his sister. He had been

384

remiss in not broaching it before. He had been so preoccupied with the march and afterwards with Harry's accident. Hoping to loosen up the atmosphere between them, he requested a drink.

'I think that I'll have that cup of tea, Kitty, if it's still on offer. I assume the embers are hot enough to boil the kettle.'

'Yes, good idea. I could do with a cup myself.' She rose from the armchair and went into the cellar-head scullery.

By the time Kitty had filled the soot-blackened kettle and returned to place it in the feeble embers of the range fire, he had made his decision. It was now or never to share with Kitty an issue that had been occupying him. He knew that it could go either way, for Kitty treasured her independence and she knew her own mind — she expressed it pretty frankly besides, as he knew to his cost on several occasions. He waited until she had placed the kettle securely on the fire and then, as she sat down, he spoke with a frankness not mustered since he had returned from the Front.

'Kitty. You know these past few months have been difficult for me. In actual fact, I have not been myself at all. But since going to see Kate, and especially now with Harry's death, I have begun to treasure the life that I have been given and to see things in a more realistic way. I am privileged to have been spared and I am determined to use my life to do some good, to make a difference to peoples' lives. I have begun identifying what my priorities should be for the future and how I can make best use of what talent I have.'

Kitty had no idea what he was going to share with her, although the fact that he had begun to identify his priorities for the future pleased her immensely.

'Well, not before time, Jimmy. You have been a bit of a challenge these past few months since you came home, you know.'

'You can say that again. I do realise that it's not been easy for you.'

'No, not really. But let's hope that is in the past now. In any case, when you love someone as I love you …' She tweaked his cheek hard, her radiant smile expressing both forgiveness and encouragement. 'Well, you know what I mean.'

'Yes, I do. And thanks. But, I sense that I'm more able to come to terms with myself now. I have taken your advice and begun to put all that behind me and to look to the future for your sake, my sake and for Kate's.'

'I'm absolutely delighted to hear it. Is there anything that I can help with?'

'You've done so much already, that I am loath to ask for more.'

'Ask away!'

'Well, I took to heart your comments about the way I treated Kate before she was taken into hospital and, well, when I went to see her … well, before I went to see her, I made the decision that I was going to … well, ask her to marry me.'

'Not before time either,' Kitty smiled sympathetically. 'But please remember that Kate is an invalid now. I don't like you to hear this, but even if she recovers — and it's a big if — well, she will probably always be …'

'Yes, I know. An invalid. Nevertheless I owe it to her.'

'I hope that you didn't ask her to marry you out of pity. I know Kate well enough to recognise that she would not wish that. She would feel humiliated.'

'No, of course not. I love her very dearly. Anyway, I took my medals to the Anchor Fent shop and pawned them. I didn't get a great deal for them from old Berkowitz. He contended that ready cash was in heavy demand and short supply, and there were medals galore on the market. And I trust him. There are lots of old soldiers fallen on hard times who are attempting to pawn their medals at the moment'

'I am not surprised that you didn't get much for them. That's why I always resisted your suggestion that I take them and pawn them.'

'Well, I got sufficient to buy that ring that Kate liked. I took it with me the last time I visited her. I asked her to put it on.'

'What did she say?'

Kitty knew Kate well. Her conviction was that women have to take the driver's seat in their own emancipation. At one stage, Kitty knew that Kate had considered marriage and all its trappings as a way of enslaving women. She considered the ring as a symbolic expression of the bondage of woman to man, which she abhorred. On the other hand, while she was still an enthusiastic advocate of women's rights, four years of war and separation had mellowed her attitude somewhat and renewed her ambition for their romance to flower.

'Well, she refused.'

'That's Kate. I always expected that she would do so in her existing condition. She would never wish to be a burden on you when she is so sick, perhaps terminally ill, even though she loves you dearly.'

Kitty wanted Jimmy to try to appreciate a woman's viewpoint. Could she help him to recognise that women had their own wishes and their own sense of responsibility? They were not just chattels to be traded and secured with a ring. How could she help him to see that the war had not just changed him? It had changed women too?

'So, what are you going to do now?'

'She confirmed that she still loves me. And I love her so very much as well. I did not know how much until she went into hospital. When I saw her there, she was so frail and yet so beautiful.'

'And?'

'I know that I have been a fool since I came home. I could have picked up my life where I left it on my return. Somehow I needed time … I couldn't come to terms … well, my experiences in the war …'

'Jimmy, you cannot expect the world to stop while you get off and make a decision.'

'Well, I am determined to marry her. I love her, and I shall wait for her for as long as it takes. I have told her so. After all, she waited for me for four long years.'

'So, she is not to have any voice in the matter, then?'

'You know, I don't intend it that way, Kitty. I just … I don't know how to put it into words. I feel like I have taken

388

my first steps on a long journey, but I can't see how to complete it.'

'Don't try, Jimmy. I think I can feel your agony.' Kitty clasped his calloused hands and held them between hers. She could see that he was not thus far fully mentally healed. Indeed, would he ever be? He was still hurting. Then again at least he was thinking constructively of the future now. She could not afford to dampen these signs of a positive movement in his attitude. 'I sense what you are battling to express. I can never fully share your pain, nor know the depths of the barbarity and human degradation that you have endured. One thing is certain, however. My love will always be there to help and sustain you in your journey back to us. There will always be a place for you, when you do return. One day you'll be whole again.'

'I'll never be truly whole again. The world has changed too much since I went away to war. But Kitty …'

'Yes?'

'There is something I need to ask you.'

'Ask away. I am not doing anything else for the rest of the afternoon. What is it?'

'When I visited Kate at the sanatorium, I asked her to take the ring.'

'Yes, and you said a moment ago that she refused to accept it.'

'Yes, though after that I persevered. I still want to marry her. I still intend to marry her. And, well, we thought of a wedding at that little church in Lynaton.'

'And was Kate happy with that idea?'

'Actually, it was she who originally suggested it. She knows that we have no money and nowhere to live. She may have gone off the idea, although I think she will come round. So I suggested that, when we get married, we could ... well, we could come and live here with you, if you were willing. I acknowledged that it could only be with your acceptance, of course.'

Kitty was dumbfounded that he had suggested it to Kate before he had even proposed it to her. This was just another example of his divorce from reality, of his ongoing disconnectedness from real life and real people. The pain and discomfort that she would have to endure at having the woman she loved living under the same roof as her with her brother. After all, there were only two bedrooms in a tiny house. And such a small scullery. It was a recipe for disaster. Two women working in that same small space and cooking on the same range? How would they organise the laundry which Kitty had always done for him? And the cooking and the housekeeping expenses?

But something held her back from her initial gut feeling that she should advise against any such arrangement. Conceivably, it was her love for both of them that eventually overcame her annoyance and deflated self-pride. If anyone could make it work, surely she and Kate could.

'Jimmy, I am sure that we can make it work. There will be some practical things to tease out, but we can all sit down and do that together.'

'You honestly mean that, Kitty?' His face lit up with a sheer happiness, which gladdened Kitty's heart.

'Well, of course. No problem in principle.'

'I can hardly believe it.' For the first time since his return home, Kitty caught sight of genuine happiness on his face.

'But Jimmy. You realise that even if Kate is well enough to come home, she will be an invalid for a long time, perhaps all her life. You do realise that, don't you?'

'Yes. I've considered that, but I am sure that we can manage. As you point out, sadly, it may not be for long.'

'Well, I am glad that you have faced that possibility.'

'However long it is for, the three of us will be happy in unison, just as we were before the war with Tommy.'

No sooner had he mentioned Tommy's name than he regretted it.

'Yes, we were always a happy group then,' Kitty smiled sadly. 'But as you affirmed a moment ago, the world has changed and we have changed with it. Things can never be the same again. There's no point in wishing that they were.'

Having seemingly exhausted each other, they sat contemplatively by the glow of the embers for a while without communicating. They were just about to pick up their conversation again when there was a knock at the door. Jimmy slowly rose and went to the door, which had already been opened by the visitor. It was Ben Feather; Jimmy invited him in without further ado.

'Would you like a nice cup of tea, Ben?' asked Kitty. 'Why don't you take off your raincoat? You look like a drowned rat.'

'Well, thanks, Kitty. Many thanks. A cup of tea would be welcome. No to your second invitation though. It is so wet that if I take it off, I'll never get it back on again.'

'Well, at least pull up to the hearth here and dry off a little whilst I make the tea.'

'Thanks. I will.'

While Kitty went into the scullery to get some water in the kettle, Ben came closer to the hearth.

'What can I do for you, Ben?' Jimmy asked.

'I've been asked to go round and contact all the members of the Council Executive to notify them that the owners have at last agreed to meet us.'

'Well, "at last" are the right words. As they say, it's better to arrive at the last minute than not to arrive at all!'

'Yes, my view too.'

'That's great news,' Jimmy commented. 'When did they propose this? And what do they suggest should be the agenda?

'Well, their position is that it is only an informal meeting. Conversely, I don't think they would be meeting us if they did not have something up their sleeve. It could even be that they have something rather momentous to propose.'

'Yes, that sounds right,' Jimmy concurred, nodding. 'Certainly, their previous position was always that they would not meet us in any circumstances, until our members went back to work. My view was that such an approach was always a bit of brinkmanship on their part.'

'That's true.'

'I proposed a casual meeting to Arthur Rowbottom early on, when I spoke to him on the telephone and he rejected it out of hand. Exceedingly superior, curt and dismissive he was.'

'Well, I would not be too hard on him. Vic told me that it was at Arthur's behest that the owners rather reluctantly accepted the idea of this meeting.'

'I suppose I always had confidence in Arthur. He's a decent fellow. Always has been straight.'

'I don't think it was entirely out of the milk of human kindness that he and the other owners made the proposal.'

'What do you mean?' Jimmy asked.

'Well, with the bad publicity they have had in the press in this town and nationally, I believe they felt the heavy weight of public opinion.'

'Yes,' Kitty added. 'The local *Observer* had a stinging lead article about the stubbornness and arrogance of the owners and there was an excellent write-up about the Trade Union march and demonstration. I think Ben is right.'

'But, to the best of my knowledge, the coup de grâce was the piece about calling in the army. The local *Observer* stated that our glorious heroes would always be welcome in our town. On the other hand, the newspaper stated emphatically that we don't need them to help us keep law and order. We have an excellent and publically respected police force for that.'

'Yes, that was a big mistake on their part,' Jimmy agreed.

'Well, the thing is, an editorial in the *Observer* has demanded to know who was responsible.'

'But the Chief Constable is not telling, is he?' Kitty asked.

'No, and he never will.'

'They'll have to if there is a judicial investigation,' Kitty suggested.

'There is no case for such an investigation, Kitty,' Ben counselled. 'After all, nothing took place.'

'Yes, though it could so easily have gone the other way. Anyway, what are the other arrangements for the meeting?'

'It is to take place on Monday in the committee room of the Mechanics' Institute. It will get underway at two thirty prompt, so we can run into the evening should the meeting need to be more protracted.'

'Anything else I should know?'

'Yes, there is. Apparently, Arthur has proposed Jacob Berenson as independent chairman of the meeting.'

'Who?' Kitty asked. 'I've never heard of him. Who is he?'

'Jacob Berenson. He's a highly successful business tycoon and the owner of the newly inaugurated motorcar company in town. He's pretty well known in business circles and well versed in industrial deal-making, although he's not in textiles. Never has been.'

'I hope he's not in league with Arthur on this one.'

'I doubt it. And he's not church! He's one of the local Jewish community and a regular at the reformed synagogue. He has cultivated the political powers that be in the town, although to be honest he has never sold out to them. He strongly endorses active citizenship and service to the local community. A man of great integrity who will never cross the moral boundary. That would be my judgement. A good choice.'

'Has Vic agreed?'

'Yes. He also felt it was a good proposition to have someone not involved in the textile industry and not from either side of the dispute,' Ben confirmed. 'And as Jacob is a well-known and respected associate of the town's business community, I gather he has agreed to act in that capacity.'

'Well, that's good enough for me,' Jimmy said. 'I respect Vic's wisdom in these matters.'

'But we must not get our hopes up too much. It is only an informal exploratory meeting to discuss possibilities. We don't know the first thing about the mill owners' strategy, and we don't have a clue what their bottom line is,' Ben cautioned.

'What do you think the prospects for a settlement are?' Jimmy asked.

'That's asking a lot for one meeting, and an exploratory one at that. Well! You never know. Nothing is excluded and nothing is included at this stage. I do hear, informally, that the owners are feeling the financial pressure with standing costs escalating and, of course, no profit. Oh and — by the way and this is hearsay, and off the record — apparently the scab labour recruited for Arthur's mill have been paid off and released. Perhaps that is the first conciliatory gesture from Arthur's side. It sounds a bit like him.'

'Yes, that sounds like good news,' Kitty confirmed.

'And good news was long overdue for us,' Jimmy complained.

'Yes, but now to more pressing matters,' Kitty said.

'And what might those be?'

'Well, the tea is ready,' Kitty smiled and handed a blue-ringed pint pot mug to Ben. 'Three sugars? That's right, isn't it, Ben? Also, that's our best mug, so don't drop it. Let's all keep our fingers crossed for a good outcome to the meeting.'

'Here's to a positive outcome!' proposed Ben, endorsing her sentiment.

Chapter Twenty-Six

'Will the meeting please come to order?'

Jacob Berenson, the rather portly and rubicund middle-aged local luminary, was lifting his hands before him in a gesture to command attention. He was calling the joint meeting of the representatives of the Workers Action Council and the Mill Owners' Association to order in his usual authoritative, suave and benign tone. The meeting was taking place in the great committee room of the Mechanics' Institute. The hubbub of conversation in the room quickly and respectfully subsided. When Jacob was confident that he had everybody's attention, he set out the terms agreed by both parties for the meeting and his own role. He opened up by addressing the assembled members of both sides of the table.

'Most of you in this room know me well, or at least know of me. When Arthur here came to me with the suggestion that I take on the role of independent chairman for this meeting, I have to admit I had great misgivings, not least since I am not of your ilk, if I can put it that way. I'm not a textile man! I am from a newcomer industry, which is quite a contrast to your own, so I was inclined to refuse.'

Jacob bided his time and regarded the group in such a way that each person in the room had the impression that he was addressing them personally. Jimmy could only admire the superb theatre in the combination of delicately understated assertions and gentle, engaging gestures.

Jacob was of course well respected. He was clearly also an accomplished committee man, a skilled politician and someone dedicated to public life and serving his community. In the post-war move from military to industrial production, he had seen the opportunities, quickly expanding his plant and turning it over to civilian car production. He was now reaping the huge benefits of that foresight and astute investment. The reinvigorated middle classes had copious supplies of cash in their pockets. They were thirsting for his streamlined and innovatively designed cars that would give them a new and cherished freedom of movement — not to mention status.

'But as usual Arthur was very persuasive,' Jacob continued. 'As he always is. Lots of you here will have felt the power of his persuasiveness in the work situation, maybe also in his benevolent endeavours for the good of this town and its citizens and in his church activities.' Another breather. 'And so, I accepted … on one condition! Namely, that my good friend, Vic here, should agree on behalf of the striking workers and their Unions.' Vic, patently fragile and subject to frequent and distressing bouts of coughing, tried to appear pleased and managed a momentary reciprocal smile, albeit a weak one.

That's both sides on board, Jimmy thought to himself.

Jacob Berenson's next statement was a masterly coup de théâtre, for Jimmy knew that those on both sides felt profound compassion at Harry's accident and death.

'I would ask members to stand and observe one minute in contemplation of our deceased friend, colleague and fellow worker in the textile industry, Harry Shufflebottom, who perished in a tragic accident last week.'

Jacob oozed sincerity and no one dissented. There was a scraping of chairs as the assembled workers and employers stood in unity and a hush descended on the meeting.

Jacob had set a climate for the rest of the meeting and had ensured that all would respect his chairmanship. *What a*

masterly stroke! This is a man, from whom I must learn,
Jimmy mused.

After the minute's silence, the members of the meeting
resumed their seats and Jacob made a short statement. 'We
all have the privilege and the honour of living and working
in this fine city. True, from time to time we have our troubles
and differences. Any group does. Having said that, I would
add that there is not a man here that I would not trust to help
me if need arose. I know both sides are committed to solving
their differences here today — otherwise they would not be
here. We all know what is wrong and what separates us. We
all know as well what it is that unites us. More of the latter
than the former, I would hold. And, gentlemen, we alone can
solve this problem together. Let's do it. And I haven't got all
afternoon. I have a business to run!'

A passing and gentle wave of amusement arose from both
sides of the table at his final comments. Jacob suggested that
both sides put forward their case in turn without interruption
at this stage. From the chair, he proposed that the employers
should go first. Neither Vic, as leader of the workers, nor
anyone else on the Trade Union side demurred.

Arthur Rowbottom stood up to put the employers' case
very astutely using every aid available to him; oral language,
gesture, humour and facial and bodily expression to assist his
presentation. With a verve, that could not but be admired,
Arthur brushstroked the employers' case, rehearsing the
litany of difficulties that the employers faced in a period of
rapid transformation from war to peace. He itemised the
additional costs of that move, including the post-war
decrease in trade and the uncompetitive nature of production,
as well as the unpredictability of basic costs such as wool
and coal, this latter with recent substantial and harmful
government increases. The world market had not only

contracted. New competitors had also arisen with much lower production costs.

'I want to clarify the employers' thinking. Our basic position is that it is better for more men to have a job at a lower wage, than fewer men to have a job at a higher wage. Those are the hard facts. Those are — and will remain — the basic hard alternatives. There is no question of the employers seeking to economise on the wage bill, as had been unfairly suggested in the local newspaper. In spite of the economic difficulties we face, the quantum of funds for wages will remain the same. The question is how it should be shared: to fewer workers at a higher rate, or to more workers at a lower rate. Our goal, the employers' goal, is to retain jobs out of a sense of responsibility to our loyal workforce and our commitment to the town and its community. The equation between jobs and wages is clear though. Higher wages mean fewer jobs. Lower wages mean more jobs. As I say. That's the equation. Either way, it does not profit the employers. In this spirit, the employers will guarantee all returning soldiers their jobs back. Not a single returning soldier, including those in this room, will be denied their old job back even though it is costing the employers a lot more to employ them than the women those men are replacing.'

Well, the notion of such altruistic munificence on the part of the employers almost had Jimmy laughing. He resisted the temptation, retained his composure and lifted his eyebrows towards Vic as Arthur continued.

'Have not employers such as myself, and my father long before me, always shown our concern for the welfare of the workers and for their advancement besides? Is there not, in this town, a tradition of employers voluntarily investing their own resources in the progress of the town, its inhabitants and its buildings? Does this very building not attest to our generosity towards the workers' advancement?'

The basic thrust of Arthur's case was that the mill owners were acting in a demonstrably responsible manner and, in the final analysis, in the interests of the workers and their families. The case was crystal clear and it was a highly appealing line of reasoning. Arthur was the ideal person to put it forward on the employers' side, for the humanity of the claims was perfectly compatible with Arthur's well-known worldview — one which was certainly not shared by all his fellow employers. It was all very reasonable and detached; the essence of his case was that the mill owners had done what they had to do in the interests of the workers.

Arthur did not use any notes and he did not speak for long. Throughout he sustained a spirited pace in his delivery, putting the arguments logically piece by eloquent piece. His major points were hammered home briefly, on occasion repetitively. Always extremely effectively. His choice of words and phrases spoke directly to the hearts and minds of the workers' side. It was a masterly performance, delivered succinctly by the most appropriate man. The employers had chosen well. Arthur had performed well.

When Arthur sat down, there was a murmur of hushed comment and conversation in the room and some congratulatory remarks from the mill owners. Jacob Berenson allowed that to last for a while, gauging the temper of the meeting and choosing the right moment to intervene and allow time for the other side's case to be presented.

After Arthur's exquisite performance, Jimmy was under no illusions about the mountain the workers' side had to climb and he was glad that, for all his ill-health, their best speaker Vic Noble was presenting their side. His satisfaction was forestalled, however, by another unforeseen event. At that point Vic began coughing violently, his whole body racked with the effort. Blood-stained sputum appeared on his lips and was wiped onto his crumpled grey rag. Clearing his throat, Vic informed the chairman in a wheezy and shaky voice that he felt rather poorly and regretfully would have to leave the meeting.

Arthur was on the point of proposing an adjournment of the meeting. Vic anticipated the danger, however, and turned plaintively to Jimmy. 'Jimmy, lad, I'm jiggered. I can't carry on. I'm sorry to drop you in it like this. Would you take over and put our case for the workers' side. Do your best for the old Pals.'

Jimmy was bemused because he had no experience of taking over the conduct of such important negotiations. Moreover, he was conscious that he had promised himself that he would visit Kate in the sanatorium to pledge his offer of marriage once more. He was about to protest, when Vic interrupted. 'I know you can do it. You're the only one who can do this for the workers. You show them, lad.'

'I will, Vic, though …' Jimmy was so worried about the likely cost of a break in the presentation of the workers' case that he chose to rise to the challenge. He could visit Kate the following day if the meeting went on too late. 'Okay, I'll do it. But you take care of yourself, Vic. We need you if we're going to win this one.'

As on the battlefields of France, fate had picked him out. First for survival and now for this.

Arthur, with humane compassion born of his intense religious conviction, commented across the table, 'Vic, you look terrible. You should get home straightaway and get to bed. Have your wife call the doctor at once. We'll carry on here without you. I am sure that Jimmy here is well versed in your case and will capably advance the case for the workers' interests.'

402

There was a moment of agonising silence before Arthur's comment was greeted by an audible murmur of assent from both sides of the table. Vic replied weakly, 'Thanks Arthur, and thanks Jimmy. I have every confidence in you both.'

'My chauffeur is waiting downstairs in the car. He can drive you home,' Arthur proposed. 'You are in no fit state to walk, let alone to take public transport. Just tell my driver that it is in order, Ben. There is no problem.'

'Thanks very much,' Vic replied, graciously accepting through necessity an offer that, being a proud man, he would otherwise have refused. 'That is kind and I shall not forget it.' To Jimmy he added, 'Go for it, son. You are my deputy and you have my full confidence.'

Ben assisted Vic to the doors and out of the room to the top of the sweeping mahogany staircase.

That brief dialogue seemed to support the co-operative atmosphere in the room from a potential confrontation to one of a recognition of a mutual interest with complementary objectives.

'I do hope it's just a severe bout of cold and not the appalling flu or worse,' Jacob exclaimed, hinting at the much feared tuberculosis. Finally, he turned his gaze back to the meeting and addressed Jimmy directly. 'If I grasp the situation correctly, Vic has asked you to put forward the case for the workers.'

'Yes, that's so,' Jimmy responded weakly through a dried mouth, feeling a million butterflies in the pit of his stomach.

'It seems to me that we should give Jimmy here some time to prepare his statement. That would only be fair, given

Vic's unfortunate indisposition and his need to retire from the meeting. Would the Union side like an adjournment of maybe half an hour? Or more if you wish? I take it the employers' side would not have any objection?'

'No, certainly not. Absolutely not,' Arthur confirmed. And addressing Jimmy directly, he added, 'Take your time.'

'What do you think? Would you like an adjournment?' Jacob asked.

Jimmy was gratified, although he hesitated in spite of that feeling. He recalled his discussions with Kate and Kitty and he recognised that he was at a crossroads. If he failed this test, he was finished. He would never get back. He had to do it now or he would never do it.

An adjournment would not serve the strikers' interests, as it risked tipping the meeting into the next working day, which meant more lost wages. And Jimmy had rehearsed the Union's position, when he outlined the case in his speech the previous weekend in Town Hall Square. He would decline Jacob's suggestion.

Impelled by a profound inner fortitude and reinforced by a steely determination, he therefore determined to cross the Rubicon. He scanned his memory to glean from the economic books they had studied at the WEA classes — Lenin, Pigou and, more recently, Marshall — but his search was in vain.

He fumbled with the ring in his pocket. *What would Kate advise? No doubt she would prefer me to be decisive. She would say I am a born leader. Seize the opportunity and fight to win. You have the words. Put the case. Your Pals are relying on you.* He would not let his pals down. He owed it as much to his dead Pals as to his surviving ones.

'Well, firstly, thank you for your compassionate response to Vic's illness and for your considerate and helpful proposal, Jacob. My thanks also to Arthur for his typically humane and sympathetic stance on the crisis. And my thanks besides to all members of the employers' side for their accord as expressed by Arthur on their behalf.'

Jimmy's comments attracted some mutterings of 'Hear, hear!' from both sides of the table, which obviously pleased the Chairman and Arthur. Both smiled in agreement. 'Which only goes to show the atmosphere of responsibility and goodwill in which this meeting is being conducted. It only serves to reinforce my philosophy that we all live under the same sky. We all have an interest in the wellbeing of our industry and the wonderful city in which we live. Therefore, I am convinced we shall have a positive outcome to our deliberations this day. The essence of that outcome will have to be compromise on the part of all sides, the Unions as much as the employers and owners.'

He halted and, for a while, allowed the silence to speak for him: a ploy he had learned on observation of Jacob's performance earlier in the meeting.

'Mr Chairman, for that reason, I would suggest that we proceed without further delay. To assemble all parties again in the near future will be immensely difficult, if not impossible. This is a dispute, the speedy resolution of which is in the interests of our joint community. The strike must not be allowed to run on. This dispute should be settled quickly in the interest of a great industry, a great community, a great town and all its people.'

'Very well. If that is what the Union side wishes, we shall proceed without delay. And maybe I shall be home in time for dinner after all! Jimmy, you have the floor.'

Jimmy recognised the strength of the case against him and the powerful — even cunning — way in which Arthur had presented his argument. He needed to pick up on the major themes of Arthur's presentation, mutuality and responsibility, and the undoubted economic predicament of the textile industry, and to use them to the workers' advantage.

He opened his address by discussing the human case against a decision to reduce wage rates that had been negotiated during a time of shared hardship. With the increase in prices of basic food that had taken place this year, and not least the six pounds a ton on coal increase approved by the government in July, the workers simply could not live with a cut in wages.

Moreover, he argued, there had been no discussion and no consultation concerning the employers' proposal. What would the mill owners think if someone, with whom they had made an agreement and concluded a binding contract, suddenly repudiated it? The employers' side had already admitted that the quantum of wages would remain the same, yet there are acknowledged savings through the fact that sadly not all the workers returned from the Front. How could those two factors be reconciled? He tried to recall as much information as possible from the economics books he had read in the local library.

'Experience shows that if you demotivate your workers, productivity falls, unit costs increase and profits fall. What more effective way of demotivating your workers could you conjure up than to unnecessarily break a previous promise and shrink their income? Gentlemen, you are cutting your financial nose off to spite your economic face. Reducing wages by ten per cent could engender a disproportionate reduction of more than ten per cent, maybe substantially more, in productivity and therefore a substantial increase in unit labour costs and a fall in profits. Gentlemen, this proposal is not even in your own best economic and commercial interests,' he repeated.

'Surely if there are real difficulties, each party has a responsibility to engage with the other so that they can jointly resolve them. As today has already shown, there is nothing that we cannot solve if we do it jointly. Think seriously about the alternatives to the proposal that you are seeking to enforce, which is not even in your own interests.'

Then Jimmy addressed the gap he had perceived in the case presented by Arthur. Of course, there were ups and down in any business, he acknowledged. Trade was improving, however, and as more and more industry returned to peacetime production, demand would automatically increase. Moreover, continuity was essential to keep the workforce up-to-date in the skills and knowledge necessary for increased production. Demotivated workers were also more likely to increase the rate of absenteeism and the costs of production.

He reiterated that a good home market was an essential base for the export market. Reducing the purchasing power of the workforce would inhibit the demand for the goods the mills were producing in the local community. A slump in demand would entail inevitable reductions in supply, in turn encompassing a reduction in the workforce, which is what the employers asserted they did not want.

'Let the mill owners show that their protestations of concern for the welfare of their workers and their town are not solely idle words. Let them show that they are aware of the human suffering and despair that currently stalks our streets. Let them demonstrate that they welcome the idea that this industry is the product of shared decision-making and not unilateral action. Autocratic action only leads to oppression and that is in no party's interest. Let them demonstrate that, just as they expect their workers to keep their word, they also have to honour their word. Let them stick to their stated wish to ensure the full quantum of wages as before. Let them act in their own best interests — interests which they actually share with their workers and their community.'

He halted briefly, scanning the occupants of the room, then switched his gaze to Arthur's fully composed face.

'The workers' side appreciates the well-stated difficulties that the owners are facing. We sympathise and want to assist them in resolving those difficulties. We're not wreckers. Rather we have a proposal that we are persuaded will help both sides. It is a win-win strategy. Given that the employers are willing to uphold the total quantum of wages, we have a suggestion for the return of all workers at the same level as before. That return would be supported by an incentive mechanism that will enable the employers to become more competitive, the workers more productive and the industry more profitable. We suggest the inception of a piecework system, which will partially or wholly link individual wages to productivity and total wages to profit.'

He took a fleeting break.

'The profits of increased productivity would be shared between workers and employers, as would the risk of a downturn. The tasks accomplished by an individual worker would be certificated by a system of work sheets. And so that the new system would not involve any additional cost, the sheets would be drawn up weekly by a Union representative and presented to management for authentication and approval. This will give every worker a stake in the efficiency of his mill. The fine print of this new scheme can be worked out in detail by a joint working party. But, in the interim, all workers previously employed at a mill will return to work tomorrow at their previous rate of pay. There will be no reductions and the new scheme will commence as soon as possible. We will marshal worker sentiment to back this scheme and guarantee its honest adherence by workers. We will help to motivate the workers. In their own best interests, will you all do the same?'

As he sat down, other members on the workers' side expressed their amazement at what he had pulled out of the hat. 'Well done, Jimmy!' some called out to him.

Wishing to expedite the business of the meeting and not to lose the apparent momentum, the chairman proposed a half hour adjournment for discussion and informal meetings among and between the members of each side. This was accepted by all, and both parties retired to separate rooms.

Hardly had the members of the workers' team finished congratulating him in their allocated room and surmising what the owner's reply would be, when there was knock on the door and Arthur Rowbottom entered. At Jimmy's invitation he sat down at the table and spoke, directly to him and within earshot of the whole group.

'Jimmy, I have a proposal to make to you from the employers' side that I consider picks up on the workers' own proposal and represents something satisfactory to both sides.'

Although incredulous that the owners could have come up with a proposal in such a brief time, Jimmy invited him to address the group. 'Fire away!'

'Thanks. Well, we mill owners have considered our position and we have recognised the force of your argument about both sides needing to co-operate in these difficult times. "Win-win" as you put it, Jimmy. After all, that's what we did so successfully during the war. Let's sink our differences in the common interest, eh?'

Jimmy nodded politely and he remained silent.

Arthur persevered. 'Off the record, I am personally sorry that the proposal for a reduction in wages was presented in the way it was. Let's be honest, just among the few of us here. It could have been seen as a bit of an ultimatum. It was never intended in that way, though. Similarly, I'm saddened by the scuffles with the police and the proposal to bring in the troops. That was neither our doing nor intention. But anyway, we're talking about a mutually satisfactory industrial relationship here, which we hope will endure for years to the benefit of both parties. Not just a temporary fix for either party. So, in the new spirit of co-operation, we are willing to reduce our request for a reduction in wages to five per cent without conditions. We take your argument that there are fewer workers. But that alone will not reduce the additional cost to the mill owners of the sixty thousand pounds a week in wages. We shall, however, have to seek to make savings elsewhere rather than in wages. Further, we shall guarantee to take all workers back, except of course those that have been convicted of a criminal offence or are so charged until any charge is dismissed. We are dubious about the Union proposal for a piecework system. We don't think it can yield the necessary economies or profits claimed for it and the associated bureaucracy will cost more.' Arthur paused before continuing.

'However, we are willing to examine it and our side will take part in a joint working party to scrutinise its feasibility and, if it can be shown to have potential, to design, implement and monitor a pilot piecework system proposed by the Unions aimed at generating greater productivity in our mills. We can test it out at first in my mill and if it proves as financially beneficial as you claim, Jimmy, we shall implement it at the other mills, subject to the approval of the owners of course. At each mill where it is shown to yield increased productivity and profits, the owners will pay the other five per cent retrospectively to the date of return. We are conscious that idle mills make no profit and continue to be a financial drain, and we accept the Union guarantee of a full, and enthusiastic, return to work from tomorrow if we can conclude a mutually satisfactory settlement today. One last thing. Apart from any bonus from the piecework scheme, the whole package will be bound by a two-year wage freeze. What do you say? That's fair and reasonable, isn't it?'

Jimmy was askance at the proposal for a two year wage moratorium. He had not expected anything like this and the Union hadn't discussed the possibility of such a proposal from the owners. He sidestepped giving an immediate reply to Arthur's proposal, wanting to consult the other members of his team first. Distrustfully, he considered that the present offer could be a negotiating ploy by the employers, feeling under pressure from a struggle for public opinion that they realised they were losing — or may have already lost.

'Thank you for your proposal, Arthur. We greatly appreciate the positive movement on the part of the mill owners and their recognition of the need for workers and employers to collaborate.' He stared Arthur directly in the face and smiled. 'We shall discuss it and come back to you promptly.'

'Thanks. And I hope that you will give the offer, which is a fair one, your earnest consideration. My colleagues took a lot of persuading to agree to this proposal. Put another way, I do not think the owners will go further than they have already. Now it is the turn of the Unions to show that they will be flexible likewise.'

411

Chapter Twenty-Seven

Quick as lightening after Arthur's departure, a tumultuous conversation erupted in the room.

'Reject it out of hand,' Bert urged emphatically. 'Stick out for the full amount and no wage freeze. They're impossible these capitalists. A wage freeze at a time of rapid inflation? We would be crazy to accept. After what they have done, I wouldn't give you tuppence for the word of these bourgeois reactionaries. Further proof, if proof were needed, of the bloody treachery and insidious collusion of the upper crust. Just think how they sent troops to Russia to rob the workers of the fruits of their revolution, even before the war on the western front had finished. All or nothing is what we want. The workers have to speak with one voice and fight to win, not to compromise.' He ended by banging the table with his fist.

'On that basis we might end up with nothing,' Ben commented. For him it was crucial to counter Bert's wild fulminations and get the members of the meeting on the track of sanity. 'In the spirit of compromise and for the benefit of our workers, their families and this town, I propose that we do all we can to pare away at the current offer. The owners have already made a U-turn on the ten per cent. I sense that there is further room for shaving down some aspects of their proposal before we conclude a final resolution. We may not get all that we want, but let's go for a little more. We've already made more progress than I reckoned was possible. After all, two weeks ago, after the fiasco at the mill, we appeared to be staring surrender and apocalypse in the face.'

Jimmy pondered Arthur's position and the opinions of his two colleagues: reject the offer totally or accept the compromise with further tweaking. Jimmy's feeling was that a realistic solution was tantalisingly close. He debated the matter in great detail, weighing up the different options.

There was still a chance to have the whole ten per cent rescinded now, rather than five per cent now and five per cent at a future date. And they might be able to bring down the duration of the wage freeze to twelve months subject to earlier review if the piecework scheme could show its worth quickly. If they did not make the effort, they would not get anything further.

'Let's take some time to think about this one,' Jimmy said. 'If you were the mill owners, would you make your final offer straightaway? No. I don't think so. We have a choice to negotiate further. We should push for our full wage, with no reduction, and a one-year freeze subject to preliminary joint review of productivity and profits after six months. We have nothing to lose by giving it a go. What do you comrades think?'

'You're right,' Ben agreed. 'I think that they are bluffing, aiming to save face, and I suggest that we call their bluff. But gently and politely. We don't want to rub their faces in it. I propose that we tell them that we are grateful for their consideration and for their revised offer. Then we add that to restore the harmonious working relationship, which unfortunately and to our great regret has been damaged by their unilateral action, only a reversion to the wage status quo will be effective and acceptable. Given that that is conceded, we will agree to a one-year wage freeze subject to review after six months in the light of the piecework scheme and the rate of inflation. To avoid any suggestion of either side having capitulated, the agreement will be announced to the press by a joint statement. That's what I propose.'

'What do you think of Ben's proposal?' Jimmy addressed the rest of the group.

413

There were murmurs of agreement from most members of the workers' team.

'It's not ideal,' Bert said. 'But on balance, and in fairness to you, I dare say what you are suggesting is about the best we shall get. I don't like the idea of a wage freeze and neither will the men. If we succeed, you'll need your gift of the gab to sell it. Ultimately though I am in accord with Ben. We have to give them something to save face.'

Jimmy counselled caution. 'If we want higher wages in the future, we have to make sure that this agreement achieves greater productivity, and profits of course. But one victory at a time, eh lads? Are we all of the same view? Do we need a formal vote?'

Bert intervened again. 'But if they don't agree to give us the full amount as before …?'

'Look, Bert, I cannot guarantee anything. All I can do is to set out the goal. And I support Ben's idea that we propose a joint statement in the local newspaper this evening, emphasising the flexibility of both sides and the cordial spirit in which the negotiations have been conducted and the ground-breaking settlement concluded. Apart from that, each side should undertake not to give separate briefings or interviews about this pioneering settlement.'

Again, there was a chorus of 'Agreed!'

'About the workers who have been taken into custody,' Bert continued. 'I believe that all must be given their jobs back. If not, none of us should go back. That's what workers' solidarity means to me. We must not allow the employers to pick off our brothers one by one.'

Jimmy knew that the employers would never accept this proposal and that it could be a potential sticking point in the negotiations, which would deprive the vast majority of workers of the fruits of their protest and strike. Those fruits were now within their grasp and Jimmy had no intention of squandering them for a small number of workers who, of their own accord and against Union policy and instructions, criminally misbehaved.

'I agree with you to a certain extent,' Jimmy said. 'It is crucial not to allow the owners to pick and choose who they take back. We should note, though, that they are not proposing to arbitrarily exclude any worker. I don't think that there will be any problem about all workers being taken back including the Union stewards who were in custody. There is, however, one exception and we are just not in a position to stand out against it.'

'What? An exception to loyalty? Never! All must go back or none. We have a duty to give succour to our fellow workers in their hour of need,' Bert interjected.

It was evident that Bert was not likely to be won over on this issue, so Jimmy decided to soldier on and appeal to his other colleagues, hoping he would be able to muster a majority if it came to a vote.

'As legitimate Unions, we cannot be seen to be flouting the law. Indeed, our explicit Union policy has been to advise all workers that protest and picketing should be peaceful and that those not participating in the dispute must be allowed to go peacefully about their legitimate business. Those men on the lorry broke the law, despite the soft drink company dropping the charges.'

Bert's face was dark as thunder.

'If we were to come out in favour of illegitimate action, we could be taken to court and sued — all of us and the Union as well,' Jimmy continued. 'In that case, there would be no more Union to support the workers. Then what would happen to our families? The employers have an irrefutable case that those who have broken the law, if convicted, cannot be taken back. Anyway, if they are convicted, those workers will not be able to return to work because they will be in the lock-up. Are we arguing that everyone should wait until they come out of jail before returning to work? I don't think so.'

'That would be totally illogical,' Ben agreed.

'I don't think that we should be slithering out of our loyalty to our fellow workers, even those who have allegedly overstepped the mark. That's not what the Union movement should be about,' Bert continued.

'You're right,' Jimmy agreed. 'But what we can do is to win this fight to return at the old rates and politely request that for reasons of compassion, justice and fairness, their families should not be made destitute. We can ask for a rider to the settlement that the women and children of those workers convicted should not be turned out of their tied homes, so long as their families' rent is paid. That would be one of our red lines. On our side, the Union Welfare Committee will, I am sure, assist the families in whatever way is necessary to pay the rent and help them to survive until their menfolk return. We can insist that any worker who is tried and found innocent should be taken back. Would that meet your worries, Bert?'

'I have to admit this about you, Jimmy Kelly: you certainly have the gift of the gab, although I still reject sacrificing these comrades. I strongly believe that we should fight for them. We have a duty to do so. We're supposed to be a Union and that requires that we are all united, no matter

416

what. One for all, all for one. Remember? The workers united will never be defeated!'

Jimmy ignored Bert's well-worn political clichés. If he could persuade his other colleagues, Bert's individual viewpoint could not win out.

There was a prolonged discussion before Ben proposed the motion. It was passed by a wide margin and Jimmy at last received the support of the vast majority of the workers to his proposal. Sadly, a few — including Bert — voted against it. However, the vote endorsed the proposal that should be made to the employers in the reconvened meeting, and the workers' side rose to return to the plenary room.

After the two parties had taken their seats in the committee room, Jimmy requested that the chairman permit him to speak first. Standing behind his chair, he felt greater self-confidence than he had done in the whole of his life. He thanked the employers for the movement in their position. For the reasons he had shared with the workers' group previously, and which he now explained to the employers' group, his side felt that they could not accept the mill owners' proposal without some amendments. The workers' counteroffer could form the basis of a compromise that would satisfy both sides, Jimmy hoped.

He respectfully requested, in the spirit of goodwill that had characterised their meeting so far, that the original wages be restored and all workers taken back. They also proposed that further discussion should be conducted to arrange the implementation of the piecework scheme as jointly and quickly as possible.

The Unions would accept a wage freeze of twelve months from this date, he suggested. Halfway through that year, the situation would be jointly reviewed and, subject to the successful introduction of the piecework scheme and its likely yield of greater productivity, additional bonuses would be paid if merited by the figures. On that basis, all workers would return the next day, including the stewards who had been wrongfully detained. Lastly, they would ask that the families of any of the workers prosecuted for misdemeanours during the strike should not be turned out of their houses provided their rent was paid.

To the surprise of the workers, Arthur almost immediately accepted the counteroffer, with the sole emphasis that those convicted of criminal offences would not be taken back. He promised that their families would not be turned out of their houses for as long as their rent was paid punctually and regularly. He also welcomed the proposal of a joint statement for the press to the effect that this unique agreement had come about through the goodwill and contributions of both parties.

Arthur sought visual endorsement from his colleagues round the table who all nodded their assent. After which, he formally accepted on behalf of the employers.

'As a further rider, so to speak, to this ground-breaking agreement and to be included in the press statement, the employers' side request an early meeting of the Allied Joint Industrial Council to put right any residual matters. In particular, they request a detailed examination of the issue of grades of wages and conditions in the future, and of course the productivity scheme. All of this on condition that the workers return from tomorrow morning — first thing, in full and on time!'

'In the spirit of friendly co-operation that has pervaded these negotiations, the workers' side has no objection whatsoever to the proposal.' Jimmy said. 'We think that the Allied Joint Industrial Council is the place to consider any

418

issues that affect either workers or management and we suggest an early meeting, even as soon as this week. With regards to the return to work we shall bend every sinew to make sure that all workers are aware of their responsibility to return tomorrow. First thing!'

The chairman put the composite proposal to the meeting, and it was carried by a large majority nem con. Not even Bert voted against. All, including those who abstained, pledged commitment to the settlement. With the agreement signed and sealed, the chairman thanked everyone for the admirable spirit with which the meeting had proceeded and congratulated both sides on their flexible negotiations and sensible conduct. He was about to close the meeting when Arthur intervened again.

'Just before we close the meeting, if I could, it seems to me that I should say something for both parties. I should like to express gratitude to our chairman, Mr Jacob Berenson, for the way in which he has chaired this meeting, contributing in great measure to its successful outcome.'

Jimmy quickly added, 'We would certainly support that sentiment and would further ask that it be included in the joint press release.'

As the chairman closed the meeting, there was a general spirit of euphoria in the room. A ritual shaking of hands took place all round amid expressions of goodwill from both sides, before both employers and employees began to depart.

Several of the departing workers came up to Jimmy and congratulated him. Even Bert approached him.

'Well done. You did well. That was a notable performance. Against tough opposition you were a star performer. You pulled it off. You have a great future in the

Trade Union movement, working in the interests of the British working class. Just don't let it go to your head, lad.'

'Well thanks, Bert. That is really generous of you. I hope that we shall be able to collaborate on that project in the future.'

'We shall just have to see. One day, when you are a seasoned performer and we have a workers' soviet, who knows?' Bert smiled roguishly and left the room.

Then Ben, who had been waiting in the background for the conversation to end, approached him and exclaimed, 'Well done! Vic will be proud of you. He clearly left it to the right man. I am only sorry that he was not here to see you in action. I'll report back to him if you wish. Tell him his instinct about you was correct.'

'Thanks, Ben. That would be good. I was stunned when even Bert came up to me and congratulated me on the outcome of the negotiations. He was quite effusive. I could scarcely believe my ears.'

'Oh, that's Bert for you. He's not a bad sort of fellow, you know. In fact, there's a lot of good in him. It's just that, like the rest of us, the war had its effects on him, some good and some bad. During his time in the army he was on punishment several times, and that may have had its influence in radicalising him too. Basically, though, he's a decent chap.'

'Let's see what comes to pass in Russia. We might already be on the road to something similar here in Britain. Who knows?'

'Well, that will have to be for the fickle judge of history to conclude. Apparently this chap Lenin is quite an agitator, and also a creative thinker. He certainly seems to be on the side of the workers,' Ben said.

'Yes, that's true from what I've read. Although somehow I do not think that is what the majority of British workers want.'

'No, that's my reading of it too. By the way, did you hear what happened in Pitt Square when Bert and his friends passed the army during the march to Town Hall Square?' Ben asked.

'No. What was it?'

'Apparently, he and his friends cocked a snook at the army … in a really subtle way.'

'How?'

'Well, they soft-soaped the soldiers by passing them singing "Soldiers of the King" and "Take me Back to Dear Old Blighty", which the soldiers found engaging, even funny. The atmosphere seemed to relax straightaway, though the singing was appalling.'

'Trust old Bert! The master craftsman of revolution through song. At least it wasn't "The Red Flag" or the "Internationale",' laughed Jimmy.

After the Union backslapping, Jimmy found Arthur and Jacob waiting outside for him. *Oh dear*, he wondered, *what is it now?*

'You conducted yourself magnificently, if I may say so,' Arthur complimented him generously. 'I am impressed. You were the unquestioned star of these negotiations. I am pleased that it has all ended like this, you know, and it was you who helped to make it happen.'

'I agree,' Jacob added. 'I could do with someone like you in my new car factory. Someone who can lead men. Someone who knows the real meaning of discipline and organisation.'

'You know, your talents are wasted working in your present job at the mill,' Arthur asserted. 'You could undoubtedly be an overlooker and one day a manager. I am sure that you would be a better one than some we have already. Why not think about joining the management side of the business? It would yield extra income for you straightaway and excellent prospects for the future. The industry needs men like you in this difficult post-war period. What do you think?'

Jimmy's reaction was expeditious and automatic. 'Thanks, Arthur. That is big-hearted. Thanks as well to you, Jacob. It's almost like the two of you are trying to compete for me,' he jibed lightly. 'I am honestly tempted. For the moment though my place is and must be with my mates. That's where my destiny lay in France and that's where it lies now. The future of this industry is not going to be easy in the post-war period, and I know they will likely need someone to lead them in Vic's absence.'

'Well, why don't you take some time to think it over?' countered Arthur. 'Come out to the house and talk about the detail if you like. You'll be welcome.'

'Thanks again, I'll think about it. For the moment the answer has to be no thanks,' he declined politely and changed the subject. 'By the way, who was it that put pressure on the Chief Constable to accept the troops?'

'Well, just put it like this,' said Arthur. 'We all make mistakes in this life. Let's leave it at that.'

'Fine,' Jimmy reciprocated. 'No harm done. And thanks again for the flattering offers.'

'No problem. You're welcome. Think about it. It's still on the table and will remain so.'

'And now I must go,' Jimmy said cheerily. 'And prepare myself for another equally — maybe more — important meeting with an adversary who will surely test me more than I have been tested here today: my future fiancée, Kate!'

Jimmy danced down the curved staircase of the Mechanics' Institute, sliding his hand down the highly polished mahogany banister as far as the carved, bare-breasted maidens at the foot of the stairs, whose bottoms he gently tapped. He winked at them and pushed open the beautiful Venetian glass doors into the dying beauty of a delightful day and to what he was in no doubt would be a happy future for himself and Kate.

Chapter Twenty-Eight

Jimmy was feeling so unusually contented with the way the meeting had gone that he decided to give himself a little treat and ride back home, using up his last few precious coppers. After all, he reasoned, if the workers were all going back tomorrow, the money would be coming in again by Friday. If that was the case, Kitty could not chide him for using up their scarce resources on unnecessary travel. Things were going his way at last and he felt more self-confident than he had done since his return.

As he waited at the stop outside the Mechanics' Institute in the still warm early evening sunshine, he juggled with the few coins. He was exultant about the outcome of the negotiations and modestly pleased with his own performance, given that it had been thrust on him at a moment's notice. His satisfaction was only restrained by his anxiety at having had to postpone his visit to Kate.

Having a conclusion to the dispute meant that he could focus more on the future with Kate and on their shared happiness — something he now felt he had too long allowed to elude him. She had borne the brunt of his changed and capricious behaviour. He now understood how self-centred and myopic he had been in his preoccupation with the past, and he intended to revise that once and for all. Kate would now be the pivot around which his continued existence would revolve.

Jimmy did not have long to wait and, with a clanking and screeching, the tram appeared and ground to a noisy halt in the middle of the road. He mounted briskly, climbing quickly up the curved staircase to the top deck. There was no one else up there and he chose to sit outside at the front in the fading sun, as though he wanted to drink up every drop of it before the end of the day. He wanted to look forward, literally and metaphorically, as the tram clinked and clattered its way up the steep hill the short distance to the top of his street. His thoughts centred on Kate and he began to quietly hum to himself, 'I'll take you home again Kathleen.'

He was feeling buoyant, working out what he was going to say and do in detail when he saw Kate. Something fundamental had changed and opened up new horizons for him. His heady excitement shaped the flight of his thoughts and they raced far ahead of the hurtling tram.

For the first time in days, he reflected on the war in a subtly unorthodox light. This time, it was not of the horror, injustice and human waste of it all. Those were yesterday's recollections. They were not appropriate for today and the new opportunities he could now envisage for himself and for Kate, and for his men. He realised he could never totally erase the horror and trauma of the war from his memory. It would still frame his future life. Nonetheless he could learn lessons from the experience and move on with a new vision for himself and for those he loved.

In his new-found elation he let his dreams run riot. In fact, nothing was beyond his imagination. He knew that the carnage of his Pals would now give new life and impetus to his actions and that of his fellow workers and fellow survivors: a determination for a better, more just and equal world. No more doffing caps to the men of money and to their often ill-gotten social status.

The war would provide a spring for his socialist ambitions and furnish the engine for his strivings, both personal and professional. In this vision, his resolution to change his relationship with Kate for the better would be paralleled by an adjustment in the relations between workers and owners to achieve greater equality in society — between men and women, between workers and employers. As

425

promised, the mills would belong to the workers. The means of production and distribution would be nationalised, so that all owned them. Today his private life and his work life seemed to meld with ease.

Jimmy was hardly interrupted in his idealistic speculation by the arrival of the cheerful conductor and the payment of his fare. With the industrial dispute now practically won thanks to the workers' discipline and good organisation, for which he had been in large measure responsible, he might even be able to get his war medals out of pawn at the Anchor Fent shop. He could wear them with pride when he went to the memorial service that was intended to take place each year on the eleventh of November at the newly inaugurated cenotaph in the middle of town. He thought how proud Kate and Kitty would be of him. And in his new role as chairman of the Union, he would count for something in their community, just as Kitty and Kate had always wanted him to before the war.

Jimmy wanted to get home as soon as possible. He would have a cold water wash in the shallow stone sink and put on a clean collar and his best tie. He would spruce himself up, brush off his threadbare jacket, polish his working boots and put on his trilby, retrieved at great financial sacrifice from the pawn shop. And he would go and tell Kate's parents what he intended to do the next day — only as a courtesy, mind you. He was not asking anyone except Kate for permission to marry her, and he would make that plain, politely of course.

The next day he would travel up the dale again to the sanatorium at Lynaton. Visiting times were pretty flexible and he would not be denied access. He would get up at the crack of dawn and take the early service to Lynaton. Once at the sanatorium he would make his formal, unforgivably belated, proposal to Kate, the love of his life. His fantasy envisaged him kneeling before her to propose their new shared life. He even found himself pre-preparing the words and phrases he would use in this make-believe scenario, although the final version would of course be settled en route to the sanatorium. He was even convinced that her total recovery from the dreaded consumption was a realistic prospect.

He fantasised that the next day would be beautiful and warm so that the patients' beds would be wheeled out onto the sun-drenched veranda again; the two of them could be together outside. Yes, it would be there that he would share his vision with her. He could imagine the scene now. Seeing her beautiful brown eyes framed by her jet-black wavy hair against the backdrop of the far slopes of the other side of the lovely sunny valley, he envisaged that they could agree all the arrangements necessary for the wedding, so that he could tell all his friends the good news when he returned to the mill. And his sister would be delighted too. This was a rare magic moment in his late life.

He could just see himself sitting on the sunlit veranda at Kate's bedside — or perhaps she would be well enough to sit in an armchair and he would sit at her side. The two of them would join hands and enjoy the panorama of the valley with the rock-strewn fells on the other side. They would watch the fell races on just such a sunny day; both of them bathed in sun and warmth; at ease in front of those floor-to-ceiling glass doors, that had seemed to finally and darkly closed behind him the last time he had visited Kate. He shuddered at its recollection. But was it just that?

As it sped out of town, swaying and lurching and accompanied by the lanolin smell of wool from the mills either side of the road, the tram approached the old central coal yard. This was where the long lines of rail coal wagons had come to deliver their loads for the grates of the whole town. The essential fuel was subsequently distributed in sacks by several independent merchants on horse drawn carts to the various households in the rows of back-to-back houses that clothed both sides of the valley. But the steam locomotives were not there anymore, or at least very few and those totally inactive, their fires quenched. Nor were there any coal-filled wagons to be seen. Indeed, with the post-war penury of coal and in consequence of the industrial action, there was little activity in the yard at that moment. 'Keep the home fires burning? What a joke! With what?' he asked himself.

As his gaze scanned the depressing, coal-dust covered scenery from the front deck, he spied the major junction of the tram-lines and overhead wires converging just beyond the coal yard entrance. He could now see the big, heavy gates, closed and bolted. An omen? He didn't believe in omens any more. He didn't need them. After all, against all the odds he had survived in France. Nothing could interrupt or gainsay his inspired revivalist reverie now. He felt himself mentally reborn. He was ready to face anything.

From the top deck, Jimmy could gradually see more over the top of the high coal yard wall, and his eyes alighted on the trunk of an old gnarled sycamore tree, twisting and striving its way out from behind the wall, its branches and verdant foliage bowering over onto the roadway. The tree had had a difficult task rooting and growing to its existing size in such a barren landscape — an alien and polluted environment where there was more coal dust than soil. In spite of having so many adversaries, against all the odds, the tree had survived. Of course it had had good luck on its side. Perhaps he could learn from and emulate that tree. Confounding probability, it had succeeded. He had stayed alive in France, whereas such a host of his workmates had perished. He would do something special with the life that had been spared. He and Kate could even think of starting a family. Not too soon of course. Only when she was strong again.

For a short while, the shadow from the tree darkened the open upper deck of the tram. The temperature dropped sharply and Jimmy shivered, feeling a sudden chill passing over him. He turned up his jacket collar and pulled his previously superfluous muffler tight around his neck.

The chill and dullness occasioned a sudden though transient alteration in his mood. Against his will, doubts about himself and his future momentarily re-presented themselves. Fortunately he quickly dismissed them and he was once again serene. He was in command again and he was resolute on the future, buoyantly certain that he had the determination to carry his intentions to fruition. They passed into the light again and quickly gathered speed.

Jimmy's street was the next stop; he rose hurriedly and prepared himself for a swift dismount. Well in advance, he went down the narrow spiral staircase in preparation for alighting. He was on the exit platform in time to see the conductor pull the leather strap to signal to the driver to halt. Before the tram came to a stop, he hopped sprightly from the platform and ran alongside it.

'Tha wants to watch out, pulling a trick like that,' the conductor called after him. 'If tha comes a cropper, it's tha fault. Just remember that.'

'Okay, I'll remember that,' he called back cheerily as he sprinted across the road. He maintained his pace round the corner and down the street, the beat of his metal hobnailed boots echoing his advance and heralding his arrival.

With the continuing warmth of the waning early evening sun, some of the neighbours were sitting on their doorsteps,

429

including John Willy, the local knocker-up. As Jimmy advanced swiftly towards him, John was surprised that he looked so carefree. Imagining that Jimmy must have already heard the bad news, John Willy was a little lost for words. Then, out of sensitivity, he decided to express something positive instead of raising a subject which he knew must be painful.

'I hear you managed to persuade the employers to accept a settlement on our terms?' John Willy queried.

'Well, more or less. Doesn't the news spread fast hereabouts? The jungle drums no doubt. How did you know?'

'Ben told me as he passed here on his way home. He was cock-a-hoop about it. A bit depressed about Vic's illness though. And I heard high praise of your own role in the stupendous success of the negotiations.'

'Well, I don't know about that. Yes, it's over. Thank god. We're all back at work tomorrow first thing, and mostly on our terms at that. Well, not me. I've got something else to do, but that's another story,' Jimmy gasped, still out of breath from his exertions.

'Well, that's a relief. At least we have that to be thankful for. It must be some compensation for you. Well done.'

Jimmy was not listening well. He had other things on his mind. Otherwise he would have detected the note of sadness, even condolence, in John Willy's voice and the pitiful reference to 'compensation', almost of personal commiseration. He could have wondered what 'compensation' he was referring to. There was always loads of tittle tattle on the street and John Willy was an arch-tattler

… he didn't have much else to do, poor chap. Anyway, maybe he was referring to the news about Vic.

'Thanks, John Willy. Much appreciated.' He responded appreciatively.

Jimmy sprinted the last few yards round the corner and down the cobbled passage, flinging open the door of the house with some gusto, intending to indicate clearly his bright feelings to Kitty.

But what his senses told him as he flung open the door was that the mood was far from celebratory. Kitty was sitting in front of the dying embers of a dull-glowing fire. Her normally radiant face was grey like the cooling ash in the grate, as she stared fixedly into the hearth. The curtains were drawn closed and the only light source in the dimness of the room was the gently hissing gas jet. In spite of the squeak the door made, his sister barely moved as he entered. He stopped in his tracks when he saw the tears twinkling in her lovely brown eyes.

What he read in her face was a sadness that he had not seen for a long time — in fact, since he returned home on leave from the Front after Tommy was killed.

'What's up, Kitty? What's up, love? What's happened? What's the matter?'

'Come in, lad. Come in and sit down.'

'What's up, Kitty? Tell me. Tell me quickly, love. Don't keep me in suspense. Is it Vic?'

Only at that point did he seize on what the worst news could be.

'Is it Kate?'

'I'm afraid that we have had some bad news, Jimmy. Please sit down.'

Only then did it finally dawn on him that he was about to hear the worst. His heart bounded unsteadily. His legs weakened near to collapse.

'What is it, Kitty? Tell me! Spare me the suspense. Put me out of my misery.'

'Jimmy, it's Kate.'

'What about Kate? Has her illness got worse? She's a fighter, you know. She'll come through it.'

'I'm afraid that it's even worse than that, love. Kate's father came round a little while ago to let us know that she … well, you know she was not strong, and the outlook was never good from the time they sent her to the sanatorium. Well, she passed away peacefully this afternoon. I'm so sorry, love.'

Jimmy felt pain of such strength — stronger than he had ever felt before, even in the trenches of France. He threw himself into the armchair opposite his sister, tossing his head back to shake off the bad news. Perhaps he had misheard. Or was Kitty mistaken? Was it someone else at the sanatorium they had mistakenly reported for Kate?

'It can't be,' he uttered in a choked voice. 'I don't believe it. Are you sure? There must have been a mistake.'

'Absolutely sure, love. I'm so sorry. Her father explained that she passed on quietly while she was having a sleep. He said that she suffered no pain.'

432

Chapter Twenty-Nine

In the blink of an eyelid, Jimmy lurched from elation to cavernous depression and utter despair. He felt as though an earthquake had struck. He began to sob uncontrollably and then, dry even of despair, he slumped into a brooding silence. He was aware at last of his failure to see what he could have had until it was no longer there for him. Empty-handed, he felt like he had been mentally poleaxed.

In a state of non-existence, he scarcely understood or perceived anything outside of his unbearable pain. How could it be? On this, his day of triumph? How could fate be so cruel? Rather he should have perished in the trenches of France than to suffer this now. And all those wasted months since his return. He was to blame.

And all this, he reflected, after Kate seemed to be getting better when he had last visited her. It was heart-rending. She'd had a bloom in her cheeks and he had hoped that was a good first sign of recovery. He'd had no idea that she was so close to death. He had willed her revival. And it had been such an important time for them together. She had helped him to sort out his life — given him a reason to live. Only moments ago, he had been so certain of the future. He'd had it all worked out, and now it lay in ruins. Everything that he had planned had been in vain. His future with Kate would never be. What could he do? What hope was there for him now? Shattered as if by a German shell, his whole future had just been blown to pieces in front of him.

With the fading light of day, the normally dank and dismal room was becoming ever darker and the chill was growing, with only a little warmth afforded by the last glowing embers in the grate. Seated, Kitty poked the coals into reluctant flame and added their sparse remainders of coal.

She rose slowly and went to the far wall. She turned up the gas mantle and gradually a dull yellow hue spread across the room. At first it showed only a small, weak glow, and then slowly it shone more brightly, throwing dark shadows like harbingers of death across the room.

Sighing deeply, Kitty returned to the hearth, knelt down on the old tab rug at the side of her brother and took his trembling hands into her own. She would share his pain. She was determined not to share his despair. She had to give him a reason to hope, a reason to live. The task that she faced was to find the words best suited to draw him out of his intense despair? She saw his face, contorted in mental agony, bravely holding back the tears that filled his glazed eyes. Why couldn't a man show his emotions and cry in front of his own sister? Why couldn't he just let it all out?

'Jimmy, I know you need time and space to grieve for your loss now,' Kitty began in a quiet and gentle voice. 'But it was always on the cards. Kate was already a sick woman, even before you came home from that damned war. It could have occurred at any time. And try to look on the positive side of things. We can be grateful for her life, fleeting as it seemed, and the humanity that she brought to us. For Kate so enriched our lives, mine as well, and we are better people through having known her and lived with her. Grieve, by all means. Then, move on. You must realise that Kate would have wished you to live your life to the full, not to waste it in fruitless remorse. She loved you deeply, you know.'

'She was a wonderful woman, Kitty. My error was that I never fully understood her until she became ill. I was just too wrapped up in my own problems. The war and ...'

'Jimmy, you mustn't blame yourself. The war changed us all and it will remain in our blood to the day we die. Then again so will Kate's legacy, and that more potently. What we suffered need not destroy us, unless we let it. We cannot go through the rest of our lives being slaves to the war. Rather we can let it strengthen our resolve to fight for those things that we all believe so strongly and want so passionately for the workers and for our society.'

Jimmy wrapped his arms around Kitty and pulled her to him. 'Oh, Kitty, what can I do? How can I live without her? I had not the slightest idea …'

'Jimmy, just listen. Kate was a wonderful woman, a woman before her time in lots and lots of ways. Refusing to be oppressed either by the social destiny of her birth in this class-ridden and snobbish society, or by the ravages of her illness, she struggled to the last. She knew that she probably did not have long. And I feel that she tried to prepare you for your new life without her the last time you went to visit her at the sanatorium.'

She looked up and gently placed her hands on either side of his face, raising it so that his eyes looked directly at her, almost childlike. She strove to console him and give him hope.

'Kate would want you to strive for the ideals and the visions that we all shared. Now that you are leading the Union, you have a unique chance to achieve what we all dreamed of: a fairer and more just society and one in which men and women are equal partners and neither subjugates the other. As we so often talked about with Kate. Demands for social reform are mounting across the board and men like you are needed to lead a campaign to show the way.'

'I don't know, Kitty. I don't know if I have it in me. I loved Kate more than I knew.'

'Jimmy, I want to tell you something now — something that Kate and I had decided we would never share with you because you would not be able to fathom it out. But, I loved Kate too. More than you will ever know. She was much more than a soulmate to me. Much more. While you were away, we came to know an alternative kind of love.'

'Kitty, why are you telling me all this?'

'So that you know that you are not the only one hurting today. I loved her too. And she loved me. During those four hard years, when you were away at the Front, we grew close to each other. You and Tommy were away and we helped and cared for each other, provided to each other the love that would otherwise have been lacking in our lives. We held hands and marched hand-in-hand in 1917 in the women's demonstration for peace. We strove to encourage those in the Labour Party who abhorred the damned war, who thirsted for peace not war, for love not hate. We only survived all those years because we were so close.'

'But, Kitty, I needed her so much, you know. By myself, well, I am just not sure that I can meet the challenge ...'

'Jimmy, listen to me. Of course you can. You can do anything you want to and put your mind to. I know you can, and more importantly Kate would want you to. That's the end of it. One day, of this I am sure, the vision that she had and that we all shared will no longer be a dream, but reality for us all — men and women, workers and owners, rich and poor alike. That will only come to pass, though, if men and women like you and me fight for those dreams. That's what she's expecting of us now.'

'Kitty, you don't know how much she was to me. I can't go on without her.'

'Nonsense, Jimmy Kelly. During the war, you showed your metal. You proved that you were a fighter. When you led those men with their complaints to the government in London, you showed you had courage, determination and high qualities of leadership. You can achieve great things for the workers and there is much more that you can do for them. You're a born leader, Jimmy, so don't waste that gift. Use it in memory of Kate and what she stood for.'

'But Kitty …'

'Listen to me Jimmy. Think beyond self. Every ending heralds a new beginning. The world is changing and the world has need of men like you to lead a new generation of workers, who for the first time have all had the benefit of a good education. We can speak to the toffs on equal terms now. Lots of the workers are now better educated than those high-born toffs. The Workers Educational Trade Union Committee has been formed this year and there are demands for the full franchise for all women and the extension of schooling for all to fifteen … and much more beside.'

'Kitty, I just don't have the heart.'

'Yes, you do, Jimmy Kelly. I'm not having you thinking that this is the ending of everything. It's not. You just gird your loins. It's the closing of one door and the opening of another. It's a time for a new birth for our people: schooling, health, social welfare, housing, medicine, finance, everything. It's not coming overnight. We shall get there with the help of men like you.'

'But Kate …'

'Kate would want you to join this fight, peacefully, to achieve our dreams for all workingmen and workingwomen. So grieve now, for sure. That's only natural. But let that grief be the seedbed to renew your strength and give you an unwavering determination to succeed in what you have to do. Don't let Kate down. Honour her memory by achieving what she wanted. Let her still be your inspiration. You have a responsibility to strive for a better world. That is the best memorial to Kate that you can construct, and to those of your Pals who did not return from the war. Make this a fit country in Kate's name and in theirs.'

Gently releasing his hands, she rose from the armchair and affectionately stroked his dark and tousled hair, knowing that he would never fully grasp the love that Kate and she had shared, or the full implication of what she had told him. Of course, she could feel his pain. She knew for certain that he could never completely share hers. But, whatever happened, she would not permit him to descend into a black hole of despair. Too many lives had already been lost for that. She had to make him move on. She would stand by him and make sure that he succeeded.

The holed gas mantle was now throwing a still weak but warmer yellow glow around the room, illuminating the cards on the mantelpiece. For an instant, she glanced at the one which carried the last message from her loved one, Tommy, who would also never return. She read out loud to Jimmy: 'There's a long, long road a-winding into the land of my dreams ....' She held the card with tears in her eyes.

'It is not just about this strike,' Kitty continued. 'It's about that long, long road of social reform for us all and how you can make a difference, to build that fit country that was promised. We all need you on that road. You have no time for despair.'

She turned away from him. 'And now I'll make us a nice cup of tea and we'll talk about the arrangements for Kate's funeral. After that, we'll talk about the meeting today and all your future activities on behalf of your mates. There is a lot for you to do, and we need to get on with it right away.'

An odd tranquillity descended on him as he sat back in the battered old armchair and reflected on Kitty's words. He took out from his waistcoat pocket Kate's tightly folded final letter to him and read her poem once more.

For my Love

And when you reach a grand old age
And life has come to its final stage
Remember then what I said to you
True love is found by only a few

Do not lament when I'm not there
Just let my love banish your care
You were fortunate for in your heart
You found true love that will never part.

Acknowledgements

I am indebted to my late father for the insight and knowledge that he gave me of his life and times during the period of war and peace covered in this book. As a youngster I learned so much by being allowed to sit in on many informal Union small-group gatherings and discussions at home and with my parents in working men's clubs. I also owe a very deep debt of gratitude to all four generations of my family and particularly to my wife, Margaret, for their forbearance, understanding, support and helpful comments during the writing of this book. I wish to express my thanks and appreciation to my son, Mark, for his indispensable sustenance for my inadequate IT skills and to my daughter Angela for her constant advice and guidance and for the final proofreading of the manuscript. A particular word of thanks is due to my youngest daughter, Colette, who accompanied me with enthusiasm on our journey of discovery through the vagaries of publishing fiction.

Appreciation is also due to my workmates at the 'Canaletto-style mill', where I learned so much about the folklore of a soon to be doomed industry. I should also thank the librarians and archivists from several cities, who so freely assisted me in consulting in situ documents, publications, newspapers and reports of charities. Finally, I should like to express my sincere thanks and appreciation to my copy editor and proof-reader Georgina Gregory for her excellent work on the manuscript.

Other Books by the Author

Parents and Teachers (with John Pimlott). Schools Council Research Studies, Macmillan

Multicultural Education, Routledge and Kegan Paul plc

Prejudice Reduction, Cassel Educational

Change in Teacher Educator (Edited with Robin J. Alexander and Maurice Craft) Praeger

Education for Citizenship in a Multicultural Society, Cassell

A Human Rights Analysis, Cassell

Cultural Diversity and The Schools (four volumes edited with Celia and Sohan Modgil), The Falmer Press

Policy and Practice in Lifelong Education, Nafferton Books

Education for Community, Macmillan Education

Education and Development: Tradition & Innovation (four volumes edited with Celia and Sohan Modgil)' Cassell

Multicultural Education in Western Societies (With James A Banks), Holt Rinehart Education

Lifelong Education and the Preparation of Educational Personnel, UNESCO Institute

The Multicultural Curriculum, Batsford Academic and Educational Ltd

Education for Citizenship in a Multicultural Society, Cassell

Teacher Education and Cultural Change, (With H Dudley Plunkett), Linnet Books

Multicultural Education in a Global Society, Cassell

Children with Special Needs in the Asia Region, The World Bank

Reformkonzeptionen der Lehererbildung in Grossbritannien, Beltz

Lehrerbildung für den Unterricht behinderter Kinder in ausgewählten Ländern (together with Professor Dr Wolfgang Mitter and Colleagues), Böhlau

Other Fiction Books by the Author

New Life in an Old Town: Part One of the Ayton Cycle (Available as e-book and paperback)

The Hydra (Available as e-book and paperback)

The Fit Country (Available as e-book and paperback)

Back-to-Back (Available as e-book and paperback)

The Final Mission (Available as e-book and paperback)

Turbulent Times: Growing up in the Edwardian Era (Available as e-book and paperback)

Deception: Part Two of the Ayton Cycle (Available as e-book and paperback)

A Boy's Story: A Novella (Available as e-book and as a paperback)

The Endless Struggle: Part Three of the Ayton Cycle (Available as e-book and paperback)

The Silent World (Available as e-book and paperback)

Armageddon: Part Four of the Ayton Cycle (Available as an e-book and paperback)

A Lifetime (In planning for availability as an e-book and paperback in late 2025)

The House on the Blind Site (In preparation for publication as an e-book and paperback in late-2024)

Happy Poems and Games for Young Children (Complete, not yet published)

About the Author

After teaching in technical education and in higher education at lecturer, senior lecturer, professorial and deanship levels, James went to the World Bank and worked in the Asia region, including Nepal, Bhutan, Bangla Desh and China, and also in some countries in francophone Africa, including Burundi, Madagascar, Rwanda and for UNESCO in Morocco. He has held Professorships in Austria, Germany, the United Kingdom and the United States and acted as a consultant to several UN agencies, including UNESCO and UNEDBAS.

He is the author, co-author or co-editor of numerous books on subjects such as cultural diversity, prejudice, human rights and multicultural education. He has also written many journal articles as well as policy papers for international organisations, such as UNEDBAS and UNESCO.

After retirement he worked for several years for the UK government as the first British technical assistance in post-genocide Rwanda. It was the advent of mantle cell lymphoma and consequent 'restriction to barracks' for health reasons that he began the process of writing novels, of which he published twelve by the time of his death.

At all stages of his life he has devoted some of his time and energy to charitable causes, voluntary activities and the welfare of others.

James is passionate about family, reading, gardening and, formerly, travel. He and his wife, Margaret Ann, live in the West of England.